SHADOW KNIGHT'S MATE

Other books by Jay Brandon:

Deadbolt (1985)

Tripwire (1987)

Predator's Waltz (1989)

Fade The Heat (1990)

Rules Of Evidence (1992)

Loose Among The Lambs (1993)

Local Rules (1995)

Defiance County (1996)

Angel of Death (1998)

After-Image (2000)

Executive Privilege (2001)

Sliver Moon (2004)

Grudge Match (2004)

Running with the Dead (2005)

Milagro Lane (2009)

SHADOW KNIGHT'S MATE

A NOVEL

JAY BRANDON

WingsPress

San Antonio, Texas
2014

Shadow Knight's Mate © 2014
by Jay Brandon

ISBN: 978-1-60940-391-1 (paperback original)

E-books:

ePub: 978-1-60940-392-8
Mobipocket/Kindle: 978-1-60940-393-5
Library PDF: 978-1-60940-394-2

Wings Press
627 E. Guenther
San Antonio, Texas 78210
Phone/fax: (210) 271-7805
On-line catalogue and ordering:
www.wingspress.com

Wings Press books are distributed to the trade by
Independent Publishers Group
www.ipgbook.com

Library of Congress Cataloging-in-Publication Data

Brandon, Jay.
  Shadow Knight's Mate : a novel / Jay Brandon.
    pages cm
  ISBN 978-1-60940-391-1 (trade pbk. : alk. paper) -- ISBN 978-1-60940-
392-8 (epub ebook) -- ISBN 978-1-60940-393-5 (Mobipocket ebook) --
ISBN 978-1-60940-394-2 (pdf ebook)
  1. United States--History--Fiction. 2. Conspiracies--United States--History
--Fiction. 2. Terrorism--United States--History --21st Century--Fiction. 3.
Secret Societies--International--Fiction. 4. United States--Politics--Fiction.
  I. Title.
  PS3552.R315R43 2014
  813'.54--dc23
                           2013046754

For Robert Morrow and Jan Morrow,
great friends of long standing.

PROLOGUE:

Exit Interview

Some historians subscribe to the Great Man theory of history. That occasionally an oversized personality comes along who changes world events from what they would have been without that person. George Washington, Napoleon, Alexander the Great. My little group believes in the person-just-outside-the-frame-of-the-picture theory of history. The unrecorded person who makes some small adjustment that makes all the difference.

Can you give me an example?

One of our greatest intrusions into American history was making sure Franklin Roosevelt ran for and got elected to a third term. 1940. A key point. We knew it. He was guided into forsaking the traditional boundaries of the presidency.

Because he was considered essential? Because he was the only person who could guide America through one of its greatest crises? Because someone else might not—?

No. Because of a man named Roger Billings.

I've never heard of him.

Exactly. Roger Billings was on the president's staff, but you haven't seen him or heard his name. If you did you didn't notice.

A key aide? A Congressional—

A dog trainer.

A what?

Roger Billings was the caretaker and trainer of Fala. Have you heard of him? The President's dog. A little scottie. You *have* seen his picture. The most famous one is of FDR down on the floor in the Oval Office, playing with Fala, coaxing him to take a biscuit. You haven't seen the whole picture, which included Roger Billings standing a few feet away. A very slender black man of average height, waiting patiently to take the dog away after the President finished playing with him. So unobtrusive you could look at him and not see him. But the president was a very sociable man. While he played with Fala, he and Roger would talk. Idle conversation. Little nothings. And occasionally, very rarely, a little something. Roger Billings would make a hint of an observation. An offhand remark. And they hit home. The Japanese in the Pacific. The cliffs of France. Who seemed trustworthy, who didn't.

FDR had to remain in office because we had him. He was a great man, but that wasn't the most important thing. We were right there with him. Never has a president of the United States been so devoted to an animal. Or so susceptible to suggestion. Roger Billings ended the Depression and won World War II. With help, of course.

The interviewer was skeptical. Who wouldn't be? *Can you give me another example? Something more recent, perhaps.*

Okay. I'll tell you one of our failures. Tom Hanks.

Tom Hanks. You somehow failed to get Tom Hanks to—

No. Tom is one of us. Unfortunately, not a very important one of us. He was supposed to be. He was being groomed for great things. He was recruited in his teens. I wasn't involved, of course, I wasn't born yet, but I understand great things were expected of Tom. He was supposed to achieve a very minor celebrity. People would vaguely remember his name as one of the stars of a short-lived TV show and a couple of silly movies. "Bachelor Party." "Turner and Hooch." But then came "Splash." We have some pretty smart people on staff, but who could have predicted this? I mean, I love Tom, but honestly, would you pick him out of a lineup as a major movie star? That wasn't supposed to be his destiny. He was supposed to go from minor actor to major behind-the-scenes player in the entertainment industry. Producer, recruiter, eventually perhaps right-hand man to a studio head. From which position he could influence what pictures got greenlighted, which ones didn't. In case you don't realize, that's how world culture is formed. Tom, and we through him, were going to guide the world into certain realizations, certain beliefs. A golden age of world enlightenment. That was the theory. If we'd had our way, "The Terminator" would never have gotten made. But damn, he became a movie star. And now that he can't move in public without attracting a crowd, what use is he to us? Oh, he does what he can, but he's not in much position to influence events subtly.

That was a lie, wasn't it?

Absolutely. Damn, how did you catch me? No, Tom—Mr. Hanks—isn't one of us. How did you know?

So you screwed up?

Happens all the time, unfortunately. We're fallible. We're not all geniuses. Far from it. And we aren't this monolithic army moving as one. For the most part the group encourages individual initiative. Each of us acts on his own, or in small groups. And we make mistakes. Sometimes minor ones. Sometimes big time.

Tell me about one of the times when you screwed up.

That one's pretty obvious, isn't it? The one that got me here.

Tell me...

It started with her. Arden. Even in that extraordinary group, she was something special. And she ruined everything.

Are you exaggerating again?

Not this time. I'll tell you....

CHAPTER 1

The little inn thirty miles outside of Paris wasn't a place to expect a chance meeting. In fact, the American ambassador had come there explicitly to avoid seeing people he knew. He had a knotty problem to work out, one that was diplomatic, strategic, and even social, and didn't want to be interrupted. He was a well-known man in the French capital—in fact, in many places around the world—but these little encounters wore on him, even though social encounters were a large part of his job. Now he sat having his third cup of coffee, looking up at the worn beams of the ceiling, beams that had been set there before the French Revolution, wondering how to keep Qatar out of the upcoming World Leaders Summit.

It was a problem that had occupied him for days, and the decision had to be made today. Qatar had a new young prince who wanted to show his independence by standing up to the Saudis and, of course, to the United States. It was a sort of national adolescent stage, challenging the last superpower. The ambassador didn't want the summit turning into that kind of theater. So he sat and brooded and tried to soak up the old wisdom of this place.

But the old atmosphere was abruptly disturbed by a passing American who nearly stepped on the ambassador's toes as he carried his own coffee from the bar. The American, a thin young man of nondescript apperance, glanced down, muttered something apologetic, then looked more sharply at the ambassador.

"Mr. Nicholas?"

The ambassador sighed, but the gracious smile was already shaping his lips, the smile that had eased millions of dollars in donations out of rich men, charmed influential women visiting from the States, and in fact had probably helped him acquire his position. Certainly the gracious smile was a necessity of his job. Sometimes Paul Nicholas hated feeling that smile on his face.

"Yes?"

"Jack Driscoll. Hi. This is weird. Do you remember me? I was your son's roommate one semester at Yale. We met at parents' weekend. I was the one who did the, you know, the little magic act at the talent show."

"Oh yes. Jack. How are you? Are you here on business, or—?"

Obviously not. The young man wore jeans, tennis shoes, a striped shirt covered by a gray hooded jacket. No way he was in business. Of course, he could have been some computer or Internet genius with a fortune already in the bank, which was why it paid to be nice to everyone, in spite of appearances. But Jack had the sort of slightly lost look of a man who would flash a lot of bills and remain unaware of the looks his wallet drew. His coffee cup clattered a little in the saucer he carried.

"No, just touristing. There's supposed to be some church around here—in fact, this is probably where people come to get away from other tourists. Sorry. Don't let me interrupt. I'll just go out on the—"

"No, that's all right. Sit down, Jack. I remember your magic act. Did the goldfish ever turn up again?" For a moment the ambassador welcomed the interruption. His thoughts were going nowhere but in circles anyway. There was something ingratiating about the young man, the way he stood already turned away, as if not expecting welcome anywhere, coffee cup sloshing a little, alone in a foreign country. Wasn't it part of the ambassador's job to help such people?

The young man did sit at the round wooden table. He had a thin face with still a few childhood freckles, dark blonde hair, pale blue eyes. Looked very young but might have been in his mid-twenties. The ambassador gave him a short study then looked off across the room, his problem still occupying his mind.

"You're a diplomat, aren't you, sir? I remember. Career Foreign Service, right? You know, you might be able to help me with something. I've got kind of a diplomatic assignment myself. Another Yalie friend of ours, Steve Reynolds—you probably didn't meet him—anyway, he's getting married this summer, and he's asked me to help with the guest list. Well, specifically he wants me to figure out how to uninvite another guy from New Haven, a guy he was roommates with for one year and is still kind of friends with, but he's one of those guys who's, you know, not a jerk or anything, really, but kind of a trouble magnet—says the wrong thing to the wrong person, still drinks like we did in college, always—well, anyway, Steve is marrying this very nice girl, old New England family, Puritans only a couple of generations back, ha ha, or as good as, you know what I mean, and he just feels like Eddie carries too much disaster potential."

Paul Nicholas was amused by the rush of words. When people approached him with problems these days, it was obliquely, and always only after a courtship of ritual and greetings with the obsequiousness factor carefully calculated on both sides, never this baldly and certainly not this rushed. His smile had turned genuine. "But—?" he asked drily.

"Well, yes sir, you get right to the point. But Steve does business with Eddie now, and in fact Eddie's the one with the contacts. I mean, people do like him, they're in the same business, he's not somebody you can piss off just because—excuse me—"

The ambassador was barely listening, the recitation having reminded him of his own problem. Besides that, his eye had been caught by someone much more prepossessing than the young American on his left. A young woman walking straight toward them, looking at Paul not with personal recognition but just as if she immediately knew him as someone important.

In his years abroad Paul had learned to spot Americans, subliminally noting their aggressive walks, the way they held their shoulders, their clothes, their prolonged eye contact, other items of national character he couldn't even describe. With this woman— little more than a girl, really, maybe twenty-one or -two—he wasn't sure. She had the American confident gaze, but the way she held her long neck was somehow European, as were her clothes. She had pale skin, dark brown hair, very noticeable red lips even when she was barely smiling, as now, an unlined complexion, bright blue

blue eyes under long dark lashes, and a nose distinctive enough in its length to give her whole face character. She walked up to the table, looking right at Paul the whole time, but when she stood directly in front of him, said, "Jack. You're not boring someone else with this wedding business, are you?"

There was a mutter of apology off to Paul's left, but he was standing to take the young woman's hand and say, "It's no bore, Miss—"

"Arden. Arden Spindler." In French she apologized for her friend's intrusion. She had a charming low voice that required Paul to bend toward her. He answered in French that the intrusion was welcome since it had allowed him to meet her.

He waved a hand, also in French, and she joined them. The table was now a social occasion. The ambassador glanced from the woman to the young man. "And are you two travelling together?"

"No," Jack said quickly, while Arden rolled her eyes in a way that conveyed a more complicated relationship, enough to make Paul chuckle. "Just one of those chance meetings abroad, you know?" Jack added, sounding sullen.

The young woman's eyes were still on Paul's. "But Jack's been obsessing over this wedding problem so much that everyone who knows him even slightly has heard about it at enormous droning length." She turned to him. "It's easy, Jack. Just don't invite the bore. And if he finds out about it later you tell him it was inadvertent, the wife's family was in charge of the invitations, blah blah."

The sullenness of the silence to Paul's left became more pronounced. Paul smiled as if performing counseling. "Doubtful that would work. Because it's not just the wedding, there are the preparations. If as you say everyone who knows Jack knows he's thinking about this, then trust me this—Eddie was it?—is going to hear about the wedding long before it happens and will probably even call up the groom to ask about it, maybe even expect to come to the bachelor party, and so forth." Paul waved a hand again to indicate complications.

"Yeah, Arden. You just think it's simple because it's not your problem."

"Well, then, get him a date who'll keep him in line. Or get him invited to something else that weekend that sounds better to him. Mr. Ambassador, I'm so sorry. Come, Jack, let's be off."

"Not at all, Arden. And call me Paul, please. So you two are here to see the Church of St. Benedicta?"

"I've heard it's nice. Authentic but not ostentatious..." Arden's voice trailed off, her blue eyes fastened on Paul Nicholas.

But he was now staring out the window. Suddenly he smiled. "Not a date," he said.

"No sir, like I said, Arden and I just happened—"

"No, no. Your boorish friend. You don't get him a date, you invite someone even worse than he is. Someone so outrageous it will make your Eddie not want to appear anything like him. You don't uninvite one, you add one. Someone who'll make the unwanted guest want to appear moderate by comparison. And we know who's got the crazy end of the bench anchored, don't we? Has had it staked out for years."

Add someone to the summit who would appear crazy and sullen, yet flamboyant. The young prince from Qatar would never want to appear to ally himself with the crazy dictator, nor would he want to appear that man's protege, as he unavoidably would if he took similar positions; he could only look subservient rather than independent. By adding someone even farther out the political spectrum, Paul would drive Qatar toward the moderate. The summit's effectiveness might be damaged, but what was it going to accomplish anyway? It was a show. And even with the craziness factor heightened, the American President would appear more statesmanlike by comparison. Even if the young prince did make noise, the President would appear above it all. And that was the ambassador's job, to create that impression.

"After all," Paul Nicholas laughed, "it's only a wedding."

"Brilliant, sir," Arden murmured.

"You inspired me," the ambassador answered. "Thank you. Sorry, I have to run. Things to arrange. Goodbye, Arden. Enjoy your church. Be sure to take the stairs to the choir loft. Goodbye—Jeff, was it?"

Jack only nodded. The ambassador rushed off between the tables, full of energy and purpose. After half a minute Jack turned his gaze on Arden. She smiled at him, blindingly. She really was a lovely young woman. Brilliant, too. With qualities that set her apart from anyone he'd ever known. He quite hated her.

"That was neatly planted," he said.

"Thank you. You might have gotten there on your own."

"But what was really impressive was that you didn't even know what I was pitching."

"It was pretty obvious."

He laughed. "The fact that you think it was—"

She shrugged. "I caught a few words of what you were saying, I wondered what the ambassador would be doing here, not meeting with anyone, when he had the planning of the summit to worry about, so I guessed—"

"Yeah. Thanks. I guess. I really didn't want—"

"Sorry. I just didn't think you were selling it."

"Sure I was. I just hadn't—"

"No. He wasn't listening. He wasn't thinking. You hadn't—"

"I think he was. Maybe it was too—"

"No. You know why?"

"I know why. Because he wasn't trying to impress me. Once a beautiful woman was sitting—"

"—i.e.—"

"Yeah, yeah." Jack looked away from her smile.

"I can't believe I got you to say it."

"Of course. It may take me a little longer without your obvious advantage—"

She patted his knee. "You could have done it without me."

He just smiled at her. Not making a rejoinder. She smiled back for a second, then frowned. "Damn. I made your argument for you. How did you—?"

He didn't smile or otherwise acknowledge the triumph of getting her to admit he hadn't needed her help. "There's something else, Arden. I hope we can fix it."

"What?"

"He doesn't remember me. Not my name, not my face. He'll never even remember he talked to a guy in a bar."

She didn't answer. She just suddenly inhaled and looked up at the ceiling, at those old beams that had witnessed a lot of scenes, a lot of conversations, few of them memorable. Jack didn't say it, neither did she, but they were both thinking of the rejoinder he could have made: *But he'll remember you.*

It wasn't how they operated. They weren't remembered, they certainly weren't acknowledged. Ever. The ambassador should never say to anyone, *I met this charming young woman, and she started me thinking…* All he should remember was that he'd been alone at an out-of-the way spot when he'd had a brilliant idea.

She didn't even say *Damn.* But they both knew. Nor did Arden say, *I'll fix that some way.* They both knew that too.

She started a new conversation. "So, you headed home too?"

When Arden said "home," it was with invisible quotation marks that Jack heard. She had spent her childhood all over America, then the best years of her adolescence in a Swiss boarding school that in some corners was much more than a finishing school, for the last three years auditing college courses in America and Europe. Home for her was a theoretical concept.

"Sure. I wouldn't miss a meeting."

"I'm on the 4 o'clock to Heathrow. You too?"

"No, the five."

"Why don't you come with me, see if you can get on mine, we can fly together."

"I've got a couple of things to do. Meet you in London?"

For a moment he gave her his undivided attention. Her explanation of how she'd stepped into the conversation with the ambassador didn't satisfy him. He wondered if she'd been spying on him. In fact, he wondered what a lot of his group wondered.

Arden looked back at him, blue eyes shiny, still with a trace of a smile, until her lips twisted in exasperation. "No, Jack, I didn't read your mind…. And I do know what people think about me." Arden glanced down at the old scarred tabletop for a moment. "Some day, maybe, I'll tell you how you make a person like me."

"I'm sure it starts in a laboratory."

She smiled, and for a moment he regretted the insult. But she'd probably manipulated him into that feeling too. Jack stood up abruptly. "See you."

"Yep." After he left, Arden let the smile drop. Her eyes were even shinier. She had no illusion Jack would be meeting her in Heathrow Airport.

Jack hurried away, didn't stop outside the door for a cab. He kept walking until he felt sure he wasn't being followed, then headed for the train station. He was headed back to America, all right, but he was taking the long way.

The next morning Jack Driscoll was in Malaysia. His current game company had sent him to what was grandly billed as the OtherWorld Gaming Convention. Jack's company thought the odd blend of philosophy and strategy in his games should have an appeal in this part of the world, and in fact at least two of the games he'd created had large cult followings in Asia. Which hadn't made Jack rich, because the editions were mostly pirated. He was also here to meet dealers in person, hoping that would make them more inclined to include him in their profits. Wishful thinking, Jack thought, but the company was paying.

Jack was a noticeable figure in the throng, though not unique. Contingents of Indians and Brits and Australians, even a few Americans, mingled with the largely Asian crowd. And a crowd it was. Jack was amazed at the numbers this convention had drawn, more than three thousand paid memberships. Game companies had opened their vaults too. The huge convention center was filled with displays, some of them the size of Broadway musicals. At one end a band billed as the hottest pop group in south Asia blasted out waves of sound, with occasional lyrics in English confirming that the words were meaningless. On another stage ninja fighters played by live actors flew through the air, only to disappear behind large screens where their digital counterparts took over the action. The use of live actors was arresting, especially since many of the people in this room looked as if they went for days at a time without seeing a real human being. Some of the audience members wore costumes themselves, though most just wore jeans and t-shirts, dedicated to favorite games or rock bands. Pink Floyd was unusually well-represented on the t-shirts. For Jack, still a little displaced, the scene seemed hallucinatory. This could have been a similar convention in any big city in America, only with some of the kids' heads digitally replaced by Asian ones.

He was pretty sure the people following him were real, though.

A game convention is no place for a paranoid to begin with, with menacing figures on every hand and company representatives leaping out of every exhibit to grab a passerby's arm. And a few people obviously recognized Jack, especially after his first autographing session. But again he felt that tickle of observation in his peripheral vision, the sign he was being watched. He knew of no good reason why anyone should be watching him, and he didn't like it.

He walked the crowded aisles, both losing himself and looking for someone. Here and there he stopped to chat with another designer he knew. Not conversations that should be recorded for posterity: "Hey, man, 's'up?" "Oh, you know—" Eyes gesturing around to show the weirdness of the scene. The other person nodding. "You gonna be in Oakland next month?" "I think so. There's this girl..." "Real girl?" "I'm not sure. That's why I'm going." "You think you'd know a real girl if you saw one?" "Ha ha, Jack."

Jack laughed and moved on. At one display he stood respectfully to the side of a line of autograph seekers. The man on the other side of the table was signing copies of posters for a game that bore his name: "Chun Lee's *Deadly Digits*." The game was about three years old, but still very popular. Chun was Korean, his broader, thicker features distinguishing him from most of the southern Asians here. Like many people in the crowd, he wore a black T-shirt, but Chun's featured Mickey Mouse holding up one white-gloved hand. On one of the white digits was a ring.

The shirt carried no printing, but Jack knew the ring on Mickey's finger very well.

Chun stood to exchange very small bows, only head-nods really, with the man for whom he'd just signed, and when Chun stood he caught sight of Jack. He showed no sign of recognition, but then Jack made a small, odd gesture, touching his temple with his little finger, as if brushing back hair. Chun's eyes lit up. Jack had heard this expression all his life, but never seen it more truly demonstrated. Beams of delight seemed to come from Chun's eyes, holding Jack in place.

The Korean designer finished signing hastily, put a sign on his table that said in Chinese that he would return soon, and vaulted over the table without touching it. This was no mean feat, since when he landed in front of Jack it became clear that Jack, at 6'2", was nearly a foot taller. Chun beamed and gripped both Jack's arms. Jack bowed his head and then tried to stay slouched so they were closer to eye level.

"Jack Driscoll! I know you, though pictures of you are hard to come by."

Jack nodded at the ring on Mickey's finger. "You've played *Back Alleys*."

Chun touched the ring on his t-shirt as if pledging allegiance. "Not just played it. It is my map of the world."

"Really?" Jack looked puzzled. "But then—"

"I know. *Deadly Digits* was hardly in the same mold. But it was what was wanted from me. It was my way of breaking in."

Back Alleys had been Jack's failed game, the one that depended on strategy and cunning rather than violence. Chun's *Deadly Digits*, by contrast, had a body count akin to the Battle of Gettysburg.

Chun took Jack's arm and walked with him. They occupied a zone of their own amid the chaos of the convention. The gaming world was very odd. One could be the designer of a game that had sold millions, yet walk unrecognized even in a crowd of fans. This had many advantages, such as now.

On the other hand, if that man and woman who had been following Jack all morning closed in, he couldn't count on any help from adoring fans. He felt a little safer, though, because Chun's bodyguards, two men dressed in jeans and white t-shirts, were also following them at a discreet distance. Chun's anxiety was well-known even beyond the gaming world. He was *North* Korean, a defector, and perpetually feared recapture.

But now Chun ignored his guards and everyone else at the convention, talking as enthusiastically as any newcomer to the gaming world, telling Jack about his experiences at the convention, his travels, how he had gotten started. Then he suddenly stopped, taking Jack's arm. "There is something I have wanted to ask you. On level 7, when you are in that alley in Helsinki and you pick up a stick to fend off your attackers, isn't that a violation of the no-weapons rule you've established?"

"Ah," Jack said, "you've played the pirated edition."

"No!"

"I'm 'fraid so. The pirates couldn't stand the lack of violence and slipped that one scene into the game."

"This is horrible!"

Jack shrugged. Chun remained outraged on his behalf, looking around as if for a complaint desk. Jack laughed. "They stole it from me, Chun. Altering it for their own market seems a lesser sin by—"

"No." Chun kept his hand on Jack's arm, looking sternly into his eyes. "If one is going to take a man's work, one must take it all, especially its principles. Anything else is an abomination."

Jack laughed again. "You have a very refined sense of ethics."

Jack was much less concerned with the years-ago theft of his intellectual property than with the fact that he could no longer see Chun's bodyguards. Amid the huge crowds in the convention center there were ebbs and flows of people, like waves. One of those tides had apparently swept over the bodyguards and pulled them out to sea. They could have just gotten momentarily separated from their principle, but Jack didn't think so.

He stood in the midst of all those people and felt isolated. No one else saw. No one would do anything. Where was security?

Earlier in the morning Jack had seen uniformed guards scattered regularly through the hall, but now saw none.

He and Chun walked on. The bodyguards did not reappear. Chun in his absorption with questioning Jack didn't seem to notice. Jack no longer saw the man and woman he thought had been following him, either, but didn't feel reassured.

"I thought perhaps picking up the stick in the alley was permissible under your rules because it was a found object, not meant as a weapon, and you didn't carry it with you."

Jack shook his head. "No weapons, that was the rule. A stick is a weapon."

"Ah." Chun puzzled at the obstacle. "What if you defended yourself with a hatrack, then, that happened to be available? What about... a credit card?"

"Chun, you're going way deeper into this than the game will really support. The point of it was not to *get* attacked. Once you're attacked you've failed."

"Ah," Chun said again. He had amazing concentration, standing completely absorbed in thought in the middle of the chaotic scene. Jack, on the other hand, was looking all around them. He felt a trap tightening, though he still didn't see the people he'd thought were pursuing him.

Then he did—the woman, her blondeness distinctive in the crowd, flitting behind a booth.

"Chun?"

"Eh?"

"Where are your men?"

Chun turned very slowly, a complete three hundred and sixty degrees. The quality of his concentration changed abruptly. His features moved alertly. His hands clenched and unclenched. Chun was trim and well-muscled, but barely over five feet tall. Jack could see over his head.

"Sometimes you can't see them," Chun said slowly of his bodyguards.

"That would be true if they were gone, too."

"Come."

Chun took Jack's elbow and guided him swiftly. Jack hoped his friend was looking for allies, but Chun just kept moving, turning from aisle to aisle, finally slipping through a relatively open space. On the other side, among a crowd of exhibits again, he said, "Two of them, yes? A man and a woman?"

Jack nodded. "Do you recognize them?"

Chun shook his head. "Only their purposefulness. Will you do me a favor, my friend?"

"Of course."

"We are going to walk down that narrow aisle over there, back into the staging area where it's less crowded. I will walk in front. Your body and your coat should cover me. Just keep walking back that direction until you are in an area empty of people. All right?"

"Isn't there anybody you could call?" Jack asked. "Back-up? Bring on the next shift of bodyguards early?"

Chun smiled at his nervousness. "You are the next shift, Jack. Heaven sent you, I think. Come."

He turned and walked, still as if strolling. Jack, following orders, walked almost directly behind him. Jack wore a long, lightweight overcoat, a variation on a style of dress still favored by some gamers, how many years after "The Matrix"? Chun seemed to compact himself even farther.

"It must be hard looking over your shoulder all the time like this. See people even when they're not there. Actually, though, it's a good mind-set for a game designer, if you think about it. Have you thought about coming up with a game based on your own situation?"

At some point, Jack realized he was talking to himself.

He hadn't had much time to formulate a plan when he'd felt followed, but now enlisting Chun seemed not to have been as brilliant as he'd thought. The little gamer was so beset by genuine dangers that he would bolt at a sign like this, as he had done. His bodyguards had proven useless, too. Jack continued to walk, armed now only with a cell phone, and no one he knew could reach him in time.

He passed a work table and quickly picked up a dowel rod, about an inch in diameter and two feet long. Jack slipped it up the sleeve of his coat. The rod was lightweight wood, but better than nothing.

At first he had heard rustling around him. Now that sound was gone, as was much of the noise of the convention. Curtains that closed off this backstage area absorbed much of it. There were the sounds of moving footsteps and murmuring voices, and Jack even saw a handful of people, but all flitting so fast they didn't seem to see him. He would have welcomed being challenged for a backstage pass and kicked out of here, but of course that didn't happen, since he wanted it.

He thought he heard the sound of a body falling, but that could have been only panic beginning to sing in his ears, painting its own scenario out of random noise.

He turned a corner and suddenly there was the woman, right in front of him. Tall, blonde, slender, with a thin face and dark eyes focused laserlike on Jack. She wore a white business suit, the legs of which tightly wrapped her own. It would be made of some fabric that allowed her to move fast. Her hands were out in front of her in what, for all Jack knew, was the killing position of lao-tze.

A person could have been caught in her gaze. Jack, though, immediately leaped to the side in the confined area. Sure enough, a foot shot through the space he had occupied a moment before. A bare foot in a blue pants leg. The man who'd been following Jack earlier had doffed his shoes and any pretense of being a member of the convention. When his kick missed its target he pivoted quickly, leg still upraised, bringing the same foot rapidly toward Jack's nose.

Six inches from its target, the foot hit the dowel rod Jack had slipped out of his sleeve. Jack cracked it smartly just where he had aimed, at the man's ankle bone. He heard the contact, like a well-hit line drive.

His attacker showed no response. His swinging foot missed Jack's face, but the attacker landed on that foot and immediately leaped off it, coming toward his target again.

"Oh, shit," Jack said, scrambling back. He had always thought these impervious-to-pain players were cheats in a game world, and he'd never imagined encountering one in real life. That smash on the ankle bone would hurt like hell, he was sure of that, but the man wouldn't give into the pain until after this fight. After Jack was down and dead.

So Jack's dowel rod wasn't going to be much help, except to fend off attack, but now the other man would be ready for that. The attacker stood for just a moment looking at Jack with a flat, dull gaze. Jack wondered if this staring at the opponent was a new form of martial arts. This man didn't seem to be trying to hypnotize him. Maybe only to memorize him.

No, it was a distraction. Even while the eyes remained on Jack, the man's foot came at him again, this time directly upward. Jack stepped back and held the stick parallel to the ground, tightly in his two hands, hoping the foot would smash on it again. He held it perfectly positioned. The foot hit right in the middle of the stick.

And broke through it, hitting Jack in the chest. Jack fell backward, onto the ground, catching himself so his hands were down on the concrete floor. His opponent's eyes smiled. Jack would not be able to rise from that position, in this small space, without making himself vulnerable for all the time his opponent would need. Jack just sat for a moment, but that was dangerous too. The attacker's foot reached out and pulled Jack's foot forward, so that his legs were extended, making it even harder to rise and leaving Jack even more exposed. Then, his fastest move yet, the man pivoted on that foot and brought his other one around in a roundhouse kick Jack didn't even have time to fall back to avoid. He cringed, beginning to slide away from the blow, hoping to evade enough of its force to stay alive and barely conscious.

The swish of flesh past his face was so close that Jack could smell the dirt under the man's toenails. One of the nails, very short, sliced Jack's nose, opening a trail of fire. Jack screamed.

Then he leaped back and up to his feet. His opponent hadn't been toying with him. He'd been interrupted by problems of his own. *A* problem, that is. Chun was back. He stood behind the attacker, having pulled him back just enough to keep his foot from connecting with Jack's head. Then he had dropped him. Chun stood there smiling slightly, hands up loosely in front of him, bouncing on the balls of his feet, looking a little ridiculous in his jeans and Mickey Mouse t-shirt and martial arts pose.

The man on the ground moved so fast he was airborne as he was turning, both his legs and hands aimed at Chun. He came at him like a rain of knives.

And Chun spun, closing momentarily through those arms and legs, inside the other man's defenses, where Chun cracked him in the nose with his elbow. There was a flurry of other moves on both parts, mostly defensive, Jack thought, and then the two fighters backed apart.

The attacker didn't shake off Chun's blow as he had Jack's. He appeared obviously dazed, blood spurting down from his nose, covering his mouth and chin. Chun began to move again.

The root of Chun's reputation in the martial-arts-gaming world, even before he'd designed a game, was that he had been North Korean and then southeast Asian karate champion three years in a row when he was eighteen, nineteen, and twenty. The digits in his *Deadly Digits* game were his own.

Jack had not struck up a conversation with him by random.

"Take the other one!" Chun yelled as he spun in to attack the man.

Jack turned to the woman, who had stayed back from the action. She looked panicked, he thought.

This lithe blonde martial arts woman was such a gaming convention. They were always turning up in the kinds of games Chun designed. In real life there were very few, and Jack didn't think whoever was following him had come up with one at short notice. The woman was just along as a distraction while the man came in for the kill. Jack gave her an appeasing look, as if to say, *Just don't do anything stupid and you'll get out of this okay.*

And the woman spun on her heel and kicked him in the head.

"Unghh." He had had just enough time to turn with the blow, slipping some of its force, but his head still rang. He jumped back, trying to gain time, and she rushed in to him. Jack still had half the broken stick in his hand, and he thrust it at her face like a knife, its jagged end capable of doing a lot of damage. She evaded it smoothly, though, twisting back and to the side, which gave Jack the opportunity to sweep his own leg behind hers and pull. This move didn't knock her down, just made her lose balance and stumble back. Jack didn't press his advantage, afraid she'd hit something vital the next time she closed with him.

"Chun!" he yelled. "I can't take this other one!"

The woman smiled. In a strange accent, sort of British-Chinese, she said, "Unfortunately for you, he is occupied."

Jack looked back past her, folded his arms across his chest, and smiled himself. "Unfortunately for you, he's not."

She didn't believe him. That was clear from her continuing confident smile. But her eyes were no longer fully on Jack, and neither were her ears. When she heard the swish of movement behind her she turned quickly, moving her head to the side. She still got clipped, though, by the small three-legged stool Chun had thrown from ten feet away, where he was just wrapping up his own opponent. The stool caught the woman on one of her cheeks. She gave to lessen the blow, bending back.

Which gave Jack the opportunity to roll suddenly to the ground and through her legs. A sort of rolling tackle, not legal in any sport, but effective. The woman went down and hit the back of her head on the concrete floor. This cracking sound was even louder than the last one. She didn't move.

A moment later Chun stood beside Jack looking down at her. "Who is she?" Jack asked.

Chun gave him a strange look. "No idea. She is not Korean, though. Neither is the man."

"Well—"

"Yes." The North Korean government certainly worked through agents of other nationalities. So did other organizations.

Chun looked at the broken stick in Jack's hand. "You used a weapon."

"No, I failed to use a weapon. That's a game rule, Chun, not one when somebody's trying to kill you. Anyway, you used the little stool."

"Yes, but it was a found object. I didn't bring it with me." Chun smiled.

They walked away without bothering to search the attackers' clothes. They wouldn't be carrying any identification, at least no accurate ones. Maybe they would still be unconscious when security came to get them.

At the curtain, Chun turned and looked back. "You know," he said quietly, "when I slipped away, neither of them followed me. They both continued to come after you."

"Probably thought you were still with me or close by. Wanted to take me out first the way they took out your guards."

"Mmmm," Chun murmured, then shook his head. "I don't think they were after me, Jack. I think they were after you."

Jack continued to look at the bodies on the floor, avoiding his new friend's eyes. "Really?" he said.

CHAPTER 2

Jack seemed to spend the next twenty-four hours on planes and in airport terminals. Only a couple of the news channels mentioned the addition of Libya to the upcoming World Summit, and those two only in crawls at the bottom of the screen. It wasn't big news, except to Jack. But he didn't take the pleasure in it he would have if he'd done it on his own, as he'd planned.

He no longer sensed pursuit, and by the time he reached LAX he felt as secure as anyone could in that place. Jack continued to exercise habitual caution, though, catching a flight to Salt Lake City and renting a car to drive to Denver.

The drive through the beautiful, nearly empty landscape helped clear his head. He gave a great deal of thought, of course, to why he had been attacked in Malaysia. Had they intended to capture him or kill him? The latter, he thought. Those two attackers hadn't appeared to be holding back. They could easily have used a tranquilizer dart or a spiked drink in that crowd if they'd just wanted to take him hostage. No, someone had hired them to kill him. Jack had no idea who would want him dead, although he was very much afraid it was one of his best friends. Maybe all his friends.

His shoulders relaxed as he drove and no one pursued, but another sort of tension began to build in him, the kind a child feels in the days before Christmas. The group meeting. Jack couldn't help grinning.

⸺ ⁂ ⸺

The medium-sized old hotel had been built a few miles east of downtown Denver, in what turned out to be a bad location. The hotel had changed hands several times in the last few years, and was now called The Lamplighter Inn, for no good reason at all. It had a spacious lobby that was usually empty, and a comfortable semi-hidden shabbiness. The gift shop was always closed. A large meeting room on the second floor could be used for receptions or speeches, but usually stood empty. Most groups would not book a meeting in this out-of-the way spot.

The hotel didn't have the high-tech security of newer hostelries, which was one reason the group had chosen it. The group's own team had swept the place a day earlier, making sure there were no recording security cameras in the meeting room and no one else's bugs either.

Starting in the early afternoon people began arriving, some in cars, some in cabs from the airport, a couple on bicycles. These latter two wore hiking boots and khaki shorts and didn't bother to change for the meeting that started at five o'clock. They didn't stand out in their appearance. A handful of men wore suits, some women wore nice dresses, jeans were common, and one couple in their late fifties wore a tuxedo and evening dress. "We have an *important* function after this one," Alicia Mortenson said, and her husband Craig laughed.

These people trickled into the spacious meeting room from about four-thirty on. There were two self-service bars at either end of the room and a few uninspired hors d'oeuvres, but no bartenders or other servers. The members were of all ages from late teens up almost to a hundred. They wore no buttons or lapel pins, and there was nothing to identify their common interest. On the hotel's register this was called a meeting of stockholders of Western Amalgamated, a name chosen to be both uninformative and too boring to provoke curiosity.

Some greeted each other with nods, others hugged enthusiastically. A man and woman who hadn't seen each other in three years but kept in near-constant e-mail communication stood side by side, their shoulders touching, and didn't say a word, just watched the others together and communicated completely by smiles and body language. Two men in their seventies, on the other hand, chattered like jays even though they had had lunch nearly every week for fifty years.

Jack sidled through the door at about five-thirty, looked over the crowd of several dozen people, and smiled gently. Janice Gentry waved at him from across the room. Janice had been his history professor at Yale and one of his early mentors in this group. She had helped teach him the Real History. She looked more like a retired fashion model than a grandmother and professor. She looked a question at him, glancing at the empty space beside him, and Jack shrugged. Thirty yards away, Professor Gentry laughed as if he'd said something witty.

Jack edged around the group, seeing people he'd known for years, but he wasn't yet ready to dive in. He couldn't stop smiling, though.

A rotund young man in an expensive suit stopped on his way to the bar, looked Jack up and down and said, "How's the kiddie porn business?"

"Awesome. Wicked good."

The young man looked at the goatee Jack had started growing in Asia, made his mouth small, and said, "It's so sad to see a chronological adult captured by a teenage fad. Or more pathetic yet for a grown man to want to appear to have the intellectual capacity of a baseball player."

Jack took out his baseball cap, the one with the company logo on it, and put it on backwards.

They both burst out laughing.

"Hi, Jack." "Hey, Ronald." Ronald hugged him one-armed, holding his drink glass out to the side. "I'm headed to a convention in Vegas after this," Jack explained his appearance. "Got to appear. There was a rumor I was going to be named Gamer of the Year this year, but at the last minute a bloc of east coast votes swept it away from me."

Ronald knew exactly what this meant. Jack had engineered his own defeat. The primary rule of this group was not to become high-profile enough to get noticed. "I'm sorry, man."

Jack shrugged. "I'll have to give up this role pretty soon anyway. Been at it long enough."

"That will be a relief, I'm sure," Ronald said. He had a smooth, preppy-sounding east coast accent which no one was quite sure was phony. But he could do other voices as well, in any of four languages. Jack had heard many of them, starting when they were at school together years earlier.

"No, I'll miss it," Jack said of being a gamer. "It's fun. I could just quit for a while and come back. In three years it'll be a whole new generation. No one will have heard of me."

"Yeah, man, but then you'll be, like, thirty." Ronald was doing a Valley Boy voice now.

"What about you? You rich again yet?"

A few years earlier Ronald, or rather a few of his companies, had made an enormous fortune in some dot-com startups. He had funneled most of the money into this group's secret coffers, then, when he was in danger of making *Fortune*'s list of billionaires, had "gone broke" in a quiet way. In answer to Jack's question, he looked sideways around the room, as if fearing eavesdroppers, and said in a completely fake voice, "Me? Nah. Nah. Just a working man. Up at dawn, milking the computers, collecting the eggs."

They both laughed again. God, it was a relief to be here.

Jack circulated, hugged old friends, genuflected to respected elders. One asked, "Did you suggest a caterer for the affair to your friend the ambassador?"

Without asking how the man knew, Jack shook his head. "No, sir. Can you recommend someone?"

The man was ready with advice. "I think you should go through Italy rather than Paris. Everyone should be more comfortable than that. And of course now you can't have a Swiss presence." Jack knew what he meant. The semi-rational dictator the American ambassador had invited to the peace conference had declared a jihad against Switzerland a few years earlier; no point in provoking him needlessly.

The man scribbled a name, and Jack took it gratefully before moving on.

A few minutes later Jack was back standing with Ronald, chatting quietly along with three other old friends, when the door opened and Arden Spindler entered. Arden wasn't particularly well-known here, having been recruited into the group only a year or so ago. But Ronald knew her, as did two other people in their small conversational group, and they all stopped talking, staring at the young woman with fascination, the way a prairie dog stares at a snake.

"What? Who?" said the fifth person. "Her? The one who just came in?"

"Don't say anything," Jack whispered.

"Don't look at her. Erase her from your thoughts," Ronald added. "Keep talking. What about this new National Security Advisor? Oh, shit, she's coming this way."

The group suddenly scattered, leaving Jack and the woman who didn't know Arden to face her alone, as the friendly young woman made her slow way across the room toward them.

Exit Interview

Three months later, after everything was smashed to pieces, the Circle destroyed and all Jack's friends gone, he began to talk to his fifth interrogator. To the first four he had said nothing, not even his name, though they knew a great deal about him already. But Jack didn't tell them anything, even after they dropped any pretense of civilized rules and began torturing him.

The interviews took place in a small windowless room that felt as if it were deep inside a much larger space. The prisoner had been interrogated many times over the last week by several different interrogators who had run the full range: best friend, bully, torturer, wheedling promiser. He hadn't given any of them anything. It was morning, but he was already tired, when he looked up to see a woman walking into the room holding a large black notebook. It matched her large black-rimmed glasses. The glasses either hid or emphasized her slightly crooked nose, and obscured rather than enlarging her mud-colored eyes. In spite of her thinness above the waist she had rather lumpy hips, looking as if she spent most of her life sitting. She also had the no-nonsense air of a woman who had spent most of her life in the company of men who resented her, so she had managed to turn off her personality as well as any sexual subtleties.

Jack thought at least she'd be a nice change of pace from the wrestler who had punched him on every third question, no matter what his answer, but after a few minutes he wasn't so sure.

We know all about your Circle. You may fill in a few gaps, but you probably have no primary information we don't already know. We know this "secret society" has operated for many years, coming to have some influence on some administrations. Currently out of favor, we believe. You were recruited by your—sixth grade teacher?

Jack didn't speak for a long minute, while the interviewer waited. Then he looked up at her and said, *Fifth.* His voice was hoarse from lack of use.

She nodded and made a note in her notebook. *An exceptionally early recruit, I understand. Congratulations. And I'm sure this organization gave you a sense of importance, the thought that—*

Jack laughed. *I never felt less important than when I was with the other members. That's what was so lovely about it.* His eyes were moist, and his voice had grown nostalgic.

The interviewer seemed to take no notice. Her voice remained clipped. *Sort of like Mensa, I suppose. Get together once a month and bolster each other's sense of superiority.*

No one ever mentioned what they were doing, unless someone else needed to know. We found out, of course. That was the one skill everyone in the group shared, gathering information.

Still sounding bored, the interviewer said, *And they were extraordinary people, certainly. What was the highest rank in government any of them had achieved?*

She sat poised with pen, mud-colored eyes focused on him. Silence reigned for a minute. Then Jack suddenly leaned across, grabbed her notebook, and tore a blank page from it. He held out his hand and after a long moment the interviewer passed him a pen. Jack wrote three figures near the top of the blank sheet: *"PQ3."*

The interviewer barely appeared to glance at what he'd written. But as the silence continued she began doodling on the paper that lay between them. Her doodles formed the characters "PB4."

Jack kept his eyes down as if contemplating. Then he looked up and said, *The highest political rank any of us had achieved? None.*

None?

No appointed positions and certainly no elected ones. None of our members has held elected office in more than two hundred years. Not even a local school board. Actually, two of our members were First Ladies of the United States, but not the two you would think. Very few of us were CEOs, either. More commonly we were the assistant to the Human Resources Director. These were the people to whom presidents and CEOs turn in times of crisis. Mycroft Holmes, not Sherlock.

And once in a while you got together to share information, such as at the meeting shortly before this crisis began.

Yes. Now a tear trickled down Jack's cheek. God, he would miss the gatherings.

So these amazing people would get together—

And you didn't have to keep up an appearance. You didn't have to dumb down or smarten up. It was such a relief. You could be yourself, even if you'd forgotten who your self was. You didn't have to put up any kind of front. It would have been useless. Everyone there had been the valedictorian of her class—or the rebel so bored he dropped out and invented a new computer language. What I mean is, you gave up that advantage here. Everyone could see eight moves ahead. Forget it. You could talk to each other like normal people. No one could impress anyone else.

She was the exception.

Jack glanced up sharply at the interviewer. She had no gleam in her eye. Her pasty white skin didn't glow with the excitement of giving away secret information. She was just doing her job.

She? Jack said. He began doodling on the blank sheet again.

The woman whose name you've been muttering in your sleep. Arden." The interviewer pronounced the name very precisely. *She was the exception.*

After another long pause Jack nodded. *She was the exception. She was a step beyond. Maybe several steps beyond. Half a dozen people I know sincerely believed she was the product of genetic manipulation. Or possibly an alien being. "Imagine being her parents," someone once said, and we all shuddered.*

Was she so frightening?

She was perfectly charming. That was part of it. We all lived by manipulating other people, to one degree or another, so that wasn't what was scary about her. Her ability to insinuate herself into a group was extraordinary, but not unprecedented. That wasn't why she scared people. It was because she did things that had nothing to do with intelligence. After talking to you casually for one minute, she could tell you that you hated your older brother, and she would always be right. She wasn't just smart, she was a mind-reader. But somehow you knew it wasn't ESP, it was her picking up signals you didn't know you were giving. Desperately you would try to stop, but be helpless. If you were having an affair, God forbid she should see you and come across the room. Within thirty seconds she would be giving you that slow smile, and you would know she knew.

Maybe she wasn't so smart, maybe she just had a very good network.

She would have had to have satellite coverage. And x-ray vision.

<hr/>

As Arden came across the room in Denver Jack tried to keep his thoughts absolutely blank, and succeeded. He'd gotten good at this since knowing her. Arden stopped and chatted with two or three people, but he knew she was coming his way. And his lone remaining conversational partner, a young woman named Elizabeth Rayona, was hurting his concentration.

"Who is she? When did you first meet her?"

"Last year. Her grandmother introduced us. I said how do you do and she just looked at me for a long few seconds, then said, 'I'm sorry.'"

Elizabeth turned to him. "What was she sorry for?"

After a long pause, Jack said, "For me. I was sad. I hadn't told anyone, but an old friend of mine had just gone missing. Not one of us. No one anyone in the circle would know."

Elizabeth's voice was growing more concerned. She was facing Jack so she was in profile to Arden, and Jack could tell that Elizabeth was trying to stand straight and not glance aside, but she couldn't help herself. Neither could he. "And she knew about your missing friend?"

"No one knew!" Jack burst out. "I hadn't talked about her and I wasn't giving anything away. But she read me. How I was feeling. And I didn't want to be read! You know? I didn't want to be—comforted."

"So did she—?"

"Hello, Jack," said a low, luminous voice. Yes, luminous: her voice gave off a soft glow, illuminating the features of her listeners so they seemed to stand apart from the others in the room, in a subtle spotlight. Or possibly that was only in Jack's imagination.

"Hello, Arden. Do you know Elizabeth Rayona?"

That was a cruel thing to do, after the build-up he'd given Arden, to unleash her immediately on the new girl. But Elizabeth had annoyed him a little by making him talk about Arden.

Arden did not turn her attention immediately to the introduction. Her blue eyes stayed on Jack. He stood perfectly still, neither smiling nor frowning, but looking back at her as if curious about *her*. "It's all right," Arden said to him, then turned to his companion. "Hello, Ms. Rayona. What school did you go to in Phoenix? Private, right? Let me think, was it—?"

"Briarcliff," the two women said together. Arden laughed. Elizabeth did not. "Do you know anyone who went there?" she asked. It didn't take mystical powers to hear the anxiety in her voice.

"Let me think, do I?" Arden said, and kept the young woman on the hook as she turned back to Jack. "I waited for you at Heathrow. By the time I got here people knew about your work with the ambassador. Of course, some people around here are a little peeved about your independence—"

"Meaning your grandmother?"

Arden nodded. "—but I've told her I thought it was a great idea."

Arden had a gentle smile, a professional sort of smile, that seemed to have nothing to do with what she'd been saying. Surely enough, she then changed the subject completely. "Did it help?"

Jack stiffened. "Help what?"

"Jack, Jack, there's no need to be hostile. The day you were in France was an anniversary for you. Did what you did there help?"

Jack turned and walked quickly away. He passed friends, some of whom spoke to him, and several raised their eyebrows, but he didn't stop walking until a hand grabbed his arm. "Jack!" a hearty voice said, while the meaty hand insistently turned him toward the speaker.

"Hello, Mr. Mortenson."

"Since you look near death I think you're old enough now to call me Craig."

"Take it easy on him, dear," Alicia Mortenson said. "He's just had a session with our resident psychic."

"Someone's giving her information!" Jack said. "She cannot just read these things from my posture and my face. Someone's feeding her."

"God, I hope so," Alicia said. "Otherwise she's a mind-reader, and I don't like that idea."

She and her husband glanced at each other and chuckled, without an exchange of words. Craig Mortenson was in his late fifties and looked older, with a fringe of white hair around a large bald head. Often he looked sleepy and bored, often irritable, but when he was at his genial best, as he seemed to be now, there was no more convivial host.

Alicia, to whom he'd been married for many years, was probably his age but looked much younger. Thin, elegant, with a firm chin and lively eyes, she looked perfectly at ease in her dark blue evening gown, while Craig looked as if he'd been forced into his tuxedo with a shoehorn.

"The trouble is," Jack said in a more thoughtful voice, "I don't know who would know the things she knows to give them to her in the first place. It's as if—"

As if someone were keeping a file on him, and had been for a long time. Jack didn't say the words aloud, but Craig Mortenson shook his head gravely. "We don't do that, Jack." He was speaking of the Circle.

"By the way," he added, changing back to his hearty tone, "great work in France. Just what the summit needs. A little precipitous, perhaps—"

"You know very well you'd been saying something exactly like that needed to be done," Alicia said. Craig shrugged agreement.

"So then I can say I had your approval?"

"Of course, dear," Alicia said, laying her hand on Jack's, while Craig only grunted thoughtfully, staring into Jack's eyes.

But Jack had had enough of having his eyes stared into meaningfully. Abruptly he excused himself. As he walked he saw Elizabeth Rayona crying, shoulders slumped, while Arden hugged her and spoke soft words of comfort. At the bar Jack made it a double.

Exit Interview

I'm sure this circle was quite extraordinary, wielded more than their share of influence over key political figures, made significant contributions that won them favors. Some were even in the diplomatic service, correct? Or had ties there? But now they're gone, Mr. Driscoll, and I'm quite sure history will proceed without noticing.

Jack closed his eyes boredly. But the landscape behind his

eyes was so barren, stretching over the horizon without relief, as his future stretched friendlessly. Only he held the Circle's legacy now. Over two hundred years of the Real History, never written, never recorded, and over now.

He knew the interviewer was challenging him so he would try to impress her, but he wanted to say something anyway. The reason for secrecy was gone now, since there would be no more secret intrusions into American history.

We brought down Communism, he said quietly.

The interviewer chuckled. *Your group, by itself, ended Communism?*

You're right, I'm exaggerating. One of us put an end to the Evil Empire. Well, two. Craig Mortenson woke up grumpy one morning, read his morning Times, *and said, "This is draining valuable resources that could be used elsewhere."*

His wife, knowing exactly what he was talking about, said, "It provides a good training ground for some of our people."

"That's not reason enough any more. Plus they're annoying me."

So he set about bringing down the Soviet Union. As he sat musing on how to begin, his wife said, "I'd start by getting a list of the College of Cardinals." "Hmm," he replied.

That was the first step, rigging the election of John Paul II. I mean, a Polish Pope? Didn't anybody get the joke? How many Poles does it take to bring down Communism?

It took him more than a decade, and he did recruit a few of us to help, but it was primarily Mortenson's doing when Mikhail Gorbachev announced the dissolution of the Evil Empire. Mortenson was toasted quietly at the next meeting.

Jack shrugged. *Well, that's Craig Mortenson. And the amazing Alicia Mortenson, of course. One of these days the trade imbalance is going to piss him off, and then China better watch its ass.*

The interviewer's voice showed its first trace of humanity as she cleared her throat and said, *Well, China can proceed without alarm for now. Mr. Mortenson—*

I know, Jack said. Craig Mortenson had been one of the first to die, even before the final cataclysm.

The interrogation continued quietly, the interviewer politely ignoring Jack's tears. He doodled more on the paper.

⸻

Denver

A group of the younger members, including Jack and Ronald, was having a good time near the bar, telling anecdotes about their jobs and recent lunches. People already knew the important facts, but got a kick out of hearing the details that couldn't be included in an e-mail, the small signals passed when a mind had been turned.

"He'd been drumming on the tabletop ever since he got there," Bill Wong was saying of a recent lunch with an undersecretary of state who had been his college roommate. "Just happy with nervous energy, you know, and as I talked about how sick I was of people stealing my ideas, or worse yet stealing them but changing them, leaving out the best parts, he was drumming more and more slowly until he stopped. Then a minute later he was just tapping on the tabletop, with his fingers like this." Bill made both his hands into the shapes of pistols, the kind small pretend cowboys make as they say, *kew, kew*, his index fingers pointing like barrels. Everyone laughed.

Some older members had joined the small crowd too, and Jack was startled to find Arden Spindler at his side. She smiled at him and didn't say a word.

"You know," a young man in a suit spoke up. The young man had been a recruit of a few years' standing, since early in college, and he had some remarkable abilities in computers, electronics, and surveillance, but in this crowd his people skills sometimes seemed limited. "I've been wondering, and maybe one of you older members can tell me, doesn't this group have a name? I mean, an organization like this, that's been around so long, you'd think at some point people would start, at least among themselves, referring to it as *some*thing. I realize there's not much structure,

31

and, and we like it that way, I know, but still it would be nice just to say to one of us quietly, 'Are you going to the meeting of the—you know, the Foundation, or something.'"

Most of the people hearing him looked amused, but a couple nodded thoughtfully, and even the amused ones shot some looks at each other, as if maybe they already had their own secret name for the group.

"I believe Aaron Burr wanted to call it the Council," one older member said quietly, "but others, I think, thought that sounded too much like a secret governing council with tentacles in—well, just not an image we wanted to cultivate, even among ourselves."

Jack said, "Professor Gentry told us that during the Civil War it was sometimes referred to as the Interdiction Committee, because of course it was intruding into both camps in order to—"

"Too many syllables," Elizabeth Rayona protested. She had apparently recovered from her brief session with Arden, though there was still a bright sheen to her eyes. "I can tell why that one didn't catch on."

The first young man said, "But it does have the weight I think this group deserves. The *gravitas*, if I don't sound too stuffy—"

"How about the Hornets?" Arden interrupted. Several people chuckled, and the young man looked offended.

"I'm serious about this, names—"

"So am I," Arden protested. "I went to school in Europe, I never got the American high school experience, and I always wanted to belong to a team called the Hornets." She shook her hands as if holding imaginary pompoms. "Go, Hornets!"

Several people echoed her cheer, laughter became general, and the stuffy young man turned away angrily. But a woman old enough to be his mother drew him back in and stood with her arm around him, looking fondly around the group.

"I've always thought of us as the Circle," she said.

Her voice was warm and binding and they realized that's how they were standing, in a circle. Some nodded, a few put their arms around each other, and the stuffy young man looked comforted.

Jack gazed around at their faces, some of them known so well to him, others only familiar from nods or legends. It may have been only in retrospect, when he remembered this scene later, but he didn't think so: looking around at their small band, he realized he was home.

The feeling was only diminished slightly by his near-certainty that at least one of these people had tried to have him killed.

Ronald clapped his hands together and said, "Let's sing favorite camp songs! Jack, lead us off!"

People chuckled, and the circle broke apart, but Jack knew the others had felt it too. There was a slight sense of embarrassment as he and Ronald stood together, so that one of them was glad to point and say, "Oh, look, here comes the Chair."

It was a joke. America has had 44 presidents. The Circle had had twelve Chairs in two hundred and twenty years. The current Chair was 87 years old, rolling across the room in a wheelchair, but that was only temporary, because of hip-replacement surgery. She could still beat any two people in the room at simultaneous visualized chess while reading a novel, and all of them knew it. This group had very little formal structure, and meetings were not called to order, but when Gladys Leaphorn rolled in they all either straightened their posture or self-consciously did not do so. Jack remained stiff-faced as she rolled right up to him. He nodded, clicking his heels together.

"Knock it off, Driscoll," she growled. "Next time you have a whim to alter the whole dynamic of a meeting of world leaders, you might check with some of us first."

"Would you have given me your approval, Madame Chair?"

"I don't know. We would have had to think about it."

"That's what I didn't think there was time for."

"There's always time for thought," she growled.

If she had ever played Halo 2, and been surrounded by hostile aliens, she would have known otherwise, Jack thought. Sometimes you just had to act. "So what do you think now?" he asked casually.

Looking as if she were just now thinking about the idea,

Gladys sat for a moment, then shrugged. "Probably didn't do irreparable damage."

Jack fluttered his hands over his chest as if his heart were going pitty-pat at her praise. Across the room, his former college professor laughed again.

"But seriously, Driscoll, all of you." The Chair raised her voice. Gladys Leaphorn was a heavy woman with dark skin and the sharp cheekbones and nose of her Cherokee ancestors, and surprisingly delicate hands. She drew attention without demanding it, and even in her wheelchair somehow dominated the room. "Our primary concern right now is the President's new National Security Advisor, one Dennis Wilkerson. Do any of you know him?"

They all looked at her, not even a murmur going around the room. The Chair sighed. "That's what I thought. This is ridiculous, unheard of. Alicia, tell us about him."

Without hesitation, Alicia Mortenson began, "Dennis Wilkerson, age 38. Raised in the midwest, attending several public schools as his father changed jobs as a salesman, finally graduating in Bloomington. Attended Wilkes-Barre College in Pennsylvania, degree in history, then entered the Air Force, where he worked in computers and digital surveillance, serving in Desert Storm but only on the very fringes."

"Nothing but fringes in Desert Storm," someone muttered.

"He did achieve a security clearance, but whether he ever saw classified documents is unknown. Released from service with the rank of captain, he worked in the security field in Cleveland for two years, and by security I mean of office buildings. Then he returned to college, at a small school in Virginia that apparently had an accelerated program—"

"—diploma mill," someone else muttered. "Download it from the 'net and print it yourself on your home computer."

"—because he achieved a Ph.D. in only two years, this time in political science. For the last several years he has taught a couple of unpopular courses at Williams College in Missouri. Until Sophie Cohen, a good friend of several people in this group, abruptly resigned as National Security Advisor and the President plucked Mr. Wilkerson from his well-deserved obscurity to take her place."

"And no one here has ever had so much as a cup of coffee with him!" the Chair said. "It's intolerable."

One member, whose contacts in academia numbered in the thousands, apparently took this personally, stepping forward to say, "Gladys, be fair. The man came out of nowhere. For God's sake, he doesn't even have tenure at that podunk college where he teaches. Apparently he wrote one paper, not even published, which he sent to the President, which so impressed President Dimsky that he lit on him for the NSA job when Sophie unexpectedly resigned. I think the President *liked* the fact that no one's ever heard of this Wilkerson character. You know he thinks himself a great judge of diamonds in the rough."

Several people, a couple of whom had known President Jefferson Witt since college, rolled their eyes. This group had helped him get elected, but not because of a high opinion of his intellect or abilities.

"Let me just be sure," Ms. Leaphorn insisted. "Not one person here or elsewhere in our group has ever met this man face to face?"

Jack scanned the group carefully. No one appeared to be hiding anything, but that didn't mean no one was.

He felt lucky that Arden was standing beside him, not looking at him.

"Why don't we approach it from another angle?" Alicia Mortenson said helpfully. "Why did Ms. Cohen resign so abruptly?"

"Again without our having a clue," the Chair muttered.

"Family health problems. Her husband."

"That's what they always say," Ronald observed.

"Oh, he has a genuine health problem," Arden smiled. "Sophie's going to kill him because she caught him cheating on her. She resigned because she was afraid the scandal was going to go public and in order to devote more time to making his life miserable."

The Chair from her seated position looked all around the room, and no one seemed to be looking down at her when they made eye contact. They knew what she was demanding now: learn everything about the Cohens' marital history, whether the husband had indulged himself this way before, and most of all learn everything there was to know about his paramour. After a moment of silence the Chair said, "I'm glad we had this chat," and rolled toward the bar.

"God, I love these meetings," Ronald said.

So did Jack. He didn't know yet that this would be the last enjoyable one, but he still enjoyed it to the fullest, still liked reminiscing about it.

CHAPTER 3

The two men went through airport security in Reno with great ease. Neither carried any luggage. They didn't even wear jackets. They slipped off their black loafers and put them through the x-ray scanner while everyone around them struggled with coats, satchels, purses, laptops, briefcases, strollers, umbrellas. The two men didn't even carry wallets. The only things they had to take out of their pockets were keys and money clips. They slipped past their fellow travellers and cleared security quickly, not having to pause to reassemble themselves.

They strolled down the concourse, one tall and thin, with blond hair buzzed close to his skull, the other shorter, bulkier, and dark, with a strong nose and even stronger brown eyes. He did the looking around while his companion just strolled. They stopped at a bar, leaning back against high stools. One ordered a Tecate, the other a Coke. When the boy brought the order he offered glasses, but neither man bothered. The blond one took a long drink of the Tecate, then frowned at his companion's drink. "Coke?"

The dark man said, "I don't like to waste good beer," and he poured his drink into a conveniently placed potted palm. His companion did the same with his beer. Then, as if having a contest, each crushed his can on the tabletop by pressing down with one hand. The cans collapsed into flattened pieces of metal. Each man tore the result in half, creating a sharp edge, then sharpened it further with a key that was a disguised file. Finally, the blond man took his keyring in his palm, and stuck three keys out from between his fingers, turning his hand into a mace. In his other hand he carried the sharpened piece of can.

Now they were armed—and they felt very secure in the airport concourse in assuming they were the only people who were. "I love security," the blond one said as they walked up toward the passenger gates.

The passenger lounge area around Gate 32 was fairly full. The two men stopped and looked over their possibilities. Several businessmen traveling separately: good possibilities. Three or four family groups they tentatively dismissed. Two thin, leggy women putting their heads together over a magazine. The blond man watched them appreciatively, until his partner nudged his arm.

There was another group of kids in their twenties at whom the men stared closely. Then a young mother with a toddler, who kept running across everyone's legs. Geeky kid with an earplug, playing what looked like a Gameboy on steroids. Middle-aged man and teenage daughter, maybe on a college trip. The dark man looked at the father more closely: take away the girl and he could be the one, their target. Two flight attendants stretching their legs, chatting quietly to each other. Don't turn your back on them: wouldn't be the first time a flight attendant turned out to be a trained killer.

They concentrated first on the people facing them, assuming the ones who were careless enough to sit with their backs to the traffic were harmless.

Jack, the "kid" playing a game on his hand-held device, wondered who the two were. They obviously didn't realize he could see them in two reflections: the glass wall in front of him and the television screen in the other lounge. The two men moved purposefully through the small crowd, obviously looking for someone. Jack appeared to continue playing his game. His cane leaned against the chair beside him. Security hadn't liked that cane, but Jack had walked in with an obvious limp and the x-ray machine hadn't shown anything inside the wooden stick, so they'd let it through.

Jack remained aware of the two men without ever looking directly at them, until they were standing over him. He felt their presence, heard their breathing, and sighed without making a sound. Jack turned off his game so he could see the two in the reflection of the small screen. Whatever happened, he wasn't moving. He felt safe surrounded by people. Until he saw the points of the keys sticking out from between the taller one's fingers. That hand was about a foot behind his neck.

Jack had some skills, but he was no martial artist. His superpower was networking. He had latched on to Chun Lee in Malaysia at just the right time, but here no one was available, there wasn't time, and he seriously doubted he could make friends with either of the assassins standing behind him.

Quickly he ticked off escapes. The gate, "guarded" by a ticket taker, but if Jack leaped down that tunnel he would find himself trapped in an airplane. Farther away there was a door that would let him out into the runway area, but these two guys, especially the taller one, looked faster than he was. They wouldn't let him get that far. The same was true of the path back down the concourse.

Couldn't go around them, then. That left one possibility.

The taller one, the one with the keys in his fist, leaned over as if to speak to him quietly. Jack didn't believe that, though. Those keys were about to come into the back of his neck, with paralyzing force. The hand was moving down.

Jack stood and turned quickly, then lost his balance without his cane and fell forward. His hand came down on the thinner man's hand, pushing it down into the seat back. The keyring as a weapon was turned on its wielder, crushing his palm inside the closed fist. The man grimaced, he was tough.

Jack gave one more hard press on the hand as he regained his balance. "Sorry," he mumbled. The taller man stepped back, shaking his hand. The other one, with a roll of his eyes, stepped forward. "Sir—" he began, as if about to deliver a confidential message. Jack leaned toward him attentively, noticing the glint of metal in the man's hand.

The two planned to kill him right here in this passenger lounge! How did they hope to get away with such a thing? Possibilities ran through his mind—maybe it was a suicide mission, maybe they had no identities—which was a distraction, but he couldn't help it. That was how his mind worked, even as he put on a dopey expression for the benefit of the burly man.

As their heads leaned toward each other, as the man's hand holding the sharpened metal came up, toward his intended victim's throat, the cane came up too, Jack raising it as if it were part of him. It blocked the man's thrust then the head of the cane rose into the man's throat, left unprotected as he leaned forward.

"Unngh," he grunted. Jack twisted the head of the cane, trying to crush his windpipe. But the man reached for the cane, and Jack knew he couldn't afford to lose his only weapon. He yanked it back and stepped away.

The burly man was choking. A woman hurried up and began tending to him, her head leaning close to his, but her ministrations didn't help. The burly man went down on one knee, then slumped to the ground.

A couple of people in the lounge watched the little drama, but most paid no attention. More people were watching the adorable blond toddler running up and down the rows. Several would have liked for him to shut up, but nobody said so, and several others smiled at him with genuine affection. Every parent in the lounge was reminded of what they had left at home.

The blond man was recovered now. He glared at Jack, whose only defense was to back up. The toddler bumped his legs, then cruised around him. The blond man closed in. He had dropped his keys, but a glint of metal remained in his right hand.

The woman who had been trying to help the other one leaned against the row of chairs, which knocked a paper cup off its small table between two chairs on Jack's side of the row. It spilled its contents, ice and soda, just as the blond man stepped forward. His foot came down on a piece of ice and he lurched. He didn't fall, he had good balance, but in trying to regain it his arm flailed. There was a sharp smack and the toddler, his cheek reddened, began screaming.

"Why did you do that?" the outraged woman shouted. The child continued to cry, his mother swooped toward him, the blond man started to explain or apologize, and the woman cried, "Don't you *dare* hit him again!"

Most of the women in the lounge and several men descended

on him as one raging parent-beast. In moments it was impossible to tell where the blond man left off and the outraged crowd began. His head bobbed for a moment atop the sea of angry adults. Apparently he was trying to explain that he hadn't done anything, but no one was listening. Someone had just found what he had in his hand.

"My God, he was going to slice him!"

"Get him! Make him drop it!"

A woman's voice shrilled, "He was with him," and part of the crowd turned its attention to the burly dark man. Once he was found to be armed as well, his conviction was complete.

Jack stood staring. The scene had turned to chaos in an instant, but a chaos unexpectedly beneficial to him. Then a hand grabbed his arm.

The woman who'd spilled the drink and accused the blond man tugged at him. Jack saw that she was Arden. How had he not recognized her? She wasn't in disguise, exactly, just a hat with her hair pulled up under it, and large glasses.

Neither of them said a word as she pulled him toward the ramp back up the terminal. There they turned to look back. Airport cops had arrived to begin sorting out the scene, and had Jack's attackers firmly grasped. The attackers looked, if anything, relieved.

"I had those two from the time they cleared security," Jack said.

"Sure you did."

"I would have left them—"

"This is better," Arden assured him.

"This—" Jack looked back at the scene in the lounge, where a dozen pointed fingers accused the two of various crimes, and obviously no one remembered that Jack had been involved, or even existed—*has aspects of greatness,* Jack finished his sentence in his mind.

"Thank you."

"Stop that." He had meant to finish his sentence, "is better." But she had answered his thought.

She put her arm through his. They could stroll out now. "In answer to your next question," Arden said, "Granny sent me to take care of you."

"'Granny'?"

"Please don't tell me you don't know that my grandmother, who brought me into this group, is Gladys Leaphorn, the Chair. I will lose all faith in your info-gathering—"

"All right, yes, I knew that. Although there's a lot I don't know, and I don't think anyone—"

"We have to go see her. Now."

"Now?"

"That was the second part of my assignment. I'm to bring you to her. Come."

"Why? I'm not going anywhere until I get some answers."

Arden glanced back. "We'll take my car."

They met Gladys Leaphorn in the painted desert, at the base of a mesa that protected their flank, a spot from which they could see miles in every other direction. Arden's car, a baby blue Cadillac from the early 70s, looked anachronistic in that setting, but not as much as one might have expected. The Chair emerged from a small stone shelter, walking shakily on two arm-canes. There was no sign of another car, nor tracks of any kind other than Arden's. Quite possibly Gladys Leaphorn had flown here under her own power. She had no entourage, not even one aide. The lines in her face looked as deeply etched as the cracks in this dry earth. But she seemed to draw strength from this landscape, standing straighter as Jack and Arden approached. One of her metal canes dropped to the ground as she hugged her granddaughter.

"Thank you, baby. Was he in trouble?"

"Just like you thought, Granny. But we got by."

"I could have handled it," Jack said.

"That is not the point," the Chair said. "Who is trying to kill you, Jack, and why?"

He looked her in the eyes and neither of them spoke for several seconds. Gladys Leaphorn's dark eyes gave him nothing but his own reflection. Of course Jack had been thinking of little else except the question she had asked. His suspicions ranged wide, and covered the Chair herself. She had saved him from this latest attack. But that didn't mean she hadn't plotted it herself, either for real or to take him into her confidence. Her mind was so twisty there was no way to follow its trails.

The way Arden had rescued him—if in fact she had—had left Jack no chance of questioning his attackers. This had occurred to him some miles back.

He turned to her. "When did you spot those two? If you had let me know you were there, we could have worked together, maybe gotten at least one of them alone and still capable of talking. Now—"

"That's the way these assassins work, Jack." Gladys answered the question. "Their attacks are in public or near-public. Either they succeed or they are taken into custody by authorities who don't know the right questions to ask. That was true of the two who attacked you in Malaysia, too, wasn't it?"

Jack had to admit that was true.

"Who are dead, by the way," Gladys added. "We made inquiries. They were 'arrested' at the convention center, but somehow never made it to jail."

While Jack pondered that, the Chair continued to study him. Arden stood a couple of feet from each of them, forming the third point of a triangle. Her arms folded, she kept her eyes mostly on her grandmother. She was more subdued in her ancestor's presence, but had an avid look on her face, studying all the time. "Tell him the rest of that story," she said.

"They were already dead when they attacked you, Jack."

His eyebrows flew up. The Chair continued, "They had been poisoned. Whether they succeeded or not, they had not long to live."

So the killer of killers was more ruthless than those he, or they, employed.

The Chair dismissed that subject. "But you're available for questioning, Jack. And I have some for you. What were you doing in Prague?"

"Prague? When?"

"Three days before you arrived in Paris."

Jack was shaking his head. "I haven't been in Prague in four years."

"You were seen there, Jack. By one of ours."

Gladys Leaphorn's voice was accusing. But Jack only listened thoughtfully, as if being handed a small puzzle. "DNA? Retinal scan? Are you saying it was just someone who looked like me?"

"You know you wouldn't have left identifying marks. What about London? Why were you there?"

"This was supposedly—?"

"The same time frame. You were spotted entering an apartment in Chelsea."

This time Jack's eyes narrowed. "Where exactly?"

Gladys gave him an address. It was impossible to tell from Jack's lack of reaction whether the address meant anything to him. Arden still stood in the same pose, her eyes going back and forth between the other two, but primarily staying on Jack. He was thinking, obviously, but didn't seem to be trying to come up with an excuse.

"The only thing I did in London on this trip was change planes. I never left Heathrow. I was there for maybe two hours."

The Chair's voice remained level but relentless. "Then you would have arrived in France three days earlier than you did."

"No one knows when I arrived in France. I travelled overland, I didn't leave a paper trail."

"Did you see anyone on your journey?"

"Ali Khatam. I wanted to get a feel for what the Kurds may be—"

"Ali Khatam's son would be dead if not for you. He would say whatever you ask."

Jack stared into her eyes and spoke flatly. "Why don't you shoot him with truth serum and then ask him, Granny?" He let her look into his eyes for a long few seconds, then added, "Of what exactly am I being accused?"

Gladys sighed. "Of nothing, Jack. Honestly. But you've been

going off on your own, acting unilaterally, and now someone is trying to kill you. What kind of mission—?"

"I did what I set out to do," Jack interrupted. "And you and everyone else knows what it was. I'm done with that now."

The sun would be setting soon, out in that western distance that appeared strangely intimate here. A breeze had sprung up, caressing their faces, its sandy touch tangible. Arden's hair lifted and settled again. The Cadillac already had sand six inches up its tires. It would not take long here for man and any of his creations to disappear.

Gladys Leaphorn was no longer interrogating him. She had known Jack for half his life, though she had never remotely been a surrogate grandparent for him. They had their roles, and had respected each other since Jack was fourteen. Gladys stared off across the desert. It was possible that her old eyes saw something coming that neither of the young people could know.

"You know the other possibility," Gladys said quietly.

Jack nodded. "Someone wanted you to believe I was in these places. They wanted to cast suspicion on me. Rather clumsily, may I say. If I wanted to go unnoticed in Prague I could. And that Chelsea address is one I know well, as you know. I wouldn't go near it, not any more."

Gladys's long eyelashes softened her eyes as she blinked slowly. "That seemed like a strong possibility. Someone wanted you portrayed. Which means that maybe your attackers—"

"—were trying to steal my identity rather than kill me. Or kill me and have someone take my place. But I have no idea why."

Abruptly the interview was over. Gladys stepped away, moving stiffly with her one arm cane. Arden had picked up the other but didn't hand it to her. Jack spoke to the Chair's back. "How do you know they didn't succeed in replacing me?"

Gladys turned, smiling, and patted his cheek. "If the day comes that I don't know you, Jack, it *will* be time to retire. I only hope it's me these schemers try to fool with a double."

Twilight had taken the mountains in the distance, turned them into grounded thunderheads. All three stared at the beauty of the darkening desert for a long few minutes. Just as they turned away, Gladys stiffened and said, "What was that?"

"What was what?" Jack asked, but Arden had obviously seen or felt it too. She and her grandmother were staring at the western horizon. "It came and went too fast," Arden whispered. "Like a flaw in the retina, a peripheral hallucination. But if you saw it too—"

"I'm not sure saw is the right word. It was too fast."

Nothing more happened, at least not in that part of America. In a few minutes they got into Arden's car, the Chair in the backseat. After they'd driven a mile, she leaned forward and put her hand on Jack's shoulder. She had never been motherly toward him. Her touch startled him.

"Stay close for a while, would you, Jack?"

Her voice was a strong combination of commanding, cajoling, and humbly requesting. There was no telling how many people it had swayed over the decades.

"Yes, ma'am," he said.

The rest of that evening was a very busy one across America. It started out tranquilly, most of the country enjoying pleasant fall weather. That's why so many people were outdoors, taking walks, sitting on porches, camping out. The adventurous were the unluckiest ones.

In a mobile home park outside Hot Springs, Arkansas, Len and Mabel Dawes had just tied down for the night. They were on their way south, slowly, from their home in Detroit. This was the first season of their retirement, Mabel from General Motors as an administrative assistant, Jack from the military and civil service. Their three retirements left them very comfortable at the ages of 66 and 68, respectively. They had children and grandchildren scattered around the country, and Detroit had seemed less and less like home the last few years. So they had sold the house, chucked the jobs, and become hobos, as Len put it. Mabel preferred "gypsies." Hitting the road, they both felt younger by decades, starting over. They held hands half the way south.

Their tie-down slot featured a tiny patch of green grass, where they sat on folding chairs with drinks in their hands. In a few minutes they might grill something, or decide to drive into town for dinner. They suddenly grinned at each other, realizing their freedom from schedules for the first time in their lives. They had been married forty-three years and felt like newlyweds.

The sky was a strange mix of vibrant blue left over from the day, gray creeping in from the east, a few dark clouds, and one bright white one, something pasted onto the night sky from a painting by Magritte.

"Southern, I guess," Len said.

Mabel nodded, thinking how wonderful it was to see a brand new sky at her age. She was about to say something along those lines when something crossed beneath that bright white cloud. It moved too fast for the eye to follow. Before one could focus on it, it was some place else. Then it was gone entirely, leaving an unsettled feeling.

"Did you see—?"

Len nodded.

"What kind of plane was that, honey?"

"I couldn't tell." Which was saying a lot for Len Dawes, who had flown every kind of military aircraft and several civilian ones, and kept up with the industry.

"You think there's some kind of experimental base near here?"

"I guess they wouldn't tell us about it if there were." Len pointed his chin at the sky. "It dropped something."

You couldn't have proven that by Mabel, who squinted and saw nothing, but if Len said such a thing it was true. He had spent twenty-two years in the Air Force, the first two as a pilot in Vietnam. His vision was still perfect, which irritated her no end.

Just as the object neared the ground it began to glow, perhaps from heat friction, so that she saw it too. A cylinder that looked small, but no telling how far away it was, except for Len. She looked at him and he said, "'bout a quarter of a mile that way. Almost seemed like I felt it thump down."

"Let's go see," Mabel said impulsively. She stood up.

Len continued to sit. Going to look at the thing, whatever it was, struck him as a bad idea. "Come on, come on," Mabel said, holding out her hand. Just like when she was a young wife trying to talk him into an adventure. He was the fighter pilot and world traveler, but Mabel was the adventurer, even if the adventure was only going to a new mall.

Len said quietly, "It might've been the pilot, honey. Some kind of new-fangled ejection seat that didn't open right."

"Oh." She dropped her hand. She certainly didn't want to see something like that.

Len looked up at her. In the dimness her gray hair looked blonde and the lines in her face were invisible even to his sharp eyes. She looked like the slender young girl he had married, mainly because she was more fun than anyone he had ever met. That was still true.

In the end, they didn't have to decide whether to go look at the fallen object. It came to them.

The mobile home park was mainly for transients, though there were a few permanent residents. Some had even planted trees, and stayed long enough to see them grow high enough to throw shade. In a few minutes there was a rustling sound like wind through the leaves, except that there was no wind. People who were sitting outside stood up. Neighbors drifted over to neighbors' yards, saying, "Did you see— Do you hear—?"

They were no longer looking up at the sky, which had grown dark, but out toward the distance, from which the rustling sound came.

The creature that came drifting along the road between the homes made everyone who saw it smile. It was a short cylinder, maybe three feet tall, with a rounded top that featured flashing lights. Wheels carried it forward. It looked, in other words, like R2 D2, from "Star Wars." Kid's toy, people thought, or maybe the movies were being re-released.

When "R2" drew to a stop, people gathered around. Mabel would have been one of the first, except that her husband stopped her. He had been in too many dangerous situations to take this one at face value. What the hell did he know about Arkansas, anyway? The tranquil setting had suddenly turned foreign to the veteran Len.

"Oh, come on, honey, it's probably going to give out movie passes. Let's not be last in line."

She tugged at him, he resisted, and their hands parted. Mabel Dawes ran toward the cute little robot.

Half a dozen people were standing right around it, pointing at the lights, trying to figure out its beeps. Another dozen people stood a little farther back, folding their arms and shaking their heads, as if the inner circle were careless children. Mabel had just broken through this ring when the little cylinder went dark. People made accusatory remarks at each other, until it rumbled and the top popped open.

"Mabel!" Len yelled then, but the top's opening made people think the prizes were about to pop out. Mabel leaned forward as curiously as the rest.

And Len turned and ran.

The spiders came crawling out of the opening of the cylinder. Golden spiders the size of a big man's hand, metallic, obviously manufactured. Nearly everyone has an instinctive fear of spiders, but these glittered like gold, like prizes. People still leaned toward them. Until they began swarming.

The man squatting in front of the cylinder was a long-time resident of the park who got a discounted rate because he was an in-house handyman. He'd been attracted to the robot because he loved tinkering with things like that, had ever since he was a kid, a real "Popular Mechanics" kind of guy. Even the spiders didn't scare him, because they were obviously machines. The first golden spider jumped right on to him, landed on his leg. His legs were spread for balance. The spider's legs suddenly extended to both the handyman's legs and clamped on. Then the body of the spider clamped onto his groin.

The handyman screamed. Not very many people had seen what happened, and most thought Ed had just caught his finger on something, as happened roughly twice a week. They'd heard Ed scream before.

But not like this. His voice went hoarse, rose to a register higher than it should have been able to reach, then abruptly went silent, though the cords stood out on the sides of his neck as if he were still screaming. His hands dug at his crotch, uselessly. Two of the spider's legs fended off the man's hands. The spider's legs were pointed like needles. Exactly like needles. Ed jerked his hand away, even while the pain in his groin held him nearly paralyzed.

The other spiders had spread through the crowd now. They scuttled up people's legs, feeling light enough to be shaken off, but that was impossible. The points of those legs stuck fast. Once they'd touched you, it didn't matter if they stayed on, anyway. The injection had happened. People would shake uncontrollably for a few seconds, then go rigid and topple over. Their faces went from red to white to gray, the gray of dead stone.

Some of the spiders—there were dozens—came spilling over the top of the open cylinder as if it were too full of them and they slopped over the top. A few came leaping out as if shot from guns, though. These caught people in the more cautious crowd holding back. They hadn't been cautious enough. One of the golden spiders landed on a woman's face, and as its claws dug in and she screamed her husband tried to pull it off, so the spider got them both.

Mabel stood frozen for long seconds. One of the spiders landed on the man next to her, and his screeching woke her up. She looked all around the scene of panic, people running, stumbling, going down under a hoard of spiders, saw there was nothing she could do to help, and looked instinctively for her husband. But Len was nowhere to be seen. He had run away. For the first time in their lives his sense of self-preservation had trumped his concern for her. That was even more disheartening to Mabel than the attack of the spiders.

She ran, jumping over bodies, hearing screams all around her, coming from farther and farther away as the spiders spread through the park with amazing speed. She kept thinking she felt something touch her, but it was only panic singing along her nerves.

Then Mabel couldn't stand it any longer, she turned and looked back. Everyone else was down, people she'd come to know slightly, others she never would. Spiders crawled over their bodies as if they would strip the flesh. Some of the bodies twitched, and a few moved, horribly, men crawling while covered with the things, as if the spiders had taken over their bodies and were animating them. Screams had been replaced by moans.

Mabel screamed, though, as she saw one of the spiders, one of the biggest ones, withdraw its stinger from a twitching body's neck and turn its little red LCD eyes on her. Then it bunched its legs together and came jumping toward her.

They could cover distance amazingly. This one scuttled faster than Mabel could run, but then it leaped, first a sort of warm-up, then its legs bunched together and she knew it could leap high enough to reach her face. Even if she turned and ran, it would land on her back, or her leg. Mabel stood frozen again, screaming. The spider leaped. It soared, coming straight toward her face.

It was a foot from her open mouth when it exploded into a hundred golden shards.

Mabel turned away from the shrapnel, took a couple of steps, stumbled, starting falling.

An arm caught her. A still-strong arm she knew well. She turned and buried her face into Len's neck. He stood with his service automatic, that hadn't been fired in twenty years. It still could, though. Len had had to rummage through a couple of boxes in the mobile home before he'd found it.

He fired two more shots at the closest spiders, then turned and pulled Mabel away. Spiders swarmed after them. Len fired over his shoulder, hitting two more. But these weren't living creatures, to be scared off by an obviously lethal weapon. The spiders had no instinct for self-preservation. They kept coming.

But Mabel and Len got into the trailer, slammed the door, held each other, and shook. "I thought you—" she shivered. "You know I'd never—" he answered.

But there was no time. They could hear the continual thumps of the little metal bodies throwing themselves against the door. Len scrambled forward, through the living space, over the table and into the driver's seat. The keys were in the ignition. He turned it on, and the sound of the big engine starting was like technological cavalry coming over the hill.

"Call 911!" he shouted. "Tell somebody about this!"

Mabel started doing so. She was a good, brave woman, she'd be all right in a minute. Len backed out without paying much attention to his mirrors, then ripped forward, tearing a couple of hoses and electrical wires. They weren't connected to the RV's engine, though. They just needed to get a few miles down the road and they could make whatever repairs were needed.

In his mirrors, in the glow of his sidelights, he could see the flashes of golden spiders falling off the vehicle. They bounced on the road, a few lying still, some struggling to catch him. They didn't have remotely enough speed, though. Len's blood raced with adrenaline. He knew he could outrun Richard Petty.

Not all the spiders fell off, though. On top of the RV, two clung, legs spread wide, then a drill came out of each body, diamond-tipped, and began drilling. The noise of the engine masked the sound, until each had made a small circular hole. Two legs of each spider lifted the metal circle aside and threw it overboard. Then each dropped through the hole.

Half a mile down the highway, the RV began to shake, rocked both by the driver's panic and by screams within. The vehicle moved even faster for another quarter of a mile, then went into a skid and finally turned over.

The sound of the crash was not particularly loud. The state highway had a fair amount of traffic, but not at that moment. The RV lay on its side in the night. Nothing emerged from it. Whatever was inside just stayed there, waiting for the rescuers who would inevitably come.

The attack in Omaha was different, but based on the same pattern. The plane too fast to be believed zoomed past, leaving a couple of cylinders in its wake. When people approached to investigate, white powder sprayed out, in a circle wide enough to catch everyone within twenty feet. "Anthrax" was one of the scariest words that could be screamed there in cattle country. The closest victims fell down, dying on the spot. Others on the fringe ran. Some who didn't even look affected at first crept away, back home, spreading the disease through their families and neighborhoods.

The cruelest happened in Louisville and Minneapolis and Tulsa. There the robots landed on playgrounds just before sunset, where parents let children continue to play in the mild evening. The robots were so familiar to the children they came flocking, and parents hardly even bothered to call them away. Many of the kids didn't have parents there, anyway. They were neighborhood playgrounds, a block or two from home, within the sound of a parent's call. And some of the children were young teens, sitting on swings and talking and feeling vaguely nostalgic for their childhoods, so few years past.

When the robots' tops opened the children were startled, then delighted as the little cylinders spewed out their cargo, spraying them in a high arc where they fell clattering among the children.

Cell phones.

They came in pink and silver and bright metallic green, and everyone grabbed for them. These were nine and ten-year-olds, just below the age of owning their own cell phones, but old enough to crave them. Even the young teenagers who already had cell phones wanted these newer models. They shoved younger kids out of the way to lunge for them. Everyone got one. A few started making calls right away. "Guess what I just got!" The cell phones were already activated. Kids played with them happily, punching buttons to find out their numbers and calling each other, making call lists, playing games. They knew how to work these devices as instinctively as their grandparents had spun tops and picked up jacks.

Most of them didn't even notice the tiny warm slithery

feeling as something was injected from the phones into their ear canals. Certainly no one displayed symptoms in that first golden hour of twilight. The most susceptible grew dizzy walking home. But by early evening they all had fevers. When news began to break about what these cylinders were doing across the country, a few cautious parents took their sick children to emergency rooms. One alarmed ER doctor even ordered a CT scan, and thereby located the tiny radioactive seed that had worked its way down the child's blood vessels into his lungs, where it was poisoning him with growing rapidity. But finding the seed didn't solve anything. There was no antidote.

By midnight the parents and caregivers and medical personnel had the "illness" too. The poisoning elements spread with amazing speed. Hundreds were infected before morning, and the infection like wildfire as emergency workers tried to contain it. Whole portions of the three cities were quarantined, but to no avail.

Cell phones lay on the floor of children's bedrooms and hospital rooms.

The culmination of the evening was a small nuclear explosion in the Nevada desert, close in fact to the area where nuclear testing had been conducted for decades. This one, though, was close enough for Las Vegans to see the mushroom cloud. The desert winds were unpredictable, no one was willing to guess whether they would blow the radioactive dust toward the city or away from it. Evacuation began haphazardly at first, then with slightly more organization, but emptying America's fastest-growing city in only a few hours' time was impossible. There weren't enough ways out. As in Houston when Hurricane Rita had approached a decade earlier, the city turned into one giant gridlock, and stayed that way for hours. No one died of radiation poisoning, but several were killed in car wrecks, and looting was widespread. Even fabled casino security broke down, as guards began helping themselves to cash along with the customers. A few kept playing the slots, deep into the night.

The President went on the air at 5:30 a.m., Eastern Time. It was still dark all across the country, and many people hadn't yet heard of the attacks. Nevertheless, President Witt had an audience of eighty million viewers, which increased when the tape was replayed on all the morning news shows.

"My fellow Americans," he began. "Some of you have heard of the mysterious attacks across this country in the last few hours. This is not a time to panic. Emergency personnel are responding. The victims are being treated and the threats ended. There have been many casualties, but we do not expect any more. The danger is being contained.

"The best thing all of you can do for your country today is to go about your normal lives. The attacks were very confined. Most American cities were not affected at all. Let us show the world the strength of Americans. We will live through this. We will prosper and grow.

"Our intelligence services have been working through the night and will continue to work to find the source of these attacks. In the first analysis, we believe this threat to our national security is not from a ... not from a terrorist nation or even a terrorist group. No group has claimed responsibility."

Now the President looked his gravest as he stared into the camera lens. Jefferson Witt had gotten elected partly because of his mature, thoughtful appearance. Exhausted by a cowboy presidency, a majority of Americans wanted someone stable and gray, even slow. Tonight Witt looked much grayer than when he'd been elected a year ago. His first visible response to the crisis was to look tired.

But there was resolve in his voice. In his next sentences he would take the first major steps of his presidency, the ones that would define him for history. And he believed deeply in what he was about to say. His eyes grew livelier and his voice stronger.

"But these attacks will not be ended by reprisals, no matter how rapidly and forcefully we respond. That kind of reaction is from another age. That page of history has been turned.

"Every nation, no matter how powerful, is vulnerable to attacks such as we have seen overnight. They will not end by our destroying some terrorist bases or even toppling regimes and occupying whole countries. We have seen the failures of such policies in recent years.

"No. We are going to do what my advisors and I had planned to do already, what I campaigned saying America should do. A large majority agreed with me. Well, now is the time.

"We are going to begin withdrawing American forces from around the globe. We are calling our men and women home. They have been stretched too thin for too long. We will not demand more of them."

The President raised one finger and shook it as if reprimanding a class. "No more will America be the world's policeman *or* the world's whipping boy. We are going to stand down. We will be an equal at the world's table. Other nations will have to solve their own problems."

The President knew the danger he faced. It was difficult to put a good face on this retreat, with dead Americans, many of them children, lying in hospitals and morgues across the country. But he and his speechwriters thought they knew how America would respond, and they counted on the fact that a large majority of Americans were exhausted from years of war and intervention. Jefferson Witt was a picture of strength, not of cowardice, as he continued to stare forcefully into the camera.

"America has never run from a fight. We have plunged into so many conflicts in order to save someone else. We are not running from this. But this is not a fight, not in any sense we have ever known. There is no other country to attack. We will continue to work to bring these attackers to justice, but that doesn't mean we have to continue to support a huge military establishment in order to protect the world. That is not our job, if it ever was. This is not a retreat, it is a consolidation. A protection of our own vital interests.

"I have ordered the immediate withdrawal of the first units of American troops from the Middle East, from Asia, from Europe.

This will not be done in haste, but in a timely way we will bring all our forces home."

The President smiled. It was a slight smile, but on his craggy face, at the end of that terrible night, it was dazzling. The President's smile reassured. His voice was hearty as he concluded, "This is the end of the age of American domination. But it is the dawn of the age of American peace. Of America taking care of itself. This will be the golden age. My fellow Americans, I ask you to join me in asking God to bless our great nation as we step forward into a bright new day. Thank you."

There seemed to be a long moment's silence across the entire country. It was broken, at least in the Circle's Colorado compound, by Gladys Leaphorn, who exclaimed, "The Age of American Selfishness. He has proclaimed it!"

"And America wants it," Jack said quietly. "That's why Witt got elected."

"This is what he's wanted to announce all along," Arden said, then her eyes shot around the room. "You don't think—"

"No." Jack shook his head, and he wasn't the only one. "He wouldn't do it like this. Even Witt isn't that stupid. If anything, these attacks probably slowed down his plans. But you know—"

"Yes," the Chair said wearily. There was much more to this than the President's public announcement. There always was. Within a few hours they should know more. "Let's wait until the others get here," Gladys added, and she rolled away for a morning nap. She was back in her wheelchair, and moving very slowly. Jack and Arden exchanged a glance, and Arden jumped up to help her grandmother to bed.

"But Witt is our man!" exclaimed a senior member of the Circle. "We helped get him elected. We have all kinds of—"

"We helped him because we knew his election was inevitable anyway," Alicia Mortenson said, and her husband nodded. They were now wearing outlandish flowered shirts and touristy shorts. No one asked if they'd been vacationing when they'd gotten the call to assemble. Maybe this was just the way they dressed around the house.

"But my point," insisted the first man, "is that we exert all kinds of influence over him. So many vectors intersect at him—"

"Perhaps we're not so influential as we think," interrupted Janice Gentry, the Yale history professor. "Someone certainly seems to have dominated him in the first reaction to this crisis."

There weren't as many members gathered as there had been at the last meeting, only a dozen or so, in the bunker at the base of the Rocky Mountains that was the group's only fall-back position, or at least the only one Jack knew about. But these dozen represented all wings of the group's power and influence: academia, diplomatic, the scientific and entertainment industries, and one junior editorial writer from the *Denver Post*.

The one who had proclaimed the group's influence was Professor Clifford Warner, currently on sabbatical at the Sorbonne, who had happened to be at an academic conference in Chicago and had rushed here when the attacks began. Warner was a tall, thin man, with long arms and legs that sometimes distracted his students from what he was saying. Today he couldn't sit still. He paced and fretted, making everyone tired. "That National Security Advisor," he exclaimed, snapping his fingers. "The one none of us knows. He must be behind this."

Jack wanted to say, "Duh," but he was much too junior in this group. Besides, icy politeness was more this group's style than outright insult. Professor Gentry applied the style as she said, "Excellent thinking, Clifford. I believe you're right. But we must stop this now. Withdrawal of our forces from around the world will be like the ocean receding, exposing things we wish to remain hidden."

Craig Mortenson said quietly, "I have one source privy to the President's plan. It's worse than he announced. Withdrawing troops is only phase one. He even wants to close our embassies. Leave no American presence in the world at all. He believes this will take away any incentive to attack us. Only American companies would continue to operate abroad. We would be the world's bankers and businessmen, but not its diplomats or soldiers."

Startled, Arden cried, "But that—!" She recovered quickly, cutting off the sentence she didn't need to say. The grave faces told her as much.

Gladys Leaphorn asked Craig, "Does your source have any influence?"

Craig answered slowly, "My source is not a policy advisor and is not one of us. If—my source—ever offered an opinion, probably the President's confidence would be withdrawn. We wouldn't even have a pipeline to his thinking."

Everyone heard the careful gender-neutrality of Craig Mortenson's statement. He wasn't usually so politically correct. They wondered just how close to the President his source was.

But that person wasn't going to be any help at the moment. "Let's go!" the Chair said. "We need to do what we do. But we need to do it more quickly than we ever have before. Some subtlety may need to be abandoned."

"On the other hand," Jack ventured to say, "perhaps we can slow down events to allow—"

Gladys snapped her fingers and pointed his direction, awarding Jack points. He didn't smile. The Chair turned to someone else in the group and said, "Call General Reynolds and our other military contacts. Surely it will not be possible to mobilize such a large withdrawal very quickly."

The member smiled. "Some of those boys can take three weeks to strike a tent. And there are always vouchers to mislay. Foot-dragging is what our forces do best. In peacetime, anyway. I'll—"

He turned away without finishing the sentence. Another couple of members had already slipped away as well. Gladys raised her voice. "We should know more in a few hours. We'll keep you informed. And you keep us informed as well. This is not SOP. We must coordinate. Work your contacts, but report here before you do anything. This must be a joint operation. No rogue missions. Understand?"

They were already leaving, some of them shuffling, some walking briskly on high heels. They were a very strange-looking task force for being assigned the job of saving the world. The median age was about fifty-five, and none of them was a secret agent or even a soldier. Nevertheless, their backs were straight, their eyes alight and most of all their brains churning. It was a brave band of siblings that headed swiftly for the exits.

"Go Hornets," Jack said quietly.

CHAPTER 4

Dennis Wilkerson, the President's new National Security Advisor, remained so largely unknown to the general American public that he could walk through the streets of Washington unnoticed. He was new enough to the high circles of government that he hadn't taken on its trappings. He had no Secret Service protection. Wilkerson liked strolling to work from his apartment at the Watergate, stopping for breakfast along the way, taking time to marshal his thoughts. This habit sometimes made him late to meetings, but he excused himself by saying, "Mr. President, if I don't have time to think there is no point to my being in the meeting at all." It was this kind of pronouncement that caused the President to listen to him so attentively when he did arrive.

So his strolling-and-breakfast routine continued even during this unprecedented crisis. At 6:45 a.m. in October the sun was not yet quite up, but the streets of Washington were full. Wilkerson walked energetically, turning from Wisconsin Avenue onto a slightly less traveled way, heading toward the small, unpopular café where the staff had come to know him. Wilkerson was about six feet tall but seemed taller because he only weighed a hundred and sixty-three pounds. A few wrinkles spread outward from his eyes, but his brown hair contained no gray. He rather regretted that. Wilkerson looked forward to being a tweedy old professor, well-respected, his opinions sought out. Maybe with a pipe.

He had lived alone his whole adult life, except for his time in the Air Force, and had grown satisfied with his own company. He looked determined as he walked, but there was really little on his mind. The President had accepted his idea, and it was the only idea Dennis Wilkerson had, or had ever had. Withdraw. Take a bow and exit the world's stage. The President had been easy to convince, and Wilkerson had nothing more to do in his role as NSA other than to keep reinforcing the idea, not let other people stop or even modify it. All-out withdrawal or nothing.

His usual table was empty. Well, so were most of the tables. The café had a small outdoor seating area. Dennis Wilkerson's table was just inside, but close to the open doors. He liked to think of himself as sitting back and taking in the day, while everyone else in the city rushed through it thoughtlessly.

Across the way, a gray-haired man in a tweed jacket seemed to be reading both a magazine and some sort of program schedule, while his eggs grew cold. The man wore thick glasses that obscured his features, but he had all the trappings of the absent-minded professor, papers fighting out of a briefcase on the chair beside him, and a white mark that could have been chalk dust on his elbow. Dennis Wilkerson smiled at how familiar this type was. The old professor which he'd once aspired to become.

The professor sipped his coffee, frowned, looked around, and came toward Wilkerson. A self-service coffee bar stood a few feet behind the NSA's usual table. The professor busied himself there for a couple of minutes, started back toward his table, then turned and said, "Professor? Wilkes, is it?"

"Dennis Wilkerson," he said, and stood up briefly.

"Yes. You are a professor, aren't you? We met at the Methods of Analysis conference two years ago in Athens. Georgia, I mean." The speaker chuckled. "Maybe that's why I was there. Greece is more my specialty."

"Yes, I remember," Wilkerson said pleasantly, not remembering in the slightest. Academic conferences were always full of types like this. He had met several.

The professor extended a hand carefully, holding his coffee cup in one hand and his magazine under the other arm. "John Owenby. Beloit College. And are you still at—Stevens, was it?"

Wilkerson avoided the name of the college where he had formerly worked. He had a little smile as he talked to Professor Owenby. This was the kind of learned man who had intimidated Dennis Wilkerson for most of his adult life. Now he had soared beyond the narrow world of academia. "No, actually I'm working here now."

"Ah. U. Va? Georgetown?"

Wilkerson nodded vaguely.

Professor Owenby said, "Good schools," then leaned closer confidentially and said, "A little too full of people a little too full of themselves, if you know what I mean."

"I think I do."

The professor still leaned close, his breath smelling like coffee-flavored mints. "Best advice is to keep to yourself for a while. Let on that you're working on a very involved research project, can't really socialize with the others 'til it's done. That will earn you some respect without your ever opening your mouth. Worked for me, I can tell you.

"Say." He leaned back, studying Wilkerson through those thick spectacles. His eyes behind them, Wilkerson noticed, were pale blue and very alert. His study of Wilkerson was penetrating as he asked, "Aren't you the fellow who wrote the paper on—what was it called?—'National Insecurity'—a couple of years ago? Yes, you sent it to the chair of my department."

"No, I didn't."

"Well, someone sent it. The chair asked me to vet it for historical content, but I got caught up in the policy ideas myself. Not my sort of thing, really." He winked and chuckled. "I'm not really interested in anything that's happened since about 123 B.C. But I found it fascinating. There are some good historical analogies, of course. Rome under Claudius. Feudal Japan. All failures more or less, but still... Where was it published?"

"It never was," Dennis Wilkerson said, and his attempt to make the sentence sound lighthearted only highlighted its bitterness. His smile was sharp and brief as he sipped coffee.

"Not surprised, to tell you the truth. It had too many ideas. Stuffy old rags like this one"—he waved the magazine under his arm, and Wilkerson saw that it was a thick academic journal— "like a lot of blather about the long dead, not policy suggestions that might actually—horrors!—have some application to the real world. They prefer my kind of thing, actually. Doddering and out of touch."

He dropped the magazine, the *Journal of Ancient Perspectives*, and Wilkerson saw John Owenby's name on the cover. "Your article was much more interesting than anything that's been published in here in ten years. It deserved wide circulation."

"Actually, it was seen by some influential people." Wilkerson enjoyed saying this with becoming modesty because of the huge irony of the sentence, known only to him.

"Excellent!" Professor Owenby shouted. "The kind of thing that might lead to a government grant, maybe? But you know, that paper should still be published. Maybe after a revision. Learn the kinds of things these rags are looking for. Or maybe even something for much greater circulation. Drop the footnotes, go for learned earnestness. I've had a few of those, too. *Atlantic Monthly*, you know."

Wilkerson was nodding. "That's a good idea." The President was going to need help selling this new policy of isolationism. A broad-circulation article could help immensely. It was exactly the sort of thing he could contribute. And now that he was National Security Advisor, his name alone should be enough to get it published.

It would help, though, to have that aura of academic respectability that he had never quite achieved in his previous career. "I'm awfully busy right now, though, and the article would need some revision to turn it into the type you're thinking of."

"Oh, I'm sure you can find a good editor. Really you need more of a collaborator, though, but I'm sure you have some colleagues...."

Wilkerson wouldn't throw a crumb to his "colleagues" at his former colleges, all of whom had dismissed him as lightweight, and he certainly couldn't collaborate with any of his current "colleagues" since they were all rivals for the President's attention. Getting this article published, some place prestigious, would remind President Witt why he had brought Dennis Wilkerson on board in the first place. It would solidify his authority.

He needed someone who could write, someone with contacts in the publishing world, and someone who would never fight him for attention. Wilkerson looked at the figure across from him, with bread crumbs on his lapel and a distracted look in his eye.

"Professor Owenby, could you help? I can almost guarantee you prestigious publication and a co-credit." Beneath Dennis Wilkerson's name and in smaller type.

The old professor looked frightened. "Me? Oh, no no no. You don't need an old codger like me. You need someone young and vigorous—"

Who would undoubtedly yank the spotlight from mild-mannered young Dennis Wilkerson. "No, sir, you're my man. But let me ask you, do you have the time, and can we work quickly?"

The gleam returned to the old man's eye. "Well, I am known as the fastest blue pencil in the east, as a matter of fact. You're so familiar with the material, and I know the style... It should be the work of only a few evenings."

Over the next few minutes, Wilkerson managed to talk the old professor into the project. Owenby seemed glad to give a boost to a much younger colleague, and clearly had no idea of the elevated position Dennis Wilkerson had attained. Well, as he'd said, he didn't care about anything that had happened in the past two millennia.

They made arrangements to get together that evening and begin their collaboration, and shook hands warmly before Wilkerson had to rush away. As he walked toward the White House, invigorated, he couldn't stop smiling, although once or twice he had a niggling little worry like a leaf floating down the edge of his peripheral vision. What had Professor Owenby said? That this policy of isolationism had always been a failure in the past? They'd have to come up with some examples of successes when they worked together.

He walked faster. By the time he reached the White House side gate his smile was so wide he didn't match the picture on his White House security badge at all, and the guard had to study him closely.

Back at the cafe, Professor Owenby's demeanor didn't change. He still appeared befuddled as he finished his coffee, gathered up his things, stuffed them into his book bag, and looked around as if trying to remember where he was. He paid his check, left a carefully-calculated tip that included nickels and pennies, and walked out to the curb. A cab conveniently waited there, and Owenby got in without glancing at the driver. "Ramada Northwest," he said, and settled into the seat. The temptation to get on the phone to the Chair was nearly overpowering, but he resisted. Not until he was alone in his hotel room.

At the next intersection the cab sat a little longer than the traffic required, until a man in a black overcoat opened the back door and climbed in, forcing Professor Owenby to slide away. "I'm afraid this one is—" he began, until the unsmiling man flashed a badge in a small carrying case at him. When the professor bent to peer at it, the man snapped the case shut.

"May I see that again? I don't think I'm familiar with that particular badge."

"Homeland Security," the man said, his mouth snapping as tightly as his badge case.

Neither the man in the overcoat nor the cab driver said another word during the rest of the drive. After a while, his protests ignored and his helpless academic act getting him nowhere, Professor Owenby shut up too.

A day later, outside Dennis Wilkerson's office, which was within shouting distance of the Oval one, Wilkerson was getting coffee at the communal urn. He had an assistant to do that sort of thing for him, more than one actually, but he still—he would never admit this to anyone on the planet—felt a little intimidated by both his elegantly appointed office and his lofty position. He liked walking out of the office to fetch his own coffee, enjoying the hum of the West Wing, the sidelong glances of people who were not exactly his subordinates but ranked far below him on any organizational chart of presidential staff. The short stroll to the coffee urn also gave him time to collect his thoughts.

A young man was already there, an earnest young man with dark hair, bright blue eyes and absolutely no lines on his face. He wore a blue blazer that was unadorned but might as well have carried the crest of his school on the pocket. Harvard, no doubt, or perhaps Princeton. This was the kind of young man so far out of Dennis Wilkerson's league that Wilkerson had never competed with such a person, hardly ever even encountered one. This young fellow had probably breezed into the kind of college, through family connections or native brilliance or both, to which Wilkerson had never even dared to apply.

Dennis Wilkerson would have loved to be a Harvard man, have that background, be able to toss off names of Cambridge hangouts easily. In meetings, which were now of the highest level, he still glanced around wondering where these people had gone to college, and feeling sure that they all looked at him askance—the Podunk U grad who had risen to the highest level of his nation's government. Wilkerson should have had a little knowing smile all the time, but thought it was the others who did.

So generally he hated bright young men like this on sight. This one, though, turned with his White House coffee mug and stared at Wilkerson with his mouth actually hanging open half an inch when he realized whom he had nearly bumped into.

"Mr. Wilkerson, sir. Can I get that for you?"

Clearly he wanted to call Wilkerson by some title but didn't know what it would be. Even Harvard men were at a loss sometimes. Wilkerson smiled graciously and handed over his cup.

The young man put two sugars and a good amount of cream into the cup, giving himself away. He had been watching Dennis Wilkerson. He handed over the cup with apparent reluctance to break the contact between the two. Wilkerson took it with gracious thanks and continued to stand there.

"My name is Bentley, sir." As Wilkerson wondered if that was a first name or a last, the young man cleared it up. "Bentley Robbins. Aide to the deputy press secretary."

"And doesn't he need your help right now, Bentley?"

"No, sir, she doesn't. She's on a little road trip, and I wasn't invited." The young man shifted his weight from foot to foot. "And what are you working on, sir, if I may ask? Or would you have to kill me if you told me?"

He smiled brightly. Wilkerson gave him a small chuckle in return. "No, not personally. I'm sure someone else would handle that. Oh, I'm—working closely with the President, actually. Refining all the aspects of the new policy. There are more details than I ever would have imagined."

Actually, other people handled all those details, which gave Wilkerson time for chats like this, except that no one in the White House ever wanted to chat with him. This young man, though, seemed fascinated by his proximity to power. He was obviously embarrassed, even intimidated, but couldn't pull himself away. "Sir, the policy, as you mentioned..."

Here it came. Dennis Wilkerson grew stiff. His posture straightened. Another critic. Since the President's announcement, Wilkerson had heard nothing but criticism, even here within the sanctuary of the White House. In meetings people argued with him outright. Out here in the hallways and bullpens people dropped remarks within his hearing. So few people seemed to understand, except the President himself. "Yes?" Wilkerson said icily.

"Well, it's brilliant, sir. The boldest stroke in a century. More. Maybe ever. Has any single man in history created such an enormous change in national policy, overnight?"

Wilkerson couldn't say anything. No one had been so effusive in praise of him and his idea, not even the President. He could only shrug modestly.

"I'm sorry, it's not my place. Forgive me for bothering you, sir. I just wanted to say that. I'm sure you're very busy, and I..."

The young man gave a little bow and turned away. "Wait," Wilkerson called after him. The young man—Bentley—turned around, looking a little frightened. "Thank you," Wilkerson said. "To tell you the truth, not many people have gotten it the way you obviously have."

"Oh, people have, sir. I have several friends who've just been swept away. We feel so privileged to be here at ground zero of the Wilkerson Doctrine."

Wilkerson didn't hear the next few words. *The Wilkerson Doctrine.* What a ring. Why hadn't he heard those words before? Because the policy idea was his. No one denied that. No one else wanted to take credit from him, frankly. And this was the kind of young man who could spread a phrase, if his flame of fandom were to be fanned just a little.

"That's very kind, Bentley," Wilkerson interrupted. "Deputy press secretary, you said? Well, I hope you get the chance to write some press releases that will spread your take on the—the doctrine."

"Absolutely, sir. I've already written a couple, but unfortunately they haven't made it into the final versions of the releases. What I need..."

The young man paused, glancing around. Wilkerson unconsciously leaned toward him. "What is it, Bentley? Anything I can help with? I have a little influence." He chuckled again.

"It's not that, sir. The problem I've encountered—and I mean even for myself—is not having quite a clear understanding of all the ramifications of the Wilkerson Doctrine. The, well, the subtleties, sir. The consequences. I'm sure you've thought all that out. Overcoming the danger of not having intelligence field operatives, for example. I've been asked about that a lot, and so far I haven't come up with a good answer."

"Believe me, the President and I have that well in hand."

"Oh, I was sure you did, sir. And I'm not asking for information. I just want to understand the basic tenets of the doctrine. I have some friends who feel the same way. We're trying to spread the good word, but don't feel entirely equipped. We feel like—disciples without a gospel, you might say."

Wilkerson was struck by the phrase, especially the word 'disciples'. "You've read my paper?"

"Oh, of course. Several times. But..."

"You want more," Wilkerson said confidentially, understanding.

"Yes, sir. That's it exactly. An expansion. A ... a commentary on the text, as it were. So far people have just seen the *Cliff's Notes* version, and I think if we had an amplification..."

Wilkerson was nodding along. "I expect to have an article coming out shortly..." he said slowly, but saw he'd disappointed his disciple.

"That will be wonderful, sir." Bentley's sincere young face said otherwise. His voice dropping, he said, "We'll wait for that."

Before he could turn away again, Wilkerson stopped him with a hand on his arm. "Wait. I have a better idea, Bentley. One article is all fine, but if there were a group of us, all spreading the word at once, we could get the explanation across much faster."

Bentley's eyes brightened again. "That's a wonderful idea, sir. A rash of articles instead of just one. A virus of information, spreading through all the media. Until people understand the Wilkerson Doctrine fully it won't gain the acceptance it deserves."

Dennis Wilkerson smiled, modestly he hoped. "Can you think of anyone you might recruit to this team?" *Perhaps eleven friends?*

"As a matter of fact, sir, I have a few friends who already meet in a sort of study group. One works in the House, one at State, things like that. All very junior, like me, but if we understand fully, we can start—"

"Spreading the word," Wilkerson said. "When's your next meeting?"

Bentley looked embarrassed. "Tonight, actually. I'm sure you already have commitments. We could certainly re-schedule—"

Wilkerson chuckled indulgently at his young disciple's earnestness. "Tonight would be fine, Bentley. Shall we say eight? Where?"

Bentley offered to bring the whole group bodily to whatever location Wilkerson might suggest, but the NSA graciously agreed to come to Bentley's apartment. The address was in Georgetown, as he would have expected. Family money supplementing an undoubtedly modest salary. That was all right. A couple of the original Disciples had come from wealthy families, hadn't they? And this group would need connections like Bentley's to spread the word. The gospel.

The young man was beaming like a child on Christmas morning as he hurried away to make calls. Wilkerson still carried the glow of adulation. His habit—no, call it a policy—of getting his own coffee had certainly paid off this morning. Later that afternoon the President asked him why he looked so happy when the country was in such grave peril. "Because of my great confidence in you, sir," Wilkerson answered at once, hearing young Bentley's earnest tones in his own voice. The President coughed gruffly, but Wilkerson thought he detected secret pleasure in his posture.

He was getting good at this game.

A few of the Circle remained at their Colorado compound. Given the communications clusters in that fortified enclave, they could monitor the worldwide situation better from there than if they'd been a thousand places in person. "Operation Footdragging seems to be proceeding well," Janice Gentry reported. "Only a few thousand troops have even received departure orders yet, and General Reynolds has canceled some of those for 'emergency' reasons. He may not be the best soldier the Army's ever seen, but at bureaucratic entanglements he is the master."

The Chair nodded approval. Jack studied her. He was watching the activity in the room, not taking part in any of it. Most of the time he just played his portable PSP, apparently paying no attention to the rest of them. Now that he was looking around carefully, he waited for a question no one asked, and finally asked it himself.

"What happened to Professor Owenby?"

"Some sort of security clearance snafu," Gladys Leaphorn answered. "Homeland Security hasn't let him make a call and we haven't been able to get anyone in to see him, but we think it will be cleared up by morning. Don't worry, we've made other contact with the NSA."

"Kind of the gangbang approach to courtship, isn't it?"

The Chair snapped a glare at him. "We don't have time for our usual subtlety. But don't worry. Young Wilkes is the best I've ever seen at this. Sort of a protégé of yours, isn't he, Jack?"

"Not really." Jack's eyes returned to his game screen. Bentley Robbins did indeed do the sycophant act better than Jack had ever seen it done, better than Jack would ever have attempted. Jack had in fact had a hand in his training, but after a while couldn't stand to be around the kid, since there was no telling when Bentley was being sincere, even when he said he needed to go to the bathroom.

"Things are well in hand," the Chair said.

Arden glanced sharply at Jack, thinking she had heard him wince, but his face was expressionless as he bent over his game.

⚬•❀•⚬

Major General Fred Reynolds, Centcom, commander of the most powerful army on earth, did not have his headquarters deep in the Green Zone of Kabul as one might expect. His command central consisted of one large building, formerly an exclusive hotel, on the edge of Sunni territory. General Reynolds liked to keep people on alert; that was his expressed reason for remaining here on the brink of danger. In fact, the general liked to make it hard for ranking officers to get to him.

The one who came striding in that morning had no problem, though. He didn't slow down for roadside IEDs, sniper fire, or salutes. He was the youngest one-star general since Custer, and always walked as if charging a line. "General Reynolds," he snapped out as soon as he entered the room, an aide who had tried to stop him trailing behind.

Reynolds returned the man's salute casually. "General Barker. This is a surprise. Why wasn't I given notice you were coming?"

"I don't know, sir. Not my department. But I have your orders with me."

"*You* have? What orders? I haven't received notice—"

"They're right here, sir."

Frank Barker had that tone, the tone of a very confident warrior addressing a senior officer perfectly respectfully, but with the full knowledge they both shared that he could kick the senior officer's ass at any combat they might attempt. His voice also had the confidence of clout.

General Reynolds was reading the order quickly. "This is not right."

"That's not up to you or me to say, General. You're relieved."

"I mean this is a mistake." General Reynolds looked up from the papers. He had always looked older than he was, which had served him well. At the age of fifty-three he had craggy features, especially a powerful brow that overhung his piercing gray eyes. Those eyes bored now into the eyes of the man sent to replace him.

But Barker's eyes deflected the stare with ease. "I believe your staff are also relieved, General. I have my own men in place already. We've set up shop somewhere else."

"Just one Goddamned minute, Frank. We're going to get on the horn to somebody about this right now."

"You do whatever you think best, General. I have command responsibilities to attend to. Good day."

He fired off another salute, this one looking like an obscene gesture, possibly Sicilian, turned smartly and stepped off as if on a parade ground.

"Come back here!" General Reynolds yelled, but his voice no longer had command. Barker gave the senior officer nothing but his back as he strode out of the room.

In the outer room, he said, "Start packing up, soldier. You've got an hour and this location will no longer be secured."

General Reynolds had spent a long career making contacts that would serve him well at just such a moment as this. He knew more powerful people, in and out of the military, than any ten other general officers. But when he started making calls he found no one would take his.

He was a general without a command.

At 7:46 that evening there was a knock on the door of Bentley Robbins' Georgetown apartment. Dennis Wilkerson already had a reputation within the White House of arriving late to appointments, so Bentley smiled now at the older man's obvious eagerness. He looked around the room at the half dozen other young men and women in attendance, and he didn't have to say "Ready?" or "Places" or anything else to announce that the play was on. They knew their parts. These young people held the positions they did at such early ages partly because of their extraordinary ability at sucking up. And at planting ideas and letting a superior think they were his or hers. They smiled confidently, then their faces went eager and admiring as Bentley opened the door.

A man and woman in suits stood on the threshold, so close they were already almost in the room when the door opened. They must have been standing with their noses pressed against it. They could have been brother and sister, with matching firm jaws, brown-eyed stares, and squared shoulders. Neither smiled.

Bentley didn't lose his welcoming smile, though it grew slightly puzzled. "Are you here with the Advisor? Or do you need to do a security sweep before he comes in?"

"Bentley Robbins?" the woman said, as if he hadn't spoken. Bentley nodded. "Step into the hall, please, sir."

Before he did, Bentley turned and swept the room with a glance that snagged on each person there. Two of them were his best friends since high school. All were close confidantes. The momentary meetings of eyes conveyed specific messages to each individual. They nodded imperceptibly in return.

Then he stepped out into the hall and the man in the suit stepped into the room, closing the door behind him. A young woman stepped forward from the group, extending her hand and smiling graciously. "Would you like coffee? Maybe a cookie? We're just having a—"

The man in the suit shook his head so minimally they could barely see the movement. "I want to see everyone's credentials," he snapped. "Now."

One of the young men stepped forward, having sensed quickly that this man was old-fashioned in his sense of purpose and probably in other ways as well. Having a female partner grated on him. He would have been more comfortable in the FBI of the 1930s, with all-male agents and only the occasional female secretary to break the solidity. All this Jamie sensed about him as he came toward him saying, "I'll handle this, Susan. I'm at the State Department, sir. Here's my ID. If you like we can get my boss on the phone right now."

The man didn't answer. He just held out one hand like a traffic cop, halting Jamie, and with the other hand moved his jacket off his hip so they could all see his gun.

———

Out in the hallway, Bentley had shifted his smile to a concerned, eager-to-be-helpful expression. "Ma'am, I don't want to make trouble, but can you identify yourself, please? Is there a security problem? I thought there might be when I invited the National Security Advisor to my apartment. I thought we might need some sort of preliminary clearance. But since the Advisor didn't seem concerned I decided not to worry about it. Should I have, Ms.—?"

She just stared at him. "Let me see your ID, Mr. Robbins."

His eyes narrowed fractionally. "How about if I see yours, Officer? Since you already know who I am, you could put us on an equal footing. I do have security clearance, you know. After all, I work at the White House."

"That may not be true by morning," the robotic young woman said, a remark that hit Bentley hard.

"What?!" he yelped, a sound of outrage that could be heard within the apartment. The woman smiled ever so slightly.

"Now. The ID," she said sharply.

Bentley frowned as he fumbled for his wallet, abandoning any attempt to win her over, going instead to intimidation. "We'll see about this shortly. As soon as Mr. Wilkerson gets here he's going to be very—"

"Stop!" the woman suddenly shouted. "Drop it! Drop it now!"

"What? What?" Bentley looked genuinely baffled. "My wallet? Here—"

He dropped the wallet as instructed, but too late. The woman in the suit had drawn her gun. Dropping into the approved knees-bent, two-handed stance, she aimed it at his chest.

"Wait," Bentley said, but before his voice could rise she fired, careful that the bullet go between his hands so there would be no defensive wounds. She was good, and it was a very short shot. The 9 mm. bullet went into the young man's chest, slamming him back.

As Bentley lay gasping on the floor, the young woman reached into her jacket pocket and pulled out a knife. Bentley's eyes fluttered, the most alarm he could show. He couldn't lift his hands in defense.

Holding the knife in her right hand, the woman cut the left arm of her suit jacket, drawing blood from the arm underneath. Then she slashed the knife across her left cheek, making no sound as the skin parted and blood welled out. She knelt quickly, opening Bentley's barely-resisting fingers and putting the knife's handle into his right hand. If he'd had his senses about him he would have recognized it as a knife from his own kitchen.

But the young man had nothing left, no sense, no last words, no time. The young woman pressed his chest, pushing out his last breath. Bentley gasped, tried to draw another, and died, on the floor in the hallway outside his starter apartment. He sent no last message, left no clue, and died without understanding why.

The young woman stepped quickly over the body and barged into the apartment, staggering as she crossed the threshold.

"He resisted," she said shakily. Her colleague drew his gun. The remaining people in the room gasped and one screamed as they saw Bentley's legs outside the doorway. Jamie broke for the bedroom door, pulling out his cell phone, and the male agent dropped him with a shot to the spine.

The others, sobbing and broken, allowed themselves to be rounded up and taken away.

In the Colorado compound, quiet efficiency had turned into uproar. People yelled into phones and at each other. There were only fifteen or so people in the room, but there seemed to be more arguments than that going on. The Chair herself was on two different speaker phones while talking fiercely to Janice Gentry. Her granddaughter Arden, who seemed to have assumed a role as her deputy, was disagreeing quietly with Alicia and Craig Mortenson.

Jack walked briskly from one computer screen to another, pressed a few keys, changed screens, then got on his own cell phone for thirty seconds. Reholstering it, he stepped up into the Chair's immediate eye-contact range, and said in a voice that cut through all the others without being loud,

"How many people are you going to lose before you stop this?"

"Stop what?" Gladys Leaphorn snapped. "Breathing? This is why we exist, young man, to come to the aid—"

Jack interrupted. "Wilkerson's being used as a magnet to pull us in, out of hiding. He's unapproachable now. I don't even think he knows he's being guarded, but the same thing's going to happen if anybody else so much as says hi to him. He's radioactive, Gladys. You have to find another way."

His use of her first name, which Jack had never done before, stopped her from immediately putting him in his place. She blinked, then twice more, and started thinking rather than reacting.

Jack looked more thoughtful too. "Of course, since he is the magnet you could try to—"

"Yes, thank you, Jack, I understand the principle of reverse polarization." They were saying that they could create a fake approach to the NSA, then follow or capture the people who responded, trying to work their way back up the chain to whomever was behind the larger crisis. Because they must be connected. The

NSA was the source of the withdrawal policy, so it followed that the people protecting him also wanted the policy protected.

No one else in the room needed to be told the facts, either. "He's right," Craig Mortenson said quietly. "We need surveillance, not just —"

Discussion broke out anew, replacing the arguments. The Chair beckoned and Jack leaned even closer to her.

"Do you want to be involved in this?" she said very quietly.

Jack stood and looked around the room. He was not a spy and he was not a diplomat, and the people in this room were connected to the most skilled operatives of both varieties. He looked back at the Chair and shook his head.

She acquiesced immediately. "Go east," she said. "I think that will be safest, heading right into the vortex and then spinning off again. After that either Miami or—well, make your own plans. You will anyway."

She had understood what Jack was going to say next, or possibly slip away without saying: he was going off on his own, to try to deal with this problem in his own way.

"Take Arden with you," Leaphorn added offhandedly.

"No!"

Arden stepped close to him and took his arm. Jack pulled away from her. "No," he repeated, speaking to Gladys, pleading with her.

"Don't then," the Chair shrugged. "You know you won't shake her." She turned away. She had just spent a minute and a half on Jack, an extraordinary compliment in the midst of the greatest crisis the Circle had ever known.

Jack turned to Arden. She beamed at him. He started to speak, discarded that thought, then another, and finally said, "*I* am in charge."

She shrugged, making wide eyes. "Of course. I don't even know what we're doing."

He turned and began walking away, shrugging her off again. But before he got many steps away he turned back, raising his voice again. "Madame Chair?"

Everyone turned to look at him, not just the Chair. "You know what this means?" Jack said. "Bentley's murder, the cone of protection around Wilkerson, the capture of anyone who makes even the most subtle contact with him?"

Gladys Leaphorn hesitated for three seconds, a very long time for her brain. Then she nodded. So did Alicia Mortenson, looking more frightened than Jack had ever seen her. In fact he had never seen her look anything but calm and gracious, until now.

What these events meant was that someone had been prepared to fend off exactly the kind of approaches in which this group specialized. That they had been outed. Someone knew about the most secret society that had ever existed in America.

Jack turned and strode out of the room, for the last time, leaving behind most of his real family.

CHAPTER 5

Exit Interview

Your group seems to have included a lot of professors, the interviewer said. *I suppose part of their mission was to indoctrinate young minds with whatever belief system your organization held.*

Not at all. They taught whatever they taught straight. We were top-heavy with teachers because that was a good job for us.

To spot new prospects?

No, because you get summers off. And if you're a college professor there are sabbaticals, especially if your dean is in on the secret. You know our greatest tool, the one thing that has allowed us to operate? Tenure.

Jack caught himself speaking in the present tense again, and felt stabbed in the heart anew. He stared down at the small, spindly table between the interviewer and him, until she wrote three figures on the scratch paper. As he pondered them, she said, *But your organization did recruit. You didn't just reproduce.*

He shook his head. *There are a few second- or more generation members, but membership isn't hereditary. Sometimes it skips a generation. Those are rather sad occurrences, I imagine, when parents have to keep a secret life hidden from their children.*

Happens all the time, the interviewer said drily. *But recruiting does go on in schools, doesn't it? Did, I mean.*

By this time the subject of the interrogation had given up any pretense of resistance. He could have been making up everything he said, but he didn't hesitate or balk. His voice remained absolutely dead, as if he had already joined his colleagues in the grave.

Most of us were recruited in college. That's when most people get away from their families for the first time. Your family may be lovely people or monsters. It doesn't matter. The first test is that you escape them, that you have the ambition and drive to work your way past the high school counselors, have the grades, the desire. College is when the world opens up for the first time.

Some few have been recruited straight out of high school, or earlier. Those are usually the real leaders, though in school they may have been troublemakers, goths, writers of underground newspapers, or dropouts. These usually turn out to be either the best of us or total busts, who have to be quietly shepherded into careers or halfway houses, and let go.

And when were you taken in by this group?

If Jack heard the double meaning in the interviewer's question, he didn't give any sign. *I was recruited in fifth grade, though I didn't know it. I was one of those kids in the back row, who seldom lifted my face out of my Gameboy, except occasionally to mutter the answer to a question no one else knew, or to say to the girl passing in the aisle to sharpen her pencil, "Nice dress, Sally. Forget what your stupid friends say. They're not good enough for you anyway."*

Why would you say such a thing, if you were such a loner? How did you even notice?

That was my mutant power, Jack said. It was the first thing like a joke he had said in this interview, but his voice remained flat. *I couldn't stop it. I just knew what people were feeling. I overheard conversations even if I didn't try. And I couldn't stop myself from trying to make someone feel better. I couldn't not say something. Sometimes it worked, sometimes Sally would smile secretly for the rest of the day. Sometimes she or someone like her would just stare at me like I was a freak. But my teacher noticed. A gamester with dual-track thinking and underground social skills caught the attention of my fifth-grade teacher, who happened to be one of us. Or actually Them, at the time. She pulled some strings and I was sent to Bruton Hall, a prep school. That's where my real education took place. I suppose Bruton's been destroyed too?*

Yes, the interviewer said flatly. Then she wrote in her notebook. Jack coughed slightly and looked away, though he remained expressionless otherwise.

Of course the Chair had been right. Jack couldn't get rid of Arden. So he grudgingly accepted her company, or appeared to do so. They took her blue Continental, and Jack caught a lightly-travelled state highway, heading southeast. After a couple of miles Arden said, "You probably didn't hear her, but Granny suggested you head due east. And I believe the nearest large airport is southwest, in Albuquerque."

Jack didn't answer. After another mile Arden said, "I can understand why you'd do the opposite of what she says, just because she said it. Maybe that's what she intended, you know?"

"Yes I do." In the rear-view mirror was a slowly-gathering, beautiful sunset. Jack kept looking back at it, making Arden turn to stare, until he finally stopped the car on the side of the road. They stood there not speaking for ten minutes, until the last brilliant colors suddenly fell out of the sky, then Jack kept driving.

By the time they reached Texas by then, and the night grew black and glittery, until a streak of stars was blotted out as something flew overhead, not very high above them, but so fast they couldn't follow it. Jack stopped the car again and stared, but there was nothing to be seen. Arden stood beside him. "Rocket?"

Jack was thinking about diverting to New Mexico. The Circle maintained a lab near Roswell, and Jack knew they must be working on the possibility that these flights were of extraterrestrial origin. Maybe they'd made contact years ago, maybe the aliens were already among us.

That would explain Arden.

"What?" she asked about his smile, and Jack was glad to know he'd had a thought she hadn't read.

From the airport in Lubbock, Texas, he called home. Arden stood close enough that she could hear both sides of the conversation on his cell phone.

"Hi, Mom. Just called to see how you're doing. Happy Mother's Day."

"Mother's Day is six months away, Jack."

"Well, I'll probably forget it when it comes, so I wanted to say it while I was thinking of it."

"Thank you, son. And happy Earth Day to you."

Arden could hear Jack's own tones in his mother's light, lilting voice, and wondered if he could.

"Are you by yourself, Jack? Have you met a nice girl yet?"

Jack glanced at Arden. "No, not any *nice* girls. Besides, Mom, I've been telling you for years. I'm gay."

"Oh, Jack, if only I could believe that. If I thought there was a chance of you settling down with some nice young man, you don't know the peace of mind that would bring me."

"All right, I'll bring him by the next time I come home. Listen, Mom, he's Thai, is that okay?"

"Jack, I'm so proud. Because I brought you up to love everyone and have no prejudices. Except of course against the Portugese. Not one of them can be trusted."

"And I've never forgotten that," he said.

Then Jack walked a few steps away from Arden. She gave him the privacy, but noted from his shoulders and head that the conversation with his mother grew more serious. He turned back toward her as he said goodbye, and put his phone away.

Neither of them said anything until they stood in front of a board announcing departing flights. This was a small, regional airport, their choices were limited. "Dallas or Houston?" Arden asked, as if they were about the same.

Jack stood lost in thought for a moment, as if doing a math problem in his head, then led the way to a ticket-dispensing machine and bought two tickets to Houston. The flight was without incident, but Jack's mind was filled with that plane, or rocket, that he hadn't quite seen, so fast it could have been created by imagination. It remained that way in his thoughts: just ahead, eluding even his mental vision, until it dropped over the horizon.

"I wonder where it landed," Arden said. "I wonder what it dropped."

Jack was wondering something else. "If the President is doing what they demanded, why are they launching another attack?"

Houston Intercontinental Airport is vast, a city. Jack got lucky. The airport lived up to its name: there was one flight to London leaving in two hours. A late flight, overnight, which left them walking the airport for only half an hour or so.

Arden asked questions about their destination, and Jack answered evasively or not at all, until she stopped. The Chair had known what she was doing, and Jack had known what she was doing too. These attacks on him might be unrelated to the larger problem, but they had to be resolved. He needed to be away from the Circle until they figured out who was trying to kill him.

Also, of course, Gladys Leaphorn didn't trust him. Not only had Jack been attacked, he had been seen in places he had no explanation for being, countries where he had denied setting foot in recent times. Maybe the Chair believed him, maybe she didn't, but she wanted him gone. With Arden watching him.

At some point he would have to ditch Arden, but he couldn't do that too soon. When it was time for Jack to bolt it would be full-out, and he wasn't ready to do that yet.

At a concourse intersection in the terminal was an old New England pub, authentic in no details. Jack and Arden sat at a table just inside its doors, eating limp salads and watching people go by, when suddenly Jack bolted upright. The next moment he was gone. Arden barely had time to grab her purse and catch up to him. Jack was moving fast but not calling attention to himself, glancing at his watch like a man late for a plane. But then he ducked behind a pillar and looked out. Arden just stood in the terminal, staring in the same direction but seeing nothing to alarm her. Jack pulled her back.

"See that man? The one at the water fountain. Now he's turning. Look."

She looked. Then she stared. Across the way was a man in rumpled, faded denim and matching jacket. He wore an elaborate wristwatch and a cell phone holster. His light brown hair appeared on both his head and his cheeks, which were stubbled, perhaps deliberately, perhaps from long travel. The man looked around the terminal sleepily.

It was Jack.

That is, it could have been Jack. It could have been his brother. "Do you have—?" Arden began.

"One brother, but he doesn't look like that."

Jack stared quickly around the terminal. If this man was here to replace him, he would have to be part of a team. His partners would have to capture Jack, or kill him, while Denim Man stepped into his shoes.

"First of all, I wouldn't dress like that," Jack said, watching the imposter critically. "Well, maybe unless I was going to a convention. But I'd never wear a watch like that."

"Unless you had to stay in touch with your entourage," Arden said, then shook her head, cutting herself off. She put her hand on Jack's arm. "Could we be coming down with a touch of paranoia, love? It's been going around lately."

"Yes, it tried to kill me in Reno, remember? Two paranoias, with weapons. And I've supposedly been seen in places I swear to you I was not." He stared around. "How did they know I'd be here? Did they have a GPS tracker on your car? But we left your car." He suddenly stared at Arden with obvious suspicion.

She shook off his look. "All roads lead to Houston," she said. "This is one of the busiest airports in the world. It makes sense that you'd come here. Or maybe they just have a double for you stationed in—" She stopped herself again. "This is ridiculous. Look how many people pass through this place. There's bound to be one who looks a little like—"

"Yeah, point out your evil twin." As he said it, Jack thought that Arden herself was the evil double. Maybe her innocent twin was somewhere here, waiting innocently to be replaced.

"I'm going to talk to him," she said suddenly.

As she walked out the set of her shoulders told Jack that she expected him to call her back in an urgent whisper, but he didn't.

He just watched. He didn't watch Arden, except from the corners of his eyes. Even with those limited glimpses he took in her act: walking distractedly across the busy terminal, glancing up at the departures sign, a woman obviously killing time before a flight. Then she saw the man in denim, registered surprise, and rushed up to him. No subterfuge, meet-cute opening line, no time for him to prepare a defense.

Jack was concentrating on everyone else in the terminal: who seemed to be watching the little scene, what men were too hard-eyed to be travelers, who was too little encumbered with carry-on luggage. He didn't spot anyone, became suddenly afraid that they were observing him, with better covers than he had, and skulked back deeper into the crowd.

He still couldn't pick out any half-concealed watchers, which kicked his paranoia into such powerful overdrive it was like a heavy coat hanging around his shoulders. Then abruptly Jack shrugged it off and was moving quickly across his side of the terminal. He ducked into a line of departing passengers, which started a minor ruckus, until he stepped out again on the other side, making an angry gesture as if he'd been ejected.

Meanwhile, forty yards away, Arden had captured Denim Man's attention. He was following her on a parallel course with Jack's, the man talking and trying to keep up with Arden, who danced just ahead of him but looking back and smiling, leading him on. And she had managed to give Jack a little signal at the same time that he interpreted as her needing his help.

There are all kinds of little niches in an airport. Empty courtesy counters, lounges from which a plane isn't due to depart for hours, empty kiosks, a shoeshine stand. This late at night, many of these things were abandoned, and there weren't nearly as many passengers as there would have been earlier in the day. Maintenance people and security guards were tired and less observant, too. Arden and her prey didn't seem to draw anyone's attention as they slipped into a darkened alcove. Jack stood looking all around, waiting for someone else to follow them in. When no one did, he slipped across the terminal, again looking at his watch—this time for real—and stood just outside the alcove. He heard a smooth voice with rough edges say, "What flight are you on, babe? Do you belong to the mile-high club?"

"It's been so long I think my membership's lapsed," Arden answered flirtatiously. "Where are you headed?"

"Miami. Land of—"

"No!" Arden squealed, like a teenager spotting a TV idol. "That's too lucky. What flight number? Let me see."

Jack heard sounds of a small scuffle that involved more than an exchange of papers, then Arden's voice came much more urgently. "Jack!"

"Yeah, that's my name, luv. How'd you—" the smooth, edgy voice was saying as Jack rushed into the alcove. The man looked up quickly: hair more blond than Jack's, probably streaked, more wrinkles around the eyes, unless Jack hadn't studied a mirror closely enough lately, but definitely his face, Jack's face. It would fool anyone outside his immediate circle, meaning it would fool almost anyone.

Those eyes narrowed, and without a moment's hesitation the man swung his right fist, catching Jack in the jaw. Jack was already skidding, trying to stop, and the punch knocked him straight to the ground. He lay there looking groggy and moaning.

Denim Man returned his attention to Arden, with an angry expression not all that different from the leer that had shaped his features a moment earlier. "So you must—" he began, reaching for her.

She hit him with her stiffened fingers in the solar plexus, just below the breastbone. She encountered muscle, hard and unyielding. This man only resembled Jack superficially. Under the clothes he was a very trained fighter.

The blow stopped his breath for a moment, but he grinned at her and caught her hand. His other hand came up quickly, aimed at her chin.

And then Jack, who lay flat on his back, his legs stretched out between his standing attacker's legs, simply brought his foot up as hard as he could. It made a satisfying crunch. The man was wearing some sort of protection, like a catcher's cup, but Jack had good leverage and his foot drove the cup up into the man's crotch, almost as effectively as if the man had been wearing nothing. Denim Man grunted hard and crouched instinctively, trying to protect himself.

And Jack brought both his knees back against his chest and kicked out into the man's gut, just as Arden swung her stiff hand at his neck, hitting his windpipe.

Both blows were effective. For a moment the man hunched, trying to protect himself everywhere at once, then collapsed.

"Hurry." Arden was already on top of him, going through his pockets. She found an ID case in a jacket pocket and pulled it out. "Look."

Jack did. He saw his own picture and name on a California driver's license. The picture looked more like him than the imposter did. He noted the address, in Riverside, sure it was fake but memorizing it anyway because he couldn't stop himself. Arden didn't find anything else useful except a ticket and boarding pass that weren't for a flight to Miami at all, but for theirs to London. "Liar," she sneered at the unconscious man.

Jack stared down at the face that was not quite his. He had an urge to kick the man in the head, stomp on his ribs. The urge made no sense at all. It was totally instinctive. This was his replacement, which made Jack unnecessary. Self-preservation made him tremble with the desire to smash this thing into unrecognizability. The same urge those people felt when looking at replicas of themselves growing in pods.

"Let's take him—" he began, while Arden said, "Is there anybody—" and they both knew what the other was going to say. Jack wanted to get the man some place where they could interrogate him, but Arden didn't think they had the time, and wondered if they could just immobilize him some place where some of their people could pick him up later.

During the second that they evaluated each other's plans, both became unworkable. Two uniformed and armed security guards suddenly stepped into the alcove from the terminal, looked down at the man on the ground who had obviously been attacked, shouted, "Hey!" and began going for their guns.

At the same time there was a clicking sound and a door at the other end of the short alcove unlocked and opened. A much beefier maintenance man came in, gaped at the scene, and stood blocking the door.

Arden was still crouched down on the floor, where she'd been going through Denim Man's pockets. Her face a mask of distress, she said, "Help me, please! He's diabetic!"

The three men reacted completely differently, which Jack noticed in less than a second. One security guard paid no attention to what Arden had said, continuing to go for his gun. The other froze for a moment, uncertain. And the maintenance man started forward, looking only at the man on the ground.

That told Jack everything he needed to know. The two security guards were confederates of the fake Jack, in on the subterfuge. One of them still had some humanitarian instincts, or maybe, just maybe, he was authentic, as the maintenance man seemed to be.

"Listen to her!" Jack snapped, and kicked the fake guard in the hand. Then he grabbed the maintenance man's arm, pulling him forward. He was a big guy, already moving forward, and his momentum turned into a lumbering fall. He sprawled into both security guards as Jack grabbed Arden's hand and said, "This way!"

She was ahead of him, already leaping toward the closing, locked door through which the maintenance man had come. Arden caught it just before it clicked back into place, and she and Jack slipped through it, quickly closing it behind them. Something slammed into it just as it closed. A fist hammered on it.

They were in a service corridor of bare steel walls, carts, tools, and discarded signs. Without speaking to each other Jack and Arden raced in the direction of their own gate. As they ran they had to jump over thick cables in places, some of which seemed to connect nowhere. It was a little scary to see how haphazard this place looked behind the scenes.

"We can't get on that flight," Arden panted. Jack had been tipping back and forth, but she made up his mind.

"We can't not! They want to trap us here. We've got to take off."

"It's already boarding," Arden said, and he had no clue how she knew that.

There was pursuit behind them. They both began opening doors along their way, trying to leave false trails. One of the doors turned out to be to a closet. As Jack thought about ducking into it he glanced into the closet and saw clothes. A maintenance worker's gray coverall and cap. He grabbed them.

"What—" Arden began, then shut up. "Out that way," Jack said, pushing her, and she went out a door. Jack lingered. He could no longer hear anyone following him. They must have figured he'd done the smart thing by now and gotten out of this confining tunnel. Showed how stupid they were, thinking him smart.

"We're going to continue our boarding of Flight 1549, overnight service to London's Heathrow Airport. This flight is about three-quarters full, so please use all the seats available. If your carry-on luggage won't fit in the overhead compartment, please ask a flight attendant..."

The passengers all glared at her spiel, one they had heard their whole lives. They crowded toward her like carnivores around a wounded zebra, ready to pounce. *Assholes*, the flight attendant thought. *Do you think you'll get there any sooner just because you get on the plane first?* The worst thing about a flight attendant's job was too many alpha types on airplanes, wanting to push ahead of everyone else even if there was nothing to be gained by it. The flight attendant lengthened her speech a little just to raise their collective blood pressure. She plastered a smile on her face.

Then the rush began. They thrust boarding passes at her, crowding almost shoulder to shoulder. She smiled at each one as she held the pass under the laser light that registered the passenger's name and seat.

The line wasn't halfway through when a maintenance worker appeared at the flight attendant's shoulder. "Sorry, Jane, spot check. It's not registering on board."

"What? What do you mean, not registering? They've all beeped—"

"But they haven't recorded," the maintenance man mumbled. He wore a cap and kept his head down, already messing with her scanner. "We're going to have to get all those passengers back off and run them through again."

The line groaned, a big sound in the late-night airport, following by mutters that sounded threatening.

"No, please," the flight attendant said urgently, under her breath. She was about to explain further to the maintenance guy when the next passenger in line thrust her boarding pass at them like a sword. She was a pretty young woman, but not at the moment, with her features contorted by anger.

"I'm in a hurry, miss," the bitch snapped.

The maintenance man barely glanced at her as he said, "Then maybe you shouldn't slow us down while we're trying to do our jobs." In that moment he became the flight attendant's hero. The angry young woman's jaw dropped, she had no response, and a few of the passengers behind her even grinned at how effectively the man in the coverall had shut her up.

"There, I think that's got it," he said a moment later, becoming *everyone's* hero. He took the angry young woman's boarding pass (two of them, as a matter of fact, though no one noticed), scanned it (them), said, "Yup," just like Clint Eastwood, and disappeared into the departure tunnel.

The bitch turned in the doorway, holding everyone up, glaring at the crowd, saying, "Wait, I dropped my ticket." People tried to push past her but she was immovable until someone grabbed the ticket folder off the ground, thrust it at her, and she went through into the boarding tunnel.

Which had given Jack time to discard his maintenance worker's coverall and cap and join the line of boarding passengers. Arden caught up to him and said under her breath, "Thanks. You just made me the most hated person on this flight."

"You probably would have accomplished it on your own anyway. But I'd advise you not to drink anything that flight attendant offers you."

But the ruse had worked. Arden's and the fake-Jack's boarding passes had been scanned, and anybody watching the departing passengers would not have seen Jack boarding the plane. If anyone checked the computer records later they would show that the imposter had boarded the plane and Jack had been left behind in Houston.

He hoped someone would be dumb enough to fall for that. It was going to be a long flight.

Jack had never been able to sleep on an airplane. He wasn't afraid of flying, exactly, he just didn't believe in it. He knew the theory—the shape of the wings, speed plus lift, all that aerodynamic theology—but his body still knew it made no sense that an object this heavy, carrying so many people and tons of luggage, could remain aloft. At least not without his concentrating very hard, keeping the plane in the air through mental effort.

"Why don't you play your game?" Arden asked. She had noticed the hand-held player that Jack had clipped to his belt, through all this.

"I can't get on-line up here. That's the only way it's interesting for me any more."

"Playing with strangers?"

Jack nodded. "Trying to figure out an opponent when you have no clues about him or her except the way he or she plays. In fact I've played a few times when I'm pretty sure the opponent was several people taking turns."

"Or a schizophrenic."

"Even better."

Arden settled back with a magazine. Even with their business-class seats made into mini-beds, Jack couldn't relax. Too much on his mind. Hanging up here in the air, giving his enemies hours to prepare for his arrival in London, set any kinds of traps for him they could devise, or simply have him arrested for assaulting Denim Man and stealing his identity—which had been Jack's to start with, but he might have a hard time explaining that—any of these was a possibility. All that kept him edgy, even after the double bourbon and water he'd ordered from the smiling flight attendant. Arden had glanced at her thirstily but then declined, with thanks.

"This was a bad idea," he muttered.

"I believe I said let's not get on board, but you overruled me. Anyway, it's too late now. It'll be fine. I'll probably have to save you again once we land, but I'm getting good at that."

Jack lay there groggily next to her, thinking that maybe she had rescued him too easily. Maybe these had been ploys designed for Arden to gain his confidence. He needed to pay careful attention to her, she might be leading him straight to destruction. But if that was the goal, Jack's death, that could have been accomplished by just *not* letting her save him. So either she was on his side after all or she was an opponent with something more devious in mind than his mere destruction.

So his thoughts circled and barked at each other. After awhile, for rest, he replayed the conversation with his mother. He pictured her standing in the kitchen of their home in Fort Wayne, with the three windows and the yellow curtains, then realized that he was picturing his mother younger than she was now, and that the kitchen might well be a different color by now. He hadn't been home in a while. But he did stay in touch. It had been more than half his short lifetime—he was twenty-six—since he had lived with his family, but they still grounded him in reality.

The mental idyll didn't last long. Inevitably he began worrying again about the reception he would face when he landed, and about the woman lying beside him. He also thought about her grandmother, the Chair, and what plans she had for him. Jack tried to remember how long it had been since he had trusted someone. Far too long. But he was lucky, he always had his family.

Arden glanced at him as if he had spoken. So he did. "Where are your parents?"

She gave the strangest answer to this commonplace question he'd ever heard: "They're dead, I think."

He just lay there blinking at her, thinking he had mis-heard, or that she hadn't heard his question right. Arden stared overhead. In a soft voice, as if to herself, she continued, "At least I'm pretty sure Mom is. She would have gotten in touch with me by now otherwise. Dad..." Her voice trailed off as if that one word said worlds.

Jack looked at her profile: smooth cheek, straight, strong nose, one clear blue eye, not meeting his. "You were estranged?"

Arden laughed very quietly. "We were never—what's the opposite of 'estranged'?—we were never really connected. I used to think that's how all fathers were, kind of—well, not there, robotic."

"Caught up in business?" Jack was good at reading people, beyond good, but he was getting nothing from Arden except sadness. He didn't have a clue to her thoughts. Maybe she could stop the subliminal signals people give off. At any rate, there was very little emotion in her voice.

"He didn't have a business. That was part of his problem, I realize now. Never really found himself. He and Mom just drifted from place to place, carrying me along. I used to be afraid I'd wake up one morning or come home from school one afternoon and they'd be gone. Then I started hoping for it. Finally one day it became true. I was too much for them to keep up with. They left me with a friend in St. Louis, one I had never met. Mom looked deep into my eyes and cried and said they'd be back for me soon. But they weren't. I'd hear from them once in a while, but in the meantime I was growing up in one home after another where I didn't have quite the status of a step-child."

"Foster care?"

"More or less," she answered.

This would account for her near-telepathic ability to read people. A child in a stranger's home has to be that sensitive, to read signals the sender tries not to send. Arden's first lessons must have been very harsh.

But something was missing from her story. "Your mother is Gladys's daughter?" Jack asked.

Arden nodded. "But they didn't have much contact. I almost never saw Granny. And Mom didn't tell her where I was when she left me. It took Granny a few years first to realize I was missing, then to find me. That was when she put me in the boarding school in Switzerland, when I was twelve. Which was heaven."

Yes, the Chair would not have had a place for a young girl in her complicated, secretive life. But she had found a safe place for her, and where Gladys had monitored her closely from a distance, Jack guessed. Arden had obviously thrived in the Swiss finishing school. But the years between eight and twelve are very, very long. They must have seemed forever to the young Arden, lost in America.

"I heard from Granny regularly when I was in Switzerland. She was evaluating me, of course, although I didn't know that then."

The school Arden had attended wasn't quite the European counterpart of his own Bruton Academy, but it did have a small gifted and talented department, consisting of one teacher and a handful of students who didn't know they were all being groomed and observed.

Now Arden was reading his thoughts. "I never heard of any of you people until Granny swooped in a couple of years ago and carried me off. But I dreamed of you. I longed for the Circle. Sometimes I think I'm still dreaming, that I imagined all of you simply by wanting it so bad. Wanting there to be something more than what I saw around me every day."

"We all felt that way before we were gathered in," Jack said. "You know that."

She nodded. "I do."

He felt as if she'd opened up to him, but her story had large missing elements. After a minute Jack asked, "Was your mother ever—?"

"Was she considered for the program? I think so. Pretty sure. But I never got the chance to ask her about it and Granny won't say a word. She clamps down completely if I bring up the subject."

The phrase "clamped down" meant a great deal when you were talking about Gladys Leaphorn. She had an emotional side, Jack guessed, but she could cut off everything—emotion, her own thoughts, a group discussion—more effectively than anyone else on earth.

Arden continued, "I always thought Dad was the restless one, moving from job to job, but now I think it may have been Mom, wanting to be part of something she imagined like I did, but never got invited to join. Probably taking up with Dad ended her possibilities of learning about the Circle forever. I think she sensed it, though. Probably that's one reason why..."

Why she hadn't been closer to her daughter, Jack thought. She envied her own child's possibilities.

At least that was how he finished up the story in his own mind. Arden didn't talk any more. He wanted to put an arm around her, but in the narrow confines of the airline chair-beds she might take that for an advance. And he had no intention of advancing on her. He did feel he'd gotten to know her much better. He continued to think about her and her life story for the next hour as he skimmed in and out of sleep. Those thoughts kept him preoccupied from the larger ones.

It wasn't until some time later that he realized she might have made up the whole estranged-parents story just to put him off guard.

It was a little after noon, British time, when they arrived at Heathrow. Jack and Arden stood awkwardly in the aisle of the plane, feeling strange with no luggage. They had no story, either, and no defenses. Police might well be waiting for them as soon as they stepped out of the exit tunnel. They both watched the flight attendants, trying to decide if they'd gotten any security calls during the flight, but if they had they were good at concealing their thoughts. The one who had taken their boarding passes in Houston still glanced at Arden hostilely when her back was turned. Only Jack saw that.

"Listen," he whispered urgently as they were in the tunnel,

"if I get arrested, there's an address in Chelsea..." He tried to give Arden the beginnings of a plan. She just frowned at him and took his arm as they came out into the light.

"Well, if we'd had the extra three days I thought we were going to have we *would* have seen 'Spamalot,'" she said angrily.

Jack answered defensively, "Is it my fault the kid runs away and freaks out the nanny? What is this, number four? I'm not the one teaching Mary that she's in charge, that she should be on the transatlantic phone to us every time..."

"If we would just stay away one time and not let her get away with this nonsense, it would do her worlds—"

The two men in black suits watching the deplaning passengers glanced at the arguing couple and looked away, as people always do. A woman and man having a spat in public put up an invisible barrier that repels others. The two plainclothes police—Jack was sure that's what they were -- gave them a close look for a moment but couldn't hold it as Jack's face grew angrier and Arden tilted her chin at an imperious angle. She spoke in a clipped sort of upper-class twit accent, not exactly British perhaps, but certainly European, giving off a flavor of travel in expensive places.

"So just let her be homeless for a while, you're saying," Jack said in a low but incredibly hostile voice as they walked past the two men. Maybe they weren't bobbies at all, or probably they were looking for someone else, but if they had been waiting for an American man traveling alone Jack and Arden had slipped by them for the moment. They hurried down the terminal.

He was mad at her. Jack wanted to strangle Arden. In their few seconds of role-playing he had felt real anger, as if they were a little-to-like couple who had been confined together too long. She glanced at him out of the corner of her eye and he saw a flash of hatred there, too. Then Arden grinned.

"That was exhilarating, wasn't it, babe?" She took his arm. "Next time let's play a young couple who have just fallen in love and see what that feels like."

Jack and Arden got through customs quickly, having no encumbering baggage. The rest of the passengers streamed toward the exits with their suitcases, greeting relatives. Jack headed back into the airport. Arden followed him without asking questions as he took a couple of turns and ended up at a row of lockers. Barely glancing at the numbers, he found one and opened it with a combination. Inside sat a large black gym bag, on end. Jack unzipped it to reveal clothes, a shaving kit, other items.

"You keep a bag in Heathrow?"

"Doesn't everyone?" Jack was rummaging in the space behind the bag and came out with a few still-wrapped flat packages. He glanced at each one critically, then at Arden's hips, finally tossed most of the packages back and handed two to her.

"Panties?" she said, noting that he'd guessed her size correctly. "And stockings?"

"Really that part of my life is in the past. I don't keep nearly the selection I used to have. Here." He also came up with a small pink kit containing a few cosmetics and other sundries.

"Pink?" Arden said critically.

"Yeah. Don't chicks still like pink? Come on."

They made their way to a ticket counter. While Jack waited in line Arden ducked into a women's room and came out *sans* packages, though her pink carrying kit now bulged. Jack rose considerably in her estimation when he didn't glance below her waist or make any remark at all. He just matter-of-factly handed her a boarding pass.

"Prague?" she said. "We're not checking out the Jack-sighting here in London first?"

He just shook his head, didn't ask whether she had overheard the conversation with her grandmother or whether Granny had shared information with her.

This flight was very short, little more than a hop, the plane not even half-full. Arden and Jack spent the time in near-complete silence, Jack lost in thought that turned into dozing. Arden stared at the seat back in front of her or out the window, feeling the tug of the continent where she had grown to adulthood. Only other expatriates know the way she felt, not a homecoming but more as if falling back into a very vivid and recurring dream. For Arden the feeling was stronger and stranger because she had spent her whole childhood on the move, never settling anywhere, so America was as much a concept as a reality to her. She had no home, never had had one until she'd found the Circle, and she knew how she was thought of there. Arden sat blankly, waiting to ... become.

Before they even left the airport in Prague, Jack found an internet connection and got on his game. Instantly he was absorbed, paying no apparent attention to the passing people or anything in the real world.

"You really are addicted, aren't you?" Arden said, standing beside him with her arms crossed.

"Czechoslovakia isn't very wired, I don't know where I'll find another connection. And it's late in the time zone where I'm playing."

She didn't care for an explanation. After a few minutes, when it became clear that Jack wasn't going to stop soon, Arden walked away. The passengers in the airport terminal were mostly men, most of them wearing suits and a large proportion of them foreign to the country where they found themselves. She could tell by looking, by the way they walked, their wristwatches.

Arden had come to Prague a couple of times while she was in school, when it was supposedly flowering in democracy, but couldn't claim to know the country well at all. She found a phone and checked in, but didn't talk long. She was staring out the large terminal windows when she sensed someone coming and turned slowly.

The man wore jeans, a universal standard, and a red polo shirt. His hair was dark and long, and he walked purposefully, unlike a European, but with an awareness of others that kept him from brushing shoulders.

It was Jack.

For a moment she was surprised, because she hadn't recognized him. His hair was wet, she realized now, he had obviously combed it with water and changed his shirt, changing his appearance subtly enough that he seemed different. Maybe he was. She didn't know him well enough. Maybe this was another doppelganger.

"Somebody shoot you with a zombie dart?" He snapped his fingers in front of her face.

No, this was Jack. She grinned at him and didn't explain why. Outside, before they got into a cab, she did ask, "Where's your headquarters here?"

"Good question," he said, and to the cab driver something in Czech, a language she didn't know. She started to ask a question, realized Jack wasn't saying anything else in front of the cabbie, and sat silent for the rest of the way into city center.

They checked into a hotel on the edge of Lesser Town, the old part of the city. Adjoining rooms: they presented themselves as business associates with a company Jack made up as he signed the register.

"Which would be more convincing if either of us had a briefcase or a laptop," Arden murmured as they walked up the two flights of stairs to their rooms.

"Airline lost our luggage," Jack said.

"Even our carry-ons?"

"Okay, we're very careless business travelers."

They opened their hotel doors, glanced in, neither felt the need of saying anything about the rooms. Arden said, "I'm going to go correct the lack of clothing and luggage situation. Want to come?"

Jack shook his head. "I'm a little beat. I'll just crash here for a while, then I think there's an internet café a couple of blocks from here."

Arden didn't say anything, didn't remind him that he'd claimed to her grandmother not to have been in Prague for three years. She just nodded, went into her room, emerged five minutes later, and went off to look for Prague fashions.

Jack did crash, though he hadn't intended to. As soon as he lay down for a moment jet lag wiped him out. His dreams were

Kafkaesque, invaded by Prague, so waking in the dark felt like continuing to sleep. He moved slowly, having trouble remembering where or when he was. Then he suddenly snapped to consciousness, on high alert that, he knew from experience, would not let him sleep any more tonight.

It was late, he knew nothing about Prague nightlife any more, but he went out. The hotel felt unbearable, for some reason. The night was cool and pleasant and frightening. His sleep had given whatever enemies Jack had here plenty of time to prepare something for him. So here he went, walking into it.

The old castle dominated the landscape as he walked uphill into Lesser Town. He had always loved that name, thinking the houses and even inhabitants would be diminutive. In other cities it would be called Old Town, because that's what it was: the original city of Prague, founded in the ninth century, though the area had been settled since Roman times. It had stayed the same for centuries, Jack had read, peasants and merchants supporting the inhabitants of the huge castle, everyone knowing their place. But since the collapse of Communism the modern world had made inroads even here. Nightclubs stood shoulder to shoulder with centuries-old hostels. Jack heard the music but had no desire to go in.

He wondered where 'he'—his double—had been spotted in this sprawling old city. What had he been doing?

For that matter, what was he doing now? Walking dreamily through the old continent, waiting for lightning to strike. Jack suddenly felt very far from home. He was never troubled by homesickness, probably because he hadn't had a home in so long, but suddenly he had a fierce longing to be back in America, just for a few minutes. *What's happening to my country?* He felt like a traitor, who had fled when the trouble started.

Jack hadn't touched his cell phone in hours, almost a day, which wasn't unusual for him. Sometimes he forgot it when he went on trips. His friends had always accused him of being an eighteenth-century kind of guy, even given his current occupation. Now he felt as if he'd travelled back in time to his rightful place.

Lesser Town was not quite deserted as midnight neared, but the streets felt heavy with sleep. Still, an occasional car passed, music drifted out of a few doorways. Jack stopped at one, read the sign in Czech over the door, and realized his walk had not been random. He went in.

The room inside was low-ceilinged, smoky, and so big he couldn't see the far walls. There were wooden tables with spindly old wooden chairs, filling the room but not cramming it. On the walls that he could see were posters, some of them peeling off, announcing rallies and concerts and even a chess championship. The lighting came from sconces on the walls and lamps on tables. There was no bar and no stage, though up at the front of the room a woman crooned softly. She had no microphone, and might have been a patron suddenly struck with an urge to perform.

Jack walked across a painted concrete floor. There were about a dozen people in the room, scattered among all those tables, some of them sitting alone, only two or three paying apparent attention to the singer. Jack sat at a table by the wall, near one of the sconces. There was no menu and no waiter appeared. Some of those people at the tables had cups sitting in front of them, but they might have brought their own. Jack sat quietly for five minutes, soaking up atmosphere, and finally walked over to a counter at the side of the room opposite the singer. He tapped his fingers quietly on the countertop, and suddenly a man popped up, a rotund man wearing an apron, who appeared old at first in the dimness but then revealed himself to be no older than Jack. The young man had a round face divided by a thin black moustache, and wide eyes that gaped blankly at Jack for a long moment.

"Coffee?" Jack said. "Or maybe a brandy?"

The man stared as if he didn't understand, then suddenly said, "I'll bring it to your table."

Jack walked slowly back. No one seemed to have looked at him. This place seemed to be a sort of European opium den, each person sunk into his or her own concerns, including even the singer, who stared upward and made no eye contact with her audience.

In a minute the man from behind the counter arrived at Jack's table bringing both a coffee cup and a brandy snifter, which Jack actually sniffed as it was set in front of him. The waiter remained standing, staring down at Jack.

"Welcome to Erenray's, señor."

Jack smiled to himself.

The waiter didn't leave. "We don't often have Americans in here," he said, in an accent that was hard to place. Certainly not Spanish, as his greeting had implied.

Jack glanced around. "I'll recommend it to my friends when I get back home." He pushed the other chair out with his foot. "Why don't you sit down, make me feel welcome."

The waiter declined, but did lean forward over the chair back so their conversation was a little more intimate. "Things are going very badly for your country," the waiter said, in a completely neutral voice that expressed neither sympathy nor satisfaction.

Jack nodded. "But I think they will get worse before they get better."

The waiter frowned. "How can they get worse?"

Jack spoke as if viewing a scene. "Rallies celebrating American withdrawals from various places in the world, turning into anti-American riots. Counter-demonstrators. But then, who knows what will be left in place once America withdraws?"

"You have some idea?" the waiter said.

Jack nodded. "A worldwide terrorist network that has succeeded in pushing America out of the world. Then what? Will they just disband? Go back to their homes and children and tend their orchards? What will come after the *pax Americana*?"

Jack didn't answer any of his own questions, just sat there musing like a young doctoral candidate in history talking about the thirteenth century. The waiter looked down at him with troubled eyes.

Jack stood up, but before he exited said one more thing: "Have you seen me in here recently?"

The waiter's look of puzzlement was answer enough. Jack moved carefully away from the table, having touched neither of his drinks. As he walked he suddenly felt observed, though no one in the café seemed to be looking at him. He stopped for a moment, then changed direction. Stopping at the next occupied table, he spoke briefly to the two men sitting there. They answered back, looking at him curiously. Jack did the same thing at the next table, and the next. At one table he simply rapped his knuckles on the tabletop in a complicated little riff. The woman there looked up at him and nodded, which was nice. Jack smiled.

Before he stepped back outside he turned to look at the singer as well, giving her a long, significant look. She lowered her eyes from the ceiling and looked back. Then Jack turned quickly and went outside.

The nighttime city street seemed different just from the short time he'd been inside, as if a major building on the block had been razed and replaced. The streetlight flickered, and the buildings shimmered like a stage set. Jack looked left and right, saw no one and no cars in either direction, and walked straight across the street. Over there he turned left, back toward his hotel, and walked quickly, shoulders back and arms swinging like a tourist out for a hike. He kept up that pace for a block, which brought him to a shopping district, where the shops had awnings and wide picture windows. Jack slowed as if window shopping. He didn't hear anything, but still had that feeling of being watched. He walked along idly for a moment, then darted around the next corner.

That set off noises. Footsteps came running. Moments after Jack rounded the corner, two men jumped around the same corner from the direction he'd come. One of the men was short and heavy, with very broad shoulders. The other was taller and thin, with hair long enough to sway as he ran. They came to a stop together and stared down the empty street. "Which way?" the shorter one asked in French, and the other answered in a strangely-accented English, "That doorway. Look."

There was a deeply-recessed doorway just past the shop under whose awning they stood. The bulky Frenchman jumped with surprising speed toward the doorway, drawing a gun as he did so. He waved it in a small half-circle, stepping all the way into the recessed doorway, and saw nothing but a door, plain and nondescript like a service entrance. The man turned and said one negative syllable to his companion.

"Maybe he picked the lock," the taller man said. He continued to speak English, but in an odd accent, one difficult to place. As his companion bent to examine the door's lock and knob, the taller man lit a cigarette and stared around the silent block thoughtfully.

———————

Above him, Jack lay stretched in the awning. He had swung himself up into it as soon as he'd rounded the corner. It was a scary hiding place because his body weight made the awning sag, and if it began to tear or he otherwise gave himself away he would be helpless. There was nowhere to go from here.

But it made a good observation post, and that was what he'd wanted, just to check out who might be following him. He'd half-thought he knew the answer, and he was right. He looked down at the thin man with the longish hair as the man lit his cigarette and Jack got a good look at his face. He recognized it.

It was Jack's face.

CHAPTER 6

Major Everett Sloane in his desert camo fatigues took the call standing up, as if he was in the presence of his commanding officer, who was actually three hundred miles away. Sloane had the call on his speaker phone so the handful of other people in the room could hear the call.

"Your withdrawal is proceeding a little slowly," came the voice of General Barker over the speaker. "I was hoping for more efficiency from you, Everett."

"Things are proceeding very efficiently here, General. But we're not withdrawing."

A long silence was followed by the single word, "What?"

"General, I'm standing in a base in Southern Afghanistan which is situated between the Sunni and Shi'ite sections. And we're not fighting. Neither are they. This is neutral ground. In the last year I have brought these sides together. I have eaten in their homes, attended their funerals. Most days I don't even wear a uniform. This base is more Switzerland than the headquarters of an occupying force, General. We have had breakthroughs—"

"That's great, Everett, and I'm sure you deserve to get written up in *Newsweek* as well as a couple of commendations, but you have different orders now."

"Yes, General, I know. That's why I've decided to resign my commission. I'll stay on here in a civilian capacity. Leaders of both factions have asked me to do so."

Another long silence sounded more hostile than the last. Major Sloane could imagine General Barker chewing on a cigar as he snapped out the next response: "Abandoning your post in wartime is an act of treason, Major."

"I'd say it's my post that's abandoning me, General. And I'd be happy to debate the definition of treason with you anywhere, including in a court martial."

Barker sounded like a man with no more time for this minor nuisance, though Major Sloane thought otherwise. He knew the commanding general of the American forces in Afghanistan had had similar problems with other battalion commanders in other parts of the country. He continued in a more placating tone, "General, we are right on the verge here. These people are talking to each other civilly, which they have never done in their history. Never. We haven't had a bombing or shooting in a month, and none committed by locals in six months, I believe. The only insurgents are those coming in from outside, and some of the locals are even helping us deal with them. Given six more months…"

"You don't have six more months," Barker snapped over the speaker phone. "You don't have six more hours. You're relieved, Major. Your replacement will be—"

"Any replacement won't get much cooperation here," another man in the room suddenly said, stepping forward from the wall. He did stand at attention.

"Who said that?" yelled General Barker. The others, who had seen Barker in the past, could picture him standing at his desk, cords standing out on his neck as he screamed into the phone.

Major Sloane tried to wave the man who had just spoken to silence, but the enlisted man ignored him. "Chief Master Sergeant George Lehane, General. I've already put in for retirement, and I'm overdue for it. I think I'll hang on here and help the major out. So will about two-thirds of my men, I think."

"You don't have that many men due for retirement. Not remotely."

"Then they'll desert, General. I'm quite sure of it."

The longest silence of all made both men wonder if General Barker had just had a stroke. When his voice resumed it was very low and bitter. "You'll be hunted down like criminals."

"Who'll do the huntin', General?" the master sergeant asked. "Since all the American forces are runnin' home with their tails between their legs? Sounds like all any criminal has to do is get beyond our borders and he's home free. Besides, you ain't got nobody—"

The major jumped in then. "I think that would be a very bad idea, General, if you don't mind some advice. Do you really want to see American forces fighting each other on CNN?"

"I think we can keep those idiots out of this," General Barker snapped. "They're all too scared to venture out of the Green Zone for more than—"

Another man in the room in Fallujah cleared his throat. "May I quote you on that, General? And do you mean all war correspondents, including the one hundred and forty who have been casualties of this conflict, or were you speaking of my network in particular?"

A short silence made them think the line had been cut. Then Barker asked quietly, "Who is that, Major?"

The man in civilian fatigues answered. "Matthew Esquivel, General. CNN. I've been imbedded with this unit for eight months now. I'm surprised you haven't seen any of my stories."

General Barker's voice ignored him and spoke directly to his subordinate. "Everett, this has been a deliberate trap for a superior officer. Insubordination of the worst kind. I'm recommending your demotion as well as removal."

"Yes sir."

"That is all for now."

"Yes sir."

A loud click ended the call. The half dozen people in the room looked at each other. The chief master sergeant was grinning. "I believe that was orders for us to carry on," said the major.

"Yes sir," snapped out everyone in the room, including, with a broad smile, the CNN correspondent.

They all left the room, leaving Major Sloane looking grim, thinking he had to start watching his back again.

Hanging in the awning three feet over the heads of his pursuers, Jack felt his weight shift, though he hadn't twitched a muscle. The awning sagged an inch lower. The Jack lookalike below him, now holding a gun like his partner, looked around alertly. Jack turned his neck ever so slowly and saw that the awning had begun to tear, next to the metal strut that held it. As he watched, the rip lengthened to six inches. He tried to distribute his weight more evenly, but that only stopped the rip for a second.

"Got it!" the burly thug said in French. And he pulled open the door in the recessed doorway and started inside.

Several things happened at once: An alarm sounded, a shrill clanging in the dead night. The awning ripped completely, dropping Jack toward the ground. His lookalike below him looked up. The burly thug froze just inside the doorway.

And Jack swung down, holding the horizontal metal support, kicking his double in the shoulders and knocking him into the doorway, pushing the door closed and trapping his partner inside.

The Jack lookalike was momentarily stunned, dropping his gun. Jack fell to the ground in a crouch and lunged toward the gun. But his double alertly kicked it to the side, and before Jack could grope for it again there was the sound of gunfire as the thug inside tried to shoot his way out through the wooden door. Both Jack and his double ducked aside as bullets flew past them. Jack turned and ran. His double took a few seconds and found his gun. Jack was running full out down the street by then, when gunfire started up again. In an idle part of his mind, the tiny part that wasn't scared to death, he noted the effect of gunshots being aimed at a person, which was much more unnerving than any video game had ever depicted. It caused panic to fly in all directions, making him want simultaneously to burrow into the ground, keep running, and fall to his knees whimpering for mercy.

He kept running, just out of momentum, darting out into the street so that a line of parked cars partially protected him. A car would have been a good idea, he wished he had one. Also a cell phone. What kind of idiot went out without one?

The gunfire had stopped, which drove his panic higher. He risked a look over his shoulder and saw that the men were no longer shooting at him. They were no longer in sight, in fact.

He skidded to a stop in the middle of the street. They were circling the block, obviously. Or had gone for a car they had nearby. Or knew that they had confederates just ahead, and Jack was running right into their arms. Jack stood there trembling, afraid to keep running, afraid to go back, afraid to turn a corner. Every choice seemed bad. He had never in his life so badly wanted to fly.

Now would be a good time for Arden to reappear, screeching around the corner in a Porsche to rescue him, as she had predicted she would have to do again. But Arden didn't appear, and he saw no way she could. He hadn't told her where he was going, hadn't even told her he was going out.

A screech of tires did happen, though. A pickup truck pulled out of the line of cars, a weird European conglomerate sort of vehicle, very boxy, but with good acceleration. It had eaten up half the distance between them before Jack had a chance to react. Then he turned and ran, to the sidewalk on the opposite side of the street from where he'd started. He looked for an opening, an alley, a fire escape, night club entrance, anything. But the street was dark and quiet. Wide glass windows showed empty display cases, their goods locked away for the night.

The car/truck had almost caught up to him now, and because it was European the passenger side was on the left, the side closest to Jack. That window was already down, and as the car nearly came abreast of him a hand emerged holding an automatic pistol. The gunman began firing before he was quite level with Jack's running position. Bullets stitched their way across the brick storefront right beside and behind him.

Jack fell. It could have been deliberate or just that his legs stopped working, but he went to his hands and face on the pavement just as the line of bullets passed over his head. The shooter didn't stop, either. The spray of gunfire continued, coming to a window and blasting it apart, showering Jack with shards of glass.

Then he heard the screech of the truck's brakes. In a subconscious part of his mind Jack had thought of the truck as a boat in a current, that would keep sailing on by, while Jack could stop on the bank. But the truck could stop too, of course. Jack made a quick calculation. He could get up and keep running, in which case the truck would catch up to him and someone inside would shoot him. He could run back the way he'd come, making the truck back up, which would be a little more difficult for the driver. And wouldn't police arrive soon, with all this gunfire and alarms going off?

Or he could run *toward* the truck, and try—

No more time for thinking. Jack stood up, still crouched, and his body took over. Right beside him, the gunman's bullets had shattered the show window of a small shop. Jack leaped through the new opening into the dark interior.

Behind him he heard car doors slam. Two of them, at least. So either the burly thug had broken out of his momentary trap, or they'd had another confederate close by. Jack fell to his hands and knees again, this time on broken glass, jumped up, and ran deeper into the darkness of the little shop. He had no idea what it sold, but apparently a lot of display cases were required. Jack banged into two, caromed off like a billiard ball, spun and kept heading toward the back of the shop. Behind him he heard feet hit the floor.

A real secret agent would duck down behind one of these cases now and set a trap for his pursuers. But a real secret agent would have a gun and some fancy high-tech equipment like maybe a cell phone. Jack had only fear and adrenaline. He kept going. Behind him, his pursuers moved more cautiously, maybe thinking he was more dangerous than he was. Jack reached the back wall of the shop and scrabbled along it. He found a door and gratefully yanked it open. Just before he went inside, though, he caught a whiff of disinfectant and realized this was a bathroom. He closed the door again and kept going.

The shop was silent in a very strange way, silent beneath the continued clanging of the alarm down the street, a silence fragile as a soap bubble, sure to burst any moment. The shuffle of a foot sounded like a lion's cough, the sliding of cloth against skin like an urgent whisper. Jack stood absolutely still for a moment and heard them closing in on him. He stepped back and could hear his own footfall, sure they could hear it too. He wanted to pick up something and toss it across the room to distract their attention, but was afraid of knocking over something if he moved his arm, giving away his position for real.

Ten feet farther along that back wall he almost fell over as he reached an open doorway. Jack went through it, hearing someone yell behind him. He found himself in a hallway even darker than the shop had been. With two directions to choose, Jack went right, immediately regretting it because that would be most obvious, at least to an American. He hoped Europeans thought differently, from years of driving on the wrong sides of roads.

By the time he reached a very narrow staircase, he could tell that his pursuers had guessed correctly, or maybe they had split up, because at least one was coming after him. And when Jack started up the stairs, making more noise than he intended, the man shouted something in Czech for his companion.

The stairway was so narrow Jack's shoulders brushed the walls on either side. He suddenly realized that the shopkeeper might live upstairs, and hoped he wasn't leading these killers into a family home. But when he got to the top there was no other hallway, just a big open room, obviously used for storage. Bulky objects lurked everywhere, undefinable in the darkness. And two of the walls had windows.

Jack ran to one, looked down, saw only a long fall to a hard street. Nevertheless, he yanked up the window and leaned out. His pursuers' truck was below, the engine still running. A police car had arrived, just as he'd prayed, and was stopped behind the truck. The police weren't getting out yet, though. Like their counterparts worldwide, they preferred to stay in the relative safety of their vehicle to take their initial surveillance of the scene.

Jack reached and grabbed something, a small chest of some kind, made of heavy wood. Without the power of adrenaline he might not have been able to lift it, but now he did easily. He hurled it out the window as far as he could, aiming for the truck, then ducked back inside without seeing what he'd hit. He did hear police voices, though, as they obviously came scrambling out of their car.

It was still the middle of the night, but closest to the

windows was where the room was lightest, because of streetlights outside. Jack moved quietly back into the interior of the room and crouched behind a cabinet. A moment later one man came hurtling into the room, in such a headlong rush that he skidded to a halt in the middle of the room without even pausing to survey the new setting.

It was the burlier of the two thugs, the one who had spoken French. So he had escaped from his brief prison after all. "*Monsieur*," he said, then continued in English, "Come out. We are your friends."

He would have been more convincing if he hadn't held his pistol at the ready position, barrel tilted upward, poised to spin in any direction where a befuddled Jack might stand up to accept his offer of friendship. But no sound came from the room, and the man cursed.

Then he saw the broken window and hurried over to it. Obviously he thought Jack had made his escape this way. The man leaned out with his gun hand leading, looking for a fire escape or ladder.

And Jack was behind him in an instant, grabbing his feet at the ankles and lifting. God, the guy was heavy. And struggling. The thug tried to twist around, but his head and shoulders had already been out the window, and there was nothing to grab out there.

Except the window frame itself. The man dropped his gun and grabbed the window's edge. He was as strong as he was heavy. His grip was implacable, even though he was already three-fourths of the way out the window. Jack pushed at him but couldn't dislodge that hand. The man glared at him, straining to pull himself back up, and succeeding.

Jack yelled in frustration, leaned forward, and dug his teeth into that hand on the window's edge. The thug screamed too, let go his hold, and fell. For a moment his ankles hooked the windowsill, but Jack lifted them off easily and his pursuer fell, still screaming, the scream cut short with a crunch.

He heard the gabble of police voices rise higher, then cut off as they separated. Presumably at least one of them was rushing inside here to look for the person who had thrown the other one out into the street. Good. That was what Jack wanted.

But he was gripped in fleeing mindset now. He couldn't stop moving even if he thought rescue was on the way. Jack crouched again and half-crawled, half duck-walked across the room to those other windows. He went along the row quickly, poking his head up to glance out each window. Very little to see. The building across a side street, narrow as an alley. Maybe ten feet away. He couldn't jump that distance, but if he could find some rope—

Then he looked down and saw a very old-fashioned fire escape below one window. He raised up higher to get a better look—

And a small, delicate cough stopped him cold. The soft sound stopped him because it was accompanied by the click of a handgun being cocked.

Jack turned very slowly to see himself. In the dim light it was like he was looking into a mirror. His counterpart smiled at him in a way Jack didn't think he himself had ever smiled: confident, satirical, with one eyebrow cocked.

"Now there are only two of us left, brother. Or should I say only one." The man chuckled, gesturing at his own face.

"What's your job now?" Jack asked. "Capture me, kill me?"

"The latter, I'm afraid. It is unfortunate, because one doesn't find a twin every day. But my instructions are very specific and leave no room for individual initiative."

He raised his gun, his smile turning regretful. Jack raised his own arms out to the sides, making a target.

"You're in an interesting position. You might even say unique."

His twin hesitated. Jack went on talking quickly. "Do you know why you're supposed to kill me? Are you supposed to take my place after that? Where are you supposed to go? Have they given you the next step yet?"

He saw that the answer to his last question was no. The man with his face frowned. He didn't know what came after this room, this murder. Jack shrugged in a way he hoped was very knowing. "It would have been more subtle of your boss to give you some bullshit story about what came next after you killed me. You might have believed they wanted you to take my place. But after my body's found here in this very public way, by those policemen who will make their way up here at any moment, well, you do the math." Jack frowned as his lookalike continued to hesitate. "You can, can't you? I hope there's a brain behind my face."

He had almost gone too far. The man glared at him. "I do hear you," he said in that strange accent. "It is just that English is not my first language. Nor my second. I have to translate in my head before..."

"Would you be more comfortable in—*Deutsche?*"

It was a quick shot in the dark, trying to prevent the man from taking an actual shot in the dark, and it hit. An educated guess on Jack's part. The man didn't sound Czech, he hadn't answered his companion in French, and he'd just said English wasn't his native language. And he didn't look Latin of any strain.

Jack had guessed right. The man suddenly began talking in German, offering Jack some kind of explanation. Unfortunately Jack's German was very sketchy. He caught the words for "family," "debt," and some kind of threat. This man obviously needed a soulmate. He hadn't had someone to tell his story to in a long while. Jack tried to look attentive, but what he was really watching was his lookalike's gun hand slowly lowering. Jack took a deep breath.

Then he shouted one of the few German words he knew, "*Achtung!*" meaning, he hoped, *Warning!* There was a sound at the door and his lookalike spun. The policeman had also heard Jack's shout, and any kind of cry sounded like a warning to him. There was a quick exchange of gunfire.

And Jack jumped out the window, shattering it, ducking just enough not to bang his head against the crosspiece. The glass was old and thin and broke easily, hardly slowing him at all. But his foot caught on the windowsill, he tipped over as he went out, and fell heavily on the fire escape outside, first onto his shin, then his shoulder. He continued rolling, bumping, reaching, trying to stop his fall but continuing to get away.

Finally, near the bottom of the metal steps he caught the rail and brought himself up short. Taking a quick breath, he stood up. Above him, the gunfire had stopped, which wasn't good, because it meant either his lookalike or the police officer could concentrate on Jack now. He ran, or rather limped, to the bottom of the fire escape then back under it deeper into the alley, away from the street.

A few seconds later, the man with Jack's face also half-fell out of the upstairs window. Bleeding, he slid down the fire escape by hanging onto the railing. He was gasping into a phone as he walked around the corner onto the street, away from his stopped truck and the police car. Within half a block a black Volkswagen pulled to the curb beside him. A door opened in the back and he stumbled into it. There was time to talk as the car moved briskly but at legal speed away from the scene of the crime. The car seemed to be safely away, several miles and minutes later, when there was another gunshot from within it. The body of Jack's lookalike was pushed out, into the gutter, and the black Volkswagen sped away.

Jack made his way back to the coffee shop where he'd been earlier. He was walking better by the time he knocked on its service door in the alley. There was a long pause. Jack felt himself observed. Then the door opened and the waiter from earlier stuck his head out, looked both ways down the alley, and pulled Jack inside, closing the door firmly behind him. A finger to his lips, the waiter pulled Jack along a short hallway, then into a pantry. He closed the door, there was a flash and a flare, and the waiter lit a very small candle. In its flickers, he and Jack looked ghostly in the confined space, as if they were holding a seance.

"I don't usually get such quick return business," the waiter said. "I didn't realize my coffee was that good."

And he grabbed Jack in a bear hug. Jack winced but hugged back. When they stepped apart the waiter had a broad grin, Jack an ironic one.

"You scared me just walking in like that earlier," the waiter said. He had plump cheeks, very black hair and now, unlike earlier, merry eyes. "It was good to see you, but *mon dieu*, you startled me. Silence, exile, cunning. Have you forgotten?"

He was reciting James Joyce's advice to writers as if it were the creed of a secret cult, which in a way was true. "I remember. I'm just not very good at cunning. Anyway, that's why I stopped at every table on my way out, in case anyone was watching me. Which I don't think they were. They were waiting outside. Man it's good to see you, Stevie."

The waiter laughed and brushed a tear from his eye. He had always been very sentimental. "No one's called me that for—I don't know. Seen any of the old crowd lately, Jack?"

"Not yet. But I'm going to need you all. Did you understand what I was saying?"

Stevie grinned. "Oh, it was subtle, but I think I puzzled it out. You want a couple of riots, then to bust open the conspiracy. Not as easy as you make it sound, Jack. And a little premature, wouldn't you say?"

"It's horribly premature. It's an abortion. But I don't have any choice, with the peace summit coming up so soon. And you know we're under attack?"

"Of course. When stealth planes cross America—."

"I don't mean that 'we,' Stevie, I mean us. The Circle. Have our communications broken down so badly you haven't—"

"Yes, Jack, I know. You think I've gotten slow in my old age? I've been following what we were taught, Jack. In a crisis like this, go to ground. Work your contacts. Avoid each other."

He said the last with a significant glance at Jack, who obviously hadn't learned this lesson. That "old age" remark of Stevie's might have been funny, too, in another context. He and Jack were the same age, mid-twenties. They'd been classmates at Bruton Academy.

"Yeah, well," Jack said ruefully. "Sometimes only old friends will do." And he and Stevie said together: "This is one of those times." They laughed. For a moment, there in the confines of the pantry, in the candlelight, it was as if they were back in school, pulling some midnight prank.

Esteban Vincenzo Romani Vosovitch—is name was a map of Europe. Stevie was Portugese but had grown up in America, spoke Spanish rather than Portugese when he wasn't speaking English, and in America had affected a Puerto Rican accent sometimes just to be more confusing, even though he had never been south of the Mason-Dixon line in the western hemisphere. He had been recruited into the Circle at nearly as early an age as Jack. Stevie was good at making friends, Jack at alienating them, so their talents had meshed well. Stevie had respect for authority, too, a virtue that Jack had spent their school years trying to change, with only limited success.

After graduation Stevie had returned to Europe for college but he and Jack had stayed in touch. Stevie was one of the few people Jack trusted completely and one of the very few who knew about Jack's recent activities.

"Did anyone come in after I left?" Jack asked. "Or leave right after I did?"

Stevie shook his head. "I heard the alarm going off after that at the building across the street, but I didn't know if that was because of you and I didn't think I could help by running over there and getting arrested. But I got rid of my customers as quickly as I could—I had the singer start singing pop hits of the eighties—and stayed near the back door. I had a feeling you might find your way back here. So you think this business is connected with the peace summit?"

"I don't know."

Stevie took Jack's shoulders again, looking at him fondly. Then he frowned. "Were you really in London recently?"

Jack nodded. As quickly as that, there were tears in his eyes. He could hardly stand to hear the sound of the word.

Stevie's grip on his shoulders tightened. "Find anything?"

Jack shrugged. "I don't know. I mean yes, I found something, but I don't know what it means. She kept—not a diary, but notes. Like clues to herself. Or maybe they would have been clues to me once she'd told me more, but she never got the chance. Stevie—I think she was part of it."

Stevie's eyes widened. His hands fell to his sides. "Are you sure?"

Jack shook his head. "I'm not sure of anything. But she certainly knew about it. Stevie, I think maybe that's why—why she took up with me. I think maybe she was trying to recruit me."

Stevie shook his head, his eyes gone fierce. "Madeline loved you, Jack. I saw it. I saw her look at you. Touch you. Nobody can fake love around me, Jack."

One tear escaped Jack's eye and ran down his cheek. When he started to speak he choked up and had to start over. "Even— Maybe that would be a reason to recruit me."

Stevie looked speculative as he worked through the emotional logic. Madeline had loved Jack. She had been part of a large plan. She must have been very devoted to it. If so, how could she not bring her two passions together?

"Unless she wasn't part of the conspiracy," he finally said. "Unless she was infiltrating it. Then she might have been afraid to bring you in. Or didn't think you were ready yet. But she didn't have time to—" His voice stopped as his eyes widened. "Oh, my God, Jack, does this mean she didn't die of cancer?"

Jack couldn't answer. Both because he couldn't speak and because he didn't know the answer.

The two old friends talked for another few minutes, while the candle burned low and began guttering. Their own shadows flew around the pantry shelves as Stevie finally asked, "Is this all connected, Jack? The conspiracy we were investigating and the attack on your country and the—someone being out to destroy the Circle?"

Just as the candle flared and went out, the waiter looked into his friend's face and saw that Jack didn't know the answer.

A few minutes later Jack was again walking the dark streets of Prague, having declined Stevie's offer of a ride. This time he was much more wary, though, so he heard the car approaching before it was upon him. Jack turned and saw something small and black and European—he was not a car person—speeding toward him. Jack already knew the hiding places around him, he had been picking out new ones every few steps, and thought maybe he could pull the same dodge again, jump through a shop window after the car's occupants shot it out. But he was weary and aching and didn't know how far he could get this time. He felt like an idiot as his death hurtled toward him.

The car braked to a quick halt, the driver's door opened on the other side of the car, and Arden stepped out, holding his cell phone.

"Next time at least take this, okay?"

She drove at an un-arrestable speed back to their hotel. On the way Jack asked, "How did you find me?"

"From the way you talked about Prague on the plane, I figured you'd go into Lesser Town. When it got late I was afraid you might be in trouble. So I borrowed the desk clerk's car and drove around until I heard an alarm going off. I figured you must be in the vicinity of that, so I kept driving around until I saw a man walking alone without a bulge anywhere on him that might be a cell phone. I figured there could only be one such person in a city this size in the twenty-first century."

Jack smiled. But Arden saw the dried tear on his cheek and knew it had nothing to do with whatever danger he'd just been though. And his smile was sad. She knew one soft sentence would open him up, but she didn't speak again until they got back to the hotel.

They were standing outside their respective doors, each with a key card in hand. But both stood there for a moment longer.

"Jack?"

He didn't say anything. His head just drooped a little lower.

"We didn't look for your double in London because there wasn't any double, was there? That was you who was there recently."

His silence admitted the truth.

"Why was Granny so sure you wouldn't have gone to that certain address? Back to it, didn't she say?"

Because no one would believe that Jack would ever again go

near that flat in Chelsea where his youth had died, along with a woman named Madeline. It held too many memories, the kind of memories that turn on you, because they were so lovely that after everything changed they became monstrous. Because he could never again be as happy as he'd been during that brief, brief time with her.

"A—a friend of mine died there."

His voice was a mumble. Arden went to him, took the key card from his hand, swiped it, and opened the door. Without turning on a light, she led Jack to the bed. She eased him down onto it, and gently removed his shoes. His legs curled up like a child's. Then Arden pulled a chair close to the bed and held his hand.

Jack was in that swirling frame of mind where he was dead-tired but not sleepy, and felt very alert even though he wasn't. He didn't even think about whether this was a good idea. Later he could rationalize telling Arden the story, but right now he just wanted to talk. She sat there without speaking for the next half hour.

"I was twenty-one, doing a post-graduate semester at Oxford. It bored me to death. I'd had too much school already in my life. I jumped ship and went to London. They sent Madeline to bring me back, or at least make sure I wasn't in trouble. By 'they' I mean the Circle, your granny. I was in that weird stage where I'd been trained within an inch of my life but I didn't know what for. I didn't know what I wanted to be when I grew up. Madeline found me walking the streets. She was one of us, of course. I'd never met her or heard of her, but I knew she was one of us as soon as I met her.

"For one thing, she didn't introduce herself. She was just standing next to me one afternoon as I was looking into a shop window. The shop sold American goods. I was looking at a baseball glove, I still remember that. Not homesick, exactly, but, I don't know, nostalgic, I guess. She knew what I was feeling even if I didn't. That was her gift. She took me to a cafe and bought me a Coke. Not tea, Coke." Jack smiled at the memory.

As if Arden had asked a question, he became more specific with details. "Madeline was thirty-five, a clothing designer at that time. You'd know her brand. Before that she'd spent a few years as an investment banker, but got to be too good at it, too well-known, you know, so she'd moved on. She was about to have to stop designing, too, or at least change her name. So we were both at loose ends. We took a little holiday from our lives. She showed me around England. London, Wales, the Isle of Man. And her flat in Chelsea."

His voice broke down for more than a minute. Arden squeezed his hand.

"That place," Jack said dreamily. "I'd never seen anything like it, but I felt home. The home that had been waiting for me all my life. I can't even describe it. It was a third floor flat, very airy and white. Lots of windows. From any room you could see treetops, not the city. Like a treehouse. It was very feminine—ruffles on the bed, flowered wallpaper, but comfortable for me, too. It wasn't cluttered, but there were interesting things in every room. Game tables with secret surfaces if you knew what lock to spring. A safe under the fireplace. Puzzle boxes and paintings with hidden pictures in plain view. You didn't have to pay attention to any of it, but if you were bored there was always something to do within reach, or just sitting and looking. Madeline wasn't a games person, but she liked layers. In her designs, in her flat. I can't imagine what she saw in me. I was so one-dimensional."

Arden knew better. Already and from this distance of years.

"Did I say what she looked like? Red hair, that soft red that changes with the light. Gray eyes. That English white skin. Average height. Not thin like one of her models. She didn't work out except for walking. Great legs. She—I don't know, she took me in. Knew how at loose ends I was feeling but didn't give me any advice. She was older and very sophisticated, but wasn't remotely motherly to me. Not remotely," he repeated, his voice lowering. "And she seemed happy. She laughed like a little girl. For a few weeks she just dropped her regular life completely and stayed with me. I don't know why."

Arden wanted to shout, *She loved you, you idiot.* She knew that much.

"No one ever meant as much to me," Jack murmured. He was crying again. "I've had great friends, I'm close to my family, but nobody ever—" He searched for words. "—ever understood me so well or was so much a part of me. We could spend a day together without speaking. Just touching and glancing."

Something had gone wrong, obviously. Arden wondered if he'd tell her that part of the story. There were already tears of sympathy in her own eyes, because she thought she knew.

"After those first couple of weeks I was just living with her. She hadn't even invited me and I hadn't asked, we were just together all the time. But after a while she started being gone once in a while. Appointments to keep. I even thought she might be seeing another man. Someone like Madeline would have had a man in her life."

No, Arden thought. Again, even this far away in time, she knew better than that.

"You know what happened next?" Jack asked. Arden nodded. He still didn't look at her, but felt the air currents shift ever so slightly, and knew which way her head had moved. "Did I mention I was twenty-one? And immature for my age? And stupid?"

"Anyone would have done it," Arden said softly. "What did you discover when you followed her?"

"She did meet with a man. An Arab man, dressed in western clothes. They met in a very out of the way place. I couldn't overhear what they were saying, but if they were lovers they were the most discreet ones I've ever seen, even when they thought they were alone. Later she met with a woman in the same secretive way, which I found very intriguing."

Arden smiled in the dark.

"Madeline began introducing me to people in public, too. Almost like a serial coming out party. At least a couple of people I knew to be Circle members, though I hadn't met them. No one spoke in anything that sounded remotely like code. They were just very gracious. I didn't feel like I was being groomed for anything, or checked out. I was getting kind of anxious to begin my life by then, but still didn't know what it would be. Madeline asked me to be patient, and she kept me—distracted. But she was gradually returning to her life, too. She began sending me off with some of these new acquaintances. I resented them, as if they were babysitters, but pretty soon I started to find their lives interesting. One woman took me to Paris, introduced me to people who worked at a couple of embassies, including the American one. They let me in on a couple of conversations that were important, that showed me how low-level clerks could influence an international policy."

"This was your real post-graduate education," Arden said.

"Yes. And I still don't know whose idea it was. Your granny denies it was hers, but she'd deny that I exist if it fit her plans. So I'm still not sure what I was trained for, or by whom. I didn't think about it much. Because it was always back to that flat in Chelsea at the end of every little adventure. There was always Madeline." Jack started crying again. Arden let him. She squeezed his hand and Jack squeezed back, but she doubted he even knew whose hand he was holding.

"You don't have to tell me any more."

He started speaking again as if she hadn't. "She started slipping away. Not just to meetings. While she was with me. She was somewhere miles away in her head. Then she'd come back and smile at me and say my name. She'd start to say something else and stop. Now I know what she was thinking. She had decided to bring me into her real life but she also wanted to keep me safe. That was her dilemma. But I already was part of it. I saw her meet with the Arab man again. This time they both saw me. I let them. They just looked at me, across a street, saw me watching them having tea in a little café far from her usual haunts. Madeline just stared at me. So did the man. Not hostilely, but curiously. Evaluating me. I thought he was speculating about me as her lover."

"Did you ask her about him?"

Jack shook his head. "Before I could she started coughing. That night she made her first trip to the emergency room."

Arden stayed quiet. Jack continued, "She got so sick so fast we barely saw it coming. One day she was okay, the next she was—" He broke off, then continued. "She had that skin so white it was almost transparent, you know. I imagined I could see the disease moving through her. Again there were times I thought she was going to have the Big Talk with me, but she didn't. I didn't care about that any more, anyway. I just wanted her to be okay again. I would have done anything, I would have gone away and never seen her again, just to know she was all right.

"But she wasn't. She never would be. One day I came home to the flat in Chelsea—I'd been to a chemist's for some pain medicine—and she was gone. I only went out because she seemed better that day, it seemed like she was recovering, but it must have been that last little boost some people get right before the end. Her eyes were open, staring at the door. I know she'd been waiting for me to come back in. That must have been her last—"

He couldn't finish that sentence. He remained silent, but his body hunched. His shoulders moved. Arden stood up from the chair and lay on the bed with him. She put her arms around him. Jack didn't seem to know who she was. He cried like a child. She wondered if this was the first time he had.

"I'm sorry," she began murmuring after a while. "I can't say anything to make it better, I know. At least you had her. Think of that. At least you found each other in the short time you were both here. Most people never..."

Jack's crying had stopped. Her words had nothing to do with it. He had just exhausted himself. His eyes were closed. He was breathing very deeply. Just before he fell asleep he said,

"You don't understand. It gets worse."

CHAPTER 7

The Circle had managed to stall the withdrawal of American forces in some instances. Near-mutinies of some troops had caused the Pentagon to slow the removal of its forces from certain hot spots. A few American diplomatic personnel had simply refused to abandon their posts—and now they could no longer speak for the American government. High-level negotiations continued, with the object of bringing all Americans home, which was just what the Circle wanted: talk. That was their weapon of choice.

The Circle was not designed for quick response to an unforeseen crisis. Their plans sometimes took generations to mature. A decade was nothing. The slow building of relationships, the "chance" meeting in college that matured into a lifelong influence, the casually-dropped remark that led one person to say something slightly different than what he'd planned to say to someone else, which led in turn to.... This was the way the Circle moved, slowly and very meticulously. They were not good at prompt reaction. None of them would be the kind to throw himself on a hand grenade that had just been thrown through the window. Their job was to make sure that the hand grenade never got thrown; indeed, that it never got manufactured.

Now something much, much bigger than a hand grenade had been thrown into their laps. Some of the members wasted too much time worrying how it had happened, how such a major catastrophe, something that obviously took years of planning, could have happened without their having a hint it was coming. There was only one precedent for that: 9/11.

The Chair kept them focused. Gladys Leaphorn seemed not to sleep. She had never needed as much sleep as an average person, and in her eighties she seemed to have given up the habit altogether. She was living on strong tea and the occasional five-minute meditation, from which she returned to work apparently completely refreshed. Craig and Alicia Mortenson looked at each other significantly when this happened. They didn't have to say what they were thinking, which was that their beloved Chair might be headed for situational psychosis: be driven quietly mad by this nightmare, so calmly that no one would notice. The Mortensons remained alert, while doing their own jobs.

One midnight, five days after the faster-than-sight planes had passed over America, Gladys dropped into a chair in frustration. "We just can't get to this damned NSA. We've lost too many people trying. And we have absolutely no one from his past to reach out to him now."

"No, that ship sailed a long time ago, it seems," Craig Mortenson said. He lit a pipe and stared into space, envisioning a different past. "One of us should have discovered his potential when he was a boy. We needed to be cultivating—"

"He didn't *have* any potential," Gladys snapped. "You've looked at his records. Everywhere he's been and everything he's done, his work has been average at best. At *best*. There was absolutely no way to predict his rise to such prominence. I almost think that infamous paper of his must have been plagiarized. But we've been scouring all our sources without—"

"There are precedents for this," Alicia said quietly. She was the only one still standing of the three, willowy in her blue dress, her eyes red-rimmed but still very alert. "General Grant springs to mind. Miserable at everything he tried except war. And who could have predicted he'd be a brilliant wartime commander until we were at war? This is somehow similar. We can't predict everything, Gladys. We can only try to keep the country on a generally correct course. We can't handle every little crisis that comes along."

"This is hardly little," Gladys Leaphorn muttered. Then she suddenly stood up. "I'm going home," she announced.

This was a big announcement. None of them had ever been to the Chair's home, or even knew exactly where it was. And if she was quitting when they were nowhere near solving this enormous problem—well, that just couldn't happen.

"Just for a little while," she said. "You two take charge. You know what we need to do."

"All except for one thing," Alicia said. "What about Jack? Why did you send him away, Gladys, and what is he supposed to be doing?"

"Doing nothing, I hope," the Chair muttered, with a flash of anger. "And you know very well why I sent him away. I don't know what he's been up to these last few years. Neither do you. I don't know if he can be trusted. If he's as resourceful as we all think he is, maybe he can accomplish something on his own. But at any rate he's out of the way. I don't think he can do much damage to the cause on another continent."

Craig and Alicia didn't even have to glance at each other to complete the thought: *Plus she's got Arden to report back to her if Jack does do something of significance.*

But even they didn't know if that was Arden's only function in the Chair's plans.

Arden and Jack went to breakfast earlier than anyone else in Prague, apparently. False dawn lured them outside, but then it was as if night fell again. They walked through a dimness that could have been the mists of time. Jack felt unwatched, unpursued. Arden seemed to have an instinct for that sort of thing, and this morning he trusted her instinct. He had cried himself out during the night, showered in darkness, and now felt very refreshed. He walked in the dark, but it was noon in his mind.

It was a beautiful old city. Somehow even shop windows were prettier than their counterparts in America: smaller, less bold, with arrangements inside that invited one to stop and peer. These shop windows compared to the arrogant displays of American commerce were the equivalent of a half-smile and darting glance compared to a shouted invitation.

Arden's shoulder bumped his occasionally, but she didn't take his hand. She respected that last night had been a vulnerable moment that didn't extend into daylight. She wouldn't take advantage of his confidences. At least not overtly.

They watched a cafe open up, as a sleepy, aproned waiter, or perhaps the owner, pulled a few tables out onto the sidewalk and set spindly-legged metal chairs around them. He smiled at them and gestured, and they took their seats as if this had been prepared solely for them. Moments later he brought them two cups of very strong, heavily flavored coffee and disappeared without taking an order. These things were done more leisurely here. Why would they be together, the waiter seemed to say, unless they wanted to be together? So he gave them a few minutes of privacy.

A breeze sprang up with the sun. The street slowly came to life. Arden moved her chair around to sit closer to Jack, maybe for warmth, maybe protection. She became more watchful. He let her. Jack's senses were exhausted in that regard. She could be his bodyguard this morning.

After their cups were emptied, the waiter returned to refill them and brought what was apparently the daily special: croissants smeared inside with a fragrant, yellowish, slightly lumpy something that could have been either dairy or fruit in origin. They didn't inquire. It tasted wonderful, but anything would have inside the freshly-baked croissants, which almost flaked into nothingness between their plates and their mouths. The breakfast seemed very delicate, but they found themselves satisfied after a few bites.

Jack sat and watched the shops opening for business, the foot traffic begin, cars move slowly down the street. He didn't feel at home, not at all, but somehow better than at home. In this setting even breakfast seemed an adventure.

He didn't feel Arden's eyes on him—she was being careful to put no pressure on him, even the pressure of attention—but he felt her curiosity. Finally he said, "How could it be worse, even after she was dead?"

She leaned toward him and her eyes fastened on him. Instantly it was as if they were back inside the dark hotel room, in the center of Jack's story again. But this time his voice was flat, as if he were again in the immediate aftermath of his lover's death, and nothing else could touch him emotionally.

"This is how it got worse. Madeline died in the summer. Two weeks later Osama Bin Laden released a videotape, condemning America, blah blah blah. Just taunting, really."

He heard Arden's unasked question: *So?*

"I was at the tail-end of two weeks of binge-drinking that had become life-threatening, with no one to intervene. I was still in London but I couldn't have told you that. One afternoon I kind of came to my senses in Madeline's apartment with the TV on and there he was, the most wanted person on earth mocking us. Mocking me personally, it seemed like. Then I noticed something strange. Maybe what had drawn my attention was a light coming on on Madeline's television. She was recording this spiel."

"How did she—?"

"That was the question, right? How did Madeline know, weeks ahead of time, when that tape would appear on the television news? Breaking into an afternoon chat show. I ran it back and played it again. It started me thinking about something other than myself for the first time in a long time. How had this man eluded American forces for so long? A six-foot-four Arab who needed dialysis? So distrinctive looking he was a walking cartoon.

"And let us not forget, I was a member of the Circle. The group whose self-assigned mission for the last two hundred-plus years has been to keep America safe, to protect our country from its own excesses *and*—" He held up a finger. "—to know everything our intelligence services know and more. Forget that Bin Laden was still free. How had he ever happened in the first place? Where was the Circle when America suffered its worst attack on our own soil *ever?*"

Arden kept watching him and shrugged. She had been a child at the time, with not yet a glimmer of the Circle's existence.

"This was the first question that engaged my attention since Madeline's death. Did we know about the attack in advance? I don't know. If we did know and still let it happen, that's unforgivable. If we didn't know, that's unforgivable."

Arden answered as if she'd heard this question debated before. "Of course, that's the kind of attack that's almost impossible to prevent. Twenty fanatics, working in a very tight-knit, homogenous group. No way to infiltrate—"

"Heavily financed and with a lot of ground support," Jack interrupted.

"True, but still only twenty crazed men. It would have been nearly impossible to infiltrate a group of that—"

Jack stopped her with an uplifted hand. "Actually only nineteen of the twenty boarded the planes."

Arden stared at him as if reading the lines of his face, then gasped. Jack nodded. "One of the supposed fanatics didn't get on board. At the last minute he had a problem or something else to do. He made sure the operation happened but escaped its consequences himself." Jack sat as if mulling over an idea, his face calm. Arden's expression grew more and more horrified. If she hadn't known about this possibility before this moment, then she was a brilliant actress. Of course, Jack thought she was. Just as she was about to speak again, he continued. "It sounds like us, doesn't it? Just the kind of role one of the Circle would play in that scenario. Actually we'd usually be much deeper in the background, but this was one that had to be guided personally, right up to the last minute. There have been all kinds of speculation about who that twentieth man was, and suspects named, but we would throw up that kind of smokescreen, wouldn't we? That is, if one of us was the twentieth fanatic."

Arden had had time to absorb the idea now. "You're just speculating."

"I was then. But since then I've spent years investigating the possibility. I've particularly wondered whether I was supposed to be personally involved."

"What?"

"Madeline meeting with the Arab man, remember? I know, I know, London is full of Arab men. But one night I woke up seeing them again, seeing the man looking at me so speculatively, weighing my possibilities. I think I was supposed to find them that day, so he could see me. Maybe he'd already studied my file, but he wanted a personal look. And Madeline just sat there with a little smile, the way she did at fashion shows where people were looking at her creations."

"Jack." Arden's hand reached for his arm, but the gesture stopped before she touched him. Jack sat appearing perfectly composed, no tears hovering in his eyes. "Yes?" he said calmly.

"You think maybe she—singled you out?"

"Do I think maybe it wasn't happenstance? That maybe it was only love at first sight on my part?" He shook his head. "I think she loved me. But that doesn't mean she didn't have another purpose in mind. To recruit me."

"To what? To be part of this cover-up? How could you have joined in that?"

Jack turned and looked directly at her. He was good at evaluating people. Beyond good. When he was on his game he could almost read thoughts. Emotions were harder. Half the time people didn't even know their own emotions. He studied Arden as he had several times over the last few days, and over the two years since he'd known her. He felt her concern, and thought he felt curiosity. That was what he wanted to know. Did she already know the deep secret he was about to reveal? Was that why she was with him, to keep him from learning anything more?

The question could be put a different way, in a form that had tormented him for more than five years: Did the Chair know what he was trying to find out? And if so, had she told her granddaughter?

The logical part of his mind was evaluating what he should do. If Arden already knew, then what was the harm in telling her? If she didn't, he might be gaining a valuable ally. The danger was in letting her know what he knew if she already was on the other side.

But he began speaking before he'd fully evaluated the risk. The other side of his brain took over. He wanted to talk.

"I believe now that there is another group within the Circle. An Inner Circle, maybe. A core group of us, allied with people outside the Circle. They may have similar goals to the original Circle's mission, but they are much more ruthless. I believe this group knew the 9-11 attack was coming, even encouraged it, maybe even first planted the idea. But at any rate made sure it happened."

His voice remained calm, but Jack stared into space and Arden knew he was far away. "You know how you can take a snapshot with your mind, and replay it again, sometimes from different angles, zoom in on something maybe you didn't notice the first time?"

Arden nodded.

"That's what I've done with that scene of Madeline and the Arab man. Nicely dressed man, Saville Row suit, hundreds like him in London. But his ear was distinctive. Pendulous lobe, flat on top. One of the hardest things to disguise. I've replayed his face in my mind a thousand times, and I've also replayed that scene that came on Madeline's TV at just the right time. I think they were the same man."

Arden gasped. "Osama in—"

Jack shook his head. "This wasn't Osama. But I think he plays him on TV. Someone keeping alive the myth of our great enemy still plotting against us. It makes sense, doesn't it? How has he eluded us so long? Because most of the time he's not Osama Bin Laden. He's a respectable-looking businessman with a legitimate passport. And Madeline was sitting there with him chatting pleasantly."

Arden stood up, stared at him, then sat again, leaning close to him. "Why on earth would any American help in such a—a mad scheme? How could you think one of us—?"

She sounded angry. The way Jack had reacted when he'd first gotten this idea. He'd had years to calm down, but it was a horrible idea, and watching Arden's reaction made him realize again the horror of it.

"Think about it," he said, emphasizing the first word. "What happened in the wake of the 9-11 attacks? There was an enormous outpouring of sympathy and good will toward America from all over the world. A new president, one most of us didn't have much confidence in, started his term with more worldwide support than

America has ever enjoyed. *Ever.* That president squandered it all over the next few years, but that wasn't our fault. The attacks made us look vulnerable but also armored us with good wishes. Maybe that day helped define our allies and our enemies in a way the Inner Circle wanted, too. I'm not sure about that part. But it accomplished what they wanted."

Arden was shaking her head. "We would never—"

Jack grabbed her arms. He talked more urgently then he ever had in his life. It was as if Arden were his own doubts made into another person. If he could convince her he could convince himself.

"No, *we* wouldn't. But I believe this other faction, this rogue component of the Circle would. Imagine it, Arden. You give people behind-the-scenes power for generations. Isn't someone bound to misuse it some time?"

She had calmed down. Her eyes tracked back and forth across the tabletop, then out to the street. Their movement slowed as her mind speeded up. Jack could see it happen, could feel her thinking as if her skin temperature had risen. Her mind explored tangents, then finally returned to him as her eyes rested on his. A smaller but more personal version of her horrified expression also returned.

"Does this mean you think they killed Madeline?"

Jack sighed. "I hope so."

Because the alternative was that his lost love had been one of the bad guys, and had been trying to recruit him as one of them.

Later they walked into the newer part of Prague. The modern office buildings and occasional McDonald's were much less eye-pleasing than Lesser Town, but also less sinister. Here the streets didn't seem to seethe with plotting. Jack wished he could go back to last night's cafe and talk to his old friend Stevie again. It had been years since he could do that. But he couldn't now. Make minimal contact, get the ball rolling, move on. That was the plan now, just as it had been for years. When he'd first suspected the existence of the Inner Circle, there'd been no one he could trust except a hardcore group of his old friends, ones he'd known since childhood. Each of them had had people they could trust too. Jack didn't, outside his own family, which was in no way part of his adult life. Now he had trusted Arden, or at least acted as if he had.

She asked, "So do you think this rogue faction as you called them launched these latest attacks against America?" She said the name of her country the same way she'd say England or Italy, like an interesting foreign place. Or maybe that was Jack's imagination.

"No," he said. "I could be wrong, but I don't think so. I think this took all of us by surprise. This is something new. I don't know the source of it yet. It may have been something the Inner Circle unwittingly set in motion. I don't know."

"And the attacks on you? The fake Jack-sightings around the world?"

"Now those I believe *are* the work of our old friends the Inner Circle. I guess they've discovered I suspect their existence. Or maybe they just wanted an excuse for the Chair to get rid of me."

Arden stopped abruptly. "You think Granny is one of them?" She wasn't looking at him.

Jack looked at her, though. She looked like a young woman startled by a terrible idea.

Jack shrugged. "I don't know. I certainly hope not. We're all in deep trouble if she's *their* leader too. But if she's not, and she's so smart, why hasn't she suspected this? Why am I the only one of us who's caught a glimmer of this?"

"Maybe you're not. Have you talked to anyone else about this? Any of the group?"

"No," Jack said. He didn't include his tiny group of old friends, whom he trusted implicitly. "How can I? Anyone I'd tell might be one of them. Even the Mortensons. Anyone I might tell might be part of the Inner Circle, and that would be the end of me."

Arden cocked an eyebrow at him. He understood. Yes. There might be others in the Circle who shared his suspicions, but none of them could afford to share them *with* anyone. Anyone who suspected the existence of this Inner Circle was isolated, trapped within himself by his own suspicions.

That was why it had been such a relief to tell Arden now. Jack felt the rush of relief through his system, relaxing him, almost making him sleepy. At that moment he didn't care if Arden's secret confederates stepped out of hiding and captured him. It felt so good to have let his great suspicion escape. It was no longer trapped within his own mind, banging back and forth against the walls of his brain.

"Do you suspect anyone in particular?"

Jack shook his head, then shrugged. "Craig Mortenson? Look how efficiently he brought down the Soviet Union. But mostly non-violently, I know. Alicia, then? Maybe they're not so joined at the cerebral cortex as everyone thinks. Maybe she guides him, a lot more subtly than he guides world events."

"I love the Mortensons!"

"So do I. Do you think evil people look monstrous? Or act it? They don't even think of themselves as evil. They just think they're doing what's necessary. From that angle, who's not a suspect? *I* suspect the only woman I've ever loved! How about Professor Trimble? He always seems to be at conferences all over the world instead of teaching. My old mentor Janice Gentry? She's been in some key locations, let me tell you. Then there's..."

Jack trailed off, but Arden knew exactly whom he meant. "Granny? You think so? Wouldn't the leader of this secret group try to stay out of the limelight within the Circle? She wouldn't put herself forward as Chair, would she?"

"No one puts herself forward as Chair. You're elected by acclamation. Wanting to turn down the job is an indication you're right for it. I don't know. I don't know."

Arden looked around, appearing surprised to find them in a modern-looking city in broad daylight. "What do we do next?"

"Leave here," Jack said. "You didn't leave anything important in the hotel, did you?"

Arden tapped the shoulder bag under her arm. If he'd planned to take her by surprise with his announcement he would have been disappointed. She appeared poised and ready. And remarkably fresh. When had she gotten more sleep than he had? Her skin was smooth and pale and her eyes gleamed. Her little secret smile had returned, too. Arden had always looked as if she were sharing a secret joke, possibly only with herself. He hadn't shocked her for long. "Where to?"

Jack started toward an underground station, and within a few paces Arden was leading the way. "Two places, I think," Jack said slowly. "The peace summit is supposed to take place in Salzburg in four days."

"Hasn't that been cancelled?"

"On the contrary, we have to make sure it takes place."

Arden frowned. She knew she'd get an explanation as they went along. "What's the other destination?"

"Israel. Or close by there, anyway."

That one obviously came as a surprise to Arden. But she shrugged and looked ready. "Which one first?"

Jack stopped and looked at her sternly. "That's not what I meant. We've got two different destinations at the same time. I need you to go to Austria."

She looked back at him, absolutely unperturbed. "We will. As soon as we finish in Israel." Jack started arguing and Arden cut him off. "Look, if I'm not with you you'll get yourself killed. Then Granny would kill me. Then there's nobody left who knows about the plot or can stop it."

She raised her eyebrows, inviting him to try to refute her logic. After a moment Jack gave up. "Come on, then."

"Back to the airport?"

"Not exactly." Train doors opened in front of them and they got in the subway.

"I hate calling in any favors at a time like this," Jack shouted over the noise of the helicopter's rotors. Arden nodded, knowing exactly what he meant. Impersonal public transportation was scary because it left them so vulnerable, but arranging more personalized transport was just as dangerous. It pinpointed them.

The pilot in his bomber's jacket and sunglasses slapped Jack on the back. "That's okay, pal, don't worry about it. Anything for the guy who wrote 'Air Gladiator.'"

Arden gave Jack a look and he shrugged. Yes, a few years earlier he'd written an air combat video game at a time when he was learning to fly himself. All he did, really, was put all his fears about flying onto a video screen, just imagine what he was about to do wrong and see if any players could get out of such a scenario. The game had been popular, not a huge breakthrough, but it remained very well-known to pilots. This one had been glad to take Jack on a hop south once he'd learned who he was.

Jack and Arden couldn't talk about any of the things they really wanted to discuss during the flight. The pilot took up the conversational slack by pointing out features of the jet helicopter to Jack, explicitly making suggestions for an "Air Gladiator II." Quite clearly he was also willing to pose for the central character. Jack and Arden had to have some kind of cover, and Arden quickly decided their roles: Jack was the internationally famous game designer and she was a groupie he'd picked up at a convention. She clung to him like ball moss to an oak branch the whole way, occasionally squealing delightedly over something he said. This scene fit the pilot's world-fantasy view so perfectly that he didn't even ask them questions. He just grinned and occasionally, very subtly he thought, winked at Jack, two men of the world. Jack gave him as manly a sly smile as he could manage in return.

After what seemed to Jack a long, long flight but in reality was only a few hours, the pilot said, "If I get much closer I'm going to have all kinds of radar locking on me." He gave Jack a look, half-apologetic, half hoping Jack would ask him to dodge incoming to get them farther inland. But Jack just said, "You've done a great job, Captain. Given me lots of great material, too. I'll be seeing you."

The helicopter set down on a beach. Most of their trip had been over the Mediterranean, but now they were on a much smaller body of water. Jack and Arden scrambled out, the pilot gave them a thumbs-up and lifted off, all within a minute. The pilot believed they were traveling under stealth cover to avoid Jack's fans, which was only partially inaccurate.

"You can let go now," Jack said once they could hear again, but as soon as Arden released his arm he felt her absence. Her coziness on the plane had been annoying and, now that it was gone, comforting. She smiled at him as if she could read his feelings, then glanced up and down the largely deserted beach. Jack, though, was watching large specks on the southern horizon growing rapidly larger.

"Where are we?" Arden asked.

"Gaza, if that pilot knew what he was doing, and I think he did. The West Bank."

"And who are those?" Because now Arden too noticed the armed convoy approaching them at a speed that seemed angry.

"Israeli troops, I think. Or maybe the Palestinian Authority. Either way, I don't think we can pass, do you?"

CHAPTER 8

"Something's happening in Salzburg," Professor Horace Trimble said over the phone from New York.

"Yes, I believe I read something about that," Craig Mortenson said drily. The front pages of every newspaper in the world had been consumed with two things in the past few days: reprises of the attack on America story, and speculation as to whether the peace summit, over a year in the planning, would still be held, now that the American President had announced that America would no longer be involved in world affairs.

"I mean," Trimble said snippily, "there's something going on behind the scenes. I'm going over to investigate."

"You're going over personally?" Craig, sitting in the Circle's western headquarters listening to Trimble over speaker phone, glanced at Alicia. She gave him a raised eyebrow in turn. "Don't you have any contacts—?"

"Of course I do," the professor snapped. "But I want face-to-face contact. Someone over there's been lying to me and everyone else on the planet, and I want to know who it is."

The Circle so far had made almost no headway in discovering who was responsible for the mysterious plane attacks. They knew from monitoring intelligence sources that the CIA and FBI didn't have a clue either. Nor could they get to the National Security Advisor; those attempts had cost them more in lost personnel than they had suffered throughout the Cold War. Instead they had now been bending all their efforts to make sure that the President still attended the summit. They hoped that somehow this would re-engage him in world events. They had influential connections with the president from several directions, and had been using all of them. Even the president's mother had called him to tell him he should go to Salzburg. They were pretty sure they had won that battle.

But now Trimble was saying there was something else wrong. "What have you found out?" Janice Gentry said to the speakerphone.

"Distressingly little," answered the professor. "I believe, though, it has something to do with our old friend Jack's appearances in recent times. He was up to something when he went to that flat in London. I'm not sure what, but I'm going over there to find out. I'm afraid our beloved Chair may have made a mistake in letting young Mr. Driscoll out of our sights. But maybe I can rectify the situation."

Craig Mortenson caught every eye around him, and found nothing but shades of apprehension. "Don't rectify anything that can't be un-rectified unless you get approval from us," he said. That was as precise as he could get, but Trimble was a subtle man. He would understand.

"I shall do no more than what is absolutely necessary," Trimble sniffed, obviously offended. "Now I have to run. My flight is boarding."

The small group pictured the tall, thin, extremely dignified professor of applied mathematics actually running down an airport concourse and knew he had been speaking figuratively. Alicia Mortenson called his name, but the line had gone dead.

Alicia looked at her husband. "You're right," he said, and stood up. "Janice, you're in charge until the Chair gets back."

"Where are you two going?" Professor Gentry asked in surprise, and Alicia Mortenson looked surprised at her surprise. "Virginia, of course." Consciously or not, her voice had slipped into a soft southern accent. Her husband nodded as if the question had been silly, and the two walked quickly out of the room. Janice Gentry sat at the console, looked around the small remaining group to see if anyone else had understood that exchange, and saw that she didn't have to feel stupid, because no one else had.

"And where the hell *is* Gladys?" she asked grumpily.

Gladys Leaphorn lay in bed. She had the temperature turned down low and lay under blankets in deepest slumber, like a child in a crib or a mystic in a trance. At headquarters she'd realized that she was making bad decisions or worse, being unable to decide at all. She had neglected her subconscious. She could get by for days without sleep if necessary, as she'd been proving, but her imagination suffered. Like most artists, she did some of her best work while unconscious. Her mind roamed from her earthbound body and sometimes returned with insights she could never have achieved awake.

So she had left good people in charge, come home, put on her favorite pajamas, and gone to bed. And it worked. The next morning, after six hours' sleep, her eyelids snapped open and she smiled grimly. She knew what she had to do. Jack Driscoll was key. Gladys needed to get in touch with her granddaughter right away, and wondered where she was. For just a moment, still under the influence of her dreams-filled sleep, she imagined she could reach out with her mind and touch Arden's.

But it was in that moment that Gladys Leaphorn realized something else.

Someone was in her house.

She climbed out of bed, groaning like an old woman, doing an excellent impression of one. Stealth was no use now. She wouldn't be able to slip past the people in her house. She had a good idea of who they were.

So instead she got out of bed, put on a robe sloppily, and shuffled in slippers out to her small living room. A man and woman waited there, wearing matching dark suits, tight mouths, and expressionless eyes. Grim as the situation was, Gladys almost grinned. Because the man's hair was slightly mussed and there was an indentation on the woman's sleeve she felt sure had been caused by a hand. These two stony-faced agents had been kissing while waiting for her to wake up. Gladys wondered how she could use that to her advantage.

"Mrs. Leaphorn," the woman said, not asking a question. "We need you to come with us."

Gladys Leaphorn didn't move. She was eighty-seven years old, and on the best day of her life she couldn't have outrun either of these two for three steps. Nor had she ever been any good with guns, and she knew these two would be. She recognized their types, if not these particular two. "Identification?" she asked.

Both immediately held out flip wallets. Yes, she'd been right: United States Secret Service. That meant nothing. They could be here on official orders or they could be under the control of someone who had infiltrated the government better than the Circle had. Or they could be rogues. It didn't matter. They had her.

She looked at the woman, at her sleeve, and her lips, then her eyes, and had the satisfaction after a moment or seeing her begin to blush. "I'll be right with you," Gladys said, and shuffled back toward her bedroom.

The woman went with her.

Jack kept saying one sentence in Hebrew, and it didn't seem to be working worth a damn. The Israeli soldiers had them face down in the sand within five seconds of reaching them, and Jack's protestation won them as much respect as if he'd been announcing he was the leader of a neo-Nazi movement. Arden tried her own more subtle methods of insinuation, which didn't require speech at all, and she thought she was getting through to a couple of the men, but unfortunately half the soldiers were women, and they just glared at Arden and handcuffed her hands behind her back. She whimpered at that, again drawing some sympathy, but only from the half of the troops with whom she'd already succeeded.

She had enough Hebrew to understand, she thought, that Jack was telling them he had some information. But the soldiers didn't seem to care. They had Jack and Arden stowed in the back of an armored personnel carrier—American-made, Arden noted wryly—and were taking them away at top speed without anyone's ever acknowledging that Jack could speak their language at all. Maybe he was getting it wrong, in fact. "What's he saying?" Arden asked in English, but that didn't work either.

The small convoy roared down the beach. Within minutes it stopped, and Jack and Arden were shoved out the back of the carrier. They found themselves in the center of a small military compound. Jack and Arden were marched up to a small tent. Arden, slightly in the rear, noted that the soldiers had completely immobilized Jack's arms with some kind of restraint with a bar that kept his elbows apart while handcuffs held his hands close together. Did they think he was some kind of X-Man, who could smash them all if he got free? The complicated restraint was kind of flattering in a way, and Arden felt slightly insulted that they'd only handcuffed her.

Then they were both shoved inside the tent. The soldiers didn't follow. A woman looked up at them from a small field desk. The woman was not very tall, and she was thin in a wiry, energetic way. Her skin was several shades darker than Arden's, with spots of color on her cheeks and surprising green eyes. Her dark brown hair was thick but cut short. Overall she had a boyish but sexy look, as well as an air of authority.

"Mr. Driscoll," she snapped. "I heard about your recent exploit in France." She stood up and spread her hands, speaking as much with them as with her voice. "So, you come to my hemisphere and you don't even call a person?"

And she ran over and hugged Jack.

With his arms awkwardly restrained he couldn't hug back, but Jack put his head down against the woman's neck and shoulder and closed his eyes. For a moment the two almost blended together. It was embarrassing to watch, which didn't keep Arden from staring open-mouthed.

The woman stepped back. Jack said, "I didn't have time that trip. I knew I'd be coming back soon. And here I am. Uh, Rachel—"

He turned around to display his restrained arms to her. Rachel frowned as if at a small puzzle.

"Ouch," she said sympathetically. "They tell me those things really hurt."

"They tell you correctly."

"What can we do about this?"

"Are you saying you don't have the key?"

"I don't have the key."

"Then could you please melt them with your laser vision? And be careful because I'd like to use my hands again some day. Like you do when you talk."

She gave him a small wicked smile, then walked over to Arden, made a twirling motion with her hand, and Arden turned around. A moment later her handcuffs came off.

"You said you didn't have a key," Jack said accusingly.

"Sue me," Rachel said. She held out her hand and said her name to Arden.

"Arden Spindler."

"Ah. I've heard of you. And how was the Chair when you left her?"

"You can imagine."

"I can, actually," Rachel said. The two women continued to look at each other. Rachel was a few years older, Jack's age. Arden was taller and heavier, Rachel a woman compressed to essentials. She looked dangerously thin, and to Arden as if she'd lost weight recently. Rachel reached out and squeezed Arden's arm in a kindly way and their introduction was done.

Rachel returned to Jack. She stood close in front of him, almost nose to nose, since he was a little hunched over, as if the harness kept him from standing upright. After a moment he said, "I didn't call because I knew I wanted to see you face to face."

All seriousness, Rachel said, "It's that bad?"

"It's that bad."

Without taking her eyes off Jack, Rachel said, "Ms. Spindler? There is a captain outside named Ari. Tell him, please, that I need the key to this contraption."

"Yes ma'am."

Arden slipped out the tent flap. She hadn't asked how she was expected to get the key if Ari didn't want to give it to her, and Rachel hadn't bothered to give further instructions. When she and Jack were alone in the tent, Rachel shook her head. "Jackie, Jackie."

"What?"

"Nothing. Your girl friend's very pretty. A little young for you, isn't she?"

"She's not my girl friend. Not remotely. I don't trust her an inch." Then he seemed to hear for the first time something else she'd said. "Rachel? Aren't we young?"

She smiled wistfully. "I think so. We're both shy of thirty. I personally am in great shape. I don't think you've reached your physical peak yet. Thing is, I thought we were grown when we were fifteen, so maybe our perspective's kind of skewed."

Jack nodded ruefully. Arden returned through the tent flap, looking unruffled and holding up a key ring. Without a word she went behind Jack and used two keys to free him. Arden took the harness, apparently studying it closely while Jack rubbed his wrists.

"How are we going to explain this?" Rachel said. "I don't want to tell my people here that you and I have some past connection."

"I conned you with some story and then overpowered you," Jack suggested.

"Be serious." Rachel paced for a moment. "You two were just lost—"

"Arriving here by jet helicopter? Yeah, we were actually on our way to the honeymoon suite at—"

"Yeah. Well, you could be the—"

"I'm tired of that one. How about if you sent—?"

Rachel shook her head. "I don't need any outside help. I'm kind of—" She shrugged. "—respected here."

"Yeah. I'm surprised to see you taking such a high profile position, Rache."

"Couldn't be helped. They needed a security consultant, and I couldn't let it be their second choice. Or third. So I had to step forward. Don't worry, I'll fade into deep background afterwards. This is very temp. The prime minister is concerned about—"

"The peace summit? More than he's usually concerned?"

"Yes." Jack looked a question and Rachel shrugged again. "He thinks the attacks on America and your president's decision to withdraw and everything else that's happened has been a ruse designed to catch him off guard and lose him an advantage at the summit." In answer to Jack's *That's ridiculous* expression, she shrugged again. "This is Israel."

Jack nodded. He started to ask another question, then noticed Arden still standing there. He told her, "Rachel and I went to school together."

"Really. You two've met before today?"

Arden remained deadpan. Rachel smiled at her. She touched Jack's arm, and her hand lingered there.

"What have you found out?" she asked then, and Jack gave her a rapid briefing. From Arden's perspective he didn't tell her everything, but that may have been because Arden was listening, and it was certainly because Rachel already knew a lot. As the two talked they sort of circled each other, staying close, Rachel's head bent sometimes as if to ease the flow of Jack's words into her ear. They brushed against each other like cats. Arden gradually lost her first impression that they were or had been lovers. They were something to each other, though, something that made her even more envious.

Jack finally said, "I need you to—" and Rachel said, "Already done. It should be three, four days at the most. In case you need to time something."

"I don't know what. I'm kind of at loose ends after this, Rachel."

"So you came to me?" She smiled. "Well, let's start with what we know."

Jack remained silent.

"That's great," Rachel said. Then more seriously, she said, "We've learned a little more about these planes that attacked your countrymen. Our scientists have been working with yours." And Rachel had the information. No one asked her how.

"Planes?" Jack said.

Rachel nodded. "There were more than one. That's how they seemed to cover so much ground. More like rockets, really. Very fast but very short range. After they accomplished their purpose they more or less vaporized, which gave the impression of travelling so fast they disappeared."

Jack nodded. That helped make sense of what had happened.

"But that must have cost billions," Arden burst out. She'd

been trying to keep quiet, be invisible, but the comment jumped out of her mouth. The other two looked at her and it was clear they'd already understood that. Arden slipped backward, trying to regain her invisible status.

"She's right," Jack said. "What country would spend that much to have America disengage with the world?"

Rachel shook her head. "Don't you think I've been puzzling over that question? I can't think of any."

"No private terrorist network has that kind of—"

"Maybe they were stolen," Arden said. "Maybe a government was working on them—"

"Without our knowing about it? Surely at least one of our people would have been involved."

"*Some*one was developing them, Jack, and we didn't know about it."

They continued to discuss the problem in low voices, and Arden understood why Jack had come here. It wasn't as if he and Rachel were one mind, but two complementary ones. They came from different angles, had different information, different perspectives. They covered speculative ground in minutes that would have taken either of them days separately. One observation led to another. Arden became lost, especially as they mentioned people and events she didn't know about.

Jack's eyes were open wide and he stood back to back with Rachel, leaning back against each other. The small woman was still talking, and Jack was envisioning what she said. "Jack!" she said suddenly, turning around so fast that Jack almost fell. "I can think of one private organization with that kind of money."

Jack questioned her silently.

"Us!" Rachel said. Her voice sounded bright, happy with the thrill of solution, then she gasped.

Jack was shaking his head. "No," he mumbled, not in contradiction but in denial. "Why would we do this? Even the rogue faction I suspect..."

They both stood silent for a few moments. Arden was afraid they'd turn to her next. She practiced innocent expressions. But after a few seconds Rachel and Jack shook their heads at the same time.

Running down the idea seemed to have refreshed them, though. They looked at each other with glowing eyes. Arden was quite sure they would have kissed at that moment except for two things: her presence and the deferential cough from outside the tent. "Colonel Greene?"

Rachel raised her voice. "I've almost finished interviewing the prisoners, Captain. Thank you for standing by."

They heard footsteps withdraw. Jack smiled. "'Colonel'?"

Rachel made a wry face. "I did this little thing last year, you wouldn't have heard about it, and got kind of a battlefield promotion. Besides, out here you have to have rank."

"What *are* you doing out here, Rache?"

"Training exercises." She glanced across the room at Arden.

"What?" Jack asked.

Rachel chewed her lip, then said it. "Our Prime Minister isn't entirely paranoid. Something bad's going to happen in Salzburg."

Jack stared at her. "You have intelligence?"

"No, just a feeling. But my feelings are usually—"

"Yes, they are."

Jack also glanced at Arden. "Is this part of the other?" He might have been asking them both. Arden shrugged.

Rachel lifted her hands in another kind of shrug. "The wrap-up, maybe. It's such an opportunity for some madman. A peace summit is the perfect place to start a war."

That was more or less the end of the conference. A few minutes later they walked out of the tent. As they did, Rachel said quietly to Jack, "I've just turned you. You're going off to Italy now thinking you're doing one thing for your own organization—"

"But you've actually duped me into doing something for yours," Jack concluded. "Duh, t'anks, Coach."

They walked on. The soldiers around the compound tried to appear not to be looking at them, and failed. Arden walked several steps behind, and for once in her life was not the object of attention. She could see from the expressions on the faces of both men and women that they held Rachel Greene in something more than respect. Arden knew her grandmother had mentioned Rachel when briefing her on Jack. The two of them had been friends at school, had gotten into some kind of trouble that had turned out all right in the end. Granny had been pretty vague about it. Whatever had happened was part of the Real History. It would never appear in any textbook, and might die with living memories.

But just as Jack had needed to come here to talk to Rachel in person, Arden had needed to see them together even to begin to understand their relationship. They gave off ideas like a nuclear reactor shedding neutrons. Arden felt bathed in their inspiration.

They walked out of sight of the camp and Rachel pointed with her shoulder. "Down there's another helicopter waiting for you."

"You ordered me a helicopter that fast?"

"It's mine, actually." They smiled at each other.

"Maybe I'll see you in—" Jack began, and Rachel nodded. They were no longer touching. Someone might be watching.

Just before he turned away, Rachel lowered her head. For the first time, she looked very young. Also tired. "Jackie?" Her voice came very low. "Who assigned us to save the world?"

"I think that was in—what?—ninth grade? And I think we aced that assignment."

Rachel looked up, her eyes alight again. "Mrs. Chavez gave us a B+, I think."

"She was just trying to keep us humble."

"Yeah? Did that work?"

They grinned at each other. After another moment Rachel said very earnestly, "Jackie? Be carefree."

He nodded. Then he turned and jogged. Arden had time for only a hurried goodbye to Rachel, then had to run to keep up with Jack. They came within sight of the helicopter and in another two minutes were in the air. The whole episode on the beach in Israel immediately assumed the quality of a dream. Except that Arden could see its effect on Jack, in renewed energy and quiet thought. She sat thinking herself, wondering what she had just learned, and how much of it she had to convey to Granny.

Exit Interview: The Real History

Once you'd been accepted into the program at Bruton—
The program for training young Circle members?
Yeah, but you didn't know that at the time. One of the first things that happened is that you went into Mrs. Stein's history course. It was always a small seminar, maybe half a dozen students. You didn't sign up for it, you just found it on your schedule.
Mrs. Stein?
Yeah. Ditsy old lady, rumor was she'd lived through half of American history herself, and she was always mumbling silly asides about the things we studied, like that Betsy Ross not only dipped snuff but had Lesbian tendencies.

For once the interviewer seemed outraged by something Jack had said. *I ought to slap you!*

Hey, I didn't say it. Some students reacted exactly the way you just did. Those students kind of got eased aside. They found themselves out of the seminar into a regular history class. And our paths began to diverge from theirs.

The interviewer frowned. *What happened to those students?*

Nothing. They went back to the normal world. While the rest of us started being taught the Real History. Jack quite carefully refrained from making air quotes with his fingers.

The "real" history. Such as?

He looked at his interviewer, obviously considering how much to say. Even now, with everything smashed and destroyed, the Real History was the Circle's greatest secret. Their legacy. It was all he had left of his friends. To give it away would be the last betrayal.

He and the interviewer stared at each other. Something in her gaze seemed to break him down, much more effectively than the back-and-forth slaps an earlier interviewer had administered. Jack's eyes filled with tears again.

Such as that Alexander Hamilton was one of our first heroes. Mrs. Stein didn't tell us about the Circle then, you had to begin to figure it out on your own. But she explained that Alexander Hamilton belonged to a group that was very committed to democracy but didn't quite believe in it.

Like the Federalists.

Jack smiled but didn't let himself be distracted. *And Aaron Burr found out about this group. He wanted to be part of it. But the group wanted no part of him. They thought he wanted to use them for his own purposes. Normally in such a situation the person who was confronted by Burr—in this case Hamilton—would have distracted him, gotten someone else to lead him down a different path. But our techniques weren't as refined then, and there wasn't time. All Hamilton could do was maneuver Burr into a duel.*

You have to remember, Aaron Burr was vice president of the United States when this happened, in 1804. He was headed for great things. And he couldn't take the secret with him. So Hamilton goaded Burr into challenging him to a duel.

Intending to kill him? the interviewer asked, leaning forward with an uncharacteristic light of curiosity in her eyes.

Maybe. No one knows for sure. But Hamilton accomplished his purpose anyway. Burr killed him, which disgraced Burr for all time. And others arranged for letters to be planted that raised dark questions about Burr's true motive. He became known as the great traitor, always trying to found his own country or otherwise gain power. He also talked for the rest of his life about a cabal that actually ran America behind the scenes, but no one believed him. He was disgraced, you see. Alexander Hamilton planned that and arranged it.

Getting killed in the process.

Jack was silent for a moment. His eyes were dry again. *Part of the point of that story was that sacrifices are required. In every generation.*

The interviewer scribbled something on the pad. Jack responded immediately. Then the interviewer frowned. *But you said some kids were eased out of this course. Was that the end of their training?*

Jack nodded. *You had to have the capacity to accept an alternate reality. Most people can't. Unfortunately, one can't know that about the candidates until they are taken partly inside. Most candidates wash out, and then they have to be dealt with. They are soothed back into the world they know.*

Brainwashed, said the interviewer knowingly.

Not really. They're just told, "We were only kidding. Things are just the way you think they are." It's a great relief to them.

And the Real History?

Jack shrugged. *I think maybe they were told that Mrs. Stein's seminar was a combination history and fiction class. Designed to stimulate their imaginations, and they'd been stimulated enough after only a couple of weeks.*

⟹•⟸

Some candidates don't make it, Jack was thinking. Some of those failed candidates are children of Circle members, which is sad for everyone. But the failed candidates might have children who have the capacity. Sometimes it skips a generation. Those grandchildren are watched closely.

He looked at Arden. She was gazing down at the sea. He had no idea what she was thinking.

Jack leaned back in the cushioned seat and tried to relax. *Be carefree*, Rachel had told him. Not careful; care-free. Because that was when Jack was at his best, when he turned his cap backward and let his thoughts roam free of restraint.

Be care-free. That was hard to do with every important person in the world out to get him and the responsibility for saving humanity on his shoulders. He shrugged, beginning to slip free. He, too, stared out to sea, seeing patterns there, faces. A supersonic aircraft that was actually several planes. And the Circle's own treasury. Who kept track of that? he wondered.

He and Arden had crossed the Mediterranean again, and it wasn't yet dusk. They were set down in the bottom of the boot of Italy and their pilot, who hadn't spoken during the entire trip, lifted off immediately, whipping them with sand and sudden loneliness.

"I assume we're heading for Salzburg?" Arden said.

"You are. I have something else to do, then I'll meet you there."

"I'm not leaving you here."

"Arden, something's going to happen there. Something very bad, and I don't have a clue what. Even worse, Rachel doesn't know, and she has the *Mossad* working for her. The best intelligence service in the world."

"Maybe nothing's—"

"She also has a feeling," Jack continued. "And Rachel's feelings are not to be ignored. I don't even know what to look for. But I need your eyes there, and I still have another stop to make. There's no time to argue."

She glared at him, but she could see that he wasn't going to move until she did. Finally she turned and started to jog. Arden still wore the small backpack Jack had given her, and she had credit cards and cash from Granny. She could hear traffic, and knew she could get away quickly. Just over the hill was a highway, she felt sure.

At the top of the rise she turned and looked back. Jack just stood there. She didn't wave, nor did he. After a moment she just turned and walked down the rise toward the highway.

Jack watched her go. Suddenly he felt very lonely. Seeing Rachel for only a few minutes was like having surgery performed on him without anaesthesia. Now his companion of the last few days was gone too. He'd never trusted her, which was one reason he'd sent her away, and she knew that. But Arden had also saved his ass at least twice. That was another reason he wanted her gone. He didn't know whether she'd really been protecting him or shepherding him, guiding his steps even while giving the illusion that Jack was in charge. Now he'd see how he did on his own.

He didn't want to be protected any more.

The first riot broke out, prematurely, while Jack was in Italy. The riot happened in, of all places, South Korea. America had kept bases there for sixty years. The strip between the Koreas was still known as the demilitarized zone, which meant it was heavily militarized on both sides. A peace treaty had never been signed to end the Korean War, which hadn't officially been a war. Tell that to all the Americans who had died there.

There was probably nowhere else on earth where neighbors were more suspicious of each other. Korea was not one country divided, not any more. On the South Korean side, the suspicion was accompanied by fear. South Koreans had actually cheered when President George W. Bush had included North Korea in his "axis of evil." North Korea was ruled by one of the most ruthless and ambitious tyrants on earth. He had nuclear aspirations, and maybe nuclear power by this time. But aside from that, he had an army millions strong. Kim Jong Un didn't have to bomb the south into submission. He just had to set his army marching. They would overrun their weaker neighbor in days.

Only one thing kept that from happening. The United States Army. America had kept thousands of troops posted near that border for decades.

When the bases began emptying some soldiers balked, as had some of their counterparts in Afghanistan. Many of them had families there, Korean wives, homes in town. They weren't going home. They *were* home.

More than that, many of them had a sense of mission. They knew they were actually protecting people, and they knew those people personally.

The riot began with a small group of South Koreans attempting to block the gates of the base, to stop the convoys taking soldiers to the airfield. At first the armored personnel carriers tried to ease through them, but when the first Korean was injured that stopped. Then they hunkered down while the commanding officer sent another convoy to another gate. Hundreds of soldiers were evacuated before the South Koreans caught on to that one. It didn't take long. The base was full of Koreans working in various capacities, and they had cell phones. The commanding officer tried to empty the base of civilians, which worked about as well as trying to sweep the ocean.

Soon the base was surrounded by civilians, hundreds deep. The demonstration made Tiananmen Square look like a couple of picketers. But this was a demonstration of affection. Of need. Even desperation. News sources soon gathered. Pictures went across the world of thousands of civilians asking American troops not to leave. It was the strangest sight many people around the globe had ever seen. Some signs read "Yankees Stay Here."

The base was immobilized.

"This would be a hell of a good time for the North to invade," the General of the Joint Chiefs said to the President during his briefing. The President glanced across at his National Security Advisor. The NSA shrugged.

"Tell General Jackson to stand down for now," the President said. "Halt the evacuation—temporarily. We'll figure out another way."

The President and NSA exchanged a glance. *But we're working against a deadline,* Dennis Wilkerson thought, and knew he didn't have to say it. The communication the night the planes had crossed America had been very explicit. This is only a warning. If you don't pull out of everywhere, the next time would be worse.

And the intelligence services had made zero headway in finding the source of that threat. It was almost as if the services had been infiltrated themselves.

"Dennis?" the President said after they were alone.

"I know, sir. I'll try to come up with something. But I could use some help." Dennis Wilkerson was feeling lonely. No one seemed to talk to him these days. At least, no one talked to him more than once.

He excused himself and returned to his office. He glared around the room, realizing he had no expertise at anything that would help resolve this crisis. Not military experience, diplomatic, strategic. He only employed strategic planning on one field.

Maybe that would help. Sometimes he felt that he drew inspiration from his one relaxation. Without any more hesitation, he opened a desk drawer, took out his PSP2, connected to the Internet, and looked to see if his most frequent opponent was online.

—•◦•—

Jack was on the train heading west when he realized he'd forgotten to ask Rachel if she'd heard of his being seen anywhere in her area. She would probably have mentioned it if she had, since she had mentioned his being in France.

He was on his way to Nice, to the home of Paul Desquat, a French architect and occasional essayist. The dual occupation was a clear sign. Paul Desquat was a Circle member.

Jack had met him through Madeline, on a short trip to Paris those few years ago that seemed so long ago, because they were on the other side of the great divide in his life. It was only later, when he'd been re-evaluating everything Madeline had done, that Jack thought she must have had a purpose in introducing him to Desquat. Letting Desquat meet him.

None of the people to whom Madeline had introduced Jack had contacted him after her death, except for a few uninspired words of condolence. That seemed a clue now too. Some of those connections should have survived Madeline. Unless her death had been specifically intended to sever them.

So Jack was going to pick up the threads again. He didn't have time to track them all down, not now. So he had returned to the flat in London. The Chelsea flat had been maintained just as Madeline had kept it, another signal. The Circle owned that flat, and they wouldn't let a civilian buy it or move into it. Madeline's mind had been too twisty. She loved puzzles too much. There was no telling how many signs she had left. People had been studying that flat very quietly ever since her death.

But she and Jack had had signals between them that no one else shared. Not many, they hadn't had a long enough history for that. And maybe everything she'd said to him had been false, even her personality made up for his benefit. But he didn't believe that, and if it was true everything else he did was pointless anyway.

On Jack's way to France, Jack *had* stopped off in London. After making sure he hadn't been followed, he had slipped into the flat in Chelsea very surreptitiously, he thought, but obviously not, since he'd been seen. The Chair had known about his going there. Maybe it was under constant surveillance. Jack hadn't spotted any cameras, but he hadn't given himself enough time to check out the place thoroughly.

Going inside the Chelsea flat was like walking through a time warp. Her things were still there. Her scent leaped into his nostrils. That must come from his memory, it couldn't still linger here. A faint aroma of violets, coupled with the scent of her own flesh. Jack swallowed and looked around coldly, but he couldn't stop his flesh from prickling with the feeling that she was about to walk through that bedroom door.

So he walked boldly in there. The bed was made up neatly, still with the flounces. Had someone found new sheets and ruffles in the same pattern, or kept the old ones all these years? The air smelled slightly musty. It circulated, but no one came here to dust regularly.

Even Madeline's sheets were puzzles. This one she had designed herself. It featured a long meandering path through gardens and villages, like a giant gameboard. Jack had tried following those paths with his mind on idle mornings when he'd awakened under those sheets and lay there waiting for Madeline to wake up too. Sometimes his finger had traced the paths, over the hollows and hills of the bed, over her body, until Madeline woke up laughing.

He drew a deep breath and let it out slowly. This place would immobilize him if he let it. He wasn't here on a memory tour.

In the next hour Jack took the place apart, neatly. He even managed to get into the safe under the fireplace, but that was too obvious a hiding place. All he found inside was some jewelry and a good bit of cash. He left it all. Once Madeline had modelled some of that jewelry for him, memorably wearing nothing else. Jewelry from an ankle bracelet to a tiara. "And I never quite figured out what to do with this," she'd smiled, fastening a long necklace around her waist. It had a pendant that hung down, strategically.

Jack studied all the paintings, the books, the wallpaper. The way the dishes were stacked and the glasses put away. No scrapbook, no mementoes of her career. No photographs. That seemed a strange absence. Someone might have taken them.

Jack had returned to the bed. If Madeline had left him a personal message it would have been here, wouldn't it? He had stood and stared at the sheet, following the path. It drew his eye downward. He had never noticed that before, possibly because his usual angle was from under the sheet. But looking at it from this perspective, he found the paths were not random at all. They went downward.

Along the way there were cottages and villages, occasionally a large country house, French Provencial style. Jack had stood trying not to move, except his eyes. They inevitably traveled down and down, to the foot of the bed. Near the bottom there was a representation of a house in a different style from everything else. A villa. Jack had stood there in the Chelsea bedroom studying that house. Had he seen it before?

He had remembered something else as he stood there. Madeline had kept a light blue coverlet at the very foot of the bed, of the softest texture Jack had ever felt. It was gone now. Now that he thought about it, he realized Madeline had gotten rid of that coverlet before her death. Right about the time she got sick it disappeared. Now it existed only in Jack's memory, but it was firmly placed there.

It had been a deep, peaceful blue, with a wavelike pattern in it that almost seemed to ripple even when it lay still. Sometimes that sheet, that coverlet had in fact moved like waves, as Jack and Madeline had set them in motion. She had laughed a couple of times when she made the comparison. The waves. And the coverlet was blue like the sea.

It had seemed too simple. Jack had stood there staring, remembering. He also remembered the jewelry, the time Madeline had worn it and nothing else. She had been laughing, describing the jewelry, some of its history. Keeping him tauntingly at bay. The jewelry had seduced his gaze downward as well. He'd reached for the pendant on the necklace, the one hanging below her waist, pretending to be curious about it. "It looks valuable," he had said with a dry mouth.

Madeline had grabbed his hand and laughed. "No. I got it from a street vendor in Nice. But it goes nicely with the necklace, doesn't it?"

"Nicely from Nice," Jack had repeated, the best joke he could manage under the circumstances.

Madeline had pulled him close, her eyes only inches from his, and she was no longer laughing. "Remember," she'd said. Then the moment of intensity had passed. She'd drawn back, laughing again. "There might be a quiz later."

But Jack did remember, years later as he stood in the otherwise empty flat again. Nice. And the path on the sheet led his eye down. Southward. To a villa that, when Madeline had lived here, had stood beside a coverlet as blue as the sea.

He also remembered the money in the safe. A thousand pounds, but the rest in francs. Before Euros.

No one else had been able to figure this out because they hadn't had the clues. Jack hadn't even needed to come here. She had tried to embed it in his memory.

She had succeeded.

Jack had stood there thinking he understood something, far from everything. He had moved carefully around the flat then, not returning to the safe or the bed. He'd stood again for a long time in front of a painting that was full of symbols, like something by Dali. He hadn't been able to make a lick of sense out of it. But if he was under surveillance, the last thing people would see him doing would be studying this painting, tracing a couple of the symbols with his finger, before he suddenly strode out of the flat as if with inspired purpose.

Now, having just sent Arden on her separate way, Jack finally had a chance to act on his hunch. He had been wanting to do so for weeks, but first he'd had to get to the ambassador, then other matters had intervened. But now, before he went to Salzburg he intended to stop in Nice, at the seaside villa of the architect Paul Desquat.

The train was fast. Jack would have liked to go by air again, but he had no more jet helicopter favors to call in and no airport was convenient. So he took a train from Italy, which was nice because it gave him time to think. Or would have if he could have turned off his nerves. Jack hardly sat on the train, he kept changing cars, standing at the back to see which passengers turned to look at him. Several did. He tried to narrow down the suspects. The teenage American girl, could he eliminate her? Not really. What about the two businessmen in suits, traveling together? Jack wasn't willing to scratch them off the list of people who might be following him either, even after one put his arm around the other's shoulders in an intimate way. What, you think there aren't any gay assassins?

He edged his way through the cars, imagining that he was gathering a wake of people out to get him. He kept studying his fellow passengers, most intently the few who looked more or less like he did. This time there were no Jack doppelgangers, at least not out in the open. Maybe they had one stashed so he could take Jake's place after they'd offed him. It would be a simple matter of pushing Jack out a door.

Because this wasn't a steam engine in the old west. This was a sleek silver European metroliner, going a hundred and twenty miles an hour between stops. There'd be no jumping off this train and rolling gently down a slope to come to a rest. If someone were propelled off this train the suction of the train's speed might pull him under the wheels. If you beat that hazard you would land on rocks at a speed of a hundred miles an hour, shattering whatever bones first hit the ground, including a skull. A very skillful adventurer, with pinpoint timing, might be able to leap from this train and suffer no worse than several compound fractures, unconsciousness, and a hospital stay. If he got lucky.

So Jack paced and jittered and had no time to plan what he would do once he got to Nice.

Rachel and Stevie had been Americans, raised in America. They'd always known they'd have to return to the countries of their origin, but by that time they'd become Americans. That was the Circle's hope.

But sometimes, once in a great while, the Circle had to recruit members from other countries, brought up there, knowing their own countries. The Circle needed that intimate familiarity with foreign places. These recruits had to be wholly foreign yet wholly members of the Circle, too. But it is very hard to create a world citizen. Teaching and training these recruits in their home countries made it harder to instill the Circle's values, which were intrinsically American. It was always a risk, and sometimes it didn't succeed. Those people had to be dealt with later.

Paul Desquat was one of those foreign-raised members. He remained a member in very good standing. Jack knew, for example, that the Chair was receiving regular reports from him during the current crisis. It was hoped that Desquat would be very useful in stabilizing Europe.

But Jack had met the architect years earlier, with Madeline. He was sure now that that meeting had meant something. Madeline hadn't done anything by accident. But Jack had heard nothing from Paul Desquat in the five years since Madeline's death. That seemed odd now. If they had thought Jack worth recruiting, why hadn't anyone tried to continue that after Madeline's death? Or had she determined that Jack wasn't material for the Inner Circle, and had waved them off?

He had a sudden thought: had Madeline faked her own death in order to start a new life somewhere else, one without Jack in it?

Members of the group had done such things before, when they'd become too well-known in a particular field. And Madeline had been a very popular designer.

Had she bailed on him?

Jack didn't believe that. That would mean everything he'd known during those few months in London had been fake. Madeline's affection for him, the glimpses of another world, the puzzles. The sex amid jewelry.

If that was true, if Madeline was still alive somewhere in the world, then there was only one thing for Jack to do. Track her down and kill her.

It was a strange thing to hope for, that his one true love had been murdered, but it was the only hope Jack had. Now, in the midst of this world crisis, he intended to find the proof one way or the other, and hope the two were connected. Who else but a ruthless Inner Circle could have pulled off such a thing? Maybe this inner group believed that America would be better off in isolation from the world. Maybe that had been the point of the 9-11 attacks, and this was another stab at the same goal.

Too many maybes. Jack had come to Nice to find answers.

He felt pretty sure he had gotten off the train unobserved. In a small cafe in Nice he resumed his Internet game. Sure enough, his best virtual friend was waiting for him. "WANNA PLAY?" Oh yes, Jack wanted to play.

An hour later he shut off, right in the middle of a maneuver that he hoped would keep his opponent off-balance for a while. Jack went into a shop and bought a bathing suit, towel, and small carrying bag. The thing about European shops was their look of permanence. Shops in buildings that looked older than the country Jack came from, possibly with the same shopkeepers. The buildings looked as if they had been remodelled from seventeenth century baronial manors, and not remodelled much. By contrast, Jack realized, stores in America, even the grandest ones, looked as if they had just been thrown up by a construction crew that morning, and might be scheduled for demolition that afternoon. How could such grand old buildings as these carry items as common as bathing trunks and gym bags? Europe made him feel that there had once been a world of grace and beauty, but it had been conquered and extinguished by the Gap. He wanted to apologize before he left.

Jack ducked into a kiosk men's room. Another odd experience, using the bathroom practically in public, with one's calves and feet exposed to view. Jack used this one only to change. When he emerged, wearing his swim suit, flipflops, and Hard Rock Cafe t-shirt, he looked as much like a native as the natives did. He strolled down toward the beach, not hurrying: that would have marked him as an American.

Nice boasted one of the most beautiful beaches in the world. It drew visitors from all over Europe and farther. Jack found a few square feet of unclaimed sand and sat down on his beach towel. It was October, cool, and the beach wasn't nearly as crowded as it would have been two months ago. There were still plenty of people, though. Women in bikinis, or topless. Some whose friends should never have let them appear in public that way, a few who should by law never be allowed to wear clothes. Jack watched openly. No one looked back. He felt invisible, which was a relief.

The sun began to go down and people began to leave. There was a tourist pier, a sort of large boardwalk that kept going into the sea. Before the light disappeared Jack walked out on that pier, to a place where it widened. There were for-pay telescopes at every corner, and luckily Jack had the right coins. He dropped them in and the view clicked open. But Jack didn't look out at the ocean. He turned the telescope inland, scanning from left to right, looking along the sand, then higher up the beach. He didn't want to ask anyone where Paul Desquat lived, he didn't want to be remembered as the man who'd asked questions, and he wasn't sure he could find the man in a phone directory. But he remembered from Madeline that the architect's villa was beside the sea. He needed to get lucky now.

The telescope found a dozen seaside houses within sight, and Jack gazed at each for a few seconds. Too big. Too small. Too ancient. Beautiful places, no doubt inhabited by beautiful people, but not the right one.

Suddenly the view of sand and houses disappeared, replaced by a pair of giant breasts. Lovely breasts even out of focus Stevie, without tan lines, but appearing threatening as they filled the view. Jack jumped back. A woman stood in front of the telescope, topless. This was one of the ones who should go through life naked. She was lithe and smooth and tan. "What are you doing?" she asked in French.

Her mouth was small, it seemed to close up when she wasn't speaking, but that was the only flaw in her face. A good chin, interesting nose, hazel eyes staring at him as if in outrage. The woman was neither young nor old, but walking confidently through her own exquisite twilight of age.

She continued, "The viewers are for looking at the sea."

Jack managed to answer in French, "I am not interested in fish."

"What are you interested in?" She sounded accusatory.

Jack resolutely kept from glancing downward as he answered. "Architecture."

The woman's mouth quirked into a smile. He had been wrong: her mouth was just the right size.

"I believe you'll find the most interesting homes down that way." She pointed eastward.

She started walking out the pier, then turned back and said, "Interesting architecturally, I mean. One of them won a competition, I believe."

She turned and kept walking, never looking back again, but her walk convinced Jack that she expected Jack to be watching her, and knew he would be. At the end of the pier she barely paused as she stepped up onto the wooden railing and dived off. Jack gasped.

Oh, Mademoiselle, he wanted to say, *please don't risk that body by diving into unknown waters.*

But she probably knew this water well. She surfaced twenty yards out and began swimming with strong strokes. Eastward, the way she had told him to go. Jack wanted to turn the viewer on her, but heard a click which meant his time had run out.

One of them won a competition, she'd said. Maybe that was the architect's villa. Jack felt he had some luck coming.

He did get lucky, and it turned out to be the worst luck he'd ever had.

Night had fallen by the time Jack reached the architecturally interesting part of the seashore. There were still a few people walking the beach, but he sensed them as movements and soft sounds. A man who stood still could go unnoticed. There was no moon.

But the villa he sought gave off its own light. Jack was sure when he saw it that he had the right one. Madeline's rendering of it on her sheet hadn't done the place justice, but it was still recognizable. The villa was made of sandstone, so it seemed to rise straight out of the beach like a sandcastle. It was low and wide, except for a crest in the center that rose up two extra stories, a small crown atop the villa. There would be a deck up there, of course, with a splendid view of the ocean. It almost looked like the mast of a cruise ship, except it curved toward the sea. A melting smokestack.

The house stood atop a rise a hundred yards back from the beach. Jack walked up that rise, avoiding the house's boardwalk. When he reached the top, the villa looked larger than it had from the beach. It dominated the view. How could a Circle member live here, in the most conspicuous house in town? *We're supposed to be unobtrusive,* he thought, and wondered if the Chair had ever seen this house. As far as Jack was concerned, the house immediately branded its owner a traitor to his group's values.

He walked around the house for half an hour, keeping his distance. There didn't seem to be any security guards, but there was an alarm system that included cameras. They might not be monitored full-time, though, they might just be making tapes that could be viewed later, after a burglary, for example. One of the cameras moved in a short semi-circle. One thing it kept in view on its circuit was some steps carved into the side of the house. Jack followed those steps upward with his eyes. He could reach that high deck without going into the house.

First he had to disable the camera, though. He crept up behind it, wondering if it had a microphone as well, and as the camera reached the farthest point of its arc to the left, Jack turned it on its pivot so it was pointing out toward the beach. Careful to stay out of its view, he made sure it was anchored there and then crept toward the house.

He hadn't seen any people through the house's large ground floor windows. But there was a car parked in the driveway in front of the house, on the side opposite the sea. A low, sleek, European sports car that called attention to itself as much as the house did. Someone must be here, but Jack didn't know where.

He climbed the sandstone steps, walked across the flat roof, and found more steps leading up to that high deck. He crept up those even more cautiously. When his head came level with the deck he peeked over quickly, then ducked down again, reviewing the mental picture he had just taken. The deck was furnished in beach-fashion, but with better taste than most people display in beach houses. Two chaise lounges with thick cushions faced the sea. A small black table between them held two cocktail glasses, with a martini shaker between them. Light curtains billowed inward from an open doorway.

He hadn't seen any people on the balcony, but they hadn't been gone long. And that open doorway told Jack where he had to go next.

Wincing, wishing he had taken some secret agent training, he stole back upward again, this time out on the deck, crouching on its surface like Gollum. He slinked across to that open doorway, and began to hear sounds. A groan and sharp intakes of breath. It sounded as if someone was being tortured. Jack reached the doorway and stared in.

A man and woman were making love. The man was on his back with his arms spread wide, the woman atop him. She had black hair and not as lovely a body as the one he had glimpsed on the pier. That was all Jack had time to notice as he ducked back away again. He sat back against the wall of the house, feeling guilty, like a voyeur with a conscience, waiting.

The breeze from the sea and the small sounds from within the house were oddly soothing. Jack had had a long, long day, beginning well before dawn. Sitting against the wall of the house, he fell into a trance that was very close to sleep. The sound of a door slamming woke him.

By the time he was alert the sound existed only in Jack's memory. He didn't know where it had come from. But a moment later he heard a voice calling from below, inside the house. "Hello? Where are you?"

Then Jack became aware of sounds much closer as well. The people in the bedroom were moving fast. Jack looked at the glasses and martini shaker on the table. Would they come out here? But he sat paralyzed, still groggy from weariness.

Luckily, no one came out onto the deck. A man's voice called, "Coming!" That started a woman giggling, and the man shushed her.

Jack crept over to the open doorway and glanced into the bedroom, his head down near the ground. He saw the man and woman who'd been making love earlier hastily dressing. By the light from a bedside lamp he could see their faces. The woman wore a smirk as she zipped herself up, and the man smiled guiltily. "We were silly," the man said in French. The woman answered, "Let's ask Alexis's opinion." The man made a silencing gesture at her as he hurried out the bedroom door into the interior of the house. The woman took her time, moving leisurely, and at the doorway turned to look back at the bed. Jack pulled back out of sight.

But he wouldn't learn anything up here. He gave the woman a few more seconds to get out, then he too crept through the bedroom. He looked around for any identifying features, such as photographs or maybe an architectural award, but saw nothing like that. He walked softly through the room and out its only other door.

Just outside the door was a staircase landing. This bedroom was the only room on the top floor of the house. Jack crept down the stairs, crouching low. The stairs wound down, and before he was halfway down he heard voices. "We were watching the sunset," the man said in French. The woman's voice answered in English, "Which set an hour ago."

There was a pause, and the man said, "You know Yvette."

In the silence that followed, Jack could picture the women's expressions: Yvette still smirking, the other woman looking at her coldly, neither offering a greeting. Probably Paul Desquat standing there with the fatuous grin men wear when alone with two women with whom he's been intimate. "Would you like a drink?" his voice asked.

"This is important. Jack Driscoll is on his way here. You need to be prepared."

This brought a flurry of voices. The man obviously knew who Jack was. After a moment Alexis's cool voice cut through the babble. "One of our people spotted him on the beach and I sent him this way. Well, we want him here, don't we?"

So Alexis was the woman who had stepped into the view of his viewfinder. Jack wondered how she was dressed now, but he didn't dare go farther down the stairs. They seemed to end right in the room where the people were talking.

"Good," Paul Desquat said, sounding more sure of himself now. "Then we will have him and he won't be able to interfere with our plans."

"He couldn't have anyway," Yvette said. "Everything is set, and your Jack has just been wandering around cluelessly."

A pause meant, Jack hoped, that the other two exchanged a glance saying Yvette didn't know what she was talking about. But her assessment wasn't far wrong.

Even without seeing them, Jack could sense the tension in

the room. The pause continued. In the silence he heard the small click and hiss of a cigarette lighter, then smelled the cigarette. Paul Desquat relaxed into a chair and tried to start a conversation.

"What intrigues me about the whole business is that no one except we few know how one day will be different from the previous, but it will affect everything. Even the language. After this everyone will say the word 'Salzburg' the way they say 'Nine-eleven' now. It could easily have been another place, but now people will think of the world in terms of before and after Salzburg."

"You talk too much," Alexis said, and from the sound of her voice she was moving. Jack had to make an instant decision, and did. Quickly but as quietly as possible, he began backing up the steps. A little more, another two, three feet, and he'd be out of sight of the bottom. He moved on feet and hands, like a child eluding bedtime. Just as he backed up near the top he heard Alexis arrive at the bottom of the stairs. Had she seen his feet? He couldn't tell. Jack stopped moving, because she had. He stopped breathing, too.

Alexis's intense gaze up into the semi-darkness at the top of the stairs almost had a sound, a crackle like a laser beam. Then her foot touched the bottom step. The stairs were metal; that one step vibrated all the way up to where Jack crouched. If he moved she would feel him move, too.

Then another voice cut across. "What are you looking for up there?" It was Yvette. Her voice was playful and mean. "I may have left my jacket up on the deck."

Jack didn't wait to hear Alexis's reply. He scuttled the rest of the way up the spiral staircase, gained his feet and hurried through the bedroom. He hated to miss what was being said in that living room, but it was even more urgent that they not know he had heard the one vital word.

The glass sliding door to the deck was still open. Jack went through it quickly, and across the deck to the steps cut into the wall, leading down. When he reached the bottom of those steps he was walking across the roof of the first floor of the house. He tried to step very lightly. He came to the edge of the roof and went down the other set of steps.

On tiptoe he ran through the blind spot he had created in Desquat's video surveillance of the house. Carefully he moved the camera back to cover the house, hoping no one would review the tapes and notice the discrepancy. Then he stood in the darkness, listening for sounds. He heard nothing, which was ominous. Some presence was quieting the insects and birds. Jack stood completely still, trying to listen and to think at the same time. Which way? Back down toward the beach? He was dressed for that, but that way was more difficult, down that sandy cliff. He could circle the house toward the front, which would probably be more unexpected. Yvette seemed like a careless person. Maybe she had left the keys in her car.

He began moving that way, around the perimeter of the cameras. The driveway was probably covered too, but that couldn't be helped. The little silver sports car was down at the end of the driveway, maybe out of camera range.

Moments later he was standing there. Peering in, he could see that surely enough the keys were in the ignition. He reached for the door handle and heard two clicks. One was of the door locking itself. The other, he saw when he turned, was Yvette cocking the semi-automatic pistol she held trained on him. She still wore the loose grin, and it was no more attractive when turned on him.

"I've always been the lucky one," she said softly, her eyelids moving languidly. "I picked the right direction. And Paul had an extra set of keys to my car."

She gestured with the pistol, indicating the direction of the house. For the moment they were alone. Jack could lunge and overpower her. But he saw her, even with the sleepy, seductive look, keeping a careful distance. She wasn't prepared for another kind of attack.

"You know he's in love with Alexis, don't you? You're just a diversion, something to make their lives interesting. You do know that, don't you?"

In an instant her lip was trembling. Her eyes darted back and forth, obviously wondering if it was true. Then she stepped toward Jack, lowering the gun.

"Could you—?" she asked hesitantly.

"Yes."

"—be more stupid?" she finished, and hit him in the stomach with the gun. The heavy metal cracked off a rib. Jack doubled over instantly. Yvette moved around, kicked him from behind, started him moving toward the house. "The great manipulator," she laughed.

A few minutes later Jack was sitting in that living room he had heard but not seen until Yvette had pushed him into it at gunpoint. It was a beautiful room, though too stark and modern for Jack's taste, with a parquet floor, half-empty white bookcases and high-tech furniture. He sat in a very modern chrome and black leather chair. The back was high enough that he couldn't turn and see anyone behind him. Jack pivoted the chair slightly so that he could see the wide windows of this room, with a view of the gardens but also a reflection of the room now at night. In that reflection he watched Alexis and Desquat enter the room from different directions, from their separate searches for the intruder. Jack looked at Yvette, saw her look first at Paul Desquat. Some women would look at their rival, comparing looks, but Yvette looked at her lover. She saw that his eyes went first to Alexis when he entered the room, involuntarily, the way a compass needle points north. Yvette's pouty little mouth hardened.

CHAPTER 9

Back in America, life went on, tensely. The morning after the attacks and the President's announcement, the Dow Jones average fell five hundred points before the board suspended trading. But days passed and nothing else happened. Habit has the force of tides; people stayed in their natural courses as rivers do. They went to work, bought groceries, took kids to school. Except in the communities most immediately affected, it was hard to tell that anything had happened.

Except in conversations. People talked of little else. At first the national response was to want to strike back, but as no immediate target of revenge became apparent, a large majority of Americans began to support the President's view. Enough of this. Let the rest of the world destroy itself. Let's stay out of it. Leave us alone.

Corporate leaders had larger views. Microsoft couldn't withdraw from the world stage, nor would Wal-Mart, nor Disney. And they didn't want to be alone out there. Executives of such companies talked of patriotism and commitment, and paid millions to public relations firms for ads extolling those virtues. But Americans, already tired of wars that lasted too long and had too little point, of screaming foreigners hating us, of being criticized even where we tried to help, switched channels.

The American Century was coming to a decisive end.

Within a very few minutes it became clear that Paul Desquat didn't know what to do with Jack, even though his partner Alexis had lured him here. Desquat was a handsome, dissipated-looking man, growing a little belly on a thin torso, the beginnings of pouches under his dark eyes. But still with a strong chin and sharp features, though now they looked puzzled.

"Why here?" he said. "Why to me? Have you been paying calls on everyone you met while you were with—?"

Alexis cleared her throat sharply, cutting him off. She was standing close to Desquat, who sat on a low black sofa matching the chair that held Jack. Alexis was fully dressed now, in black slacks and a black filmy blouse, giving dramatic effect to her pale skin and black hair.

"He knows," Desquat said to her dismissively. "Everything he's been doing is about Madeline. As if she left him directions."

"It certainly took him a long time to decipher those directions," Alexis said, still staring at Jack. In Jack's peripheral vision he saw, off to the side, Yvette glaring at the two of them, neither of whom seemed to notice.

"He doesn't know all that—" Yvette said, and Desquat interrupted her, which was perfect.

"Maybe he didn't need to do anything about it until now."

Yvette scowled. Jack pretended to ignore her, as the other two were doing. "Maybe I didn't want in until now." He leaned forward, noticing how that move heightened Yvette's interest in him, and her gun's interest. The chair in which he sat was too low to spring out of suddenly. Jack said, "I believe I've learned everything I can from my—early tutors. Madeline was going to introduce me to others."

Alexis and Desquat studied him. Alexis had her arms folded. "I don't think so," she finally said.

Jack studied her in turn, with frank curiosity. "I don't know you. Haven't even heard your name. Are you—" He turned to direct the unfinished question at Desquat. To Jack's hidden delight, the architect looked guilty. "So you've been recruiting outside the—" Jack deliberately cut himself off, as if he'd said too much.

Alexis strode forward. "I know all about your precious Circle," she sneered.

"Do you? What's the password? Show me the secret handshake." Jack held out his hand at an odd angle. Alexis kicked at it. Jack's hand twisted, caught her ankle, pulled, and dumped her on her ass on the hard parquet floor.

Yvette smiled, and didn't raise the gun in his direction. Jack jumped to his feet, but Paul Desquat didn't move. "Where will you go?" he said quietly. "You came here to learn, didn't you?"

That stopped Jack. Alexis regained her feet, with as much dignity as she could muster. Her face was even whiter, all the blood having drained southward. She looked like a vampire with her blazing blue eyes. Without any other warning she slapped Jack hard across the cheek.

He could have grabbed her then, used her as a shield and a hostage, maybe escaped. Instead Jack just pursed his lips at her in a simper. "Bitch."

Yvette had to stifle a laugh.

Jack sat down slowly, looked up at Alexis, waited for her to walk away. Then he returned his attention to Desquat. "Tell me why I should want in," Jack said slowly.

"No one's invited you." When Jack didn't respond, Desquat shrugged. He repeated Jack's question, with an eloquent French gesture that took in the beautiful room, the house, Nice, his life.

Jack acknowledged what he wasn't saying. "You have a villa in Nice. How nice. All the money you could spend in more than a lifetime. Comfortable furniture. Lovely friends. Why would you want more than this? You do have Internet, right?"

Desquat smiled. "I have a wine cellar. A lovely beach, where the most beautiful women in the world come to play nearly naked. More comforts than the most powerful Caesar could have had. Why isn't this enough, Jack?"

"I don't know."

"Yes you do." Desquat waited, but when Jack didn't take the bait he answered, "Because nothing is ever enough. We are the monkeys who climbed to the top of the highest tree, Jack. But from there we can see the mountains."

Jack nodded slowly, as if convinced. "All right. You've got me."

Desquat smiled sadly. "I'm sorry, Jack."

"Madeline trusted me."

"Really? What did she tell you?"

"Your name. She was ready to bring me in."

"If she gave you my name, why has it taken you all these years to come to me?"

"Not to find you. Just to decide I wanted in."

"I'm sorry, Jack. You need a sponsor to come in. You don't have a sponsor."

Jack noticed that Alexis had disappeared. He had shamed her out of the room. Desquat probably wasn't going to buy his turncoat act, and Alexis clearly wouldn't. So he turned serious. His voice turning hard, he said, "Did you kill her?"

Desquat merely sighed. "I'm sorry. I really am. Maybe Madeline would have brought you in. But not now. You're too wild a card, my friend. I think you don't want this. You want to stop us."

Jack lifted his arms from the uncomfortable chair arms. "I don't have a gun. And I'm sure my knowledge of martial arts is less than yours. I'm not a threat to you."

"You have your mind. It is one of the twistiest we have ever known. No one can trust you." Desquat gazed off into the distance, considering. "But... I don't think—" He almost said a name. Jack listened tensely. But Desquat stopped himself. "What are we to do with—?" He looked around and saw for the first time that Alexis was gone. As he realized it, she came striding back into the room. "That's simple," she said. "He's a burglar, isn't he?" A doorbell chimed. "That will be the police."

The others went more tense than Jack did. At least Alexis and Desquat looked tense. Yvette seemed to enjoy their sudden and quick quarrel. She glanced at Jack with a conspiratorial smile. He didn't try to send her any message.

Desquat's and Alexis's argument was quick and only half-spoken. "We can't turn him over—" "What's he going to say? That he's discovered some worldwide—" Alexis turned and laughed at Jack. "Go ahead. They'll bury you in the crazy ward."

Jack smiled back at her ever so politely, like a guest at a cocktail party who knows no one.

Then came the sound of the front door crashing inward.

One would expect that an elegant resort city in the south of France might occasionally need to incarcerate celebrities, or at least rich people. One could hope that their jails, therefore, would be several cuts above the American equivalent. But if that was the case, these gendarmes obviously didn't think Jack worthy of the presidential suite. The small cell into which they threw him unceremoniously had a rough cement floor—he could attest to the roughness—a small cot, and a constant stench. Its only luxury was solitude. Maybe they thought he would infect the other prisoners with his craziness. Or maybe this was solitary confinement.

It could have been, in fact, that those were no police who had taken him from Paul Desquat's house and that this was no jail. At least no official one. It could be that that barred door would never open again, and there would be no official record of this discarded American.

Jack curled up on the cot, which immediately sank so that his side was touching the floor. He was wearier than he had ever been. The only useful thing he could do in here was sleep, but he didn't. He thought.

For the first time since this crisis began, Jack had time to think. He was alone, he had no one else to worry about. And he didn't have to think about evading pursuit, because he had already been caught. Lying on that cot, his mind roved back over the days, and he realized that since the night the planes had crossed America, obstacles and puzzles had been thrown in his way that had kept him from concentrating on the big picture. He had been separated from his group; he couldn't contribute to their discussions nor get their insights. Was it accidental that Jack alone had been cut off from the Circle?

What had brought him here? Those sightings of him in Europe. Some genuine, several false. He had seen the fake Jacks himself. They weren't close enough to fool anyone who really knew him. Someone could have used plastic surgery to create near-perfect Jack clones if they had wanted, but what could they do with such replicas? Even if they looked exactly like Jack, they couldn't fool anyone who mattered for long. Not the Chair, not his friends. His face mattered to so few people. Even if his name was fairly well-known in the gaming world, his face wasn't. What had those fake Jacks accomplished?

No, that wasn't question. The question was the one Arden had asked: *Why you?* Jack suddenly sat up in the darkness. Those Jack-sightings had separated him from the Circle and brought him here, that's what they had accomplished. They had kept him on the move and on the dodge, unable to think until now.

Someone wanted him out of the picture and coping with lesser puzzles. Why? What did he know? And oddly, the Jack sightings had brought him to Europe, which seemed to be the heart of the conspiracy, if he could believe what he had heard Desquat say. Salzburg. Where the peace summit was going to take place. It could have been a lie, Desquat might have already known Jack was listening. But Rachel had had a feeling about the same thing, and he trusted Rachel's feelings.

Whoever had plotted this wasn't a gamer. This was a bad game. In a good game one clue leads to another. Conquering one level admits you to the next level. What was happening now was circular instead, each revelation leading back around. No way out.

Jack paced as far as he could pace in the small cell, reached the wall and paced back. No one knew the National Security Advisor, except that Jack had a way to get to him. The NSA seemed to have been plucked out of anonymity and installed in the White House just for this reason: to isolate further an isolationist president. And someone had created a figure of enormous influence who was completely unknown to Circle members. A near impossibility.

What had those planes accomplished? A huge fortune had been spent on that one night of terror. It had made a president decide to draw back from the world. Who could profit from that? Some terrorists, perhaps, though most would rather have the Great Satan blundering about in the world, giving them recruitment material.

Think. What else had been accomplished? And how would it be furthered by some event at a meeting of world leaders in Salzburg? It seemed that Jack was the one who could figure this out, because he was the sole target of the invisible enemy's scheming.

But Arden had also been cut off from the group. Sent to babysit Jack. Had that been intended?

Jack lay back down on the cot, which weariness made comfortable. There was a way out of this puzzle. Stop thinking two-dimensionally. Rise above the board. He began to drift off, his thoughts growing wilder and longer, the figures in his life flitting like distorted masks. Madeline. Arden. Rachel. Stevie. The Chair. Mrs. Stein. Jack smiled in his grogginess as he pictured her at the front of the class, telling them about Robert E. Lee's young adjutant, a name lost to history, but who had set the general's glasses down in such a way that when he reached for them they focused on a town called Gettysburg. It was such a crazy concept it had made Jack laugh even then. And glancing out the classroom windows he saw someone peeking in. A boy who wasn't in the class, who had been excluded.

Bruno Benjamin had been the smartest boy not only at Bruton Academy but in the memory of his teachers. No one since Craig Mortenson had tested so high in IQ, in the Circle's own tests, the ones that mattered. But there was something they didn't trust about Bruno. He was smart, yes, but he was also lacking in that empathy for other people that was the essential weapon of the Circle. They had brought him to Bruton for observation, but had shied away from bringing him fully inside. He was not, for example, placed in Mrs. Stein's history class.

But the Circle, those self-styled masters of the American destiny, hadn't counted on Bruno's ingenuity, his deviousness. He began to learn about the special classes even though he wasn't in them. Jack's first mission for the Circle, one too big for a schoolboy but that could only be done by a classmate, had been to steer Bruno away from his suspicions– an assignment Jack had bungled so badly he had almost given them all away. That was the first time he came to the attention of the Chair, and not in a good way.

Bruno was eventually transferred to another prep school, a much better known one. Jack had asked about him years later and been told that the Circle had seen that he got admitted to Yale, and even inducted into Skull and Bones, which should assuage his hunger for secret societies. The Circle had once again congratulated itself on its managerial genius. But Jack wondered now if anyone had kept up with Bruno's subsequent career.

Did anyone keep track of those Circle rejects who had been shuttled aside? Because there on the edge of sleep Jack realized what those planes had accomplished, what a disaster at Salzburg would seal for good. Those events had undone everything the Circle had been designed to achieve.

He sat up again. Think about it from a different angle. What if all this business had been aimed not at America but at the Circle itself? If so, it had been a smashing success. The Circle isolated, some of them arrested, others scattered, their mission of maintaining American supremacy in the world in tatters. It would take generations for the Circle to undo this, if they continued to exist at all.

If this was right, the person behind it would, first of all, have to know about the Circle, and hate all its members. He or she would have to have enormous resources and an amazing intellect. Jack could only think of one candidate: that boy he'd seen peeking through the classroom window fifteen years ago.

And Bruno would have known that only one person might be able to figure out who was behind this scheme: Jack. For this to work, he would have to isolate Jack from the rest of the group, set him apart and on the run, so he couldn't think straight.

Exactly what had been accomplished in the last week.

It was scary to have thoughts ranging this widely across time and space while trapped in a small cell. Jack was getting too cosmic for his own good. If Rachel had been here she would have told him he was suffering from rest-deprivation. But once his mind started clicking along these paths, he couldn't turn it off. There was nothing he could do right now with the idea that his old pal Bruno was behind the cataclysm going on in the world. But he could trace back and see if it made other things fit.

Did Bruno have other Circle members on his team? That would be almost essential. Sleeper agents in their midst. People Jack knew and loved. And good old Bruno would be sure to plant someone right next to Jack, if he could, both to guide him astray and to keep a leash on him.

Arden.

Why had she been assigned to him? Had that been an idle thought of the Chair's, or had it been planted in her mind in some subtle, sinister way? As Jack began to think, he realized how little he knew about Arden Spindler, how little any of them knew. She had been raised here in Europe. That was the most dangerous thing the Circle ever undertook, to try to bring up a member loyal to the good old U.S. of A. without being raised there. Sometimes it failed, as Paul Desquat demonstrated. Maybe it had failed with Arden as well. At the very least, being raised in Europe had put her closer to the influence of someone planning a disaster at Salzburg.

But he liked her so much.

What? Where had that come from? Jack's mind was playing him weird. As he lay there in the tiny, smelly cell, the darkness was peopled with Arden: watching him as he talked on the phone to his mother; standing silently aside at his reunion with Rachel; coming around the corner in a car to rescue him; spotting him across a crowded room; her laughing face as she turned and caught sight of him.

But just before sleep finally took him down, Jack realized something else. If the construct he'd created in the last few minutes was true, then Bruno wouldn't be content to leave Jack here in this cell while he pulled off his most spectacular scheme. He would want Jack as a witness. Which meant he had to free Jack. And that didn't seem possible.

Arden had rescued him several times already. She had been there when it was barely possible for a human to know about his peril. But now she was gone. There was no way she could learn about his imprisonment here, and nothing she could do about it if she did.

Unless Bruno Benjamin was behind his current incarceration, and Arden was on his team.

His last thought: If Arden showed up to rescue him again, she was on the other side.

Sunlight woke him. The little cell did have one small window, a little higher than a man's head, so the sun must have been high already to hit Jack's face. Now he could see his surroundings, which were more disgusting even than his nose had told him the night before. He was at the end of a row of three cells; the other two were unoccupied. Outside the door a short hallway led to a simple wooden door. Down beyond the third cell was some kind of storage area where apparently manure and straw were stored until needed. A paradise for flies and probably worse vermin.

He had to get out of here. He had to get his PlayStation. He had to contact the Circle. He had to call home. But it looked as if no one intended to let him do anything he needed to do. No one, for example, had brought him breakfast, or let him out for a bathroom break. There was a bucket in the corner. Jack stayed as far from it as he could.

Half an hour later that wooden door opened. Arden walked through.

Jack stared at her expressionlessly. He thought he was hallucinating, especially since she showed no reaction to seeing him. Her face was as blank as his. Blanker. She looked like a mannequin of herself. Jack thought, she's given up the pretense. She knows I'm on to her.

Then Arden came farther along the hallway and Jack saw the man behind her, the man in uniform holding a gun on her. He marched her forward, pushed her aside, opened the door of the cell next to Jack's, and shoved her inside. Arden turned and gave the guard a look that Jack took for complicity. Arden and the guard were in something together. But the uniformed man just stared back at her, then locked the cell and marched out without a word.

"Jack!" Arden flung herself against the bars, reaching through them, so he had no choice but to go and give her an extremely awkward hug. Jack kept his emotions tightly contained. He knew now she was waiting to betray him. He could give nothing away.

Nevertheless, her arms felt surprisingly good.

He asked her how she'd found him, but barely listened to her explanation: decided he would need her, followed him to Nice, heard about an American arrested for invading a home, blah blah blah. Jack waited out the story, then asked, "How are we getting out of here?"

Arden looked longingly at that wooden door. "Hell if I know."

"You don't have a plan?"

"I don't even know exactly where we are."

Which put a tiny hole in his suspicions. If she didn't have a way out, maybe she *wasn't* on the other side. But just give her time, Jack thought. She'd come up with something ingenious. "You sort of made friends with that guard, didn't you?"

"I thought we made a little connection," Arden answered, worry putting lines in her forehead. "But I sure couldn't tell it by the way he shoved me in here." Her nose wrinkled. She looked around the accommodations, and her expression was horrified. "My God, Jack, I only left you alone for like a day. What did you do to get put in this hellhole?"

Jack was still watching her. She seemed genuinely to be as trapped as he was. "We have to get out of here," she said, sounding a little desperate.

"Yes, and very soon."

"Why?" She looked at him with real curiosity. "What's happening?"

"I'm starting to think real seriously about that bucket in the corner."

Two hours convinced him that Arden had no idea how to get out of here. Lunchtime passed as had breakfast time, with no intrusion from the outside world. By climbing the bars between their cells, then leaning far back and to the side, Jack could grab the bars of the only window and hold himself up long enough to see out. There was little to see. The window seemed to be facing an alley. He couldn't see all the way to the ground from his angle, but he could see another wall a short distance away, and could hear no human voices nearby, although there were the sounds of cars and foot traffic from off to his left. No one close by, though. No one whose sympathies he could enlist.

When he dropped down he said angrily to Arden, "You know what to do in this situation, don't you? Find an ally before you get captured. Or create one. Didn't you?" Because Jack was getting very anxious and more than a little paranoid. He wanted this to be over. She should go ahead and reveal herself and drop the pretense.

"I didn't have time. I was worried about you."

She spoke very quietly. Jack turned to look at her and found Arden looking down at the floor. He waited, but she didn't look up. She'd sounded sincere. Which meant they were truly trapped here. Jack wondered if he'd be taken before a magistrate. Certainly no one had offered him a phone call.

An hour later they were slumped against the bars of their cells, back to back. The slight human contact was nevertheless warming. Jack thought he could hear her thinking. But everything they did was about manipulating others. In this solitude, they had nothing to work with. Instead they found themselves reminiscing, as if this might be the last time. Arden spoke of her parents again. Jack told her about school. "Really?" she'd say, as if everything ordinary sounded like an adventure. "One time Rachel and I sneaked into the library late one night, looking for a book that was kept locked away. We didn't know what was in it, we just knew it must be great if they wouldn't let us see it. And four teachers were having a meeting in the library, all huddled around one little lamp." He could hear Arden picturing it, not the same scene he'd seen, but *a* scene, one transposed into her own school library, probably. He could feel her back against his as he told the story. It *had* been an adventure. He and Rachel had graduated thinking they'd prepared themselves for the grandest adventures of all, world-guiding. They hadn't had a clue. World-saving was smelly, uncomfortable work, not grand at all.

When he finished talking Arden said one word: "Wow." And he found she was holding his hand.

Some time about midafternoon that wooden door opened. The young man in uniform who had brought Arden in stepped into the passageway. Jack smiled inwardly. Here it came. Arden's plan beginning. When she got them out she would also reveal herself.

"You have a visitor," the guard said. Jack waited for Arden to stand up. She didn't move. Jack turned his head in exasperation and saw the guard looking at *him*. The man gestured impatiently.

Jack scrambled to his feet. No one would come visiting him. Unless the Circle had somehow managed to—

He looked through the now-open door and saw Yvette. The young woman from the night before. She stepped through the door, and her nose wrinkled at the stench from his cell.

Jack glanced at Arden, who was staring at Yvette. He had to admit she was worth a stare. Yvette had changed into tight silvery pants that ended about mid-calf. It was hard to tell where slacks stopped and skin began, they were so tight. Good legs. On top she wore a cowl-neck royal blue sweater that brought out her eyes.

"Jack, darling!" she said, and threw her arms around his neck. There she whispered, "You were right. And you're the only man who can make Paul jealous. I have to have you out."

Drawing back, she said more loudly, "I wanted to bring you something, darling, but they searched me. *Quite* thoroughly." She looked accusingly at the guard, who smirked. He was a young man, swarthy, with a very small moustache and a very large sidearm. He turned to look in the remaining cell at Arden and Jack saw, hanging from the guard's wide belt, a dagger. It looked ceremonial, something stolen from a museum, or a costume shop. But Jack didn't stop to criticize. He jumped forward and grabbed the dagger's hilt.

The guard turned quickly. The thing to do then was to run the blade across his throat, silencing him and killing him. But Jack had no experience of killing, and he had nothing against this young man. It takes a very rare kind of person to make and act on the decision to kill a stranger, and Jack was not one of those people.

But he jabbed the dagger hilt first into the guard's stomach, making him grab there. Jack snatched the keys off his belt. He tossed them through the bars to Arden, who quickly began working on the lock.

"Who's she?" Yvette said. Then several things happened in about a second. The barred door swung open and Arden stepped out. The guard straightened and grabbed his pistol. And Jack jumped behind Yvette, putting the dagger to her throat. Then they all froze.

"Are you insane?" the guard asked in accented English. "Who is that woman to me? I'll kill both of you."

"Waste this?" Jack asked unbelievingly. "Look at her." The young guard did, still frowning. Yvette turned toward Jack with a protest. And Arden gave a long sigh and swooned.

She did it in a very dramatic, silent-movie fashion, putting the back of her hand to her forehead and swaying like a kite string before falling sideways. Atop the guard's gun. He tried to break her fall—she *had* gotten to him, at least a little—and Arden grabbed the gun. Jack stepped forward and punched the guard in the face. With the weight of the dagger still in his fist, it was a strong blow, and nearly broke his own fingers. The guard fell, but managed to hang onto his gun.

Arden grabbed Yvette, tripped her, and threw her down on the guard. Then she had Jack's arm, pulling him out the door. Jack looked back and saw Yvette giving him an outraged look. He didn't even have time to shrug in response.

Arden slammed the door closed, locked it, and threw the keys across the alley. "Come on!"

Instantly, the world seemed alive with the sounds of pursuit. "This way!" they both shouted, and Jack let Arden tug him her direction, thinking she'd had more time to check out the area before getting herself arrested. She ran in the direction of crowds, thinking they could lose themselves. To Jack they looked like everyone else in town, in jeans and tennis shoes, but the gendarme coming out the front door of the police station looked straight at Jack and Arden and yelled for them to stop. They didn't. No longer hand in hand, they ran, turned the corner, jumped through people. They were in a shopping district, but not in the touristy part of town. Produce was being offered from wooden stands, and small shops sold essentials.

Arden darted into one, pulling his hand. This was a cafe, with only five small tables. Sleepy-eyed men barely glanced at them. Arden began arguing with Jack in French too rapid for him to follow, moving her arms and shoulders expressively. One man at a table smiled, but no one else seemed to pay attention. Jack slumped his shoulders, looking hangdog, but his act was wasted. No one was looking at him. The French didn't seem embarrassed by a public quarrel the way Americans would be, nor did they seem interested in it.

Arden kept moving, through a swinging door into a small kitchen crowded already with a middle-aged couple. The man began shouting, adding to the general clamor, but the woman just leaned her cheek on her hand and frankly listened to Arden's tirade, with a faint reminiscent smile.

Keep moving, that was the secret. They never stopped. Arden acted as if other people were mannequins in a stage set backing her performance. They went out the back door of the kitchen into another alley, where they turned left. Arden kept up whatever she was saying as they ran across the alley, tried two doors, and went through a third. They found themselves in a small storage room where they stopped to catch their breath. They were chest to chest, breathing hard.

"Which way is the—?" Jack panted.

"The what?"

"I don't know, don't you have a car or a way out?"

"I'm pretty sure they impounded my car when they arrested me." She glanced at him. "Don't give me that look. I got us out, didn't I?"

"No, I think I did."

They started out through another small shop, and saw a half-open door. Arden moaned. "Oh, look, a bathroom. I'm sorry, I've got to—"

"Go."

"You first. You were inside longer, I can—"

"Go!"

She went inside. Jack was almost jumping from foot to foot now. He looked around the cluttered room. There was a small plant in a two-foot copper stand. The soil inside looked deep, and dry. Jack stared out the windows. They were alone.

Two minutes later Arden came out. "Okay, your turn. I'll keep watch."

"It's okay. Come on."

"Don't you—?"

"No! Come on."

"Macho man. God, James Bond. I can—"

"Come on!"

"Okay, okay. Wait a minute. What's that smell?"

"Out, out, we've got to get out of here." He grabbed her hand, hurried her toward the front door. This shop seemed to be closed, or at least empty of people, with the clerk taking a break. Arden looked out the small window beside the front door. A police car pulled up, with that whah-whah-whah European cop car thing. Without another word they ran back inside. They ran toward the back door, heard that same sound.

They looked at each other. No way out. One of them would have to sacrifice himself. Jack saw a small door down a narrow hall. "Quick!" She followed him as he ran. The small door gave, as he knew it would, onto a narrow staircase, going up.

"Come on!"

"Why?" She tugged at his hand. "There's no way out up there. Why?"

"I don't know. I always go up."

As they pounded up the stairs, she asked, "Has this worked out for you in the past?"

Well, no. It was just an instinct. Monkey to the top of the

tree. They were probably trapping themselves. But he couldn't stop. At the top of the stairs they burst out into a hallway, ran down it. Doors left and right. Jack went left, Arden right. A few seconds later they ran into each other back in the hall. "No way—!" they both shouted.

At the end of the hall was a window. They were at it in a second. Down below, there were crashing sounds. Jack raised the window. There was a narrow alley below. Cobblestone street. The promise of broken legs.

They turned back the other way, heard the sounds of people filling the floor below. They stared at each other, the same thoughts crossing both their minds. Too many cops, no way to make a personal connection. "I'll—" But no plan emerged.

They turned back to the window. Now there was a sound from below. Something filling the alleyway. A small truck that seemed to be filled with straw. Perfect. Jack looked behind them. Arden looked at him. He shook his head. Her eyes met his. They took each other's hands, each put a foot up on the windowsill, and they stepped out the window. Arden screamed as they stepped.

The scream brought a French police officer, then another, up the stairs and down that hall to the window. The gendarme looked out and saw the truck going by. He screamed, the loudest sound on a noisy street, and everyone looked up at him. Some of his men appeared at the mouth of the alley and halted the truck. The policeman in the window made hand signals. Then he turned and gave explicit instructions to his subordinate, indicating the open doors along the wall. "Make sure they're not hiding in the rooms, trying to fool us." The young recruit nodded wisely, eyes narrowing. He stalked into the first bedroom as his captain turned and ran out down the hall.

When the captain reached the ground floor his men had the truck surrounded, the driver out on the sidewalk waving his arms and shouting while everyone ignored him. Another officer explained quickly that all the doors along this alley had been locked. "And we had men at both ends of the alley. There is no way they could have gotten past us."

The captain nodded intently. He dropped to the ground and peered under the truck. He was a man who didn't mind getting his uniform dirty in the performance of his duty. No one was clinging to the underside of the truck, but there was some kind of structure there, an extra appendage hanging down.

Plus all that straw in the back. And the cab of the truck itself. "Take it apart," the captain said brusquely.

There was a shout from the open window that the fugitives had leaped through. The young recruit stood in it, waving his arm. "Not up here," he cried. The captain waved him down, then stood frozen. Beside the young recruit, attached to the wall, was an old wooden fire escape. It went down, but also up, to the roof. It wasn't vibrating, there was no obvious sign of passage. Nonetheless, the captain screamed in rage, looking up toward that roof.

As he ran that direction, splitting up his men, he thought, *The scream*. The woman's scream. That's what had drawn him into what he'd done, without even looking upward until now: the scream of a woman jumping out a window, even fading as if she were falling.

It had been perfect.

Two blocks away, Jack and Arden, having gone over the roof of the building and down the other side, had escaped capture for the moment, but they were on foot. Within a minute Arden found a Citroen with keys in it. "Two blocks," Jack said. "We'll just drive it a couple of blocks. I'm not stealing a car."

They got in and took off, Arden driving. Jack looked back and saw a police officer emerge from a side street, putting his hands on his hips and staring first the other direction, then this way. Jack ducked his head. "Six blocks, tops," he said.

"What do you think, Butch?" Arden and Jack huddled in a shop doorway across from a train station. "Hop a freight, or bluff our way on board?"

"The thing is," Jack answered immediately, "I really don't know how to 'hop' a train. I don't even think you can any more. I mean, look at them."

The few trains they could see waiting in the yard were silver cylinders with no apparent handholds. Sleek and slippery and within a few yards of pulling out they would be going eighty miles an hour. Eventually a hundred and twenty. And no cattle cars or open baggage cars. Probably no unlocked doors one could open from the outside. The movies on which Jack and, apparently, Arden had been raised seemed useless here as training films.

"How hot are we?" Jack asked.

"I feel a little feverish."

"I mean, I'm just a burglar, and you're just someone who came to see me. Or did you do something else to get thrown in jail?"

Arden shrugged, which made him give her a double take. "I killed DeGaulle," she confessed.

"So there's really probably not that big a manhunt for us. Let's just go in and buy tickets."

"You got money? Because they took mine when—"

"Excuse me a second." Jack went into a men's room and was gone for a while. When he came out his face was very blank. In one hand he clutched some Euros, and in the other he carried a small key ring. Arden stared at him. "How did you do that? How did you keep anything through a police search?"

"Forget it."

As he walked past, Arden turned and continued to stare. "I mean, the folding money I understand. But the keys?"

She followed him into the train station and past the ticket windows to a row of lockers. "You're kidding," she said aloud.

Jack said nothing. He went into the second row of lockers, mostly hidden from view of passersby, and straight to an upper one. He opened it with the small key and pulled out a wallet, a small cell phone and charger, and an overnight case, black leather, the kind a sophisticated traveler would carry. Jack put the phone into the bag and peered into the locker. He seemed to be looking for something, but didn't find it.

Arden, hands on hips, said, "You keep a stash in the train depot in Nice?"

Jack closed the locker door. "Doesn't everybody?"

Jack bought them tickets, feeling as if he were glowing radioactively. Security was much tighter than it had been pre-9/11, but not like an airport. As they moved toward the train Jack looked fidgety.

"What's the matter?"

"I wish I had my PSPII." Jack's fingers were moving involuntarily.

"Just as well you're leaving it behind," Arden said carelessly. "That's probably how they were tracing you all over Europe."

Jack stopped and stared blankly. As they mounted the stairs he turned and looked back at the moderately busy station. No one seemed to look back at him. Nevertheless, Jack gave his head and shoulders a paranoid duck as he went through the door.

Jack had spent the extra money for a very small private carriage. They didn't say much until the train was moving. Jack looked out the window, musing. Arden didn't know everything he had been through in the last twenty-four hours, and didn't know what he planned now. She had to ask what he was thinking.

Jack looked up at her. "You left Yvette locked in the jail."

"We needed to distract the guard."

"We could have knocked him unconscious, taken his gun, and brought her with us. She could have been useful."

Arden stood up and looked back at him over her shoulder. "Oops," she said, and went out the door of the compartment, heading for the communal bathroom.

CHAPTER 10

Alicia Mortenson called Janice Gentry once Alicia and Craig were on their way. "I'm sorry, dear, that was inexcusable, the way we just walked out."

"Thank you," Janice agreed.

"The fact is, we didn't want to announce exactly what we're doing to everyone in the room, and to Craig and me it was obvious. You know too, don't you?"

Back at headquarters, Janice stood with the landline phone to her ear. She was exhausted, but somehow Alicia's voice conveyed energy. Janice stood up straighter. She let her mind go blank. A soft breeze seemed to blow across her face, pleasantly scented.

Eyes closed, she smiled. "Of course," she said.

It was as if Alicia had projected an image into Janice's mind, across miles of phone line. Because Janice was certain she knew what she meant, and where the couple had gone.

"There you go, dear," Alicia said in that voice that would have made her the greatest kindergarten teacher of all time.

"All right, well, you two be careful."

"We will. And don't worry about the Chair, Janice. I think she may be all right. Maybe she just had to go put in an appearance at her day job. It is important to look normal."

"Yes," Janice said slowly, wondering if Alicia was conveying her another message and Janice wasn't getting it. She wasn't sure exactly what the eighty-seven year old Gladys Leaphorn's "day job" was. She had worked at Langley for years, as an administrative assistant on whom a series of deputy CIA chiefs had come to rely. Shortly before her retirement she had transferred out west here, to North American Defense Command. But in this crisis could she just go pop in at NORAD and say, "Hi, I think I left something in the closet"?

Well, anyway. At least she knew Alicia and Craig were safe. And what they were doing.

The Mortensons set up shop at one of their old stands in Vienna, Virginia, a very upscale suburb of D.C. A million-dollar home in this neighborhood was mid-size. Nice but nothing fancy. They stayed in one such, the vacation home of an old friend who was staying huddled in California until someone explained what was happening now. Then the Mortensons started placing phone calls to friends and acquaintances, most of whom sounded glad to hear from them. The Mortensons were listening for the sound of someone who was not.

Craig managed to reach Don Trimble, but it took a while. "How are things in Salzburg?"

"Ominously quiet," Trimble answered. "Huge security apparatus, of course, but not much trust among the various groups, so they're overlapping and leaving gaps."

"Seen anyone we know?" Craig meant other Circle members, perhaps of the European branches. They would seem inevitably drawn to the city that was soon to be the political center of Earth.

"A few acquaintances, no one who seems to have a clue."

"Jack?"

"No. Have any of you heard from him?"

"I don't think so. We're temporarily away from headquarters."

"You are?" Trimble said quickly. Craig frowned at Alicia. She frowned back as if she had heard not only the whole conversation but also what her husband was thinking. "Where are you?" Trimble asked.

Alicia shook her head at Craig, which was hardly necessary. "California," Craig said. "Thinking about hopping to Malaysia. I think maybe Jack was up to more there than he let on."

"Good idea," Trimble said. "But everyone else is still at headquarters, aren't they?"

"Most all."

They ended the call a few minutes later without chitchat or farewells. Alicia said immediately, "What's wrong?"

"I don't know. Next time you call him and listen to his voice. He just seemed a little too anxious to know where everyone is. And he had absolutely nothing useful to tell me even though he's at ground zero on the scene."

"Maybe he just hasn't learned anything. I never did think Don was the fastest horse in the stable."

Craig laughed. "Or maybe there's nothing to learn there." He looked at his dead cell phone. "Damn it, Don, that was badly played. You should have given me something, something to let me know you're still on the team."

Alicia said, without conviction, "Maybe he was being overheard."

Craig took her hand and gave it a quick kiss. "I'm going to lunch with the Russian ambassador. You?"

"Just some shopping."

He looked at her sharply. Alicia smiled. "With the Secretary of State's mistress."

They parted without goodbyes or backward glances. They were so close they didn't even feel apart when they weren't together. They almost thought with the same mind. But unfortunately they didn't share eyes.

About 10 p.m. a porter came by and made the small train compartment into two beds, one above and one below. Jack and Arden stood in the narrow corridor looking at each other while he worked, neither of them speaking. They had had a hectic, exhilarating hour before boarding the train, but before that they had just sat in a cell for hours. Neither was physically tired. They were very keyed up, and not just from fear of pursuit. Jack's eyes stayed on her face. Arden looked very young, only tracings of lines beginning around her eyes. Her blue eyes took him in, absorbed him, drew him in to her. He wondered what she was seeing. He felt so much older than he had a month ago. Old and suspicious. She looked at him with what he should have known was affection, but he didn't trust her at all. Couldn't. His body did, though. He found himself drawing closer to her.

The porter coughed discreetly, moving between them and out of the way. Jack tipped him a bill without looking at it, probably way too much, from the way the porter chuckled. Or maybe that was just from looking at the two of them.

Arden swallowed. He could see her throat move. "I'm going for a walk," she said.

"Good idea." He stopped swaying toward her.

She took off, moving briskly and swinging her arms. Jack got undressed, mostly. His overnight bag hadn't contained pajamas for either of them. He turned on the small light at the head of the bed and tried to read the one paperback in English he'd found left on the train, a Danielle Steele novel. He had already read enough to understand why someone had left it behind, but there was nothing else to do. Soon he came to a love scene, put the book aside, turned off his light, put his hands behind his head, and looked out the window. France flashed by, dim and smeared by speed. Farmland, widely scattered houses. Like all lonely people, Jack imagined that the people inside those houses were happy. Tired from honest labor, ignorant of sinister forces at work in the world, unconcerned about anything larger than produce prices. So he imagined, and he envied them.

He wished he were back in school, so he could talk to Stevie or Rachel. Jack smiled wryly in the darkness. Sharing his dilemma over another woman with Rachel would be a complicated business, but that was part of the fun.

He wondered what time it was in his home town, what his parents and brother and sisters were doing. His mother would be worried about him, and rightfully so, but her voice wouldn't show it when he called her first thing the next morning.

The door of their compartment slid open. Arden stood there, letting her eyes adjust to the darkness. She didn't speak. There was only a very narrow space between the door and the bunks, perhaps two feet. Arden stepped out of her flat shoes, slipped them to the side. She wore a pleated skirt and a thin sweater with three-quarter sleeves. After a moment she slipped off the skirt, opened the very narrow closet door, and hung it inside. Then she lifted off the sweater, slowly, standing there for a long moment with the sweater around her head while she pulled her arms out. Then she pulled her head free, folded the sweater, and put it on a shelf. The closet door closed with a click that was loud in the silent room.

Arden wore a bra and panties, and Jack couldn't tell anything about their material in the dimness, but they looked filmy. Some moonlight came through the uncurtained window, enough for him to see well, but then he'd been lying in the darkness for a while. Arden must not be able to see at all. Maybe she thought he was already asleep.

He could swear she was looking at him, though. He saw her eyes.

She reached behind her and the bra fell to the floor. She cupped her breasts, which were not large but well-shaped and gravity-resistant. She moved her thumbs along their undersides. When she moved her hands away her nipples were alert.

Jack was sure then that she knew he was watching. He didn't know whether to move or cough or applaud. Very deliberately, Arden hooked her thumbs in the panties, bent at the waist, and pulled them down her legs. As she straightened up she ran her hands up her thighs.

Then she stood for a long moment, palms on her thighs, very pale in the moonlight. He couldn't see any tan lines. Jack sat up slightly, resting his head on his hand, and just stared. She apparently wanted to be seen, and he wanted to see. God, it was going to be hard to sleep after this.

Very deliberately then, Arden hooked her thumbs in her panties and snapped the waistband. Then she looked toward him in the darkness and said, "How long are you going to pretend to be asleep?"

"I'm not. I'm lying here watching you."

He could have sworn she hesitated then. As she did, he moved out of bed and stood in front of her, inches apart. He reached out to the left, the length of his arm, and opened the shades. Moonlight flooded the compartment, seeming very bright. She wouldn't look up until he lifted her chin, then her eyes shone.

They interrupted each other with his saying, "May I—?" and Arden saying, "Would you like—?" Then Jack just nodded, kept looking into her eyes, stepped forward, and put his mouth on hers.

"Hmmph," she said some time later. By then her arms were around his neck, his around her waist.

"Yes," he said. "Arden? Do you really—?" She stopped him with her mouth on his. Also by pulling down his briefs. "My," she said, reaching down.

The train made it perfect. There was that steady rhythm under them. They joined it, first standing then in the bunk. By then they could both see clearly by the shifting moonlight through the window. Jack looked down at her and she covered herself modestly for a moment. Was it mocking? He didn't know. But when he pulled her arms down she didn't resist.

She pushed him back on the bunk, or possibly he pulled her, but in any event he was on his back, she on top of him, looking into each other's eyes. This time he didn't speak, just widened his eyes. She nodded.

Entry was slow, then quick. She made an intake of breath that seemed very loud in the cabin, except it was matched by his. Then they locked eyes again. Then they began moving.

"Oh God," she said, some time later. Jack stroked her hair and just nodded against her bare shoulder, her nipple indenting his chest. "Are you—?" he began, then they both fell instantly asleep, but that kind of sleep where each was aware of the other all the time, their hands stroking each other. Some time in the night they half-woke at the same time and tried again. It was better, or just as good, which was just as good. They ended up staring into each other's eyes until they began blinking and nodded off again.

The miles rolled by.

The library clerk in the American embassy in Munich said to the ambassador's secretary, "I've got to go home, Alice. I've got a headache."

The thin, efficient, middle-aged lady looked up sympathetically and said, "One of your bad ones?"

The clerk nodded. He was a heavy man, which, with his shaved head, made his age hard to determine.

"Well, it's pretty dead here. All the activity is shifting to Salzburg. You take care of yourself, Bruno."

"Thank you, Alice." He liked her, which was one reason why he was leaving this place.

Bruno walked out of the embassy for the last time, walking almost on tiptoe, like a man trying to minimize pain, and didn't stop the act even when he was outside. He eased into his car, a Volkswagen Jetta that was almost too small for him. Then Bruno Benjamin drove away, but only a few blocks.

A few minutes later the ambassador's private cell phone rang. "Yes?" he said impatiently, expecting his wife.

"This is the man who called before. Do you recognize my voice?"

"Yes. Sounds garbled, though. Where are you?" No answer. "Look, I don't have time today. You must know there's a lot going on. You said before this was a security issue. Well, thanks for caring, but we've got plenty of security. You've never seen so much—"

"I'm talking about your personal security, Mr. Ambassador. Do I need to say her name?"

During a long pause, the ambassador looked across his office to the mirror on the wall, checking his hair, which was perfect, slightly wavy with a little gray at the temples. He had always been handsome, and now he was tending toward distinguished. "If you think I'm going to pay you—" he began.

"I'm calling on her behalf. This is just about separation terms. We're not talking about money. She has a position to protect too. She wants to make sure you're not going to—damage each other."

"Of course not. Look. I don't know what we can—"

"This will only take a few minutes of your time, sir. On your way to lunch. Across from the restaurant, there is an alley."

"So?"

"Meet me there. One meeting. She wants me to return a couple of things that are very recognizably yours. And you have something of hers as well, don't you?"

The ambassador thought quickly. He'd feared blackmail, but no longer did. The man's calling him "sir" subconsciously convinced him of the superiority of his position. As a matter of fact he did have Suzanne's day book, which had dropped from her purse at their last tryst. At least he had found it when he was leaving. She would want that back. The meeting made sense. And it was thoughtfully arranged, too.

"All right. Twelve-twenty-five. I'll only have a minute."

"Yes, sir."

⸺•◦•⸺

When the ambassador went into the alley he saw a man walking quickly down it away from him—a burly man whose shape seemed recognizable. He walked with a heavy walking stick. "Hello?" the ambassador called, but the man just kept walking, looking back fearfully over his shoulder as if the ambassador might be a mugger. That was amusing.

About halfway down the narrow alley the man stopped. When the ambassador walked up he turned. The ambassador stopped, then laughed.

"Bruno. You're kidding. What are you doing here?"

"I'm the one who called." Bruno was thinking what a dolt this man was, not to have recognized the voice of a subordinate who had worked in his building for as long as he had.

"You're kidding," the ambassador said again. "What a funny little guy. So you were calling for—her?"

"No, I was calling for myself—sir."

He touched something, the end of the cane fell off, revealing a small, thin blade. Moving quickly, Bruno stabbed the ambassador in the kneecap, with enough force to break it. The ambassador screamed harshly, reaching down. Bruno slashed his hand.

Both wounds were painful but not life-threatening. The knee, especially, was agonizing. The ambassador remained bent over, staring up at his library clerk, the ambassador's face twisted out of any semblance of handsomeness.

"What do you want?" he finally managed to gasp.

"This. To watch you in pain." Bruno smiled. He had worked at the embassy for nearly two years. After so long an imposture as a subordinate, this felt wonderful. The ambassador, a smug rich man who'd gotten his position through campaign contributions, obviously didn't understand at all. The man was a pig, who just happened to have been blessed with good looks and inherited money, which had turned him ugly. He treated everyone around him like a servant. Bruno hated him personally, but also for the way he treated his secretary, who was his superior in every way except wealth and status.

"Are you crazy?" The ambassador lifted his head to shout. Bruno stabbed him in the stomach, stopping his cry. The wound bled, too much, weakening him too fast. Bruno watched with interest. The ambassador tried to speak, beckoned with his right hand as if asking Bruno to lean over so he could whisper to him. But Bruno wasn't interested in his last words. The ambassador doubled over in pain again, and Bruno pushed him with his foot so he fell over on his side, so he could see his face. The ambassador had a look of great curiosity, as if straining to understand not just this moment but his whole life.

"You're too stupid to understand," Bruno told him, staring down. Then he heard noises behind him, down near the mouth of the alley. He sighed. Couldn't wait any longer. With the sword cane he slashed the ambassador's throat. Blood gushed bright red, then darker, then slowed to a trickle. Bruno thought he could see the moment of the man's death when the ambassador tried to shift his eyes toward him and they stopped, then glazed.

Bruno watched him for another few seconds. That hadn't been as satisfying as he'd hoped. But that was okay, he had more satisfaction ahead. This had just been a last job that had to be done, his resignation from the embassy.

He didn't expect anyone to notice his disappearance from the job. Soon there would be no more American embassies. Bruno smiled. He retrieved the concealing sheath of his cane, fixed it back in place, and walked out of the alley the other direction, strolling. He left the woman's date book in the ambassador's pocket. Bruno didn't care for her either.

As Bruno strolled out his mind was already on his much more important plans. He didn't give much thought to whether this murder would speed up or impede the American withdrawal from the world. It was just something he had promised himself he would do someday, since his first week on the job. It was what had kept him working in his imposture as an underling.

He chuckled as he walked out of the alley, smiling like a man who had read something amusing in the morning paper.

Now to Salzburg.

They overslept Salzburg, which turned out to be just as well. The station there was crawling with security. If Jack and Arden had done what they planned and exited there they almost surely would have been detained, American tourists in a place that didn't draw many tourists, at an occasion that would have almost no public events. Everyone disembarking from the train in Salzburg had their ID's examined and recorded. Jack would probably have been arrested.

As it was, the two of them slept peacefully through the stop in Salzburg, snuggling together. The train lurching out of the station woke them. Jack glanced out the window, saw a station, wondered idly where they were. Then Arden was awake too, moving kittenishly in his arms. She looked at him with clear eyes. His own eyes must have shown what he felt, guilt, because she reached over and touched his cheek and shook her head. "My idea, remember?"

She kissed him, slowly, starting with a mere brush of lips, but not doing anything else simultaneously. Putting some thought into it. Two minutes later she said, "Okay, you want me out of here. I know it."

Over his denials she got up, pulled on her blouse and skirt, and went out the door into the tiny corridor, toward the bathroom. Jack sat on the bed, realized they'd missed their stop, and didn't much care.

So they got off at the next station, thirty miles on, a sleepy little town that never drew tourists, and had drawn very little security attention this week, either. Jack and Arden, very lightly encumbered with luggage, hopped off the train and went quickly, and separately, to find places where they could use their cell phones.

At the end of the platform, Arden's call was very brief. "We're right on schedule. Goodbye."

She walked back to find Jack just around the corner of the small station, his back to her. She stopped and listened, the corner separating them. From the tone of his voice she knew he was talking to his mother.

"No, she's really nothing special. I'm *try*ing to be nice. But she just is always coming up with something obnoxious. Like, well—no, I can't tell you that one. Well, here's one. She does this awful thing of always listening outside before she steps into a room or comes around a corner. I know, it's irritating as hell. She has no concept of privacy. Probably because she was raised in a girls' school. You know, girls—"

"You bastard." She came around the corner and put her hands on her hips.

Barely glancing at her, Jack started laughing like a seventh-grade boy. Into the phone he said, "Listen, pretend we were talking about something else. Yeah, she is. No, she's not mad. She's a great sport about that kind of—ow! No, it'll be okay. I think I still remember how to make a tourniquet. Does it work on a neck wound, though?"

She walked away, giving him a semblance of privacy. Arden

put her arms around herself, feeling warmed by his voice, even warmer than she'd felt last night. The murmur of his voice was warm. She heard him click off. When she turned around he was looking at her funny, sort of smiling.

"Mom says she likes you."

This was one of the most genuinely puzzling things anyone had ever said to her. "She hasn't set eyes on me. Or heard my voice, for that matter."

"She says she likes the way I sound when I'm with you."

Jack looked embarrassed, fumbled putting away his phone, and pretended they had much more luggage to organize than the one small gym bag.

Arden just stood watching him, feeling something very strange, a hollowness at her center that was rapidly being filled by the churn of many emotions. She loved him. She was sure of it, even though she had never felt this before.

She only wished she could take back now the things she'd done, but there was no way to undo events that had been set in motion, or the fact that she had already betrayed him.

"Come on," Jack said, regaining some of his gruffness. "I've got to find a PSP, and fast."

Men are such boys. Arden followed him sadly.

Craig Mortenson strode along K Street into Georgetown. He liked striding in D.C. The city had an aura, as strong as any he'd ever known. D.C.'s aura was about power: having it, using it, the hunger for it. Craig breathed it in and it invigorated him like strong coffee.

He had spent several years here, as a bureaucrat then consultant, and frequent visitor as he'd worked to destroy the Soviet Union. Many people here were still loyal to him, or at least friendly, and some very few, mostly out of power now, knew what he'd accomplished.

He and Alicia had been fixtures on the dinner party circuit for a while, including giving their own. They were great places to pick up information, especially the kind that Alicia used best: who was interested in whom, who weren't speaking, who felt slighted and was looking for revenge. Watching her quiet smile at such a party, he could see the pieces breaking apart and re-forming in her head, in that intuitive way that would have made her a great matchmaker. *Make sure the Polish ambassador overhears that waiter over by the kitchen door.* Craig wouldn't know what she was talking about—they had just met the Polish ambassador this evening, and he'd never noticed that waiter before—but she was never wrong. A lever would be pushed down in a Georgetown dining room and a boulder would rise from a river half a world away.

But Craig wasn't trying to lift boulders today, nothing so complicated. He and Alicia had just decided, simultaneously back at headquarters, that the action of the world's stage was about to shift to D.C., and they wanted to be there for it. Establish contacts. Thus today's lunch with his old friend the Russian ambassador— who had been a dissident history professor in and out of Moscow prisons before the collapse of the Soviet Union.

Craig knew the heart of the problem was this National Security Adviser, the one nobody had heard of. The Circle's attempts to get near him had been disastrous so far. Craig loved such a challenge. He felt sure he could reach the man. Go around this way, out of the city, out into academia, back through a family connection.... Craig shook his head. This D.C. air was heady, all right. Made a man feel as if he could do anything. Bourbon, not coffee. But Craig had better sense than that. He wasn't going anywhere near this NSA.

He strolled on to his appointment, walking thoughtfully. No longer striding.

"He is so frustrated," Elena Valenciana said. "He says it is like living through 'Invasion of the Body Snatchers.' At first everyone in the cabinet and most of the staff were arguing against the president's withdrawal policy, but now one and then another becomes a pod person. 'Their eyes literally lose their light.' Then he'll grip me and say, 'Elena, promise me that if you see me with dead eyes you'll do something about it. Put a stiletto through my heart if nothing else.'" Elena laughed. "He has this fantasy that I am an international woman of mystery. An assassin, perhaps."

Her blue eyes flashed at Alicia Mortenson. No one would ever accuse Elena Valenciana of having dead eyes. She was Spanish, with a gypsy mix. Her skin was pale, but its base color was not white. Pale copper. When she and Alicia had met at a spa years ago Alicia had wondered what Elena was doing there, because she was already a woman of incredible beauty. As they'd become friends she'd discovered that Elena had a spirit to match her looks. She was wild but resourceful. *She will never be any man's wife*, Alicia had thought at the time, and so far she was right. Elena didn't enter into marriages, she ruined them. She went through phases, and now liked men of power. The current Secretary of State had been the CEO of an international corporation, so already familiar with many heads of state when he'd gotten his appointment. And his travel schedule often left room for an extra passenger.

"Maybe he should give in himself," Elena said. "Lead the charge the other way. If one is going to lose this battle anyway..."

Alicia's expression was a little pained, enough to cause larger pain on her companion's face. "No, if I do that I will be convincing him to join the herd. Also to do away with his own values. Even if I convinced him, he would hate me for it."

Alicia smiled approvingly, as if liking an item she saw on the menu. The restaurant was one of those light, airy cafes Georgetown does so well, even on an out-of-the-way side street. Elena didn't have to hide out from anyone. She was, within her own limits, very discreet. In her first days in Georgetown, years ago, Elena had learned that a particular woman was gossiping about her ferociously. Elena had taken the woman's husband away for a wonderful weekend in the Shenandoah Valley. People didn't gossip about her any more, except in an admiring way.

So they sat at a back table, but not hiding. A basket of fresh daisies hung near their table, not only giving off their pleasant scent but subtly affecting the light. Daisies, Alicia thought, how refreshing.

Alicia didn't mind being seen with Elena. She had many friends, and was a funny conversationalist. Elena had too many contacts for anyone to think that lunch with her was aimed at any other particular person. This was much safer, for example, than having lunch with the First Lady, which Alicia had also considered.

"But just encouraging him in what he already thinks is boring," Elena pouted. "And it doesn't give me any credit." She smiled at Alicia's arched eyebrow. "Yes, it is all about me. You know, darling, if a giant asteroid were coming to smash the Earth into pieces, I would be quite sure it was coming to pick me up."

"And I'm sure you'd be right, dear." They clinked white wine glasses. "Outside events are shaped to your will, not the other way around." Alicia looked up at the waiter. "Salad Nicoise, I think."

She handed away her menu while Elena kept gripping hers. She finally felt the waiter's stare on her and said, "Steak tartare," as if it were an incriminating statement dragged out of her.

When the waiter had gone Elena muttered, "That's it, of course. Everyone's been thinking too small. It's this damned District of Columbia, it reduces everything to personal pettiness. But out in the world—"

"I don't follow."

When Elena turned to her, her eyes were so bright that they *could* have been dead moments earlier by comparison. "Albert needs forces in the outside world. That riot in Korea the other day made a few people start questioning this withdrawal idea. Albert said he saw the President waver, but then the NSA and other pro-withdrawal forces swooped down and captured him again. If only something like that could happen again." She gripped her friend's hand. "If only he could *predict* something like that happening again."

"Hmm," Alicia said thoughtfully.

The two women talked of other things for a while, fashions and shows and the births of babies. Alicia introduced that last topic, which clearly bored Elena, so when their food came she switched back to the first. "You hear things sometimes, Alicia. I don't know how, but you do. If you could give me an alert, even of just a day... Albert would look brilliant and he would want to reward me." She smiled. "He does that very well, when he's well motivated."

Alicia shrugged. "If I hear of anything, of course, darling. Sometimes someone drops a word. Nothing on a schedule, of course. My other thought is—" She gazed off into a white corner of the restaurant, which looked cool. "—to discredit the source. If this National Security Adviser is made to look like a fool personally, wouldn't that make the president question his advice? I've heard the man is quite a clod. Perhaps a dinner party—"

Elena was shaking her head. "Believe me, Albert has thought of that. But the President thinks of this Wilkerson man as sort of a backwoods prodigy, like Abraham Lincoln or Davy Crockett. Every time he uses the wrong fork or drinks from his water bowl, the President is more convinced that he is a genius. And he's the President's own genius, you know? He likes him more because he thinks he discovered him. The way I was with that tenor." She gave a little shiver of disgust. "Believe me, those illusions have great power."

"Oh well," Alicia said, shrugging. "I should just give up trying to give my friends advice. It never works."

"But you're such pleasant company," Elena said, squeezing her hand. "And somehow, I don't know, I just seem to think better around you."

Alicia dipped her eyes in gratitude. She waved off the dessert menu. Her work was done here, and for dessert she'd picked up a couple of tidbits of information she hadn't had before.

Leaving the table, she said, quite without irony, "Say hello to Imogen for me."

"Oh, I will. Thank you, darling." Imogen was the Secretary of State's wife—and Elena Valenciana's sister.

Craig Mortenson liked stuffy old clubs. There were too few of them any more, except in recent years they were making a slight comeback. Aging baby boomers embraced some of the fantasies of their parents' early lives, such as old men with cigars ruling the world from comfortable wingbacked chairs while a waiter brought brandy.

Craig, who was as often as not somewhere else in his mind, liked the comfort of noticing his surroundings and finding them so clichéd. The Russians did these things quite well. Sergei had found the perfect place, a short cab ride from his embassy. The two men sat in cozy isolation in a room full of heavy furniture, discreetly placed ferns, and tables of people who seemed equally disinclined to be overheard.

Alicia was the subtle member of the Mortenson family. Craig leaned back in his leather chair and said, "So, Sergei, will you people take over the world once we've withdrawn from it?"

Sergei Eisenstein looked pained. "Who wants it? Thank you for the headaches, no. You take it."

"Can we palm the whole thing off on the Chinese?"

Sergei shook his head, taking the joke seriously. "Even they are no longer unsophisticated enough to want world domination. No, it would have to be some madman, the kind the middle east and Africa seem to produce so well."

"Well, that won't do anyone any good. Come on, we want reasonable people running the store. Japan?"

Both men broke into laughter. It was a very pleasant lunch.

Jack managed to find an electronics store, even in this out of the way place, and bought a new personal game player. He looked over their stock of games, bought one, but then slipped one of his own out of his gym bag and put it in the machine. To Arden he said, "I need a few minutes to configure this. Why don't you see if you can scare up some transportation for us?"

"Yes, sir."

Jack smiled down at his game, smiling for her without looking up. Arden went wandering. Jack watched her depart, wondering if she was aware of his gaze, wondering so many things. When she had come into the jail he had been sure she was on the other side, because there was no other way she could rescue him. But then *she* hadn't rescued them; he had, more than she. It was very neatly managed, if it was, to let him think he'd pulled off the escape.

But there remained the fact that she had found him in the jail in the first place. That would not have been possible for a normal person, in normal ways.

Then Arden had ditched the French girl, an act of jealousy, humanizing her, then they had made love, which shouldn't have made a difference but did. His head spun.

But he had work to do. While Arden was gone Jack made other calls, first to his old friend Ronald, a valued member of the Circle who had contributed much to their coffers with fortunes made in the dot com world. His first words were, "Ronnie, are you safe?"

"Well, safer than some of us, because I'm not trying to contact that damned National Security Advisor."

"Yeah." Jack glanced down at his game. They conferred hastily about what each was doing to dig the Circle out of its current hole. Ronald was unsurprised to hear that Jack was near Salzburg. Then Jack asked, "Ronald, where's our money?"

"The Circle's? The Hornet treasury? Here and there. Why?"

Jack told him what he had learned about the planes that passed through America that one night. "I've already passed this on to the Chair and the Mortensons, etc., and no one can find a connection to any country. I've thought of one other organization that could have afforded that kind of project."

"Microsoft? Google?"

"Us, Ronald. We could afford it." Because the Circle was, among other things, a multi-billion dollar non-organization. "So I repeat. Where's our money?"

Three seconds' silence on the line showed how hard this idea had gripped Ronald, because Ronald could think very deeply while talking at the same time. In three languages. "Let me check."

"You do that, Warren."

Ronald chuckled. "Warren" was Jack's pet name for him, only Jack's. It referred both to Warren Buffett and to Warren

Worthington the III, who was the Angel in the X-Men, as well as the scion of a very wealthy family. It was a financial nickname.

Ronald would be on this quickly. Jack had given him what he liked best, a money angle to a huge puzzle.

Next Jack called Craig Mortenson, who answered the phone sounding jovial, which was odd. Oh, wait, no. Their world was coming to an end, America faced its worst crisis ever, villainy was both afoot and unknown. Yes, Craig would be having a high old time.

"Hello, Craig, it's Jack." Jack still had a hard time calling him by his first name, but "sir" would sound smarmy. "Quick question. Do we have a treasurer?"

"A treasurer? Do you need to send in your dues, Jack?"

"But seriously, folks."

"Yes. Well, of course the Chair oversees everything, but you can't reach her. I guess if we have anyone else who might hold that honorary title it would be Don Trimble."

"Professor Trimble? I never knew. Where can I reach him?"

"He's in Salzburg, dear boy."

"Salzburg!"

"Yes. And he's either learned everything by now or he's bumbling around helplessly. Why don't you look him up?"

"Maybe I will, if I get the chance. Anyone else I know on the scene?"

"Not that I know of. Alicia might know, especially by this time. Is that your phone beeping?"

Jack took the phone from his ear, glanced at the screen, and said, "That's her calling now, Craig. I'll—"

"Give her my love," Craig Mortenson said, and clicked off just as Jack was saying, "Where—?" So he took the other call. "Alicia, hi! It's so good to hear you. Are you calling from the White House?"

She chuckled, a mature woman's acknowledgment of a compliment. "I never go near the center of power, dear. The periphery is much more fun."

They talked for a minute of what sounded like idle chitchat but was actually a coded, densely-packed exchange of information. "Can I bring you anything from Europe?" Jack finally asked, prelude to ending the conversation.

"Yes, actually. You remember the trinket from Korea? The border stone? Do they have anything like that in Europe?"

"As a matter of fact..."

"Sooner would be much better than later, my dear. And can you give me a heads up when it's coming? I'm planning a party, and I'd like to wear it."

Jack thought quickly. He wasn't sure where he would be in an hour, let alone three days from now, and it would be much better to cut out the middle man, anyway. In the next sentence he dropped a phrase, "Alps peddler," which sounded perhaps like a reference to the Tour de France, but would actually put Alicia Mortenson in touch with his old friend Stevie, if— Jack laughed quietly to himself. He had almost thought, *If Alicia caught the hint.* As if Alicia Mortenson had ever missed a clue in her life.

Alicia's voice colored like a slight blush. "Thank you, dear boy," she said, accepting a compliment, as if she had heard his mental exchange with himself.

"I'll try to stay in touch," Jack said. "But don't worry if I don't. By the way, I was just talking to Craig. He sends his love."

"Did he? That's odd, I'm on my way to meet him now. He could tell me himself."

"Does he?" Jack asked, his voice sounding childlike, unable to stop himself from asking for a little insight into the most intriguing couple he knew, the most complete marriage.

Alicia laughed again. "Oh, there may be a bit of blather about what a fascinating creature I am, especially if he had a brandy after lunch. That never hurts. Take care, Jack."

Jack looked up into Arden's eyes. She had returned sooner than he had expected. That next to last sentence of Alicia's sounded like advice. Jack didn't smile, nor did Arden. Their eyes held on each other's. Jack's lips began to curl upward. Hers didn't.

Into the phone, he said. "'Bye, Alicia. Be—" He'd planned to say *Be careful*, but that would be silly. Just in time he finished the sentence, "—happy."

After he'd hung up, Arden said, "The Mortensons? What are they up to?"

"They didn't say." Jack put his phone away. "Couldn't find a way to get to Salzburg?"

Alicia gave him a frowning smile, as if he'd told a joke that wasn't funny. She gestured toward the curb, where a baby blue Mercedes 360 sat idling.

"That's great," Jack said, "except renting a car is going to leave a trail that might be prob—"

"Oh, thanks, Professor. Teach me more. And should I buy a pop-up ad on Yahoo saying 'Arden and Jack ask any assassins in the vicinity of Salzburg, German, to contact them'?"

"Sorry. But then did—" He didn't want to suggest she'd stolen the car, which would undoubtedly set her off again.

"A man loaned it to me. And no, Jack, I didn't give him my real name. *Or* give him anything significant in exchange." She frowned at him, and Jack spread his hands, apologizing for a remark he hadn't made.

They climbed into the car. The padded seats accepted them like lovers who had stayed away too long. "But you were only gone, like, twenty-eight minutes," Jack said.

"Do you want me to tell you all about how I got the car?"

"Sure, that would be entertaining," Jack said, doubting her story would have many intersecting points with the truth. By this time he understood that Arden was quite aware of her air of mystery. She cultivated it. Of course, they all did, to different extents, but not with each other. That was one way she was different, outside the Circle, extraordinary.

Jack took her hand for a moment, raised it to his lips and kissed her knuckles. He smiled, out at the road, not at her, as if a lovely memory had just crossed his mind. From the corner of his eye he could see Arden smiling too, but still with that sadness in the heart of the smile. She was one of those women who started thinking about the end even while a relationship was still new, he thought.

"Salzburg?"

Jack nodded. "But first I need an Internet connection, and fast."

CHAPTER 11

Level 5

There was an Internet cafe on the outskirts of Salzburg. There was always an Internet cafe, or a hotel offering free connections, or a wireless network to breach. It would not be long before the Internet would simply be in the air, you could think your way into it. And it into you. It was a tempting fantasy. But Jack, one of the best-wired people on Earth, would hate that. He wanted his thoughts to himself.

As he was launching the game in the café, leaving Arden the task of ordering German coffee, he began searching for his usual partner on-line. As Arden sat beside him, he muttered a curse.

"Am I not giving you enough space?"

"The person I usually play with isn't there."

"Is that so important? I thought you just liked the game. Is it a competition thing?"

Jack turned to her. Her eyes were close to his. They looked different now, her blue, patterned eyes. He thought he could see a little deeper into them. Sex gives that illusion. On the other hand, he'd been as close to Madeline as any person he'd ever known, or thought he had been, and now he didn't know if he'd known her at all.

Arden must have seen something change in his eyes. She took his hand, under the tabletop of the booth, and raised one eyebrow. Now she looked amused. His eyes had gone sad with memory and that had made Arden happy. He wondered if they were going to be like that, on an emotional seesaw. The expression didn't just mean up and down, it meant that one was *going* up as the other went down. There could be only a finite amount of happiness between them, it had to be shared.

He smiled. Somehow having been intimate with Arden made him feel bad—sad or guilty or untrustworthy or maybe just uneasy. But she was a lovely girl, and much more. She had depths and twisty byways to her mind he could explore for decades. They could be like Alicia and Craig Mortenson, except that those two knew each other so well that one stood up before the other even said *Let's leave*, and he thought he could spend a lifetime with Arden and never know her mind. Why was that?

"It's all right, Jack," she said softly, still with that little smile.

"I wish you wouldn't say that—forgiving me in advance for whatever I might do, as if it's no big thing. Let me tell you something about myself, Arden, especially since we haven't had much conversation. I've never lost a friend except to death. Well, that's not true, but certainly not over sex. I'm still friends with everyone I ever liked who liked me."

"Are you telling me you and I will always be friends?"

"If we ever get to be."

Her smile broadened. "Like you and Rachel?"

Jack tilted his head, reprimanding her. "I don't betray my friends' trust, either."

Her smile lost its power for an instant. He thought she was jealous. "I guess that tells me the answer."

He shook his head. "No, it doesn't. Maybe Rachel or I, or both of us, wouldn't want people to think we *didn't* ever make love. Maybe one of us is gay, or both of us, and we're the only people who know it about each other. Maybe there was a lost—" He faltered. "—time, or—I'm not going to explore all the possibilities with you, that's the point. Why don't we talk about you and me instead?"

"Okay." But she leaned back from him and took her hand from his. This was page one, chapter one of the body language textbook. Why didn't Arden want to talk? Did she not want to talk about herself, or about him? Interesting...

His game beeped. Jack glanced at the screen, which now said, "WANNA PLAY?"

He tapped a Y in reply. What time was it in America?

Arden sighed. Without glancing at her, Jack said, "You didn't want to talk anyway. And this is important, I'm sorry."

She was silenced for a moment, an extraordinary event, not knowing which of his statements to answer. Then she leaned against his shoulder as he tapped keys. *Want to play Level 5?* he asked his unseen opponent.

"How can this be important? Is it the championship?"

Jack laughed quietly. At some point thick white mugs of coffee had appeared in front of them. He hoped it hadn't been while he was revealing world secrets. Jack took a quick sip and liked the cup. Heavy, substantial, no flimsy Starbucks plastic or paper. The cup was better than the coffee, in fact.

The answer to his question appeared on his screen: *There is no Level 5.*

Jack grinned. *I have the European edition,* he typed. *Follow me.*

It was almost as if he had his opponent by the hand as they jumped to the level they'd already been playing, and the other character followed Jack's assassin-with-no-loyalties character to a secret door behind the refrigerator in a run-down café. Not unlike the one in which Jack and Arden sat, as a matter of fact.

Jack had designed Level 5 himself, very hastily, partly in his mind while he was alone in jail, then on the train while Arden slept. So it was a hazy level, not very well filled-in. But 'twas enough, 'twould serve.

There was a pause while his opponent read the rules of this level. What was important at this part of the game was that the two characters would be separated. Each would have a home base, which he could take as much time as he wanted to explore and even alter to some extent, before venturing out in search of his adversary.

While his opponent read, Jack turned to Arden again. "I don't get it," she said.

He shrugged. "Not much to it. I really don't know what to do next in Salzburg, and this relaxes me, helps me think."

"I could relax you, I think."

It was funny the way she said that, trying to be sexy and trying not to sound as if she were trying. Jack smiled at her, not trying to convey an erotic response at all himself. Arden shrugged, looking more girlish, and smiled at herself. "That would be wonderful," he said, but in a way that sounded even to himself kind of dismissive.

Arden stood up. "I'll go look around. How long will you be?"

Jack glanced at his screen, where his opponent was tiptoeing through his own territory. Even on-screen, Jack could see his wariness. He grinned. "Half an hour, tops."

Rachel Green liked being part of a team. It had been a long time. Being a Circle member on foreign assignment—or a foreign member of the Circle, she was never sure which; it had led her into philosophical discussions in her own mind, which she had never resolved, such as Was the Circle a country unto itself?—was inherently lonely. Anyone who might act friendly to you could be a foe. Most of the time when you tried to make friends with someone, it was for a reason, which meant the ensuing "friendship" was an artificial construct, even if she genuinely liked the person. You never have friendships again like in school days. At least that was Rachel's experience. As for lovers—well, it was like she imagined being a spy in the Cold War days. Give yourself to someone wholeheartedly, but with a knife under the pillow and an escape plan.

The way some men were naturally, she chuckled to herself.

Her second in command, Captain Bernard Lowenstein, raised an eyebrow at her, asking her to share the joke. "Nervous chuckle," she whispered.

He nodded understandingly. "I get gas from nervousness."

"Great time to tell me." Because they were walking through a concrete culvert, a very large pipe, barely wide enough for two people to walk abreast.

"It's why I always have new partners," Captain Bernard Lowenstein said, and they both laughed.

To say Bernie was her second in command was misleading. Rachel had an honorary rank of Colonel, but no place in the chain of command. Her title was Consultant. Not Security Consultant or any other specification. Bernie had pointed this out and assumed it meant Rachel was an expert on everything. "There's this girl I like who works in a flower shop. What should I take her if I ask her out on a first date? Chocolates?"

"Flowers," Rachel had answered. "You know she likes them."

"But then what if she asks me where I got them and I have to say I bought them from a rival so I could surprise her? Don't you think that would make her mad?"

Rachel had spread her hands, indicating the discussion had gotten too silly for her. But Bernie had persisted, shrugging and quoting. "If you have two Jews, you'll have five opinions. You owe me at least one more opinion, consultant."

That was what Rachel missed about being part of a team: banter; easy camaraderie. The unspoken, unthought belief that they were all on the same team. Your colleague had your back, and vice versa. This feeling grew from talk as silly as flowers and first dates.

Now such a feeling was important, as she and Captain Bernie went slowly through the conduit, which was getting smaller. This drainage line, according to Salzburg city diagrams, eventually turned and went under the public square where the chief executives of eight nations would be meeting in the only public forum of this conference. Surely someone had checked it out, but Rachel wanted to be sure.

The concrete tube got shorter and narrower, until the two of them couldn't go side by side. "Which of us will go in front?" Captain Lowenstein asked.

"Which do you think, farter?"

While Bernie laughed again, Rachel got down on hands and knees and crawled ahead. She hated this part. Anyone who didn't wouldn't be human, in her opinion. She began to have fantasies that she was crawling back into the womb, or the heart of the earth. Behind her, Lowenstein was just grunting, his head occasionally bumping her feet.

Then she stopped dead. There were sounds ahead. When she stopped the sounds persisted for a second or two, then also stopped. Rachel started slowly forward, and the sounds started slowly up again. Must be echoes. But she didn't believe it. This echo had an odor.

She turned on a flashlight just as someone else did. The two beams clashed like light sabers, revealing nothing but the lights. Rachel lowered hers, so that it would illumine her face. That took as much courage as anything she had ever done. In this confined space, her partner couldn't provide her any cover, and she couldn't see to defend herself.

"Israeli?" came a male voice from only a few feet ahead of her.

Rachel nodded. The voice laughed. Then the man turned his own light on himself, revealing craggy but youthful features, curly dark hair, and very dark eyes. "Syrian," he said with an odd sort of sneer, then added, "Ill met by flashlight."

The tunnel seemed to shrink even more. Their two countries had been bombing each other two months ago. At the moment—as of ten minutes ago, that is—a very fragile cease-fire prevailed, which militants on both sides were trying to destroy. This was one of the primary reasons for the peace summit. But few people believed there would ever be peace between these countries. Certainly there would never be any trust between their armed forces.

Rachel heard guns being eased out of holsters. She left her own in place. This was a situation for a voice. But her throat had gone completely dry. Behind her, she could hear Bernie trying to wriggle forward, but her body blocked his. When the Syrians shot her, maybe Bernie could use her as a shield, to fire back.

"What's back down that way?" she asked in a hoarse voice, stalling for time.

"Nothing," said the Syrian. Then after a pause, "Do you believe me?"

Something was wrong here. Rachel's mind raced. Then she realized what was so odd. They were both speaking English. And his "ill-met" remark had a very English source: Shakespeare.

She turned her flashlight back on her own face. "Princeton," she said distinctly.

There was a moment of silence, as if she had said something incomprehensible. Then there was an explosive laugh from the darkness in front of her. The Syrian pointed his flashlight at his own face. "Columbia," he laughed.

They crawled forward, almost face to face, and shook hands in the old student-power way. It was hard to study each other's faces in the moving shadows, but she thought he looked familiar. He may have thought the same thing. "Hassan," he said, and Rachel told him not only her name but her year of graduation. Very briefly they reminisced. "What do you miss most?" Rachel asked, and Hassan sighed. "New York. Central Park. Chinatown." "The Museum of Modern Art," Rachel said, and he nodded. Then Hassan looked up, at the culvert barely overhead. "Sleeping through the night," he murmured.

Rachel nodded too. Then she spoke in a businesslike way. "Both our Presidents are going to be on that platform. Does this culvert go directly under it?"

"Close enough, if the bomb is powerful enough."

After a moment she sighed. "I have to go through. Make sure you didn't leave anything."

"And I have to do the same."

"We are carrying only sidearms," Rachel pointed out.

"As are we. Do you want to frisk me?"

"I suppose there's no other choice. How far is the other end?"

"Perhaps eighty meters. Thirty meters past the closest point to the stage."

Rachel pointed back the way she'd come with a gesture of her head. "The other exit's about fifty meters back. You've got the better deal."

The Syrian grinned. "I don't know about that. Ready?"

"Meet you up top," Rachel said, and began moving forward very slowly.

By shifting to the side, they could pass each other with their bodies sliding along each other. Hassan took the opportunity to feel her all over, including spots where she could not possibly have been carrying a bomb big enough. But Rachel did the same. Sure, they'd made nice in the tunnel, but how could she completely trust someone who'd gone to Columbia?

The four got past each other nervously, and in the case of the men who frisked each other, with great embarrassment. By contrast, slithering the rest of the way down the drainage tunnel was simple. Rachel and Captain Bernie kept their flashlights on and did their jobs, checking the tunnel thoroughly. Rachel had equipment, some of it of her own design, that would supposedly detect explosives even if they were made of plastic. They found nothing.

Rachel could count on the fingers of one hand such relief as she'd felt when she emerged from the other end of that tunnel. The relief was physical, composed of the nerve endings in her skin exhilarating with freedom, the smell of fresh air, even her scraped elbows feeling good at no longer grinding along concrete. But there was more to the relief than that. She had been afraid this end of the tunnel would be blocked, that they would have to crawl back the way they'd come, and by the time they got there the Syrian would have blocked the only other exit, too.

But they were free, they had done their jobs, and she felt confident that this path, at least, was closed to terrorists.

"Stay here," she said to Bernie. Then she walked back across the square. In another day and a half this area would be filled with people, watching eight world leaders appear onstage together, some of whom had never been that close together before. Tonight the place was just crawling with security people. That was the problem. There were uniforms from nearly a dozen countries, some of those countries nearly at war with each other, others mistrustful. Too much security was worse than too little. They all had to keep checking, then checking what the other security teams had checked.

She thought she recognized the body of the man walking to meet her. She had known it intimately, but only in the dark and for a minute or so. But he smiled as he drew closer, and she knew he'd been thinking the same thing. Hassan swept off his cap and bowed. He was unshaven, dark, wearing an olive uniform that didn't tell her much. Rachel was thinking how bad she must look, and possibly smell.

"Hello, Princeton," he said. "Now what?"

"Seal those two exits, right now, while we know the tunnel's safe. I left my captain back there. You left your man at the other end?"

"Of course."

Rachel looked around. The place looked strangely like a military compound, but one put together by a boy who didn't have enough soldiers of the same uniform to make a full army, so he had mixed them all together. "Let's get two people from two other security forces to accompany us, and go and seal them now."

"That's three countries per end?" Hassan nodded. "Sounds about right. I pick French."

"All right. I pick British."

"Ah, you're just trying to throw me off. You were sure I thought you would say American."

Rachel smiled up at him. "You and I are the Americans, Hassan."

He chuckled, but made no move to walk away. "What?" Rachel said.

"It was hard to see down there," the Syrian said quietly, studying her. Rachel, who had an unfortunate tendency to blush in such moments, tried to control her skin. "I was afraid we would get up top and I would be embarrassed at having been so close to someone who—you know, I wouldn't want to be seen with in public."

"God, you must have women crawling all over you back home. Mr. Smooth. Look, I just slithered a hundred and thirty meters through a drainage tunnel. I'm not—"

He must have thought she was apologizing for her appearance, which was not at all where she was going with the sentence. "Oh no," Hassan said, reaching out to touch her arm. "I just wanted to say that you are someone I would be happy to grope even not in the line of duty."

"Catch me if I swoon." Then Rachel chuckled in spite of herself. "Okay, Columbia. After we get the tunnel spiked, you want to get a beer?"

After all, it was part of her lifelong job to make contacts, wherever she could. Rachel had her limits, but having a beer with an enemy who might be a potential friend was well within those limits.

Hassan smiled at her. "Boola boola," he said.

Rachel kept her eyes on him. "I think that's Yale."

He grinned. "I was giving you a test. I was checking you out."

"I think you did that already, about twenty feet below where we're standing."

He saluted her with another grin, and they went off to find other soldiers.

"You wouldn't believe the problem I'm having," Stevie said.

"It's too easy?" Alicia Mortenson guessed.

Stevie stared at his computer screen. At this distance there was a lag time of a second or two. He waited to see Mrs. Mortenson's smirk. When her face hadn't changed its expression of polite interest—slightly raised eyebrows, slightly cocked head, slightly smiling lips—he concluded she actually hadn't changed expressions. "All right, I guess you *can* believe it," he said grumpily.

"I'm sorry, Stevie. I've just been at this a bit longer than you have. And I hope I understand the world a little bit."

But I'm here on the scene and you're not, Stevie thought. Oh well. "Yes, it's a little too easy. I'm finding a lot more pro-American sentiment here in Poland than I thought. The same as in Prague. There are more people than you'd think—well, than most people would think—who remember Communism, and think America put an end to it. I'm trying just to put a lid on it, because Jack said to wait until I—"

"Stevie?" Alicia interrupted. Her face shimmered on his MacBook screen. He might be about to lose his connection. "Take the lid off," she said.

"Oh. Really? Is Jack—"

"It will be okay. I promise."

"Yes, ma'am. I'd say day after tomorrow. Maybe Friday. Some people want to wait for the weekend to riot, you know."

"That will work fine. Good work, young man."

"Thank you. Mrs. Mortenson?"

She raised that one eyebrow a tad higher. It occurred to Stevie that Alicia Mortenson read people so well, and had been doing it for so long, that she must have turned down the volume of her own expressions and body language. She expected her listener—at least, a listener like Stevie—to read her well.

"Where's Jack?" Stevie finished. "I haven't heard from him since he was here. He's okay, isn't he?"

"Oh yes. I just talked to him."

But for a moment he had seen something flicker across her face. A blink, a pause. The lowered eyelids of anxiety. Maybe it was just a trick of the time lag. Because if someone like Alicia Mortenson was scared, it was time to panic.

She reassured him again, and as he was asking about her husband the connection was broken. Stevie shrugged, closed his laptop, and went back to his job of talking ugly about America in cafes and union halls. He thought he would set off the demonstration within two days, and just hoped he didn't get beaten up in the process.

Craig was early to meet his wife. They were to meet on the mall near six o'clock, in the shadow of the Jefferson Memorial. Corny, but Craig liked corny. He stood for a few minutes staring up at the standing statue, the slightly lidded eyes that really looked as if thoughts were passing behind them. Thomas Jefferson had not been a member of the Circle, but Craig had a private theory that Jefferson had inspired its formation—behind the scenes, more subtle than the masters of subtlety. There was absolutely no evidence of this, which to Craig confirmed his theory. Because if a man like Jefferson set out to do something secretly, there *wouldn't* be any evidence, would there? Except for those children of Sally Hemmings', of course, but that was a different matter. Craig held another extremely private theory that Jefferson had wanted to be found out on that score, as well.

Brooding about the founding of nations and the secrets of

founding fathers, he began to have an idea. As he thought he walked, something he often did, and quite unconsciously. It was not unusual for him to find himself miles from home and with a few lost hours at the end of some deep meditation.

His mind turned, as it often did, to the middle east. There seemed no way out of the Palestinian-Israeli conflict: two peoples claimed the same land as home. But Craig Mortenson didn't believe in insoluble problems. This, after all, was the man who had brought down Communism. Something needed to be done to lift all the combatants' eyes from their immediate conflict. Give them a larger conflict, perhaps? *My enemy's enemy is my friend.* Could there be a common enemy for the Jews and Arabs? Who would that be, and who would be willing to play that role, perhaps for a generation?

Craig continued to think, his feet continued to wander, and by the time he had solved the middle east problem he realized that it was dark and he didn't know where he was. Looking around, he no longer saw crowds. Slowly—coming back from miles and years—he oriented himself. He had walked down toward Lafayette Park. Alicia would be waiting for him. With that amused look of hers. She would spend the time communing with Mr. Jefferson and her own thoughts and wouldn't be angry, especially after he told her what he'd come up with on his ramble.

He turned and the shorter, paler of the two thugs stuck a gun into his stomach. "Wallet!" he snapped.

"Certainly," Craig said, holding his hands out to the sides in a placating manner. *Idiot,* he thought to himself. Wandering into a dangerous area like a tourist. And looking lost in thought, the perfect target.

So he stopped looking like that. His eyes hardened. He looked into the robber's face. The man was thin and pale, blond hair poking out from beneath a navy watch cap. His hand holding the gun was steady, and there was no nervousness in his gaze. *Oh, shit.* This was an experienced criminal, not a druggie with an impulse. But maybe Craig could use that to advantage.

"My wallet contains very little cash, and only one credit card with a small limit and large identity theft protection. You could do better than this."

He looked past the man holding the gun on him. The partner was larger, African-American, equally calm, with almost dead-looking eyes. His hands were in the pockets of his coat, which looked as if it had come from Goodwill after two or three owners. But something didn't fit. Black-and-white teams were common in the movies and police forces, much less so among criminals in real life. Criminals usually came from classes that harbored prejudices, and if they had spent time in prison, as most criminals had, they would have fallen into groups segregated by gang membership.

Glancing down as if at his wallet, Craig saw the black man's shoes. They were black loafers, polished and tasseled.

"My gratitude would be worth a great deal more than the contents of this wallet. If you wouldn't mind escorting me back to my hotel..."

The gunman grinned. He didn't even glance over his shoulder at his supposed partner. "Sure. Let's go."

Craig turned, taking a quick survey of the area. They were at the bottom of a small hill. There were people within a hundred yards, but not many. He was quite sure these two wouldn't let him get to the top of the rise. Was there any message he could send, any clue he could leave?

But as they continued to walk he came to a worse realization than that he was about to be murdered. They were using him to lure Alicia. They would let him get back to the Jefferson Memorial, let her see him, before they made their move. Crowds of sightseers wouldn't matter to these two.

Craig stumbled and fell. Neither man made a move to help him. In fact they stepped back. The one with the gun growled, "Get up," and his partner took his hands out of his pockets.

Craig came up much faster than they expected, with two handfuls of mud. He flung them both as he kicked at the gunman's gun hand.

He had been right about the African-American man, who had a fastidious sort of look. He flinched away from the thrown mud. The gunman didn't, so it hit him right in the face, obscuring his vision as Craig spun to the side. The gun fired, but Craig was no longer standing where he had been. The shot missed. He kicked the man in the crotch, reaching for the gun. He was much faster than they'd expected.

But that was why they'd brought back-up. The black man lifted the automatic in his own hand and fired twice. Both shots hit Craig Mortenson in the chest.

And a scream pierced the night.

The sound didn't come from the victim. It froze the two assassins for a second, then they turned and looked up. Alicia Mortenson stood at the top of the hill, an expression of utmost horror on her face. The two men started running toward her.

Alicia had accomplished what she'd wanted, distracted the men from her husband. Could Craig survive two shots? At least they weren't shooting him any more.

But now the men came relentlessly toward her.

Level 5

In Phase 2 of Level 5, Jack typed on his screen, *we switch strongholds.*

Words appeared slowly on his screen: *you didn't tell me that rule.*

Jack made the symbol for a shrug. *it's just a game. here we go.*

The figures of the opponents disappeared from the screen. Seconds later each player found his character in the other character's headquarters. The other player, who Jack was certain now was Dennis Wilkerson, the National Security Advisor, began looking around his new environment curiously. Jack sat unmoving. On his split screen, his character just stood, hands at his sides.

It didn't take long. Within five seconds the NSA's character took a wrong step, the floor dropped out from under him, and he fell to his death on a bed of spikes. The character reappeared, having lost that round. This time he opened a door, just trying to get out, and a swinging blade cut off his head.

In his own mind, Jack could hear the NSA screaming in outrage. *What's happening?* Jack typed on the screen, *I told you you could alter your home court.* And he closed his game on his opponent's protests.

That was as much as he could do. Jack felt helpless. He looked around and wondered where he was. Arden had left him here. Where had she gone? Jack went outside and began walking toward the heart of Salzburg. He didn't want to get too close. Security would grow tighter with every hundred yards he traveled now. But he hoped to find Rachel. He sensed she was here.

The night seemed darker than it should be, the streets less crowded. He heard a strange murmur that he couldn't quite shape into words. Maybe the European wind spoke a different language. Jack had the feeling of being surrounded by an invisible crowd. In fact, there were very few people on the streets, which seemed odd.

Down at the corner a policeman in a light blue uniform watched Jack steadily, to the exclusion of all else on the street. Jack's instinct was to walk straight toward the man, until he remembered he might actually be wanted for the incident in Nice. So he turned instead and crossed the street, as if toward a restaurant that looked like the only open business on the block.

The street felt old under his feet, worn down smooth. The buildings were old too, but strong and stylish, stones with modest curlicues of architecture. As much time as he had spent abroad, Jack was American to his bones, and Salzburg made him feel strange. He expected to be stopped and asked for his "papers" at any moment. The citizens who passed averted their eyes, and if there were two of them they muttered just below the level of Jack's hearing. A good place to start a case of paranoia if you didn't already have one.

He didn't want to go into that café. Its door looked like a mouth, a trap from which he would not emerge. He could break right instead, dart down the street. The policeman would blow his whistle and a dozen more might appear. Just as he thought he'd try it anyway, a woman in a trench coat came around that corner to his right and just stood there. She was slender and young and Jack might have been able to take her, but then again maybe not, as he watched the efficient movements of her hands as she lit a cigarette. Also a slight droop in a pocket that ruined the drape of her overcoat.

He went into the restaurant. There would be a back way out. Maybe he could call Arden.

Jack stopped just inside the doorway, took a quick scan of the tables, started to move through them, then his mind did a quick rewind and he stopped dead again. He thought he'd recognized the portion of a man's cheek he'd glimpsed beneath a hat. But mentally Jack shook his head. Couldn't be. And even if it was, he needed to steer away.

But then the man he'd thought he recognized was smiling and waving him over. Jack stood there thinking hard, wanting to get away, but then saw that the man was about to stand up and call his name, so Jack hurried over and sat down. He stuck out his hand and said as quietly as possible, but with surprise in his voice, "Professor Trimble? What are you doing here?"

"Jack! Well met. Didn't expect you here. Why didn't someone tell me? We could have joined forces. Good show you came, actually. See those men in the corner? I've been surveilling them. Now it looks as if I was waiting to meet a friend instead of following them in here. I think they might have been starting to get suspicious."

In nearly every other situation, Don Trimble would have been one of the least suspicious people on earth. He had been an Economics professor at Yale when Jack went there, and also a Circle member. Jack had taken one class from him, been impressed by the man's brilliance but barely able to stay awake til the end of the semester. But Trimble was deep inside the leadership of the Circle, much deeper than Jack, in both recruitment and long-term planning.

No one would ever have used him for a field agent, though. He was tall and thin and somewhat clumsy, his hands and feet like the unruly children of distracted parents. With his height and his baldness he stood out in a crowd; his long nose seemed to tremble when he was excited. At least he was wearing a hat now, and a trench coat. Secret Agent Man.

"Who are they?" Jack asked. He made some sort of gesture at the waiter, which perhaps didn't translate well. Moments later a beer appeared at his elbow, in an elaborate stein.

"Not sure," Trimble murmured, staring straight at the small group at the corner table. "Two of them are affiliated with Al-Quaeda, but one is French and two others Asian. An odd grouping, and at least three of them affiliated with terrorist organizations. I've been following them for two days."

If that were so, the men must have spotted the professor a day and nine-tenths ago. Now they saw Jack, too. Jack turned his back on them. "What do you think they're up to?" he muttered.

"Pretty plain. That summit begins tomorrow. It's our one chance to lure the President out of this ridiculous turtle-posture he's put us in. To get him to re-engage with the world. Groups like Al-Quaeda would do anything to stop that. When he comes they plan to kill him, pure and simple." Professor Trimble looked feverish for a moment. He had never been this animated as a teacher. "It is absolutely imperative that we head off any such terrorist plot *and* that the President comes here. If he doesn't, we've lost. The mission with which we've been entrusted for generations is a failure. If he comes and gets killed we've lost too. We've got to take out whatever all the terrorists on earth are planning, and we have less than twenty-four hours."

Jack said, "Absolutely," without much enthusiasm, then looked around again. "Any other leads here?"

Trimble calmed down and straightened his coat. His forehead creased. "Just in the last few hours I've noticed a young woman flitting about. Very young. Light brown hair, blue eyes, a quick step, a little reminiscent smile on her face once in a while. She's been in and out of the area too fast for me to—"

"That would be Arden," Jack said. He couldn't help smiling himself at the "reminiscent smile" in Professor Trimble's description. "Arden Spindler."

"Ah. Knew she looked familiar. She's up to something,

though. I'm not sure she's absolutely to be trusted. Have you ever done anything with her?"

For a moment the question left Jack at a loss. Then he managed, "As a matter of fact, we're working together right now."

"Oh. Well, then you'll know what she's up to. I saw her earlier, going into a building down the street. Odd sort of place. I called to her, but she didn't hear me. Anyway, I've had to concentrate on these fellows."

"Have you seen Rachel here, Professor? Rachel Greene?"

"Rachel? Oh yes, the Israeli girl. Your friend back in school, wasn't she, Jack? No, haven't heard a thing about her. Is she supposed to be here?" Trimble looked away from him as he spoke.

"I thought so, but maybe she's coming later." Jack slumped a little more in his chair. He looked all around the restaurant. Six occupied tables, out of a possible dozen. The bartender was cleaning a glass with a bar rag—the same glass he'd been cleaning since Jack had walked in. The restaurant patrons were couples or groups, but mostly men. None of them looked overtly at Jack.

"I need to ask you something," Jack said softly to Don Trimble, which caused the professor to look at him intently. "But I need more urgently to find the men's room. Know where it is?"

Trimble gestured a direction with his head, a gesture broad enough for everyone in the restaurant to see, as Jack had hoped. "Down that little hallway, I think."

"Thanks. Be right back."

Jack stood up, moving like a man with a rather urgent mission, not meeting any eyes. He entered the short hallway, momentarily out of sight of everyone. Two doors at the end of the hall had symbols on them, broad enough to understand. Jack instead took the first door he came to on the right. It was locked, but not very sturdily. A few moments' manipulation got him through it. Jack went inside, found himself in a dark, empty office, and opened the door a crack to look back out into the corridor he'd just left. In only a few seconds three men came into the hallway. They all walked resolutely toward the doors at the far end. Two of them went into the men's room and one into the women's.

Jack closed the office door and looked around. Heavy curtains hung behind the desk. Jack went and pulled them open and found a window, to his relief. He raised it shakily, trying to be quiet, and slipped out. He stood for a moment in the alley and closed the window behind him. He glanced down the alley that would lead to the back of the restaurant, but that was the direction the men who had gone into the restrooms would be going. So Jack turned and ran, fast, the other direction, toward the street from which he'd come, hoping that anyone who'd been watching him would have shifted to have a view of the restaurant.

They hadn't. When he was within twenty yards of the street that young woman stepped around the corner and stood waiting for him, hands in her trenchcoat pockets. She didn't smile or otherwise acknowledge that he was coming.

Jack skidded to a halt. Trench coat woman wouldn't be alone. He turned, saw a fire escape back that way, and headed toward it. Just as he reached the bottom, though, he looked up and saw the man on the roof at the top of the fire escape. These people knew his habits.

A bullet pinged off the metal next to him. Jack ran the only direction he could, across the alley, where another window beckoned. Covering his head with his arms, Jack dived through it.

Forces scrambled into motion. The woman disappeared, heading around to find another entrance to the building. At the other end of the building, half a dozen more men headed into it from that direction. They would have the first floor blanketed in seconds, then close in.

In a large room a few blocks away, Bruno Benjamin sat in an overstuffed chair and smiled at one of the screens in front of him. "This is so much fun," he said aloud to no one. "What kind of idiot gets any satisfaction out of a video game?" He turned a knob and spoke into a small microphone. "He'll re-emerge from the same window. Be ready."

On the screen, after a beat of four or five seconds, Jack's head came out of the window he'd dived through. He looked both ways down the alley, which seemed quiet now. Slowly, trying not to make a sound, Jack climbed back out and dropped down into the alley.

"Jack, old friend, you are so predictable," Bruno said, and sat back and folded his hands over his stomach and enjoyed himself, watching the screen.

Jack felt safe for the moment. But which way? They were down there to the left, down to the right, they might have left people in place while they searched the building at his back. He would have to bluff or be faster than a bullet...

Wait a minute. What about going back into the restaurant the same way he'd come out? Find another way out on the other side of the building. No one would ever suspect him of going back to his starting place.

Acting on the thought as soon as he had it, Jack started quickly across the alley, on tiptoes. He tripped on something and fell to the left, which saved his life, as a bullet went through the space where he'd just been standing.

Uh. Jack heard the shot, heard the bullet slam off the pavement, but didn't know where it had come from. He looked both ways down the alley, saw no one. Then he remembered, just in time, the other direction. He jumped to the side just as another bullet filled the space he'd just vacated.

This time Jack looked up. The guy at the top of the fire escape had stayed in position. His handgun at the end of his arm, he fired again.

Jack ran the only direction he could, to right under the fire escape. It cut off the guy's angle. But Jack had nowhere to go. The window into the restaurant office was six feet away, a gap that would kill him, because the shooter above was focused on it. Nor could Jack stay safely where he was. The trembling of the metal ladder beside him told him the shooter was descending.

As Jack hesitated, his situation only got worse. The gunman above him paused long enough to fire into the window through which Jack had dived across the alley. The bullet was loud, ricocheting and echoing within the building. It would alert the people inside. The man fired three more times, just to make as much noise as possible. Then Jack heard the clatter as the automatic weapon's clip fell to pavement beside him.

That meant he had a second to act. Jack leaped out, headed toward the nearest window. But as he did, he heard the distinct click from above of the weapon being reloaded. Jack was still a few seconds away from that window, which he had so carefully closed. He knew he wouldn't make it.

Well, maybe it was time to take a bullet. See if he could survive that. If he couldn't, all this would be someone else's problem. He had already done all he could.

The problem was, he *didn't* think anyone else could handle the world's situation.

Before he leaped he glanced upward again, to see exactly where his assailant was. The man was coming down the fire escape rapidly, holding his gun pointed skyward. Then Jack looked past him, and was amazed. There was another head up there on the roof, looking over.

Jack leaned outward to get a better look, stepping out of the shelter of the fire escape. That made the gunman pause in his descent and lean outward too, to get a better aim. Jack seemed so distracted that the shooter took his time, aiming downward carefully. Just as he pulled the trigger the concrete block fell on his head. The concrete block Arden had just dropped from the roof above.

The man's hand jerked, the shot went astray, and the gun fell. Jack caught it in mid-air and began scrambling up the fire escape. After one flight he stuck the gun in his waistband, because the former gunman was clearly unconscious, slumped over the rail. As Jack passed him on the fire escape he resisted the slight urge to push the man over. Instead he left him there dangling, and went on up to the roof. Arden's face had disappeared, but she was still up there when he jumped over the low balustrade onto the roof.

"Where did you come from?"

"Another fire escape on the other side," she said shortly.

"But how? How did you know?"

Arden was scrambling up the steep roof and Jack followed, staring at her butt that was hiked into the air as she went up the roof on hands and feet.

"Saw the people assembled around this building and thought you must be the target inside. Especially since this is the only restaurant open for blocks around. Come on."

In his armchair several blocks away, Bruno sat forward, leaning toward the screen. "A new player," he said musingly. "Will she save Jack? Yet again?" He turned to a console close to his right hand, drew out a phone, but let it dangle in his hand as he continued to stare at the screen, as at the good part of a favorite movie.

At the peak of the roof Jack stopped and looked over the other side. The other side of the roof was just as steep, and there was no balustrade at the bottom to stop their descent, just the edge of the roof and a long drop. They needed a rope. He turned to Arden to ask if she'd come prepared for this. She, though, paused for just a moment, standing on the very tip of the roof in a way that made him nervous, then she moved a foot to the left, sat down, said, "I think it's about here," and gave herself a gentle push. She began sliding down the steep roof, picking up speed. At the bottom she didn't even try to grab the edge, just threw up her hands as she went over, shooting out far too far to grab any fire escape attached to the wall.

"Arden!" Jack screamed. A sickening feeling spread from his stomach, as if he were the one falling. He felt as if he were.

He lurched toward the spot where she'd disappeared, almost fell over himself, barely recovered his balance. He wanted to get to her, wanted to save her as she had saved him so many times. But there was no good way down from this roof peak. The roof was too steep. That's what had caused Arden's downfall. Jack turned around so that he hung feet first toward that drop, stretched out as long as he could while holding onto the roof peak, then let go.

He started sliding down, hitting his face, his elbows, his knees, clutching for handholds. He slowed himself with his feet and his hands, at the cost of skin scraped raw, but he was still sliding too fast. He couldn't look down at the way he was going, didn't know how close he was to the edge. Trying to turn himself sideways, he almost started rolling, which would have been fatal. Jack grabbed out in every direction, frantic, feeling the world drop under him in imagination, and managed to get himself straightened out again, sliding down feet first.

He was crying.

But his fall had accelerated. A moment later his feet were sticking out into the air. Jack grabbed at the roof as hard as he could, breaking his fingernails, then ripping them out. He dropped completely over the edge, his whole body, but there was a rain gutter, thank God, and he managed to grab it. The sudden stop sprained his wrists, and he had banged his chin on the gutter, so he hung almost unconscious. But he was stopped! He dangled, dangerously but not dead. For a moment in his panic he had become completely self-absorbed, forgetting Arden. But as he hung from the gutter he remembered her and was afraid to look down, dreading the sight of her body splattered on the concrete. How many flights of fire escape had he climbed? He was at least four stories up. And far from safe yet.

Then he heard the strangest thing he had ever heard. A threat. A challenge. Both couched in laughter.

"Why don't you let go?"

Jack managed to turn and look down over his own shoulder. Arden stood there, hands on hips, thigh-deep in trash inside a Dumpster. This apparently was what she'd been aiming for when she'd shot off the roof. The inside surface of the trash container looked about eight feet by four feet. A very small target, especially from forty feet in the air. Jack continued to stare at the damned girl. Did she have no fear at all?

He did. Instead of accepting her challenge, he edged along the roof, holding tightly to the rain gutter, until he reached the fire escape on this side. He swung back and forth and dropped onto it. Even that short drop almost made him throw up. He could never have done what Arden did. Forget the danger of missing. He couldn't let go and let himself fall that far even if he knew he had a sure landing. Jack went down the metal fire escape nursing his injuries and his pride. As he neared the bottom he remembered there were all kinds of people chasing him, which was almost as frightening as facing this girl.

Down in the alley, Arden was staring at him curiously, having climbed out of the Dumpster. Frowning, she said, "You went down on your front? Doesn't that hurt your face and your chest and—well, everything?"

"Not so much," Jack said, refusing to rub any of his two or three dozen aching body parts. "Beats smelling like eau de Dumpster. Especially a Dumpster behind a restaurant."

Arden shrugged. "Come on, there's a car over here with the keys in it."

"There is? Then why didn't you come rescue me in it?"

"Didn't know where you were. Thought I should go up on the roof and look over the situation. Good thing for you, huh?"

Jack didn't answer. He walked behind her, watching the swing of her hips, and wanted to grab her, in spite of any garbage taint. She turned and grinned at him, knowing exactly what he was thinking. He hated that.

He grabbed her anyway.

Bruno watched with an odd mix of emotions on his face. "Enjoy yourself, Jack. 'The condemned man ate a hearty meal.' Or whatever."

Arden and Jack clung to each other in the alley so hard they almost burrowed into each other. Jack's hands hurt like hell, but he held her anyway. Her leg went around his. He didn't reprimand her for being too fast this time. There is no aphrodisiac like near-death. Jack's hands went inside her blouse, hers inside his shirt.

Then she pulled back and said, "Don't we need to get out of here?"

Jack's hands stopped moving, but he didn't answer. After a couple of seconds passed she raised an eyebrow.

"I'm thinking, I'm thinking.... All right, yes, damn it. But don't forget where we left off."

They ran to a dark blue Lexus parked in the alley. Maybe the restaurant owner's car. Jack felt hollow from strangeness, from the rush of emotions. He dropped into the passenger's seat without any protest over who was driving. Then as the car took off he wondered where they were going.

"I have no idea what to do now. Head for city centre, I guess, try to find Rachel, see what she—"

Arden was shaking her head. "Do you know who that was chasing you, Jack?"

"No idea."

She gave him a sidelong look. Master spy. Where had she acquired all this self-confidence?

"Those were German security forces. Undercover. Mixed, I think, with Interpol."

He frowned. His little contretemps in Nice wouldn't have called out such a response. "Who did they think I was?"

"They think you're you, Jack. I can't tell you why, but while you've been playing your game I've been doing a little reconnoitering. You are like suspect number one here. If there's any kind of plot about the summit, they think you're behind it."

"How can that be? I haven't been anywhere near—"

He stopped suddenly. The Jack doubles throughout Europe. Had they been doing something other than just luring him here?

They drove sedately through the night, Rachel trying not to draw attention to the two of them in their stolen car. She wasn't driving toward the heart of Salzburg, he noticed, but merely turning from street to street in this suburb in which they'd found themselves. Going in circles.

He glanced at her young, sharp profile, softened slightly by her cheeks. Arden looked beautiful to him now. He couldn't remember how she'd looked before, before he'd known her, so long ago. Two weeks.

She glanced at him and smiled, raising one eyebrow to ask for instructions.

"What do you think we should do?" Jack asked carefully.

"Find a place to go to ground for tonight," she answered immediately. "Tomorrow just find a way to get out. Your presence here disrupts things. We have people in place here. Leave it to Professor Trimble. He's organized."

"You've talked to Professor Trimble?"

"Just briefly, before you did. He's been here longer than we have and seems to be on top of things."

Jack sat silent. Once again she seemed to read his thoughts. Arden said with a touch of sternness, "If you try to get to Rachel you'll just get yourself arrested. Even trying to call her would be dangerous. You wouldn't believe the high-tech interception equipment they've got all around the summit site. And she's right in the thick of it."

Jack nodded. He turned to look at the old buildings passing slowly by. Silent, stolid, immovable by centuries. But now everything seemed fragile to him, as fragile as a child's drawing on construction paper. He stayed turned away from Arden, hoping the set of his shoulders wouldn't give him away, trying as hard as he could not to let her know what he was thinking.

"Your plan is good. Do you have some place in mind? We probably shouldn't be seen together, if I'm so hot. Maybe you should drop me off somewhere along here. I'll meet you wherever you say."

He felt her scrutiny on his back, but stayed turned away as if studying the nighttime city. Jack could almost see Arden's suspicious stare. But when he turned back to her quickly she was just driving, watching the road carefully. "You're our best hope now," Jack said, touching her cheek. He was thinking, *I love you. I want you out of this.* Thinking it as hard as he could.

Arden obviously read his thoughts, and the touch of his hand. "Let me stay with you," she said softly.

Jack shook his head. "I'm done here, I'm no use to us. You don't want to get tainted with me. I'll fall back, see if I can do anything from the outside. The President's not here yet."

Arden's expression grew harder, focused on the job. "He has to come, Jack. Nothing can interfere with that. This is the only way to draw him out of his ridiculous isolationism."

"I know. Maybe I can make sure nothing interferes with that. Anyway, I've got to get away before anyone spots you with me. What will you do?"

"Find Professor Trimble, I guess. Work with him."

The interior of the car was its own little piece of nighttime, darker than the one outside. Jack and Arden cast no shadows in here. They were shadows themselves. *I may never see you again,* Jack thought. Thought it hard. It made his face very solemn, even as he tried to smile.

They kissed, for what seemed a long time. Any cop walking by would have indulged them. The kiss made Jack wish they could start all over again, from the beginning of the relationship, building it somewhere else, away from all this. He sensed the same feeling on her part.

"Somehow I think you're heading for the seat of power," she whispered as they broke apart. "I'll find you." Jack only nodded.

She let him out in the dark middle of a quiet block. There were no sounds of pursuit, no alarms going off. Still, Jack felt very nervous as soon as he emerged from the car, which gave at least the illusion of safety.

He looked into the car, let Arden see him nod and shrug, then he began walking. He heard the car move forward and turn at another street. He didn't turn to wave goodbye. In spite of what Arden had said, Jack wanted more than anything to get in touch with Rachel.

But Jack wasn't going to be seeing Rachel.

But he did manage to call her. "Rache, I'm going into a difficult situation. If I don't get out of it, there are several people I want you to kill."

"Okay."

"Starting with a couple of people in Nice."

"I know about them. I'm on it. But does it have to be death?"

"It absolutely does. Has to be."

"You're saying that impoverishment and international, albeit totally private, humiliation wouldn't work just as well?"

"Damn. You remain as ever the mistress of the hard bargain."

"It's already begun."

"This is a tough call. Can I get back to you?"

"Always punting the tough calls, eh, Jack?"

His voice changed in the middle of the sentence. "Rachel, only when I can leave it up to you."

"Jack?"

"I know. Thanks."

They hung up, and Jack felt very alone again. He walked, having no idea where he was going. After a few steps Jack began to hear his footsteps echoed. It was getting late. His stomach rumbled.

The street was beautiful, the buildings like a stage set. No, much better than a stage set. Medieval but very real. Ancient Europe. Mozart had walked these streets, maybe run his hand along this wall, glanced into this shop window.

There was no one across the street.

That's what Jack had been looking into the window for. He felt pursued, and wondered how wide the net was. At least he had no pursuers across the street, unless they were vampires.

At the next corner he turned, glancing back as he did so. There was no one behind him, either. Jack frowned but kept walking. He heard footsteps. Where were they? He even began to hear the murmur of voices, as if he were a human cell phone, connected to the ethernet.

He took out his own phone, punched in Arden's number. But as it began to ring, a man stepped into view at the end of the street, facing Jack. Jack froze for a moment, then walked toward him. Then faster. The man was Jack. One of his doppelgangers. The man just stood staring at him with a blank expression as Jack ran faster. Then the man turned, slowly, and disappeared back around the corner.

Bruno Benjamin was grinning now. He hadn't had this much fun in years. "I could lead you around the world," he said to the screen, which showed Jack running. "In fact, I have." He chuckled quietly to himself. Slowly, over the course of a year, Bruno had transformed the neighborhood around Jack into his own theater, with not only hidden cameras but speakers. He could make a man hear footsteps or whispered voices where there was no one. Bruno was very good with equipment.

He rose and looked around the spacious room. "Now we have to get ready," he said, as if to a pet cat. In fact, Bruno detested animals. His only pet was his own mind, which was also his only companion for the most part. Bruno could be charming in short bursts, as he had been with the secretary at the embassy, but it wearied him.

Jack came to a metal door, through which his double had obviously disappeared. It still trembled slightly under Jack's hand. He stared at it for a long few seconds, thinking he was within sight of the end, one way or the other. For a few moments Jack just stood there, then he finished punching Arden's number into his cell phone. She didn't answer. To her voice mail he said, "I'm following a lead. It's one of my doubles, so it seems to be aimed at me. I hope you can hone in on my signal somehow. Otherwise I'm afraid you're going to be on your own. I love you, Arden."

He wished he had time for one more call, to America, but he didn't. Using his elementary burglary skills and tools, Jack went through the door.

Inside was blackness, dark as the inside of a skull. The kind of darkness that made a man think the floor was about to drop out from under him, or bright lights come on and people scream "Surprise!"

Instead the darkness gradually lightened until he could tell he was in a narrow hallway. After thirty yards it ended in a very small room, like an elevator lobby. There were two doors there. They stood side by side, possibly leading into the same room, but Jack didn't think so. This time Jack didn't put his hands on the doors, or lean against them to listen. Instead he looked all around the room, searching for another way.

Bruno's eyes as he watched the screen were more narrowed. He had a heavy, jowled face, but his body wasn't as uselessly plump as it first appeared. When Bruno's eyes narrowed a good observer could see a much thinner, hungrier man within. Tonight he wore black, blending into the big, black leather chair, almost into the dimness of the control room where he sat. As he stared at the screen he was almost reduced to a pair of eyes.

"Come on, Jack, the lady or the tiger. Which is it?" As nothing continued to happen, Bruno smirked. "Your legendary people skills aren't much use here, are they?"

———

Jack saw no obvious other way out, except the way he had come. But he didn't trust those doors. His training had taught him, whenever there are two ways to go, find a third.

The ceiling was low in this room, composed of large soundproofing tiles. By jumping as high as he could, Jack could touch the tiles, even push them up a little out of the metal grid holding them. No way he could get up into there, though.

He looked around. No tools to work with, not one. The room was absolutely barren of adornment. Jack only had two things to work with other than his brain and his body. Maybe it was game-playing that had taught him to look at objects in different ways, or maybe it had been his own inherent instinct. At any rate, it had taken him only moments to realize that sometimes a doorknob can be used as something other than a doorknob. The doors were so close together that their knobs were only a couple of feet apart. Jack put his right foot up on the knob on the right, jumped, pushed his hands right through the tiles of the ceiling, found the other doorknob with his left foot, and stood there for a second recovering his balance. Then he jumped off the doorknobs up into the ceiling.

It took him a moment to assure himself that he was stable. He put the tiles carefully back into place, and began crawling.

"Damn it!" Bruno yelled, jumping up from his chair. "I should have put the damned tiger up in the ceiling." "The tiger" was merely an expression. He probably didn't really have one on the scene, though his unseen listener couldn't be sure.

Bruno ran around the room frantically, bringing screens to life, checking other sensors. He did not have cameras up in the ceiling, or any other way of tracking Jack's progress. There was really nothing Jack could do up there—Bruno thought, but then he hadn't thought Jack could get out of the two-door room any other way, either. It took him only seconds to consider and discard all the weapons at his disposal. Then he turned to the corner of the room. "You'll bring him," he said coldly.

Jack was crawling through dimness, feeling pleased with himself even with no idea where he was going, when he heard a scream. It was piercing, maddening, a scream of terror and pain. And he was quite sure it was Arden's scream, though he had never heard her so much as raise her voice. The scream froze him for a moment, but not with indecision. When he unfroze he started crawling quickly, toward the source of the scream.

After some distance he slowed and halted. He was afraid he was giving away his position. Worse, he knew he was about to do something very stupid. He stopped, catching his breath, and took out his phone. The screen showed he had signal. Quickly he punched in some numbers. After a moment he got Rachel's voice mail. Could she be sleeping? More likely she was using her phone.

Jack wasn't even aware of the tenderness in his voice as he spoke. "Rachel, it's me again. Listen, there's something else you have to do. No, two things, and I hope to God you know what they are, because I can't tell you from here. There are also some people you have to watch out for, starting with Professor Trimble. You'd be surprised to hear about the other two, I think—"

But before he could finish, the tile below him splintered and gave way. Then the whole ceiling around Jack collapsed. The collapse hadn't been caused by his weight, though. Metallic arms reached up and grabbed him from his exposed position. The arms pulled him out of the ceiling then dropped him. He landed standing, then fell on his ass. His cell phone skittered away somewhere under the rubble around him. Jack coughed and blinked. The large room in which he sat seemed bright by comparison with where he'd been, though in fact it was dimly lighted. The wall in front of him was covered by a large console, with at least a dozen screens and as many keyboards, plus a vast array of buttons and switches. The room had an angled ceiling that ended high at that end, with a catwalk up on the wall above the console.

The rest of the room was furnished rather like an old-fashioned study, or a parody of one. Heavy, overstuffed leather furniture, a thick coffee table, floor lamps.

There were no people in sight. Then the one chair at the console turned, and the fat, bald man in the chair sat smiling at the dishevelled drop-in visitor.

"As you've realized by now, I just needed to make you hurry through the ceiling, so your noise would give away your position." He flipped a switch close at hand and the scream rang out again, nerve-shredding even though it was only a recording. The man flicked the switch off again. "I don't actually have her here now, though I did have to make her scream the first time we met. I thought it might come in handy to record it." He sat beaming at his visitor, with his hands folded in his lap. Jack had never felt such warm regard.

"Hello, Jack."

"Hello, Bruno."

"Please don't act as if you're not surprised to see me."

"I mentioned your name to people three days ago."

Bruno narrowed his eyes, studying the man he hadn't seen in a dozen years. Then he smiled in satisfaction. "No, you didn't. I am a complete astonishment to you."

Jack shrugged.

"You had forgotten me completely, hadn't you?"

"No one could forget you, Bruno. I've thought about you often, believe it or not. I've always wondered when I'd be seeing you again."

"Liar."

Jack shrugged again. What he'd said was true, though. He had first met Bruno half their lifetimes ago, at Bruton Academy. Bruno had realized what the place was before Jack had, but in the end Jack had been inducted into the inner mystery and Bruno hadn't. As a consequence, Jack thought, Bruno must have harbored the belief all these years that the Circle was something other than what it was: that it was the conclave of the Secret Masters of the World. That naked yearning for power as much as anything was what had kept Bruno out. But Jack had always suspected, as he'd said, that Bruno wouldn't forget them.

He walked a little, which didn't seem to bother Bruno at all. He didn't even swivel to keep Jack in the center of his attention. In fact, he was looking past him, with a slight frown.

"How did you get the money out of our treasury to fund your project, Bruno? How'd you turn Professor Trimble?"

"Oh, that was easy. I've been cultivating him for years. He actually thinks I'm part of your group, Jack. Part of the 'Inner Circle,' so deep undercover that I don't attend meetings or have contacts with anyone else. He believes he's working for the good of mankind, whatever that means."

"And the technology? For your miracle planes and spiders and all?"

"For the Night of Terror?" Bruno smiled. The fact that Jack knew so much about him obviously didn't disturb Bruno. "Well, I've always been good with machines, Jack, I don't know if you remember that. Good enough that I could meet some of the people who are *really* good. All that technology, as you called it, is stuff that's been on drawing boards around the world for years. There are more mad scientists than you'd think. They just didn't have the funding or the motivation actually to build the things before I came along."

Jack wandered closer to the console, until he was close enough to touch it. He pressed a couple of switches, changed camera angles on screens. Bruno didn't move to stop him. Jack didn't hear much sound beyond this room, either. No scurrying army of minions. Except for his equipment, Bruno seemed to be alone.

Jack turned his attention to his old classmate. Aside from balding, Bruno didn't look much older than he'd looked as a chubby teenager. His eyes were black and deep and hard to read. He continued to chuckle, but something smoldered far down in his eyes. Jack sighed. "Bruno, let me tell you something true. I thought they did you a favor when they didn't bring you into the Circle. I thought you could accomplish so much more in the real world. Really become something. Famous like you wanted, instead of the invisible creatures we are. Like vampires behind the—"

Bruno's fist slammed down on the console. The whole room seemed to shake. It was a large fist, Jack noted, with tremendous force driving it. The metal console was actually dented under it.

And now the hatred had appeared on Bruno's face. The flesh seemed to fall away, exposing sharp cheekbones and a thin nose, the face of someone eaten up by obsession. The smile was gone completely. "What would have been the point?" he snarled.

Jack gave him a look of non-comprehension. Bruno stood up, half a head taller than Jack. "Do you know what it's like to feel the whole world shimmery and insubstantial around you because you don't know the real truth of it?"

"Actually, yes," Jack said quietly.

"To feel that whatever you might accomplish is overshadowed by someone whose name you'll never know? To think that even if you conquer the world, it will only be because someone else planned it to happen?"

"We're really not that good."

Bruno leaned into his face. "Now you'll be nothing. I'll be part of the Real History. I'll be controlling it."

Bruno recovered some of his composure, straightening up and smoothing down his black jacket. "Yes, I know everything," he said, trying to smile again. But he was looking past Jack again, all around the room, up into that dark space above the ceiling.

Jack knew now too, knew how high the stakes were here, not just for him personally, but for the world. He'd known that intellectually for days, but here in this room he felt the pulse of hatred so strongly it almost knocked him backwards. Enough hatred to smash everything to pieces. "You've done all this just to destroy us?"

Bruno laughed. "Not just to destroy you, Jack. To expose you and humiliate you. The Circle was designed to protect America's place in the world. Now America has no place. Once the President gets here and is assassinated, America's isolation will be complete. The world will come in to feast on the corpse."

He sat again. Bruno obviously wanted to tell his story. "In less than fifteen years I've put together a better team than yours, Jack. Yes, some of them are washouts like me, but not as many as you'd think. The Circle has overlooked some powerful talents in the world. And I've trained them. In many ways it's better to have a solid foundation of belief than to know the 'real' history." Unfortunately, Jack could not only hear the quotation marks in Bruno's voice, but Bruno made them in the air.

"Your precious Circle was a failure anyway, even without my speeding up the process. Look at the world you were protecting and tell me they were fulfilling their mission."

Jack thought he sounded like a lapsed Christian, a man losing his religion and angry about it; angry at God for not existing.

"I created David Wilkerson, you know. The National Security Advisor? I guided him to power right under your noses, right past all of you. I even wrote his silly paper years ago, the one that brought him to the President's attention. I'm sure he doesn't remember it, but I did."

Jack realized that he was very unlikely to leave this room alive, but on the off chance he did he needed to gather as much information as possible. *Lie to me*, he thought at Bruno. *Show me what a lie looks like.*

"Arden brought me here," Jack said slowly. "How long have you been cultivating her?"

Bruno smiled again. "Longer than you can imagine, old pal. Where is she, by the way? I thought she'd be following you. Well, no matter." That accounted for his looks past Jack and around the room. For the first time since he'd fallen out of the ceiling, Jack had an inkling of hope. But then Bruno resumed his story. "First I was her stern but kind-hearted math teacher at finishing school. Since then I've been feeding her information little bits at a time. She is completely mine."

"It's too bad you can't trust her completely. She could have been even more of a help to you."

"I do trust her completely," Bruno said. His face was absolutely still as he said it. Nothing flickered. Then he gave the tiniest of smirks. "Anyway, it doesn't matter whether I trust her. How did you know, by the way?"

That was good, Jack thought. *First a lie, then the truth.* Bruno would never trust any human being completely.

"She was too good," Jack answered. "Always there when I needed her, always rescuing me when things seemed hopeless. Of course, I didn't trust her from the beginning, because she'd been assigned to me. Then tonight she told me I couldn't get in touch with Rachel and that she'd rely on Don Trimble. I'd already suspected him, partly because he's the treasurer. And he told me he hadn't talked to Arden. She said they have. They needed to coordinate their story. Trimble hasn't bothered to get in touch with Rachel, either, even though he's been here for days. He's obviously working for a different team." He studied Bruno's face. "So is Arden. So she's been yours all along? Ever since she was in school in Switzerland?"

Bruno's smile was so self-satisfied it could almost live on its own, lift off his face and hover in the air, a UFO of smugness.

So Arden had been bombarded from all sides, for years, to believe that Jack is the villain. "She was even told you couldn't be trusted by her beloved grandmother. Who, you may have noticed, has been MIA for a while."

Jack stared. He was beginning to lose himself. This had been an intellectual exercise until now, a game, even with the world at stake. Because the world didn't matter, only the people you cared about. And Gladys Leaphorn was like an immortal, a repository of so much history and wisdom she was irreplaceable.. Murdering her would be like going into an art museum swinging a flame thrower. He didn't believe even Bruno capable of that. "You didn't—" he sputtered, but broke off at the transformation of Bruno's face.

Bruno's voice remained smug but very hard. He stared at Jack, waiting for him to attempt something. All boyishness had left his expression. "Not until I no longer needed her," he said grimly. "I know, you think I couldn't do it. I think I could. After all she wasn't my beloved headmistress, not in the way she was yours. Anyway, I found people who could do it." Offhandedly he added, "Arden thinks you're responsible for her demise, by the way."

Jack wanted to leap at him and get his hands around his throat. In fact he felt sure Bruno was waiting for that. He wanted to goad Jack out of intellectual response. Instead Jack did something off-kilter. He closed his eyes for a moment, putting Bruno's existence and everything he'd said out of his mind for a moment, then took his modified PSII off his belt. Jack's fingers scampered over the keys. Yes, he had a connection.

Bruno went back to smiling. "Yes, I have wireless here. Go ahead, check your sources, Jack. Find out how thoroughly everyone mistrusts you. I don't think you'll even get a response from Rocky Mountain headquarters."

Jack allowed his shoulders to jerk a little as Bruno revealed even more of what he knew. He had obviously devoted his life to a study of the Circle. What a waste.

Jack found his screen filled with angry invective. The National Security Advisor felt he'd been cheated. At an earlier time in his life, like ten minutes ago, Jack would have grinned at the mental havoc he'd caused. Now he just replied with a short message: *you've been playing the game, imperialist. I've been playing you.*

And he signed off for good. "Nothing," he said aloud, just to give Bruno another grin.

"So now what?" he asked, dropping the game so that his hands dangled loose at his sides.

"I thought I'd just let you go," Bruno said. "Let you go try to stop me. Like one of your games. See how ineffectual you are."

"I've already stopped you. You just don't know it yet."

Bruno blinked, staring at Jack's calm face. "You mean your little riots that are about to break out? Crowds chanting for America to re-engage with the world? Are your friends busy writing the signs now? It won't matter, Jack. That will just be the punctuation on your failure."

That shot hurt. Jack didn't disguise the fact. His shoulders slumped a little more, and his eyes began moving around the room more frantically, looking for some way out or a way to sabotage this madman's plans, even while continuing to talk to him.

Jack's voice turned gentle, almost pleading. "It doesn't matter, Bruno, what you do to me. There are still so many of us, some much smarter—"

"Such as, say, Craig Mortenson?" Bruno purred. He sat down again, the better to enjoy his old acquaintance's reaction.

Jack stopped moving, stopped breathing, almost stopped living. He absolutely believed what Bruno was implying. The smirk confirmed it. He had murdered Craig Mortenson. Jack could see the scene played out in his mind. Not the scene that had actually happened, but something similar.

The thing was, each of the Circle members was so vulnerable, individually. They had the world's best network ever. But they had no armies, no Secret Service, no individual bodyguards. It would be so easy, really, to take any of them out. If anyone knew who they were. If anyone even knew to look. Bruno had exploited that weakness.

Jack's eyes were wet. His head hung down. But he continued to study Bruno from under his brows. "So then Alicia too?"

"Yes," Bruno said. "Also dead, a little later in another place."

But Jack had seen, not a flicker in his eyes, but the absence of a flicker. Bruno holding his face immobile. So it was a lie. At least in Bruno's mind, Alicia Mortenson still lived. Jack didn't understand how that was possible. If Alicia had been there she would have tried to prevent the murder, at the cost of her own life if necessary. If she hadn't been there, she would have hunted down everyone responsible by now.

"So forget about your back-up," Bruno said almost sympathetically. "It's just you, Jack, and you're completely stymied. I could release you from here right now and you couldn't stop me. You could run screaming into that compound that there's a conspiracy to kill the leaders and they'd shoot you down like a rabid dog before you got three words out. Every security force there has your picture. Your doubles have been doing some nasty things around Europe. Law enforcement officials of a dozen countries know your face and your name."

Bruno shifted in his chair, making himself more comfortable. "I know what you're thinking now. You could slip in, infiltrate. Mess with some minds. Tell them you have secret information. They'll ask what's your source. I've primed everyone, man. Your doubles have done enough to make everyone mistrust you. To counteract that mistrust, you would have to reveal every secret you have. Either you reveal the entire history of your secret information, or you're a raving lunatic. These are your choices, Jack. You save your group or you save the world. You can't have it both ways. Either way, I win."

Jack's fingers twitched. Bruno saw him considering options. He actually laughed out loud.

"You won't let me go," Jack said. "You're not that confident."

Bruno considered, then shook his head. "No, you're probably right about that. Let's just sit here, enjoy a pleasant evening, watch the show, then when you know how badly you've failed—well, I wouldn't want you to have to live with that pain."

Bruno saw panic growing on Jack's face, in his posture. Saw him consider running, saw him realize there was no way out. He dug the knife a little deeper.

"After you're gone, I may even bring Rachel into the operation. She can help me run the world. In a subordinate capacity, of course. Just wanted you to know that."

Jack's breathing was tight, so his voice came thinly. His face was turning red. "Once you kill me, the only sign you'll ever have of Rachel Greene, maybe, is the sound of her breath behind your back just before you lose consciousness. If you hear anything."

Bruno laughed with utter confidence. "No one will ever know I did you, Jack. I'll be the person most ardently out to avenge you. Rachel and I will join forces. I imagine they'll even bring me in to the group once their forces are so diminished. What do you think, can I make it as a Substitute Legionnaire?"

"I don't think you can make it as a human being."

Bruno's rage suddenly boiled over. He stood up, dropping the pleasant tone. "I could have been anything! I was the best of the lot at school, you know that. I would have been a legend. *The legend of the Circle: Bruno of Bruton Hall.* I would have been the culmination. I was bred for it. Did you know that?"

"No. And I really don't have time—"

"Now it's Bruton Hall Twenty Years After."

"Not quite."

"No, it didn't take me that long. Have a seat, Jack. You've got the best view there is for the end of the world."

CHAPTER 12

The engines of Air Force One shifted as the plane lost altitude slightly, preparing for the long, slow descent to Munich. The changed rumble woke those few people on board who had been dozing. In the conference room, President Witt was huddled with his Secretary of State and a few others, preparing for the summit. There was a subtle sense of relief in the room, career diplomats ready for a big assignment, a chance they'd thought they had already lost. Even the president was throwing himself into the discussion with some enthusiasm. Ever since announcing his new policy of American isolationism, he had missed something, as if some favorite person were gone from his life, or a treasured heirloom. Jefferson Witt was not an introspective man, so he hadn't explored this feeling, but what he had missed was a sense of being the most powerful person in the world. Now he was going to reassert himself.

"We can concede nothing on Jerusalem," said Sylvia Rescone, who as ambassador to Italy should have no official position on that subject. But everyone knew that Sylvia had friends and sources all over her half of the world—and opinions on everything.

"Not my job," the President said confidently. That was going to be his refrain at this conference. America would no longer be the world's referee. "We're not going there to talk specifics."

"Well," Secretary of State Lawrence Jackson demurred quietly. "Maybe a few specifics, behind the scenes. These people are calling on us, Mr. President. Not just these summit leaders, but the world. As I predicted, demonstrations are erupting all over Europe, *pro*-American demonstrations, the first anyone has seen since World War II. We have to assure the world—"

"I'd call them riots," said the Commander of NATO. The military shouldn't have had a place at this table, but the NATO commander was unofficial chief of presidential security on this trip. "And I don't trust them. Anyone can stage a riot. That doesn't tell you what's behind them. They may just be luring us in."

Except for Secretary of State Larry Jackson, everyone in the room grinned furtively. The President of the United States had the best security in the world, it hadn't been breached in a long time, and procedures were more thorough now. The summit site was being scoured by security specialists from a dozen countries. The President felt secure on that score.

In a lounge not far away, Dennis Wilkerson stared down at the shattered pieces of his PlayStation2. "Cheater," he kept muttering. *Changing the damned rules in the middle of the game. European edition, what bullshit.* Wilkerson had enjoyed playing this opponent more than anything else in his life. Wilkerson could win if he really worked at it, even though his opponent was a very skilled player.

So he'd changed the rules to win. Wilkerson called that cheating.

The cracked little machine still retained some power. Wilkerson could still read the mocking last message. *you were playing the game, imperialist. i was playing you* What the hell did that mean? You're always playing against the other player, it wasn't an automatic game of playing against the machine. Of course the two players had been playing each other.

The shift in air speed and direction of the plane shifted Wilkerson's thoughts as well. Now that his game was smashed, with its connection to his only companion, he felt more of an outcast than ever on this plane. No one listened to him. The Secretary of State had beaten him in influence with the president once these pro-American riots had started. They were meaningless, Wilkerson knew, possibly contrived by allies of Larry Jackson himself. But they had worked to push Wilkerson aside. The president kept assuring him that he was not abandoning the policy—Dennis Wilkerson's policy, the Wilkerson Doctrine—of American isolationism. He was just moderating it, taking it in stages.

But this first stage was a world stage. Sitting with other world leaders in smiling unanimity. Wilkerson wanted America watching such an event on television, disdainfully turning it off after a few minutes, not participating. Why had everyone worked so hard to get President Witt here anyway?

The remains of the game flickered and buzzed. A few letters burned brightly, then the whole thing shorted out. The last word he'd seen had been *you. I've been playing you.* But what else had the little screen said? *imperialist* Where had that come from?

Who had he been playing against all this time? Who had been playing him?

Wilkerson sat back down in furious thought. This final message was a taunt, the kind terrorists gave, when they were so sure of themselves they knew they couldn't be stopped, that their enemy was too stupid to figure them out.

What had he learned from the game, from the so-called "European edition"? Switching home courts. That the other player had all the time in the world to turn his home court into a deathtrap, where it was impossible to—

Oh, my God.

Secret Service protection went pretty lax aboard Air Force One, where everyone on board had been checked very thoroughly. But the screaming progress of the National Security Advisor brought the president's detail to full alertness. Dennis Wilkerson was lucky not to die as he burst into the conference room.

"Sir!"

President Witt was on his feet, looking concerned, not alarmed. Everyone else in the room glared at Wilkerson as if he were crazy. "It's all right, men," the president said with a calming gesture. "Dennis, you're not really supposed to be part of this meeting—"

"Sir, we have to turn around! This summit is a trick! It's a trap."

Larry Jackson sighed and rolled his eyes. Sylvia Rescone made a disgusted noise.

The president lowered his voice, making the conversation private between himself and his NSA. "Dennis, we've worked all this out. Security is being provided by forces from—"

"—from a dozen countries, some of which are hostile to us, and all of which have radical elements who would like nothing better than to pull off a huge terrorist coup like this. Have *our* people been able to check out all *their* people?"

The president glanced a question at Jackson, who shrugged angrily. "We can't intrude into other countries' militaries. We've been assured that all these personnel have been thoroughly vetted."

"'Assured'!" Wilkerson scoffed. "By the very people who would love to do this man damage. Sir." He turned back to President Witt, excluding everyone else. "This is a trap. I promise you. Why did they insist that this summit take place in Europe? Far from home for us. Cut off from the great bulk of our forces. They want to cut off our head, sir. They want to humiliate you and then kill you."

The president was listening closely. "Dennis, you have specific information?"

Wilkerson drew himself up and managed to sound both calm and stern. "I am your National Security Advisor, Sir. I have operatives in the field. Good operatives, my own people. Yes sir, I have specific information. The three most powerful terrorist organizations in the world have banded together for this one. They will capture you, hold you hostage, humiliate you publicly, then kill you on international television. It is something they have been planning for years."

President Witt shot a look at Larry Jackson, whose expression was no longer dismissive once the president spoke. "Larry, do we have anything—?"

"Of course not, Sir. If we did you'd know about it. It's all fabrication."

To his chief of staff Witt said, "Sandra, get me the CIA chief. If he's asleep, wake him. I want to know if there's anything that corroborates what Dennis is saying."

Dennis Wilkerson began to feel he had the upper hand. "Sure," he sneered, "let's check with those wonderful folks who brought you Nine-Eleven."

"You shut your mouth!" Larry Jackson snapped. Even with all the security present, the scene threatened to break down into a playground scuffle. The president pulled the NSA aside. Almost whispering, he said, "Dennis, you have specific information about this?"

"Yes sir, I do. Deep background chatter. We picked up pieces. Now in the last twenty-four hours these networks have gone absolutely silent. That means they're in place. These are forces you would never suspect, sir. Sleeper agents buried so deeply their own relatives don't know about them. Waiting for this one chance. The cusp of history, they call it. They hate the idea of America withdrawing from the world stage, because it takes away their great Satan, the fuel for their recruiting and fundraising. They are convinced by assassinating you, in the most horrible way possible, they will draw a savage response from us that will set the world on fire. That's what they want, sir. These are not countries. They are wild-eyed firebrands, with no guiding principles at all. They just want anarchy, and this summit is going to be their finest opportunity. As if they decided it themselves." Wilkerson glanced back over his shoulder. "Which I think may be a possibility."

The president stared at him. "You have hard proof of this?"

"At home I do, sir. Here on board the plane it's just electronic transmissions. I couldn't risk bringing everything on board. But I just received a message from one of my agents that confirmed our fears. Sir, it is horrible. Do you want me to tell you what they plan to do to you, on live television?"

He was making things up wildly now, but Wilkerson was so sure of himself, so sure he'd read the message on his game player correctly, that he felt justified in saying anything. Though he was inventing the details, he was sure he was correct in the essential truth of what he was saying—and that he would be proven right soon.

"Sir!" the Secretary of State called from across the room. "You cannot turn back now, sir. We made promises. We will lose enormous prestige."

"We don't want world prestige any more," Wilkerson snapped. "Remember? Sir, I beg you. It's not just your safety that's at stake."

The president stood silent, everyone staring at him. The plane's engines rumbled, shifting to a lower speed.

At the summit site, taking a last stroll with Hassan, Rachel Green said, "Shouldn't the American President be here by now?"

"I like the way you say that," Hassan chuckled. "As if he means nothing to you. 'The American President.'" He laughed again.

Rachel didn't get the joke. "And how is *your* president doing?"

"Wonderfully. Installed in his suites, with every comfort. It is said of President Hassid that he enjoys a certain delicacy before occasions such as this."

Rachel was surprised. "Drugs?"

Hassan grinned. She had discovered that he was a great gossip. In the few hours they'd known each other, she had learned more about everyone in the camp than she'd learned through intensive study for weeks. Of course, he could have been making it all up, to impress her. Hassan had made no secret of his desire for her. Rachel actually found his attention flattering rather than disgusting, which hadn't happened to her in a while. She had no intention of indulging him, but she did enjoy his company.

"I can say no more," Hassan smiled, imitating a spy in an old movie. "I have said too much already. No, not drugs."

Rachel was not the gossip her companion was, but she was not without her own sources. "His teenage nephew?"

Hassan gasped. "How can you know such a thing? But no, this scandalous rumor is completely untrue. I know, because I started it myself."

They both laughed, and resumed their stroll around the square. Rachel was unarmed. She may have been the only person within a square mile in that condition. "You know the hardest part of this summit?" she asked.

Hassan nodded. Together they said, "Which president will come out on stage first."

She looked toward the American Secret Service detail. They all seemed to be speaking at once, and not to each other. There was some consternation there.

"I think the American president has been delayed," Hassan said, looking where she was.

Rachel was frowning. Something was happening. She wanted to talk to Jack. "He'll be here," she said. "He has to come." And she walked quickly away from her companion.

"He'll come," Bruno said comfortably. "And when he does he will be assassinated. By someone who can be traced back to at least three countries. America will be chasing its tail for the next decade. There will be no revenge it can take. It will retreat back into its shell, headless now."

"You haven't been in America for a while, have you, Bruno?" Jack said. He stood tensely at the console, watching the same screens Bruno was watching. One showed the progress of Air Force one, almost to the coast of England.

"I know the historical forces," Bruno said. "I know what I've designed. He will come. All his advisors are telling him so now."

Jack wondered. From the steady progress of that blip on the screen, it looked like Bruno was right.

President Witt and Dennis Wilkerson shared a special relationship. Bruno had created this relationship without quite being aware he was doing so. In the late stages of his presidential campaign and his first months in office, Witt had completely shared his true agenda with no one but his NSA. The two men had their great plan to themselves. The night of terror had allowed them to implement it sooner than they had thought they could.

But those months of isolation together had given them a strange bond. Dennis Wilkerson had had no one else in his life; Bruno had seen to that. Witt had had no one else he trusted with his grandest ambition. The two had been like boyhood friends, the only members of a secret club.

That feeling lingered, even now after the president had shared his bold vision with the world. Emotionally, the two men remained connected. Witt stared into Dennis Wilkerson's eyes and said, "Dennis, are you sure about this?"

"Absolutely, Sir."

"But I can't turn back now. I'll look like—"

"Not after I release my information, sir. Besides, you're not cancelling the summit, you're only postponing it. And moving the venue. Let it be on American soil, sir. This will emphasize your message. If the world wants us, the world will have to come to us. Make them come to you, Mr. President. Only your own home turf is safe."

The NSA had been laying this groundwork of paranoia for a long time. The president looked up at him with the first gleam of optimism he'd shown in a long time. He felt energized. "Home turf." Somehow he liked the sound of it.

He stepped away from his National Security Advisor, talking to the room at large.

"Turn the plane around."

"No!" Rachel gasped. She was in the Israeli security headquarters. Word had just come that the American President was bailing out of the summit. Chaos began to reign. She could hear people running across the compound outside.

"Did he say something about a threat?"

"Not specifically," Captain Lowenstein answered. "The president's message just said he had urgent business at home and he prefers that this summit be conducted there."

"This is dissing the whole world," someone said. "Pack up. Our premier is not going to play second string."

"No!" Rachel said urgently. She wasn't sure why. "Wait. Wait. We're not going to run. Let us wait and see."

"NO!" Bruno screamed, watching the blip of Air Force One make a wide half-circle and begin heading for home. He leaped to his console and began throwing switches frantically. "I'll blow it out of the air! Where are my missiles?"

"Missiles," Jack sneered quietly.

Very, very slowly, Bruno Benjamin turned. In his black outfit he looked like an animated piece of the night, the part that could move. He seemed bulkier now. He seemed to grow taller as he stared at Jack. Jack saw his old classmate's face change. It darkened as blood rushed into it, but more than that. Bruno looked older, with creases in his cheeks. He looked like a man consumed by a lifetime of passion. But his eyes were dead and black.

"We never use missiles," Jack boasted. "Not even Hornets." He laughed at his little inside joke. Bruno didn't even look puzzled.

"You did this," he said.

"I told you I'd already beaten you."

Bruno's chest moved as he made himself breathe. He began walking slowly toward Jack. "You are so far from beating me you are like a child throwing toys. I have so many back-up plans you couldn't count them. This is nothing."

"I think it's something," Jack said, glancing at the screen. He made his voice sound calm, but he was beginning to worry. In addition to Bruno's other character flaws, he had been something of a bully. Good with his fists. This might not remain an intellectual exercise much longer.

"You've become just like our teachers. So smug, so sure of yourself. *You* kept me out, didn't you? Because I was your only real rival. The only one who might have competed with you for the leadership. Stop that!"

Jack was shaking his head. Bruno's face went even darker. His fists clenched.

"They steered me back to the stupid track," he said. "They taught me that George Washington was the first president of the United States."

"Technically true," Jack said soothingly.

"Technically, technically. They thought I couldn't handle the real truth. The secret history. The real history."

Jack snapped, "Of course they knew you could handle the secret history, Bruno. You longed for it. You lusted after it. The secrets known only to the precious few. That's not why you washed out. You know why."

Bruno's advance had stopped. His forehead crinkled with thought. "Yes, I know. Because I wanted real power. They thought I couldn't be trusted."

Jack shook his head sadly. "What's your mother's phone number, Bruno?"

"My mother? Is she a member—?"

"What's her phone number?" Jack asked again, sounding like an impatient teacher calling on a slow student.

"I don't know. It's in my Blackberry."

"I bet it's not. What were the first rules? What was the first thing we were taught at Bruton Hall?"

Bruno's anger was tempered by puzzlement, as if he were being annoyed by gnats. "Always look behind the scenes. Be two steps ahead. No, three, I know—STOP DOING THAT."

Jack was shaking his head again. "The very first things they told us, they told everyone, on the first day. What were the primary rules?" He waited and got no answer. He answered his own question, slowly, as if for the mentally disqualified. "Talk to your mother every week. Listen to your father. When you're not sure what to do, think what your family—"

"That summer camp shit? I know, I know. But the real rules—"

"Those were the real rules, Bruno. Keep in touch with your family. Know the real world. Love, Bruno. Stay grounded in the real world. That's why you washed out. From the first day, you wanted to lift off the ground and commune with the gods on Olympus. But there are no gods. No great men. There are only mothers and sons, and fathers and daughters. There are only families and friends. If you don't know that, then you have no business—"

"Shut up."

"You don't know people, Bruno. You only know machines. You think you can program people the way you can computers. You never consider—"

"Shut up!" Bruno screamed, and he began to rise.

Jack stared. Bruno's rage seemed to be blowing him up. His head was ten feet above Jack's in an instant. Then Jack realized that Bruno's legs were elongating. An extra set of arms ripped out of Bruno's black shirt. Mechanical arms, like the ones that had dragged Jack out of the ceiling.

He had made himself into a machine. He had wanted to be all-powerful, and this was how he had done it.

Jack jumped back as one of those arms snaked at him, missed him, and smashed one of the screens.

"Bruno!" Jack yelled, having nothing to say, just trying to appeal to his old acquaintance's humanity.

But it seemed to have vanished. In one step Bruno was towering over Jack, then reached down and lifted him off the ground.

His face had calmed now, in his power. He said, "I wanted you to see the end, but now I realize you're too dangerous. That's a tribute, Jack. I have to kill you. Take it as a compliment."

And he flung him across the room. Jack's arms and legs flailed and only luck kept him from being disabled by the throw. He slammed into a chair, rolled back over it, and fell onto the couch. He scrambled to his feet, looking for a weapon.

Arden had saved him from this kind of situation before. Jack knew now that she had only been with him to steer him to this scene of destruction, but somehow he still expected her to appear. She had been here with Bruno. He had schooled her. He hadn't revealed all his plans to her, Jack was sure of that, but he would have boasted of his power. He would have shown her how things worked.

Jack kicked a desk chair on wheels across the floor. Bruno didn't even bother to step over it, just let it hit his mechanical legs and roll away. Then he started forward again.

Jack dodged aside, tried to make it to the door, but Bruno cut off his escape, moving easily. He stumbled a little, but righted himself.

Bruno was not the kind to practice at something. He considered himself the master of anything he attempted. He had given himself this mechanical power, but he wouldn't have worked to master it. Jack ran hard, right at him. Bruno shuffled on his legs, then stood firm and reached with the mechanical arms to grab Jack again.

Jack let himself be picked up. He had an idea, but it involved pain, and he suddenly realized he might not survive one more throw. He struggled. The arms gripped him tightly, then raised him over Bruno's head and hurled him.

Jack shot through the air even faster than last time, and this time there was no soft landing. He managed to turn in the air and cover his head with his arms, but he smashed into the console, his elbows shattering another screen. Already bruised from his slide down the roof earlier, his body began throbbing. Jack rolled off the console and shook his head.

Bruno just stood there, waiting to see if he'd killed him. His face turned grimmer when he realized he hadn't. His face was pale now. Bruno's mechanical arms and legs were powerful, but his flesh and blood body still had to manipulate them. Jack climbed to his feet. He kicked another chair at Bruno. The giant figure let it bounce off him again.

Arden had left him a way out. He felt sure of it. Jack knew he wasn't such a wonderful lover that one night of passion with him would make a woman his love slave. But he had made a human connection with her, and Bruno couldn't have. He didn't have that capacity. Arden had betrayed Jack, she had led him here, but she would have had doubts, too. She would have given him a clue, if he was smart enough to think of it. She would have made it a test.

Jack ran forward again. But he stopped before he got within five feet of Bruno, and skipped to the side. Bruno lifted one long leg to cut him off and Jack skipped to the other side. Bruno's legs moved again, crossing each other. Failing the dance step, he almost tripped over his legs.

Jack picked up the end table beside the wing chair and threw it at his host's head. Instinctively, Bruno ducked. The long arms moved, but sluggishly and too slowly. The table glanced off Bruno's shoulder. He partially blocked it with his own human arm. Next Jack threw the lamp. This time one of the mechanical arms caught it. The strain showed on Bruno's face.

What had Arden said just before she'd let Jack out of the car? Something about approaching the seat of power. Strange phrase. Jack looked frantically around the room and realized that Bruno had stayed in one chair during their whole encounter. The throne-like chair close to the console. Even now he stood in front of it, blocking it.

There was only one door to this room. But Bruno wouldn't leave himself only one way out of anywhere. Two steps ahead, he had said. Or three. He would protect his escape. The way he was protecting that chair now.

The arms reached for Jack. They elongated. Bruno could reach him without ever giving up his position in front of the chair. Jack skittered backward, then to the side. Sure enough, Bruno turned but didn't move.

One arm grabbed Jack's ankle, and he fell to the ground, then jerked free. But the arms had him blocked. Jack scooted forward on hands and knees, but he reached the wall and the arms were still within reach.

"Lazy bastard," he snarled. Bruno had contrived a way to be in power without moving.

Over there close to Bruno the metal struts still dangled where Jack had been ripped out of the ceiling. They almost formed a ladderwork.

This was a terrible idea, but Jack had no choice. He scrambled up and ran, again right at Bruno. Bruno braced himself, pulling his arms back defensively, and waited.

And Jack grabbed the struts and swung himself upward. They started pulling loose, coming down, but somewhere above his head the metal strips remained attached. Jack kept pulling himself upward, and the thin metal held.

Bruno realized what he was doing, and the arms went toward the ceiling, trying to block Jack or pull loose his improvised ladder. Both arms gripped the metal.

And Jack swung on the last strut holding. He was almost to the ceiling now, and when he let go with his feet he swung fast. Jack pulled himself as hard as he could with his arms, swung in an arc, and let go.

He smashed feet first into Bruno's chest. The mechanical arms remained otherwise occupied, and Bruno couldn't manipulate them well enough to protect himself. He put up his own arms, but Jack slammed into them. Atop the long metal legs, Bruno's balance was delicate to begin with. And he was tired. Jack had seen that in his face. All his arms flailing, Bruno went over backwards.

Jack dropped off as they fell. Bruno tried to right himself, and tripped over his chair. He went over it and fell hard.

And Jack dropped into the chair.

"NO!" Bruno screamed, even louder than before. Jack frantically looked for controls. His fingers skittered uselessly over the chair's arms as he heard Bruno heaving himself upward.

Nothing worked. Jack forced himself to stop and think for a moment. Was there a code phrase? This was Bruno. He had already said his own name aloud and nothing had happened. What else would he do?

This was Bruno. Jack tried to place himself in that life. He only had moments to do so. Bruno, who had labored in hatred and hiding for most of his life. Angry, manic, enraged. Jack slammed his fists down on the chair's padded arms and thought he felt something click. But nothing happened.

Bruno. Furtive, secretive, trusting no one.

The chair faced outward into the room, the way Bruno had been sitting in it during his conversation with Jack. Jack put his feet down and spun the chair around, so its back was to the room, hiding the occupant.

This time something definitely clicked. The chair locked into place.

Bruno had regained his feet, two yards away. He lunged forward, his face completely contorted with hatred. Jack screamed defensively and put up his arms over his face.

But a panel had opened on the arm of the chair. Glancing down, Jack saw buttons and a switch. There were no labels, he had no idea what the controls did.

The switch was the most prominent control, the one a person could trip without looking at the buttons. Jack's hand shot downward and he pushed the switch.

Nothing happened. Now Bruno's mechanical arms gripped the chair, trapping Jack in place. Bruno pulled himself forward. Now his real arms were within reach of Jack. Bruno pulled back a fist. Jack had nowhere to duck. The mechanical arms held him in place like a small, tight cage.

Then there was a rumble beneath him. Some force had been building, silently, since he'd thrown the switch. Padded restraints came out of the chair's wings, holding Jack in place even more tightly than the mechanical arms had. There was a quiet explosion and the floor of the small dais opened beneath him.

Jack in the chair was falling. Bruno screamed again. He tumbled forward as Jack fell down a large tube, chair and all.

Bruno must have had no trace of claustrophobia. Jack did. The tunnel was just big enough to accommodate the chair. If Jack hadn't been held in place he would have been clawing at the tube's metal walls. He was crying, whimpering, his flesh contorted by the speed of his fall. There was faint light at first, then complete darkness and falling.

And Jack thought, Maybe this wasn't a way out. Maybe it was a way for Bruno to dispose of an enemy, in some horrible fashion.

Day had broken in the public square where the world leaders were to appear, revealing what appeared to be an antbed, tiny figures scurrying everywhere. It had been confirmed now that the American President wasn't coming. No one knew what to do. America wasn't the host, but was there any point to the summit without them? At least two countries were already packing up to go home.

Rachel knew that shouldn't happen. She didn't know how she knew, but she trusted her instincts. Hurrying to her own president's suites, she passed Hassan. He made an elaborate shrug. Rachel stopped. "Are we all his supporting players?" she asked. "Is there no show without him?"

She stared at the Syrian. He saw her determination. As he walked away, his own shoulders lifted and squared.

Along her way she scattered as many such comments as she could, hoping they would spread. She didn't have time to start a whispering campaign properly, because she had to talk to her own president.

That went badly. "I am not dealing with Syria in this fashion," the president said sternly. "The American President has as good as said this is a plot of terrorists. I am not condoning it. I am going home."

"Slinking home," Rachel said, and he glared at her. Immediately she said, "I apologize, sir. That was not my thought. I was just thinking how it would be reported." As she went out she muttered to an aide, "Snow White didn't come so the seven dwarfs couldn't have a party."

She went out again. What could she do? She was one young person surrounded by soldiers and diplomats. How could she—?

Across the compound she saw something odd. A small disturbance in a scene of many disturbances. But Rachel was drawn to this one. She walked that way, then began running.

A young woman was trying to get past a knot of security people. Rachel recognized her as Jack's friend, the one she had met on the beach. "Arden," she said quietly, and the girl's eyes fastened on her.

"I told you!" Arden said to the man restraining her. "She has my credential." And she pushed past the man, who let her go.

Rachel waved her own security clearance from the chain around her neck, and reached into her belly pack for another one. The man didn't even wait for her to produce it. He knew Rachel. After all, she had been here for three days. She had made connections. "Whatever," he said, and went back to harassing another group. Security was growing rapidly more lax as it began to appear the summit wasn't going to happen.

Rachel pulled Arden away from the perimeter. The young woman looked slight, but Rachel felt a steeliness in her arm she wouldn't have expected. "What are you doing here? Where's Jack?"

"He can't be here. Everyone is looking for him. Besides, he's—" She stopped herself. "And what are *you* doing, Rachel Greene?"

She sounded odd. Well, they all did. "Trying to keep this tent from folding," Rachel answered.

"Why?" Arden looked around at all the scurrying activity curiously. Over there across the way was a small American contingent of functionaries. They looked especially lost, their president having pulled the rug out from under them abruptly, when they had been somewhat confused to begin with, their German ambassador having been murdered shortly before the summit. Did that have something to do with why the President had pulled out?

"I don't know," Rachel answered Arden's question. "I just feel like if this falls apart someone bad has won."

She was watching Arden closely as she spoke. The young woman looked confused. Rachel had only seen her once, but she had exchanged emails with Jack about her, and he had spoken of her enormous self-possession. What had happened to her?

Rachel just kept staring. Arden caught her, looked away, then her eyes snapped back. "What?!"

Rachel just looked at her. A very young woman, who had grown up virtually parentless, then thrust into the heart of the most secret society that had ever existed. A woman of complete self-control, who could almost read minds. Rachel's expression was open and curious, inviting reading.

Arden studied her for a moment, then blushed.

"You betrayed him," Rachel said wonderingly.

Arden didn't deny it. She put her arms around herself, holding tightly. She couldn't hold Rachel's eyes, and looked away across the compound.

"And what are you here to do now?" Rachel asked in a harsher voice.

Don't let it be water, Jack thought. Please God don't let the chair splash down into a deep pool, with Jack still restrained. The thought of drowning terrified him, and somehow he feared Bruno would know that.

The chair seemed to fall faster. Jack had no reference points, because he couldn't see anything. His arms were held firmly against his chest. He sensed a huge obstacle out there ahead of him, and was certain that the chair's fall was going to end by slamming into a wall. Jack was screaming without knowing it. The chair accelerated faster and faster, eager to smash him. Things seemed to brush at him in the darkness. Every moment felt like his last.

Then his fall began to slow. The chair suddenly took a steep turn, which slowed it further, and it was sliding forward, to come to a stop. The chair fell over sideways, which completely terrified him, then its constraints popped free of his arms. Jack pushed against the wall in front of him and it gave way. He stumbled up and out into an alley. On the outside the walls looked like one of those old-fashioned freight elevators that come out of the ground. Jack staggered free of it and the doors closed, leaving him alone and completely disoriented.

He walked away a few steps, rubbed his hands over his face. It was November in northern Europe, and colder than January where he came from. Thin sunlight didn't help. Jack had been up all night, most of it spent in Bruno's sanctuary. He turned in a slow circle, trying to find a landmark.

A couple of blocks away a three- or four-story building, the tallest structure in this suburb, caught his eye. It was the most modern building in sight, glass walls rising out of the old, old town. The windows reflected the sights around them, so the building appeared to be wearing a coat of older architecture. It was an interesting effect, as if the building were hiding in plain sight. At night it would be nearly invisible.

The building held him. Three stories. Had he climbed that high through the ceiling? Somehow the building looked to him like Bruno, intrusive and secretive at the same time. The building was narrower at the top, in what could have been a penthouse. Or a control room.

As Jack watched, the top floor of the building exploded. It was a quiet explosion, self-contained, and if Jack hadn't been staring right at it, he wouldn't have known where the sound came from. The walls didn't shatter and send glass flying. One window burst, but the others just collapsed inward, an implosion that collapsed that whole top floor in a matter of seconds.

That hadn't just been an eject button Jack had hit. It had been a self-destruct switch. An emergency escape from Bruno's sky bunker in case he was invaded by overwhelming force, and needed to get away and destroy his attackers.

Jack's mouth fell open as he stared. The explosion would have been most thorough, he felt sure, destroying all traces of his old classmate's renegade operation.

"Goodbye, Bruno," Jack whispered.

He felt sure Bruno would have wanted it this way. He wouldn't have wanted to live with defeat. In fact, this whole scheme might have been an elaborate suicide plot.

But Bruno had said something ominous. *I have more back-up plans than you can count.* Something like that. And at least one of those schemes might already have been set in motion.

Jack started running, looking for a phone and a car.

Rachel Greene's eyes kept returning to the American contingent, standing befuddled. One woman was holding a drape of the presidential seal, the kind that would hang on a podium. "Stay here," Rachel said softly, and walked across the square. The middle-aged woman holding the presidential drape began to watch her as Rachel drew closer. The woman was a little frumpy, but with efficient-looking arms and wrists. There was something familiar about her eyes, an insightful determination. She was the kind who would make the perfect executive secretary. While everyone else had lost their heads, she had remembered the seal, but now couldn't think of anything to do with it.

"May I?" Rachel asked, holding out her hands. The woman's faded blue eyes stared into Rachel's soft brown ones. She looked puzzled and even a little angry, but she was used to taking orders. Her fingers eased their grip and she let Rachel gently pull the cloth from her hands.

"Thank you," Rachel said, and walked on. She glanced back over her shoulder and saw Arden watching her. *Are you so smart, girl?*, Rachel thought. *Do you know what I'm going to do?* Jack had trusted this girl, at least to an extent, but Rachel did not.

The stage was already set up in front of her. There was no central podium, just eight chairs on the stage. A great deal of planning had gone into that arrangement. If the chairs were put in a line, two people would be on the ends, shuffled off to the sides. Someone would be central, someone not. There were other considerations. Israel could not be next to Syria, the U.S. not next to Britain. (They didn't want to look too insider-ish.) War had almost broken out at the peace summit over the arrangement of the chairs. In the end—Rachel's subtle suggestion to a chief of protocol—the chairs had been arranged in a horseshoe shape, with two up high and the others in two arms circling around, so that the ones on "top" were farthest from the audience and the two on the ends were closest, positions of prominence. This had satisfied everyone, and the various presidents pretended it had been a tempest over nothing, that they couldn't care less where they sat.

Rachel mounted the steps beside the stage, walking slowly. Two Secret Service agents in the wings, along with security personnel from other countries, watched her closely, but there were no presidents on the stage, so who cared about a young woman providing window dressing?

Rachel chose one of the chairs near the top of the horseshoe and carefully draped the American presidential seal over its back, facing the audience. Now the chair was more prominent than all the others. It was dressed and they were naked. The chair also looked expectant. Let's get on with the show. Rachel backed away, checked to make sure the seal was on straight, then walked quickly away.

She had done everything she could.

As Rachel walked back toward Arden, the character of the square changed. The American contingent looked pleased: a small victory for American diplomacy. The woman from whom Rachel had taken the drape smiled at her, then kept her eyes on her. Photographers from dozens of news organizations watched curiously, unlimbering their cameras.

The effect on the members of other nations' representatives was most pronounced. The aides and attaches in the square began whispering to each other, then getting on phones and walkie-talkies. The confused, almost idle air of the square, a place where obviously nothing was about to happen, became purposeful.

The first head of state to appear on the stage, three minutes and forty-three seconds after Rachel had placed the presidential seal, was the French president. President DeVinces almost skidded to a stop in his haste, then checked himself to make sure his dignity was intact. An aide followed closely, but the president waved him away. With great deliberation, the French president seated himself in a chair across from the presidential seal, smiled out at the crowd, and waited.

The president of Israel was next, followed very closely by the president of Syria. The men exchanged words, apparently not unpleasant ones, and took their seats on either side of the chair adorned by the American presidential seal.

Within ten minutes all the chairs except one were filled. The British prime minister was the last one to take the stage, but he did so talking on a cell phone, perhaps as if in intimate conversation with his friend the American president. The P.M. seemed nonplussed for a moment to have only one chair to choose from, but then took the chair on one end of the horseshoe with good grace.

For a moment they all sat, smiling , posing. That's when all the cameras went off. The next day the front page of every newspaper in the world would carry that picture: the most important heads of state in the world coming together to try to solve the world's problems, with one empty seat among them, that seat prominently displaying the American presidential seal.

Then the presidents and prime ministers and premiers stopped posing and started talking. The Syrian and Israeli presidents leaned across the empty chair to chat amiably. England and Russia got into an animated discussion, the Russian president sweeping back her long blond hair at one point. Germany, France, and China leaned close to each other, chatting and nodding as if they were all multilingual.

The conversations began to look less chatty and more purposeful. There were undisguised frowns, but no apparent angry words. Clearly positions were being taken, then changed. The conversational groups shifted. The heads looked thoughtful, forceful, flexible. Watching them—and the whole world was watching—anyone would have longed to be part of that conversation. It shifted and flowed. Apparently hearing something he liked, the British prime minister nodded, then got up and walked a few steps to the chair displaying the American presidential seal, sat in it, and engaged the Syrian and Israeli presidents in animated discussions, obviously conveying information, or perhaps an offer.

Now the American contingent was not pleased at all. The executive secretary frowned at Rachel. Then her gaze shifted and she looked puzzled for a moment.

Rachel took her place beside Arden and stood quietly, ignored by everyone else.

"My God," Arden muttered. A compliment. Rachel nodded in acceptance.

"May I sit at your feet and be your disciple?" Arden added after a moment, looking around in awe.

Rachel turned to her with her hard look back in place. "No. And let me tell you why—"

Her cell phone rang.

Rachel answered, holding the phone tightly to her ear.

"Rachel," Jack said, out of breath. "I got away. I'm on my way. I don't know where Arden is, she was supposed to—"

"Don't worry," Rachel said tightly, not wanting to give anything away. But she could tell from the girl's pleading eyes that she had known who was calling from the moment Rachel answered the phone.

Rachel started to tell Jack what had happened, but somehow he knew about the American president's change of heart. "Something else is going to happen," he said quickly. Obviously Jack was running as he talked. "Something to make it look like the president was right to leave. Some plot—"

"Jack, this is the most thoroughly checked-out site on earth. Unless there's a missile strike on the way, there's no way—"

"Then it's something else. Bruno said he had back-ups, and I believe him."

"Bruno? From school?"

Rachel looked at Arden as she talked. Arden appeared unsurprised by anything.

After a quick explanation, Jack said, "I'll be there as fast as I can. We've got—"

"No!" Rachel and Arden said simultaneously. Rachel stared at the girl again. Either she had extraordinary hearing or she could read minds. Either way, it seemed useless to try to keep the conversation from her. Rachel eased the phone away from her head so they could both hear.

Then she told Jack, "You're still extremely *persona non wanted* around here. If you rush over here now, it will look like *you're* the security threat the president was warned about."

"Damn." Miles away, Jack skidded to a halt. When Rachel said something, he believed it instantly. There had been times in the past when he had failed to believe her, and he regretted nearly all of them now. "Then what can I—?" he looked around helplessly. "Where's Arden?" he muttered. "Bruno thought she'd be here. Maybe if I could—"

"She's here," Rachel said quietly. Into the phone's speaker Arden said, "Hello, Jack," very softly. Then all three were silent for a moment. Arden cleared her throat, about to say something like, *I'm glad you got away*, but knew before she said it how lame it would be. The other two heard what she'd thought about saying and knew the same thing.

After a long moment Jack's voice said from the phone's speaker, "All right. Rachel, there's something lethal there. You have to find it, stop it, and leave no sign that there was ever any danger."

Rachel's eyes swept the square. There was activity everywhere now, people moving, speaking, with dozens of security agents watching everything better than she possibly could. "Okay," she said slowly, "and you can offer me—"

"I don't have a clue."

Arden chimed in, "He's not good with people. Bruno, I mean. It couldn't be someone he's induced to do something. It must be a machine."

"He was pretty good with you," Jack said, with some bitterness, but it sounded feigned to Rachel. She looked again at the girl, in a different appraising kind of way.

"I never really—"

"Oh, right, you never bought into his—"

"Really I didn't, Jack. I just wanted to find out what he was—"

"Sure. Arden the spy. And you didn't bother to tell me what I was walking into because that would have..."

Their bickering sounded familiar to Rachel. And it gave her an idea. Speaking of Bruno, she said, "He's good with the excluded."

"And orphans," Arden chimed in.

Jack had fallen silent.

"Outcasts," Arden and Rachel said together, beginning to look around the square again. But how, out of all these people, could they spot the person Bruno had planted here?

"What? What?" Jack was saying into his phone. He felt very excluded himself.

A block away from him, those below-ground elevator doors opened again. A battered figure, stripped of mechanical arms and legs, crawled out into the alley. Then he fell onto his back and lay there, breathing in the free air.

"Give me a hint, Jack," Rachel said into her phone. She and Arden were standing shoulder to shoulder, slowly turning in a circle, taking in everyone. "By land or sea or air? A bomb, you think? I'm telling you, there can't be anything on or under that stage. It's been checked so thoroughly, and I sealed off underground access to it myself. If there's another killer plane on the way, surely the Air Force will give us some warning. Besides, if it's one of these people, Jack there are too many. We can't possibly—"

Wait, wait. Jack ducked his head, pinched the bridge of his nose, and thought. How, from miles away, could he stop a plan that Bruno had been brooding over for years? And do it so efficiently and quietly no one would ever know there had been a problem?

Because that was the way the Circle operated. More smoothly than the most accomplished magician. They vanished not only the lady but themselves, and any memory that there had even been a performance.

There was nothing. He had nothing. Bruno had too many back-ups. Someone there was either under his influence or perhaps even acting on a post-hypnotic suggestion, that would be triggered by an event bound to occur at the summit, such as the playing of a certain national anthem. But if Rachel and Arden disturbed the ceremonies, the president could use that to spin his retreat. And Jack wanted that retreat to have no justification at all, to be an utter whimpering flight in panic.

Well, maybe he couldn't have everything he wanted. "Arden," he said resignedly, about to tell her maybe to try to stop the band, or something else to disrupt the ceremonies.

Then he stopped. "What is it, Jack?" Rachel's voice crackled out of his cell phone.

"Arden," he said again, then more forcefully: "You're not supposed to be there, Arden. Bruno thought you'd be here. He wasn't sure he had you completely, but he damned sure thought he could predict you well enough to know you'd come in with me. In fact, maybe he never thought he'd turned you at all. Maybe he was convinced of your secret loyalty to me. So he counted on your being here." Jack's mind was spinning wildly now. He thought he understood Bruno. Bruno would never have confidence in any other human being; his face had told Jack that. He had manipulated Arden, yes, but how? Toward what end?

He started talking again. "There are only two 'seats of power'—thank you, Arden—in this town. He wanted you to be here. That means—"

"He didn't want me to be here," Arden said. She looked around wonderingly. "But why not? What could I possibly—? Oh my God."

She was staring at that executive secretary, as the woman turned to look out over the crowd. Her eyes didn't settle on Arden, but Arden got a good look at her for the first time.

"Orphans," she muttered. "Outcasts."

Arden was staring across the compound. She and Rachel were on a small rise, so they could see over the heads of the milling reporters, civilians, and security people. The middle-aged secretary from the American crowd was moving toward the stage. Her posture had changed. She no longer looked frumpy, or aged. She stood very straight, staring at the presidents on the stage. Her hands clenched and unclenched.

"There was something familiar about her," Rachel muttered.

"Because you've met me," Arden answered dreamily. "It's my mother."

Arden swayed as she stood. She couldn't have been more stunned if a meteor had landed on her. She hadn't seen her mother in years, but she knew this was she. Her young, slender, always a little frantic mother had turned into this slightly overweight, competent-looking professional. She had come to resemble her own mother, Gladys Leaphorn, the Chair of the Circle.

The group from which Arden's mother had been excluded her whole life.

Arden hadn't realized it at the time, but her mother Alice had spent years on the run trying to fill the craving she could never satisfy, the craving to belong, to be part of something important. Maybe she didn't know the whole truth, but she felt its loss. Somehow Bruno had figured this out and had gotten to Alice. Arden knew it. He had tried to get to Arden, and had to a certain extent, but she had been prepared for him. Granny had rescued her from her feelings of being left out. She was not such easy prey for Bruno Benjamin as he had thought. But her mother had been.

The woman was no longer staring at the stage. She was moving purposefully, in her efficient executive secretary mode.

"They'll stop her," Arden whispered. "They won't let her get near—"

"It doesn't matter if they stop her!" Jack yelled into the phone. "If she looks like a legitimate assassin the president can say he knew about her. This is why he left. Rachel, there can't be any disturbance! Do you understand?"

Rachel had an inkling of what Jack meant, but more to the point she took him at his word no matter what.

"All right, Jack, but what do you want me to do?" Rachel just stared as the woman started to make her way toward the side of the stage. She was harmless enough anyway. What was she going to do, stab someone with an earring? There was nothing remotely dangerous on that stage. Even the microphones were wireless. Rachel and all the other security forces had made sure there couldn't be even an improvised weapon—

Rachel gasped. Oh, she was an idiot.

There was one new thing on that stage. One thing that hadn't been checked out by anybody. It was deep blue with yellow fringe, and it featured an eagle with a very determined expression.

"Damn it! I'm the fool," Rachel said, as the other two questioned her. For a moment Rachel wondered if she herself was under the influence of a post-hypnotic suggestion. But no, if she hadn't placed the seal the executive secretary would have. Arden's mother. Because she was a deeply-imbedded, probably longstanding functionary of the American diplomatic contingent. Which is why no one would question her now as she walked across that stage. Probably just wanted to straighten the seal, the guards would think. Or remove it. What harm could she be?

But Rachel understood. The seal was flammable. Maybe even explosive. And the woman must have a detonator, or simply a book of matches. She was up on the side of the stage now. In seconds she would be there. Maybe she was close enough already.

Rachel saw standing nearby sharpshooters who could take the woman down from here. And at least two of them would do it at a word from Rachel. She had developed that much trust in the last few days. But then everything would be shattered. The woman's body would be examined, then the seal. The plot would be uncovered, the plot that could have destroyed seven heads of state. And the American president would be able to say he'd been warned about it in advance. His not being here would be explained. And Jack didn't want that. She wasn't sure why, but she believed him.

Rachel stood frozen. Arden stared at her mother. She must not have seen her in years. Rachel glanced at her, then back to the woman on the stage. Her eyes widened. Her frustration peaked. Rachel took a deep breath and closed her eyes.

Then she screamed.

Rachel was not a screamer. She seldom even raised her voice. She was known among her friends, in fact, for her repression. A raised eyebrow on Rachel's face was the equivalent of someone else's launching into a shouting tirade. People cringed at her mutter.

So perhaps this had been building in her for a long time. Because this was a world-class scream. It froze everyone around her, raising hairs on arms and the backs of necks. Everyone turned and stared. And because Rachel and Arden were on that slight rise, everyone saw her.

Jack heard the scream clearly through his cell phone and wondered if his old friend had lost her mind. The tension had made her snap. He started saying, "Rachel, when I said you can't disrupt the ceremonies, what I meant was—," but no one was listening to him.

With everyone staring, and hands reaching for guns, Rachel said quietly to Arden, "Don't look at me. Look at her."

Arden understood. She stood straight, as if in a spotlight, and stared across that crowded square at the woman who was now on the stage.

The woman stared back.

Rachel began stamping her feet. "Bugs," she said loudly. "Is it an ant bed? No." She reached down and picked up a small, befuddled lizard, holding it high, then tossing it away. "Yuck," she said, shivered all over, and indulged in other such girlish behaviors, things she had never done in her life. She was brushing off her clothing, looking distressed. More than one man started toward her aid. Guns were eased back into holsters. Eyes rolled. Hand signals told security personnel everything was okay. Just a silly girl overreacting to local reptilian life. A few people chuckled. That was the most notice Rachel's scream would draw. It was the kind of small, foolish event that seemed enormous for a few seconds, but wouldn't be reported by any news outlet. Rachel quickly slipped out of sight in the crowd. Within minutes, no one would even be able to say who had screamed.

So Arden stood alone on the rise, with no one looking at her any more. No one except that woman on the stage. Their eyes remained locked. The woman put her fist to her mouth. Her eyes watered. Arden lifted one pale hand in greeting to her and the woman forgot everything else she'd been doing or planning. She hurried down from the stage and into the crowd.

Rachel started leading Arden away, over to the edge. The woman would follow. They would draw her completely out of the square. Rachel felt like a fly fisher, flicking Arden across the surface of the crowd, letting her continue to be seen. A ripple through the crowd showed the rapid advance of the executive secretary.

Rachel said into her phone, "Jack, I have to say I was brilliant. I think things are okay here now. We'll—"

"That's great," Jack said quickly, as if he hadn't harbored any doubts about her ability to handle the small problem of stopping a mass assassination without anyone's knowing. "Just one more question, Rache. Is Professor Trimble there?"

"Professor—? No, I haven't seen him here at all, Jack. Why? Why should he—?"

"Damn," Jack said. "Good job. I'll see you two later."

And he clicked off. Moments later the woman from the American delegation caught up to them, and the way the two women threw themselves on each other, the way they clung and wept, held Rachel's attention for minutes. She had tears in her own eyes as Arden said "Mommy" and the older woman whispered "my baby." Obviously whatever influence or post-hypnotic suggestion had been guiding the woman had fallen away completely at her first sight in years of her child. They didn't offer each other any explanations, they wouldn't start talking for some time to come, but they hugged and whispered and cried. It was one of the sweetest moments Rachel had ever seen. She just stood and watched, a spectator to familial joy.

When she tried to call Jack back ten minutes later she couldn't reach him.

CHAPTER 13

The White House, the next day

The desk in the Oval Office, as well as the coffee table, were scattered with newspapers from around the world, including the U.S. They all carried that same photo, of the summit leaders gathered around an empty chair adorned with the American seal. That's what the President of the United States had become on the world stage: an empty chair.

"Nothing happened," the president said. "The summit went off brilliantly. Agreements have been reached. There are new statesmen today."

"You could go now," Dennis Wilkerson said. "There's still lots of work to be done. Everyone would be—"

The president glared him to silence. The glare was more effective because only the two of them were in the room at the moment. When the President started speaking, it was obviously a speech that had been building in him for hours.

"You made me look like a fool on the world stage. Worse, in front of my own people, at a time of the greatest national crisis we have ever faced. You are fired. You will not be allowed to take anything from your office. You will be escorted out of the building and to your apartment where Secret Service agents will watch you pack and take you to the airport. If you are lucky, I will not have your plane blown up in the air. You have one hour to get out of town."

"Sir! I can still be of value to you. I have contacts no one else has. Secret information—"

"Who? Name one source."

The NSA thought of his PlayStation2, smashed to pieces on Air Force One. "I'm sorry. I cannot reveal my—"

The President pressed a button on his desk. Two men in very black suits entered the Oval Office. "I was wrong," the President said. "You have thirty minutes."

Dennis Wilkerson left under escort, almost whimpering. The President didn't even watch his departure. He was on the intercom to his assistant. "Get me the chief of staff and the secretary of state. Now."

Twenty-six Days Later

All the president's men tried to spin it as a continuation of the summit, this time on American soil. Their motto was "America: where the world comes to finalize agreements," but no one picked it up. It sounded too much like the work of a committee.

They couldn't get all the other seven heads of state. They claimed to have countries to run. Surprisingly, the Russian and French presidents agreed to come, while the British and Israeli heads begged off, though promising to come on another occasion.

So the American President's "peace summit" looked more like a press conference, with the Russian and French presidents smiling behind him, the men clasping hands in three-way clenches, so that the photo looked as if the President had managed to resolve hostilities between France and Russia.

But importantly, it was a coming out party. The riots, the successful summit, Dennis Wilkerson's making him look like a coward, all had convinced President Witt that his isolationist policy had been wrong. This occasion in Virginia was going to amount to his creeping back out onto the world stage, and he wanted someone holding his hand while he did that.

This was exactly what the Circle would have arranged.

The location was a small college, Galt University, which was actually the alma mater of the Secretary of State, who had suggested the location. The area was semi-rural, semi-suburban, or "bucolic," as the school billed it, not too far from Washington but not in the shadow of U. Va. Not many presidents would have the nerve to make a major policy announcement with Mr. Jefferson looking over their shoulders. Galt College was perfect: small enough for security to be controlled closely, stately old buildings including the auditorium where the press conference would be held, enthusiastic students, and professors who had told those students that their institution was about to become a historic site. "The place where America reclaimed the world stage," more than one of them had put it. They hoped this President was up to the job of marking the occasion.

Security offered some problems, because the foreign presidents insisted on having their security forces involved, and the President's handlers insisted on a big audience for the opening press conference. Students and professors and journalists had credentials, including foreign journalists, but they all had to be checked, usually by more than one security person, and this occasion had been put together so hastily the Secret Service hadn't had a lot of time to inspect the auditorium. They managed to keep out suspicious strangers, but not the determined assassin with visiting-professor status.

Professor Don Trimble looked so much the part of a professor—which he had been playing for three decades—that hardly anyone bothered to check his ID. He carried a notebook, had a pipe in his mouth, his thinning blond-gray hair was disheveled, his tweed jacket had patches on the elbows. He took so long to find his ID that the impatient guard, a university cop, finally just pushed him through the metal detector. He cleared, that was good enough.

The professor made his way through the crowd, smiling and stopping to chat with colleagues, nod to students. The press conference was due to start in three minutes, which meant he had all the time in the world. He strolled around, enmeshed himself in the crowd, then made his way out to the lobby. There were security people scattered around, some of them obvious, a few not, but they didn't know the place nearly as well as Trimble did. Behind the box office was a nondescript unmarked door. Trimble made his way to it, not looking around, opened the door with a key, and slipped inside. He waited for his eyes to adjust to the semi-darkness, then started up the narrow stairs inside.

The Secret Service had not entirely neglected this staircase, though. At the top a young man in a nylon jacket turned and looked at the professor in surprise, reaching under his jacket.

"I'm sorry," Trimble said in his befuddled way, "I've got some extra students and wanted to see if there's any room up here in the extra balcony."

This was less a balcony than a large private box, above and to the left side of the floor of the auditorium and the stage. It had been reserved for foreign dignitaries who weren't coming, but no one had bothered to un-reserve it.

"Sir, I'm sorry, we're not allowing anyone to be seated up here. It's too un-secured a location. If you'll just—"

The guard was holding out his hands, because the professor was such a befuddled type that he kept advancing as if he didn't understand the language. Plus the guy had the obvious appearance of someone who'd been telling people what to do for so long that he didn't think rules applied to him.

"I understand," Trimble said in his hazy way. "Plus I'm having a problem with this thing..."

He was fumbling with his pipe. The guard looked down at it, a little surprised the professor had been allowed to bring it in, but the people downstairs were pressed for time and the pipe looked as if it belonged in Trimble's hands or mouth. As the guard looked down, Trimble brought the pipe up, pressed a switch underneath, and shot a tiny dart into the guard's throat.

The guard almost got out the syllable "Uh," but the poison was very fast-acting. Curare. Trimble had always wanted to use it. It paralyzed everything, including the lungs, so that the victim was immobilized as he choked to death, trapped inside the shell of his no-longer-functioning body. Trimble looked curiously into the man's eyes and saw the panic there. What Trimble had always wondered, in his scholarly way, was whether the victim of curare poisoning went mad with fear before dying. Looking into the security guard's eyes, he thought the answer was yes.

Trimble eased the man down into a seat, so he was still in a way guarding this private box. Then the professor looked down at the auditorium from his vantage point. The seats below were completely filled, while would-be audience members still clogged the aisles and the space at the back of the auditorium. That wasn't supposed to happen. The seats had supposedly been precisely allocated. But with the presidential staffs of three countries doing favors for friends, they had overbooked. The floor was a solid carpet of people.

Onstage the show was just getting started. A staff person came out and checked the podium and microphone. There was a bulletproof plastic shield in front of the podium, as always. From this vantage point Don Trimble could see the three presidents in the wings, chatting for a moment as they awaited their entrance.

The professor's watery blue eyes hardened. A vein at his temple began to pulse. Even his flaky pale skin seemed to be melting away, revealing sharper features. Trimble wasn't in disguise, but he was shedding the look of indecision he'd worn for years.

But Trimble didn't stay where he was standing. The box wasn't his destination. It was too obvious, too John Wilkes Booth. Trimble went back out into the small hallway outside and found the even more secret staircase that went higher.

Behind another nondescript door, this staircase was so tiny he had to turn sideways to go up it. At the top of the stairs was a small catwalk, a space for lighting. The professor walked briskly to a panel on the opposite wall, a panel that looked like the others, but when the professor put a tiny key into a hole two feet above it the panel dropped open. Inside was a sniper's rifle.

Trimble quickly assembled the rifle, including its silencer, while listening and watching. On this catwalk he could stand up straight, but barely. Banks of small spotlights threatened his head at every step. He had a perfect view of the stage, including the wings if he moved to either side. This workspace had been built when the building was originally put up a hundred years ago, when a student would have to position these spotlights by hand. Everything was automated now, but the space remained.

Someone from the president's staff came out onto the stage, took the podium, and did a little preliminary throat-clearing, introductory remarks to which no one listened. The crowd's noise grew even louder. Closer at hand, Professor Trimble heard what he'd been listening for: footsteps coming up those narrow stairs.

This time he wasn't subtle and didn't do the befuddled-professor look. No time. The Secret Service agent's eyes hadn't had time to adjust. The professor knew that if he stood still he'd be almost invisible in the gloom of this small space.

Sure enough, the agent in his black garb stuck his head up, peered around, then said into the air, "All clear. I'll check on Stanley again and be back. Craig out."

As soon as "Craig" was off the air, Professor Trimble shot him. It was a perfect shot, right in the throat, making the man mute before killing him. The agent gasped for air, fell to his knees, then rolled over and didn't move again.

Trimble checked his watch. There wasn't much time now. That death would bring other agents to check on the missing one within minutes. But they'd all be preoccupied right now, because the President of the United States was taking the stage.

He strode boldly across—"bold" was the new watchword in the White House—unaccompanied for the moment by the other presidents or any of his own staff. The audience applauded, which was less a sign of approval than gratitude that the show was starting, and the President gave one broad wave. His face remained serious, though.

Trimble moved into position. From up here he could send a bullet either over or around that plastic shield. In moments he would make history in a way the Circle never had. Nor would they have approved. That's why a new Circle had been needed. One that was not only decisive but prepared to act. Not dropping hints any more, not even subtly guiding others to kill. Once in a while a bolder move was needed. Don Trimble had believed that for a long time before he realized there were others who thought as he did. Once he'd been invited into the inner circle, he'd joined with alacrity.

Their inner security was so tight he wasn't even sure who the other members were. As with the larger Circle, each member operated fairly independently. So Trimble had been on hand in Salzburg, knowing there was a plan afoot and ready to help out. But as soon as Jack Driscoll had shown up there, Trimble had been afraid things would go awry, as they obviously had. Trimble had quietly slipped away before the end, knowing there would be a next act.

This one he had set up on his own. He had all kinds of contacts in the diplomatic and academic worlds. It hadn't been very difficult to get early word of what the President was planning and where the announcement would take place. The location had been perfect for Trimble, who could find a colleague at nearly any college in America who would be willing to designate him a visiting professor.

He had been on campus for a week setting up this moment. His escape would be easy too, but even if something went wrong, he was prepared to give up his life for this. The President was about to turn around his own isolationist policy, the policy the inner circle had pursued for years, secretly even from the rest of the Circle. The world was too difficult and unpredictable a place, and had become much too dangerous. Too many centers of power, too many fanatics. It would all blow up soon, that was inevitable. Better for America to be out of that scene completely, staying safe behind its own borders until time to pick up the pieces.

In another few seconds, with one shot, Don Trimble would accomplish that. The President who was about to change course yet again would be murdered at home. There could be no clearer signal that the world was unsafe. The vice president, who had been cultivated for years by inner circle people, would resume the isolationist policy his predecessor had announced. Especially after the lesson had been driven home yet again that foreign involvement was too dangerous.

The President was talking. Making a little self-deprecating joke, from his expression. Professor Trimble raised his rifle and sighted through the scope. It was strange to have just that tiny circle of vantage point, jumping all over: the curtains, a Secret Service agent's chest, the First Lady's head, the President's arm, then his face. Trimble did not look the part, but for years he had been practicing for this moment. He was an excellent shot, as he had proven twice in the last few minutes.

There was a rumble beneath his feet. Trimble lowered the rifle. The metal catwalk on which he stood trembled. Trimble shot a sharp look down at the stage. He couldn't afford noise until he made the shot. A Secret Service agent was looking up this way, but obviously couldn't see anything in the dark catwalk area. But he spoke into his shirt cuff, asking a question or giving an order.

The professor started to raise the rifle again, when the source of the vibrations revealed itself. Beneath the catwalk, down on the curving metal floor itself, a panel lifted away. It was set aside quietly, then a human figure sat up. "Phew," it said, sharply but quietly.

Professor Trimble stood immobilized. He could have killed the interloper immediately, but curiosity got the better of him. Maybe this was one of his own team, ready to help.

But no. The figure rolled completely out of its tiny hiding place, staying below the catwalk, then rolled over and looked up.

It was Jack Driscoll.

Jack moved slowly and stiffly. He had obviously been hidden in his tiny space for some time. Trimble didn't move. His breathing stopped.

Was Jack on his team after all? The inner circle were all so secretive, no one was sure who was in and who wasn't. Trimble had been certain in Salzburg that Jack was the enemy, but here he was again, and the pistol in his hand seemed to indicate an intention to carry out the same kind of plan as Trimble. Trimble waited.

Jack crept out to the edge of the space and looked over it, down toward the stage. But then he did nothing. He didn't take a sniper's position, he didn't ready the pistol. From his head movements, he didn't seem even to be concentrating on the president.

In a moment Trimble understood. Jack wasn't here to perform an assassination. He was here to prevent one.

But for once he was one step behind. Don Trimble smiled, lowered his rifle, and very deliberately cleared his throat.

It was a small sound, but it went through Jack like electricity. His head swivelled then stopped, as he saw for the first time the tall man looming over him. Jack was in an awkward position, looking back over his right shoulder, his right hand holding the gun. He couldn't move that arm any further back, he would have to roll onto his back to get a clear shot, and that would give Professor Trimble more than enough time to shoot him dead, since Trimble already had his high-powered rifle pointed at Jack's back. Somehow he looked as if he knew what he was doing with the gun, too.

"Professor."

Trimble nodded, still smiling. "Jack."

They both kept their voices down, but could hear each other clearly in the confined space. Jack said, "I didn't expect to see you here."

"Yes. You never had any inkling I might be part of another design, did you?"

"Oh, I knew you were part of the group that had other plans. I just thought you'd be skilled enough to guide someone else into doing your dirty work."

Trimble's smile disappeared. His eyes narrowed. "Bullshit. You didn't know anything."

"You're right," Jack said, indicating his own position. "I'm just a figment of your imagination."

He was still stuck in an awkward position, looking over his shoulder. His left hand was out of sight beneath him.

"How long have you been here?" the professor said, curiosity overcoming him.

"Ten days. You wouldn't happen to have a can of Lysol spray on you, would you?"

"You've known about this conference for ten days?" That was two days longer than Trimble had known.

Jack nodded. "Barely in time to get here ahead of all the security and position myself, so I'd already be here before they made their security sweeps. And how did you get in?"

Trimble moved his chin, and Jack glanced down toward the end of the catwalk, seeing the body of the Secret Service agent lying there. In that moment everything changed. Jack had been trying to figure out how to get the President, the professor, and himself all out of here alive, with the professor sedated for later questioning. But when he saw the agent, obviously dead, his plan changed. When he turned his head to look at his old professor again, his eyes were cold.

The eye of the rifle was on him. "I'm afraid I need to take you out first," Don Trimble said, with both amusement and regret in his voice. "What, by the way, did you think you were going to do with that pistol, which I see has no silencer on it? If you somehow managed to shoot me with it, you'd bring so many Secret Service agents up here, you'd be dead in seconds. Were you going to sacrifice yourself nobly for the sake of the mission?"

Jack shook his head. He moved slowly, pulling his left hand out into view.

"Do you see what I have in my other hand? Not the gun, this hand. It's the light switch. See, I'm pushing it down now. If I let it go abruptly, such as if you shoot me, all the lights will come on up here. You'll be spotlighted, with a rifle in your hands. On the other hand, if I let it go very gently, nothing will happen. Your move."

The professor, in spite of having cast himself as a quick-thinking assassin in control of all the elements, was not very quick on the uptake. He took his eyes off Jack and looked upward and around, suddenly noticing the strategically-placed spotlights. His eyes widened.

While he stood frozen, Jack released the switch. Abruptly. And fired his un-silenced pistol.

The sound of the shot, which went harmlessly into the curtains behind the president, was almost drowned out by all the answering shots. Perhaps 2.8 seconds. Certainly a response time well under five seconds. Those Secret Service agents were good.

One moment Professor Trimble was a tall, efficient-looking man holding a silenced rifle, in the glare of six spotlights. The next he was an emptying bag of cooling meat.

Everything else in the building was chaotic movement. Jack moved as quickly as the agents, switching off the lights as he climbed to Trimble's level, reaching Trimble's body and shoving it gently to the edge of the catwalk. For a moment the body turned and Trimble seemed to be looking at him in surprise. Then the body went over the edge.

Jack heard screams, knew people had spotted the falling body, and hoped it didn't land on anyone. Agents would be rushing toward it. Some would be on their way up here, too, but not as quickly now that they knew the danger was over. Jack dropped his pistol. That gun had a history, and now it would be Don Trimble's history as well. It would tie him to a well-known extremist group, leading to speculation that terrorists had wanted to keep America isolated. Jack trusted this would steel the President's, and the country's, determination to rejoin the world.

He ran the opposite way down the catwalk, opened another door in the wall, revealing a metal ladder. Jack jumped onto it, closed the door behind him, and slid down the ladder, barely touching the rungs. He landed with a thump on the ground floor, behind a door hidden by a heavy curtain. The architect of this building had been inspired by the magicians who were so popular in the early 1900s when this auditorium went up. Jack had read the architectural plans, probably the first person to do so in over a hundred years. It served him well now.

He stepped out from behind the curtain and was immediately engulfed in a throng of students, some rushing to get out of the building, some to get closer to the stage, some just trying to hold their ground and watch the drama. It took twenty minutes, but the security people got them moving out of the building. Jack blended right in. He had one of those faces. No one would remember him.

But Jack would remember. Being herded toward the exit along with all the other civilians, he took a moment to look back, staring toward the spot where his victim lay. Jack hadn't fired a shot at anyone, but he had quite deliberately committed murder. History would exonerate him, except that history wouldn't remember at all.

But Jack knew his role. He had done what had to be done, without hesitation and now without remorse. When he had been the only person in a position to act, and only one action would serve, he had done it.

He was the twentieth fanatic. Not the person who had launched the terror attack, but the kind who could. The ruthless kind.

Until today he hadn't known that about himself.

CHAPTER 14

Two Days Later

It took Jack two days to reach headquarters, because he took a very circuitous route, a couple of hops by plane, mostly by cars. It took him that long to get over the idea that he was the most wanted man on earth. He managed to follow the evolving story of the attempted assassination, and never heard anyone suggest, even through back channels, that there had been a second assassin. Still, the Secret Service might be the least of his worries.

One worry was that during the two days he was on the run he couldn't reach anyone. Not anyone on the inside. At headquarters he only got the ominous message, "The number you are trying to reach is not in service." That was all right, they might have turned off the phones, changed numbers, even closed down the operation for the time being. But he couldn't reach any of them on their own lines, either. Not the Chair, Alicia Mortenson, Janice Gentry, his old friend Ronald.

He did manage to raise Rachel, who was back in Israel. She filled him in rapidly on events in Salzburg, assuming he already knew them. "Didn't Arden—?"

"I haven't talked to her since you and she—"

"I assumed she came to find you." Rachel sounded puzzled. Jack knew that she was playing back in her mind her last conversation with Arden, in precise detail. Not just the words and facial expressions, but the tells and tics as well. "She said she had to leave. Even left her mother after just being reunited with her. Where did she go, Jack?"

Not to him. Maybe back to headquarters. Maybe to find her grandmother. Maybe that had been a lost cause.

Rachel said, "I'll—"

"No! You stay away, Rache. You and Stevie may be the last of us. You have to—"

"Stevie and I have to regenerate the Circle? Not through reproduction, I hope."

Jack laughed. Good old Rachel. They finished each other's sentences, even in their heads, and she was the only person on earth who could reliably make him laugh, even now.

Jack began to have long thoughts as he drove down the empty western highway. Obviously Rachel was having them too. As her voice began to fade on his cell phone she said, "I feel that an age is ending. This is what—the fourth age?"

"But there will be a fifth."

"Yes, and you know what, Jack? There will be two people just like you and me in it."

"I plan to be there myself."

"I knew—"

"I know—"

"—you were going to say that," the finished together. They laughed, on different continents, as he lost her signal completely.

Then Jack drove alone. He felt like the last survivor of a worldwide catastrophe, though in fact life was returning to normal all over the world. America was dominant again, and safe, at least for today. The Circle had succeeded.

So maybe everyone had just adopted the safety plan. Don't answer your phone. Separate. Disappear into your normal life, or a new one you already had in storage.

Two more hours of driving left him feeling very alone. Headquarters came into view, or at least it should have. The headquarters "building" looked like a desert mesa from the outside. Parking was underground, and in fact the road died away five miles from the entrance. The last slow driving was over scrub land, dry cracked earth that would reveal no tracks. Jack sensed no activity. His cell phone remained dead, even though the Circle had had its own disguised tower out here.

And he should have seen the mesa by now, but he didn't. Was he so addled he'd gotten lost? It would be easy to do out here in the western vastness. But no, he recognized a tree, and an unusually-shaped boulder. He was almost at the front door.

Jack's car drifted to a stop and he got out. "No," he whispered.

Ahead of him was a canyon. A huge hole in the ground. A new one. Right where the mesa had stood.

Jack ran. The wind whipped at him, nothing to block it for hundreds of miles. It could have lifted him off his feet and flown him away. At the edge of the canyon he fell to his knees and skidded to a stop.

The edges of the hole were ragged and black. Nature hadn't scoured this. Jack peered over the edge in the dying light. Roots had been blasted apart. The sides of the hole were black and flat, almost glassy. This was what was left after a huge explosion. Earth had caved in at the bottom, but Jack could see evidences of human life. Electronic parts, burned papers, pieces of furniture. A woman's shoe.

He was crying though he didn't know it. Crying and furious. All this brilliance destroyed. Again he heard Bruno's words. *I have so many back-up plans you couldn't count them.* He had been intent on destroying the Circle any way he could. If humiliation didn't work, he would throw away subtlety and use bombs. He had had enough technology left for one huge strike.

Jack slammed his fists down and screamed out over that canyon. "NOOOOOO!!!" Echoes captured the cry and made it their own. Jack put his forehead down on the ground and wept uncontrollably.

That was when the man and woman dressed in black appeared behind him. They must have been in the underground parking area all along. For FBI agents, they showed amazing empathy and were surprisingly gentle. "We've been hoping one of you was left," the man said.

"You'll have to come with us, sir," the woman added.

Jack let them lift him up and escort him away.

"And that was the end," Jack said. He had just brought his interrogator up to date, as of five days ago when he'd been captured, or arrested, or whatever he was.

"That's everything?" she said. Her voice didn't hold the sympathy of the agents who'd arrested him. She sat there as if she'd been hoping the tale had a bigger finish, and he had disappointed her. This was an interrogation technique, he knew, but it still irritated him. He had just told her that his world had come to an end and the real world was going to be a much more dismal place as a result, and she acted bored. He thought she was overplaying her role.

In fact, that wasn't quite everything. He hadn't told her about Rachel, or Stevie, in fact hadn't named any names at all, just given a broad outline. He was prepared to take personal details to his grave, or into lifelong prison.

In a more cheerful voice he said, "Nothing else except to add that everything I've said is a lie. I was just hiking through the desert when those agents grabbed me and I made up a story to keep my brain occupied."

The woman didn't smile. She wrote three symbols on her pad. Jack waited a moment, feeling the vibrations of her fingers tapping out another message, then answered her on the paper. After he did she wrote a K with a slash through it. Jack nodded.

They were sitting staring at each other when the door slid noiselessly to the side and a woman in a wheelchair rolled into the room. The door closed behind her. The woman pointed a small control in her hand at the room's video camera and clicked.

Jack jumped to his feet. The woman in the wheelchair looked at him impassively. "We never talk," she said. "Never. Not under any circumstances. We never reveal ourselves to outsiders. Never for any reason. Isn't that the first thing you were taught?"

"Mrs. Leaphorn!"

She nodded, her expression bored at his obviousness.

"I thought you were dead," Jack said happily.

"Even then we don't talk." Then she relented and gave him a little. "I wasn't arrested, just isolated. After half a century in government service, I have a reputation as a consultant. During the crisis, our government in its wisdom wanted me consulting. And the security here makes Langley look like an outdoor playground. I couldn't get word to anyone. Luckily, I did have enough pull to have you brought here."

"But not to stop—"

Gladys Leaphorn shook her had minutely. Apparently she didn't trust that she had turned off all the surveillance in this room.

Jack looked at the interviewer. The Chair had already said too much in front of a civilian. Looking at the woman in the chair opposite him, Jack said, "Go Hornets?"

The woman nodded.

"Damn." He turned his attention back to Gladys. "But people got away."

She gave him another tiny nod.

"So what Bruno told me about Craig Mortenson—?"

"That, sadly, was true. Craig is dead. I think."

"You think?"

Gladys wore a little frown, the way she did when confronted with something inexplicable. For an old Indian shaman, she had absolutely no supernatural beliefs. "Alicia says he's not dead. Oh, his body is certainly deceased, we've confirmed that. But Alicia escaped, as you surmised. And after she dispatched his murderers, she would not leave without her husband. She says she didn't. Alicia says she caught Craig's dying breath, and took his mind into her own. No one ever understood their symbiosis. Now it's complete. She says Craig was tired of his body anyway, and is quite happy in hers."

Jack was staring at her. Gladys shrugged irritably. "You should hear her talk to herself. But it's a harmless psychosis, and makes her happy."

In a toneless voice, Jack said, "Alicia told me where the

conference was going to be. That college in Virginia. That's how I was able to set up there before anyone else."

"How could she have known that?"

"She said she and Craig figured it out."

They both stared into space. Then the Chair shook her head and her eyes drilled into Jack again. "But none of this excuses what you've just done, Jack. You can't be trusted."

Jack stood perfectly still. He wondered if she was going to arrange his death. That's probably what it would have to be. Mere lifelong incarceration wouldn't keep him from talking. She had the power to do it any number of ways.

He could tell from Gladys' expression that she hated what she had to do. "I kept listening for some sign that you knew, that you were just leading us on, knowing we were the ones interrogating you. But I never did."

The woman in the chair sat up straight. She had begun taking off her makeup, removing implants from inside her mouth. Her face slimmed down. She took off the lifeless wig, shook out her hair, which was much shorter than the last time he'd seen it, but the same light brown. She removed contact lenses and her eyes were their old piercing blue. Arden stood up and unself-consciously reached up under her dress, pulling out the padding. Jack just watched her.

"He did know, though," she said matter-of-factly.

"What?" Her grandmother's head snapped toward her.

"He was dropping clues all along, Granny. Didn't you catch any of them?"

"When?"

"Oh, please. That part about making love to me. The detail." She rolled her eyes. "Implying that I wasn't very good at it. Please. That was to goad me out of my role."

Gladys was thinking hard. "No. You're making excuses for him now."

Arden said nonchalantly, "Plus he's been playing me the chess match I won against the computer when I was in school in Grenoble. Move for move."

Gladys sat there, only her eyes moving. Obviously she'd been seeing the scribbles on the pads and hadn't bothered interpreting them. Now she ran back in her memory all those moves of the last three hours. "My God, you're right."

Arden said, "It is only the deep respect in which I hold you that prevents my saying, 'Duh.'"

Jack stood at ease, letting the women work it out. Gladys Leaphorn obviously hadn't been persuaded. "You told him," she accused her granddaughter. "You gave him some kind of signals. You winked at him."

"I did not! Run the tape."

"I'm sure you would have it altered somehow by the time we played it back. But it doesn't matter. He has proven he can't be trusted."

Jack finally stepped in. "What are you going to do then, Granny? Mind-wipe me?"

Gladys sounded disgusted. "I doubt it would take in your case. You would be left a drooling idiot roaming the streets babbling insanities. Questions would be asked. No, Jack. You are out." She shot a look at her granddaughter. "Both of you. You deserve each other. You will never again be privy to our councils. The Circle is dead anyway. You are the last remnants. We are disbanded."

Her eyelid flickered, so swiftly it could never be caught on videotape.

Jack hung his head. He put up a little argument, but Gladys Leaphorn was adamant.

Arden said, "I guess I have to re-frump."

"Put it on," her grandmother said. "When you look like that you become one of the women men don't see."

"Really?"

"Just do it."

Arden reconfigured her disguise, lifting her skirt to put the padding back on. Jack watched her without pretending to do otherwise. She sighed as she reinserted the contacts and cheek pads. Then the three of them left the interrogation room. No agents waited outside. Gladys escorted them out of the secured area, flashing her badge a few times—sure enough, the men glanced at Arden then she seemed to become invisible to them—to a waiting car that had no driver. "Go," Gladys said, and turned and rolled back into the building without ceremony.

Jack drove. In a few miles they came to a small town, and abandoned the car. They walked toward a tiny train station. If there wasn't a train due soon, Arden would get a car for them.

She transformed herself back into Arden again. This time Jack watched appreciatively as she reached under her dress and pulled out the padding.

"Thanks for the signals," he said as they started walking again.

"Thanks for entertaining me with that BS about me being lousy in the sack."

He turned and looked at her in surprise. "Such language from a nice schoolgirl. I have never used such a crude expression in my life."

"But it's what you meant."

"No, I didn't." He put his arm around her. "I think you have talent. And enthusiasm, which—"

"Shut up."

"All you need is—"

"Practice," they said together, then Arden added, "Then let's hurry up and get to a large population center so I can—"

"Oh, right. As if anyone could—"

"There would be—"

He laughed. She jabbed him in the ribs with her elbow. They were both laughing. By the time they got to the train station they were interrupting each other's sentences after one or two words. It sounded as if they were talking in code.

— THE END —

ABOUT THE AUTHOR

J ay Brandon is a successful attorney and a prolific, award-winning mystery novelist. He holds a Master's Degree in writing from Johns Hopkins University and a law degree from the University of Texas. Except for *Shadow Knight's Mate,* all of Brandon's novels are set in San Antonio and South Texas. His extensive experience as an attorney with the District Attorney's office in Bexar County and with the Fourth Court of Appeals has provided him with plenty of insights into the workings of the legal system, and how what is "accepted history" is often a long way from the "real history." A native Texan, Brandon lives in San Antonio, Texas.

Colophon

This first edition of *Shadow Knight's Mate*, by Jay Brandon, has been printed on 70 pound Edwards Brothers text paper containing a percentage of recycled fiber. Titles have been set in Charlemagne and Copperplate type, the text in Adobe Caslon type. All Wings Press books are designed and produced by Bryce Milligan.

On-line catalogue and ordering:
www.wingspress.com

Wings Press titles are distributed
to the trade by the
Independent Publishers Group
www.ipgbook.com
and in Europe by
www.gazellebookservices.co.uk

Also available as an ebook.